Fractured Weapons

Stability is fickle, perceptions are not.

Written by

D. L. Farmer

Edited by

Karen Robinson

Page break artwork by

Magda Cygan

Book cover artwork by

David Leahey

127,504 words

<u>Special thanks for helping to review the story before its release:</u>
Alexandra Farmer

Gerry Pinkerton

Laurie Farmer

Mark Smith

Matthew Farmer

Robbie Pinkerton

Sarah Farmer

Toni Boyes

Chapter one – Sunset

Fourth eclipse, eighteenth day

The fur on his knees brushed against the purple feathers of his beloved steed while his eyes stared at the hills of pale blues and greens. The gentle breeze flowed across the familiar landscape, brushing aside the sand trapped in his black fur. The forgotten aroma of blossoming flowers and harvested wheat entered his nostrils. The darkening clouds in the evening sky enveloped the surrounding southern and northern peaks of this once innocent land.

Memories of his youthful days filled his mind. Memories of welcoming cheerful miners returning to the surface, of climbing mountains with his once-pale hands and of dancing with his girlfriend when they were both still unbeastly. Yet no satisfaction nor any notion of peace came to him, for his round ears heard only the vengeful voices of his brethren behind him. His grip on the scale-laced reins remained tight, for once the sun set, he intended to use the viciously spiked pole axe strapped to his back.

With a gentle breeze blowing through her short, scruffy hair, Iyna grinned, for her trained red eyes saw her friend hadn't learned anything from their duels. He still held the straw training spear like a sword and even stood with the setting sun shining in his blue eyes. It was a shame all the villagers were too busy to watch tonight, but few of them would trek to the top of the green hill just to witness Vernon lose again.

Her confident gaze darted to the featureless grass between them and returned to his face. "You ready?"

He nodded.

She leapt forward, thrusting her straw spear at him before he could react, cushioning the soft tip onto his chest, and nearly forcing him off balance.

Iyna grinned. "Too slow." She stepped back, readying herself for another duel.

He sighed and gave a small smile. He readied his stance and made a wide, predictable swing at her. Iyna dodged it with ease and jabbed through the opening he left.

Several more one-sided duels later, he wearily gave in. "That's … enough."

"Come on, Vernon," she pleaded. "We can keep going."

He shook his head.

"Tell you what, I'll use only one arm. Okay?"

Vernon simply held out his training spear.

She took it, grunting. "All right, fine."

Iyna watched him amble over to the book he had left nearby and let out a loud sigh for him to hear. Seeing him ignore her irritation, she slumped down on the dry grass, resting the spears on her lap.

She stared blankly at the shallow stream that snaked its way around their hill. Her gaze traced the water backwards, through the empty fields to the small moat accompanying their village's grey wall. As her eyes followed the ramparts, she smiled when she spotted each of the five spear guards patrolling the wall. Vernon sat beside her, opening his book.

Her gaze widened to view Edenor as a whole. It was like a calm yellow pond, from the way the curved straw roofs rippled out from the stone clearing at its centre to the short grey wall that encircled the village. Even the mill near the gate, with its slowly turning green spirals, resembled strands of grass jutting high above the water. Aside from Vernon's house at the far end, whose second floor stood above Edenor's perimeter wall and the other homes, Iyna saw it as the quietest, most peaceful place imaginable. Therefore, as soon as she got permission, she would leave.

Vernon's voice brought Iyna out of her daydream. "Looks like they've almost finished the offering."

She glanced at the cobblestone clearing at the village centre and saw one of their neighbours pouring seed into the straw stack. Iyna leaned back on the grass. "Looks that way." She heard the sound of pages turning and said, "I don't want to read tonight."

"It's important to learn," he said.

"But it's not. No matter how much I learn about past battles and stories, it won't affect anything we do today."

"I couldn't disagree more." Vernon's voice quivered with excitement. "Learning the past not only helps us understand the world much better but improves our actions today."

"But I already know how the world works." Iyna turned her head to face him. "And how is reading supposed to make me a better fighter?"

He smirked. "These stories feature all kinds of fighters you can look up to."

Iyna felt a wave of bitter sadness hit her, and she turned her gaze away, mumbling, "I already have someone I can look up to."

After a moment of silence, Vernon apologised.

"Don't worry about it." Iyna didn't want to dwell on it. "You look up to that guy in your book, don't you?"

"I do indeed." Vernon closed the book and stared at its cover. "He truly was a great man."

Iyna heard a familiar girl's voice call out to them from the base of the hill.

Hopping over the little stream, Niyaa ran up the hill, shouting to her friends, "Iyna! Vernon!" They were sitting together at the very top, and she wondered if she was interrupting another reading lesson. She called out to them again, "The festival's starting soon!"

Iyna turned to the setting sun on the horizon, with a hand shadowing her eyes. "We got loads of time!"

Those words made Niyaa's task harder, and she reluctantly reached the top of the hill. Standing before them, she darted her yellow eyes back to Edenor and watched the last of the seed fall into the offering. "But my dad told me to come get you two."

"We got time." Iyna jumped to her feet, holding out both training spears. "You wanna have a go?"

Niyaa shook her head. "I'm sorry, but we don't have time."

Iyna shrugged. "I'm sure no one will mind."

Niyaa couldn't find the words to convince them, leaving an awkward pause in the air.

Vernon calmly stood. "It's all right, Niyaa. We'll head back."

Iyna sighed and dropped the training spears on the ground. "Fine."

Niyaa smiled, relieved. "Thanks." With each step, her excitement grew. When they crossed the little stream, she glanced back to them. "I can't wait to see you both try my mom and dad's ale."

Vernon asked, "So have they made a new batch for tonight?"

Niyaa nodded but looked away. "They both said I have to wait till I'm older before I can help brew it with them or even have more than a sip."

"Trust me." Vernon smiled. "The time will pass before you know it."

Niyaa ruffled the back of her long hair. "I guess."

Iyna said, "You could always try making some where your parents won't see. That way you can prove to them you're old enough."

Niyaa sighed. "Dad told me only ale from a clean brewing pot will taste right."

"Almost certainly the safer way," Vernon said. "Wouldn't want to poison anyone."

"All right." Iyna shrugged. "Guess you'll just have to wait for permission."

Vernon said again, "Believe me, the time will pass by."

The girl's little sandals pranced on the tiny stone bridge over the peaceful moat as the three approached the open gate. Niyaa glanced across the flaking, green bars and smiled at the thought of painting with such pale greens. It was unlike the scratched green of the guard's chestplate, thin helmet and spear handle, which gave Niyaa an uneasy feeling. Still they were better colours than the rusted greys of the man's dented triangle shield and spearpoint.

Iyna greeted him. "Hey, Errad, is Cairsie on the eastern side tonight?"

"Think she is." He stroked his thick grey beard. "Anyways, it won't be long till sundown, so you three better head to the centre."

"Will do," Iyna replied.

They entered Edenor, and the gate squeaked on its small hinges as Errad slowly shut the stiff bolt behind them.

Walking along the short dirt street, Niyaa gazed up at the many red, orange and yellow disks above them, strung with yarn between the straw roofs. The handful of blue and green lanterns up ahead were being lit, brightening the darkening cobblestones with beautiful colours.

"I can't wait for the festival to start," she said, her legs moving faster.

Vernon nodded. "It certainly will be good to see the farmers' hard work pay off tonight."

Iyna said, "Don't forget about your hard work."

"*My* hard work?" Vernon asked.

"Yeah," she said. "Those assignments your father has you complete."

"Oh," he said.

Niyaa tried to lift their spirits. "Don't forget about the reading lessons."

Iyna glanced away. "Well ... I guess."

"A very good point." Vernon's smile returned. "Both of your reading skills have come a very long way since we started."

Niyaa thought back to the first day Vernon had smuggled one of his few books for them to read. "Well, Iyna's doing much better than me. I bet one day *she'll* be the one reading to me."

Iyna laughed. "That'll be the day, won't it?"

Most of their neighbours had already gathered in the clearing, faces filled with pride and joy. Niyaa turned to the offering standing before the small chapel; the straw stack was as high as an adult with the wheat seeds almost overflowing from the top. It was definitely bigger than the last harvest.

Her dad was lifting their old glass and wicker dining table out of their brewery. She ran to him. "Found them, Dad."

"That's great." He wiped his brow. "Now why don't you kids hang around 'ere for a bit till everything's up?"

Iyna sighed. "Could've spent a bit longer out there."

Niyaa darted her eyes away. "Yeah, sorry about that."

"It's all right," Iyna said. "I wanted to see Cairsie before the festival anyway,"

Vernon said, "And I need to return this book before Jornis finds it missing again."

"All right then." Niyaa let out a relieved breath. "I'll have a tankard filled for the both of you."

Her dad said, "Afraid they'll have to wait till after the priest makes his big speech."

"I know," Niyaa replied as her friends walked away. "But I can at least get them ready."

"I don't see a problem in that," he said. "Just don't let others see it. Otherwise we might have the whole village asking for their own prepped drinks."

"I won't." Niyaa turned to their empty dining table. "I'll go help mum clean the tankards."

"That'll be a big help," he said. "You know, it still amazes me how your mum and I managed to raise the kindest person in the whole world."

Niyaa's smile grew, and she eagerly rushed to the brewery house.

With the book under his arm, Vernon paused before the black iron door to his house. Every time he saw the nation's emblem bolted onto its surface, the muscles throughout his body tensed. The irony that the nation of Felliet would have as its emblem a shield on its side, as though safeguarding the common people, was truly absurd. To have this deceitful symbol bolted onto a black surface, the colour of greatness, was for Vernon a worse insult than having the emblem on his door to begin with.

Putting his resentment aside, Vernon carefully lifted the latch and pushed open the door, lest the noise cause another row with his father.

10

Peering down the empty hallway, Vernon rolled his eyes at the lone candlelight flickering from his father's cramped, windowless study. Jornis preferred the company of his grey candle and neatened stacks of parchments than the villagers he was supposed to govern. Vernon shifted his gaze to the fur-rugged lounge at the end of the hall and moved across the slate floor without bothering to glance into the doorless study.

With only sparse light emerging from the two thick, lounge windows to his right, Vernon marched across the soft fur carpet, passing three abandoned armchairs till he reached the spotless glass wall shelves adjacent to the dust-covered fireplace built into Edenor's wall. His gaze drifted across the titles of his few precious texts: *The Mysteries of the Therra, Gildren's Prosperous Rise*, and *Myklinn's Great Struggle.* Reading those titles brought back pleasant memories spent in the city's library tightening his grasp on his favourite book. He retraced his steps back across the lounge and through the hallway with *The Foundations* still under his arm.

"Having fun, are we?" Jornis asked from the study without turning his head away from his desk.

Vernon sighed. "I have finished my studying today, so I am heading out to enjoy tonight's celebration."

Without a change in the rhythm of his ink feather, Jornis replied, "This festival is an extravagance Edenor cannot afford."

Vernon rolled his eyes. "It's for the omniscient mother. So that she would—"

"Vernon," Jornis said, finally turning to face his son. "Do you honestly believe the Goddess would bestow guidance in return for our offering of a handful of grain?"

"And how else would one show their devotion, if not by sacrificing food?" Vernon asked.

Jornis returned to drafting his letter. "An all-seeing God should not require any sacrifices, of time or resources." In the brief moment of awkward silence, the only sound was that of the ink feather lightly scribbling against the brown parchment. "You are not to take that book outside."

Vernon narrowed his eyes at the command, and without a word, he stormed out, shutting the black iron door behind him, book in hand.

Running in the darkening shadow of the wall, Iyna finally spotted Cairsie atop the small battlements, staring at the eastern landscape. Strangely, she had a firm grasp of her iron triangle shield and an even tighter grip around her inherited spear.

Iyna shouted, "Hey, Cairsie, I beat Vernon again!"

Cairsie jumped and turned to Iyna. "Startled me there." She brushed her ginger fringe away from the faded jagged scar across her forehead and perched on the wall's edge. "Don't go too hard on him, you hear."

"I won't." Iyna grinned. "Besides, he's easy to beat."

"I see." Cairsie smiled. "So how's that reading he's been trying to teach ya?"

Iyna looked away. "It's … goin' well." She spun her gaze back to Cairsie. "But I won't need that stuff in the future anyway."

"Maybe not." She shrugged. "But it won't hurt, will it?"

"I guess," Iyna said.

Cairsie stood up and turned toward the village centre. "You better hurry. The sun will be setting any moment now."

"You aren't coming?" Iyna asked.

She shook her head. "I can watch the fire from here."

"But…" Iyna stared at her. "You were there last harvest."

"Yeah, I know, but…" Cairsie darted her eyes away with a distracted look. "This time I've got to stay here, all right?"

Iyna felt her body weaken at the thought of a lonely festival night.

Cairsie glanced down at Iyna, bent her knees holding out the spear horizontally, and said, "Tell you what. Midday tomorrow, I'll let you practise with your mother's spear."

Iyna screamed. "Really?!"

"I think you've waited long enough," Cairsie said. "Now head back, lest you miss the fire."

Overwhelmed with unexpected joy, Iyna stared wide eyed at the weathered spear. "Thank … thank you." She sprinted back to the cobblestones with a thrilled smile across her face.

All the blue and green lanterns were lit, the brewers table was packed with tankards around a hefty green cask and the two villager cart haulers had brought a leather lap drum and an iron mini harp. The gathered hundred or so villagers waited for the elderly priest, dressed in his pearl white hooded robes, to finish watching the sun lower beneath Edenor's short wall.

Iyna looked around at the farmers and craftsmen as they chatted and laughed. She spotted Vernon sat reading beside one of the green wall lanterns and ran to him. "Guess what? I'm gonna be using my mother's spear tomorrow."

Vernon closed his book. "That's great."

"I know, isn't it?" Iyna sat beside him, excitedly jittering. "I can't believe I finally get to use my mom's spear."

"Not against me I hope." Vernon darted his eyes away and opened his mouth as if ready to say something else only to close it again without a single word.

Iyna realised how insensitive her words had been, given he didn't have anything of *his* mother. "Sorry."

"It's fine," he replied, bringing an awkward silence between the two of them.

Iyna desperately tried to think of anything to say to break the uncomfortable moment.

Thankfully, the priest turned to the villagers, unveiling his pure white hood. "Loyal people of her guiding warmth, I welcome you to bear witness to the offering your labour has wrought."

The crowd quietened as they turned their attention to him and the reddening horizon flowing beyond the small wall.

"On the night of this bountiful harvest, we offer our food to the all-seeing mother as a sign of our endless gratitude to her gentle guidance over our lives."

Like the rest of the villagers, Iyna devoutly raised her head towards the offering, and though she tried to keep her mind on the offering, she kept picturing using her mother's spear.

The priest knelt beside the offering, and with a scrap of flint against iron, sparks flew onto the dry straw. Flames sprouted and flourished across the stack, and he steadily lifted his aged body to his feet. As the sound of cracking seeds filled the air, he stepped away and raised his voice. "May this light that shines as she sleeps act as a symbol of her inextinguishable support for us all."

With the warmth of the roaring fire radiating out, the priest bowed his head towards the sun as she finally disappeared below the horizon. "May we strive to better the world and its numerous souls towards a brighter tomorrow." A moment later the last yellow glow of the sun faded from the darkened sky, whereupon the priest turned to the crowd. "Thank you."

As the last two words left his lips, nearly all of the villagers brought their attention to the free ale, and not a moment later the two cart haulers readied their instruments.

Vernon relaxed and turned at Iyna. "I think I'll get a drink. Do you want one?"

Iyna shook her head. "Need a clear head for tomorrow."

"This is a night to celebrate," Vernon said. "And you have an especially good reason to enjoy yourself tonight."

The cart haulers began playing, with Rioree's hands beating a light rhythm against his lap drum followed by the swift twangs of Pern's harp sending a flurry of music dancing into the evening air.

Iyna took a deep breath. "All right, but just the one."

"That's the spirit," Vernon replied.

Before long, the two of them were standing in the midst of the crowd with tankards of yellowish ale overhearing all kinds of merry chatter between the playful rhythm of the drum and harp. Though Cairsie wasn't there, Iyna still enjoyed the atmosphere of the festival even if she was daydreaming through most of Vernon's unending talk of the federation's first emperor. The offering had burned to a perfect red mound but still flooded the cobblestone centre with a pleasant warmth and a bright glow for all to see.

Taking a sip of her barely touched ale, Iyna thought back to the first festival she and Cairsie had enjoyed in this place. She couldn't help but smile at all the grand stories, fitness training and sparing lessons that had prepared her for this moment.

Without warning, an agonisingly long scream bellowed from the gate, silencing the drum and harp. The joyous atmosphere vanished as all eyes turned to the pitch black street leading to the gate. Iyna tried squinting past the bright lanterns surrounding the cobblestones only to see nothing but shadows. Glancing up to the night sky, she realised neither moon had yet risen, worsening her unease.

All around her, the crowd was muttering in voices of confusion, worry and indifference, only for them all to be hushed by a loud, strange whistle echoing from the gate across Edenor.

A short, dreaded moment followed, before several figures in red scaly armour crept from the shadowy surroundings, bringing terror to the farmers and craftsmen. As the defenceless crowd drew closer together, Iyna struggled to see. Her eyes widened with shock, and her tankard fell from her loose grip, clattering against the cobblestones.

Any previous image conjured in her mind from Cairsie's tales did little to reflect their nightmarish appearance. One had the large, unblinking eyes of a mountain owl while another possessed the towering white legs of a tusked goat. A bowman's bulbous shoulders pulsated like a heartbeat while a pikeman's snakelike skin shimmered in the firelight. For a long while, Iyna stood unable to move at the horrific sight. Her thoughts turned to Cairsie's safety, and Iyna looked for a way to escape these Beast Riders.

Further monstrous figures emerged from the surrounding shadows, bringing the villagers even closer together, packing them in a tight crowd. A long stillness hung in the air as the surrounding Beast Riders stared wordlessly at the stunned crowd. A singular set of hooves walking from Edenor's gate drew everyone's attention. A dark violet steed whose chest grew long lilac feathers approached, a single curved antler jutting forward beneath its chin. Though its narrow sapphire eyes glistened in the flickering shadows, Iyna's wide gaze was drawn to its enormous bear-like rider and the gargantuan reddened halberd he effortlessly held.

The fur-covered rider moved his steed onto the cobblestones, and without a word, slowly circled the frightened villagers till he was overlooking the burning offering.

The monstrous figure turned his attention away from the red fire and towards the villagers. "I see you all enjoy the same carefree lives as though nothing happened. You still burn your food, still celebrate your harvest, still live lives bathed in ignorance." He narrowed his pure black eyes, darting them from one face to the next as his breath became ragged. He pointed the spike of his halberd towards the white-robed priest. "You! Step closer."

The elderly man quivered in terror as he stepped from the safety of the crowd towards the spike.

Once the frail man was within arm's reach of the spike, one of the black eyes of the monstrous rider twitched. "How old are you?"

"Seventy … seventy-three." The priest's legs shook.

"So you lived through the culling?" The humongous rider moved his steed forward, bringing the spike within a finger's length of the old man's face. "Perhaps you even put many of us to the chopping block yourself."

The priest shook his head, trying to speak. "I-I-I wasn't—"

"Liar."

Iyna watched as the bear-like rider drove the spike into the old man's chest, bringing him screaming to the ground. The village centre filled with panic as the crowd ran in a maddening frenzy towards the gate, and the other Beast Riders watched in cruel delight. Iyna found her body moving in the frenzied flow of the terrified crowd with Vernon by her side, his book having fallen to the ground.

Iyna heard the priest's screams grow louder and glanced back just as the bear-like rider brought the axe part of his halberd down against the old man, silencing him. She shot her gaze ahead just as the same Beast Rider yelled, "Take what you deserve!"

It became a mad scramble towards the gate, with people desperately pushing past one another as the sounds of windows smashing and doors breaking filled the evening air.

Nearing the open gate, Iyna was brought to a horrified stop as she glimpsed Errad's mangled body through the crowd of fleeing villagers. Her mind thought only of Cairsie, and without hesitating, she left the crowd, running alongside the wall, ignoring Vernon calling to her.

Hearing the panic-stricken screams outside his residence, Jornis understood what had occurred. He thought of the wall ladder near his home that he could use to climb atop the ramparts and over the accompanying moat but rejected the idea of foolishly charging into the open dark street. Knowing such an action to be foolhardy, he rushed to the front door, bolting it shut, fully aware it would merely slow any intruders. Jornis pondered the first-floor window overlooking Edenor's wall and shook his head at the moronic idea of falling onto the wall below. One lone idea came to him.

He rushed back to his study and heaved the stone desk away from the wall, scattering the parchment stacks across the black floor. From where one of the back legs had stood, he prised up a small slate piece, revealing his hidden stockpile of documents and, more importantly, his precious stamp. As he took the latter from the hole, he heard the latch being tried against the door and hastily set the stone and desk back into place. A hammer against the black iron door echoed down the hallway, quickening Jornis to take a fresh parchment and grasp his ink feather. He took a deep, calming breath and brought his steadied writing hand against the page.

The battering refused to slow and was soon accompanied by someone striking the lounge's strengthened windows. Jornis briefly paused to recover his breathing, for his hand must remain unwavering, lest the letter appear amateurish.

He ended the letter with an old but cherished signature not of his original making. As he carefully folded the parchment, he heard a metal hinge strike the slate floor.

With only moments to act, Jornis scraped his stamp across the grey wax of his candle and sealed the letter with the emblem of Felliet. As he watched the wax dry, the thunderous sound of the metal door crashing in the hallway rung in his ears. Jornis tucked the stamp up his sleeve and broke the scarcely dried seal.

He heard footsteps approaching the study and took another deep breath to calm his nerves.

"Hello mate," a man's voice called out.

Letter in hand, Jornis calmly turned to the intruder. His large, unblinking eyes were carefully examining the small room while loosely holding in his right hand a rusted, spiked ball mace.

The Beast Rider tapped the wall with the mace. "So why don't you tell us where your valuables are … lest I get annoyed."

Unflinchingly maintaining eye contact, Jornis took a small leather purse from his pocket. "This contains eleven bronze and twelve brass coins. I assure you this is my entire fortune."

The intruder held out the palm of his free hand, into which Jornis placed the coin purse, bringing a victorious grin across the intruder's face. Another Beast Rider with bulbous throbbing shoulders that seemed ready to draw his ivy woven bow appeared. "Saw some books in the other room."

The owl-eyed man rattled the purse. "All yours. I'm fine 'ere."

As the bowman left for the lounge, the mace wielder darted his wide gaze down at the papers strewn across the floor. "Seems a little messy in 'ere. You sure you weren' hidin' anything more?"

Jornis held up the letter. "It took me a while to find this amongst the other documents."

"Oh?" the intruder said. "And what value does that have then?"

"For you and your companions, everything." Jornis held the parchment to him. "It is a letter from Ellity. It states that a group of thirty tribowmen will be arriving in Edenor at sunrise."

All confidence quickly vanished from the intruder's expression as he snatched the letter and stared bitterly at its contents.

Seeing the frustration build in the man's altered face, Jornis attempted to translate. "It reads that the Elite Dictorate are aware—"

"I can read!" the intruder shouted, and his strange pupils darted up and down the page. He glared at Jornis. "How do I know this to be real?"

"Examine the letter's seal," Jornis said. "It can only be made by the highest members of the Elite Dictorate, which even the governors of the large towns could never possess, let alone one leading a small village at the edge of the world."

The intruder turned the paper, narrowing his eyes at the dry, grey seal as his grip on the parchment further crumpled its edges. "So how come you've given me this then?"

Keeping eye contact, Jornis replied, "If those reinforcements arrive while your band is still in Edenor, you will be forced to barricade yourselves within our walls until every one of you is killed and I am blamed."

"Looking out for yourself then." The mace-wielding intruder stood for a long troublesome moment as he visibly pondered the situation. He stormed out of the study, letter in hand, and shouted down the hallway. "Kiran! We're leaving."

The bowman, books stacked in his large arms, followed the owl-eyed man out. With their departure, Jornis knew it was time to use the outside wall ladder.

Iyna grew increasingly distant as Vernon struggled to follow her alongside the wall.

"Iyna! Iyna!" he shouted in vain. "Iyna, slow down!"

Her frantic pace didn't slow, even as that same whistle sounded from the village centre, forcing Vernon to push his body harder as he desperately tried to keep her in sight. When he thought he would lose her, she stopped and he finally caught up with her.

Clutching his knees, Vernon thought only of trying to keep his breath as he spoke. "Iyna … you need to…" He looked up and saw Cairsie, face up on the ground with an arrow jutting from her bloodied neck.

Vernon's mind went blank at the sight, and he turned to Iyna who stood frozen in place, legs shaking. Her knees gave way, and she fell next to the body.

Tears silently poured down her stunned face, and Vernon wondered what he should do. He looked around, hoping he wouldn't spot any of the attackers emerging from the shadowy surroundings, and crouched in her line of vision, whispering, "We need to leave."

She didn't move.

Vernon heard the crackling of burning straw, far greater than the offering, and hurried to his feet. Horror gripped him as he glimpsed flames rising above the central rooftops, and he rushed to her again, urgently raising his voice. "Iyna! Please, we need to go."

Yet again, she didn't move.

He grabbed her hand, trying to tug her to her feet, only for her to angrily yank her hand back. "Just go away!"

Vernon glanced at the growing flames and frantically looked around, hoping for a solution. He spotted the spear lying near the body. Thinking of no alternative, he picked it up, crouched in front of Iyna and held it before her. She shifted her gaze from Cairsie's body to her mother's spear and moved her quivering hand towards its flaking green handle.

As soon as her fingers gently wrapped around the weathered green metal, Vernon said, "Take it."

Iyna looked at him with disbelief.

He said, "She wanted you to practice with it, correct?"

She slowly nodded.

"Well" Vernon let the spear fall into her grasp, "It's yours now, and Cairsie would want you to survive tonight so you can use it tomorrow."

Tears flowed freely down her cheeks and her hands tightened their grip. She gave a single reluctant nod.

The crackling of the straw roofs grew louder. Vernon rose to his feet, pulling her up with him. "We need to hurry."

Once they started running, she took her hand away from his and their pace quickened, but unlike before, they ran together. The sounds of many sets of hooves galloped past the other side of the wall, and he returned his attention to the curved path alongside the wall as grey smoke drifted through the air.

Before long, fire had spread to every rooftop, transforming Edenor into an inferno and leaving the air tasting of ash as smoke bellowed from every home, blowing across the entire village.

The two of them sprinted through the gate, emerging into the fresh, cool air outside the village, yet their pace refused to slow across the empty fields or when they crossed the stream. Only when they reached the pinnacle of their hill where many others had fled, did they stop to witness the sight of Edenor.

Exhausted in both mind and body, Vernon felt his weary muscles give way, and he collapsed onto the dry grass as his eyes stared at the engulfed village, knowing this horror could have been prevented.

Standing far from any obvious location a fleeing civilian might take, Jornis witnessed the village he was tasked to protect burn before his eyes and saw an opportunity.

With a single burning thought engulfing her mind, Iyna brought her mother's spear close to her chest as her bitter, watery eyes stared through the thick smoke at the monstrous figures riding away.

Far from the chaos and surrounded by their terrified neighbours, Niyaa's family stopped running, and the young girl's innocent eyes filled with tears as she looked back at the flames dancing above her home.

Chapter two – Morning

Fourth eclipse, nineteenth day

As dawn broke, the fires had subsided, revealing nothing but ash and blackened walls for the residents to return to. Iyna stepped through the broken gate. Spear tightly in hand, she could taste the dust and ash clinging to the chilling air, and hear aged wheels turning as the two cart haulers took Errad's body towards the cobblestones.

Turning to the scorch marks staining the stone walls along the ash-covered street, she felt her arms tense and realised Vernon's pitying eyes were focused on her. Iyna avoided his gaze and marched ahead, passing a handful of people sifting through the rubble of their ruined, roofless homes.

Treading on the cobblestones, she found her sandals overcome with the ash blanketing the centre, greying her toes. Slowly she turned to the large ash mound that had been the offering and watched the two cart haulers carefully place Errad's body alongside the priest's. Dread and sadness overcame Iyna, for she knew Cairsie would be placed there, her soul forever released.

"I will come with you if you like," Vernon said.

"No." Iyna kept her eyes trained on the pyre. "I don't need any help."

His voice softened. "Very well."

Taking in a long, deep breath, she marched alone towards the two cart haulers as they placed singed straw around the two bodies. "Cairsie…" Iyna's throat stiffened and her voice quaked. "Cairsie is by the eastern wall."

Pern asked, "Could you show us?"

Iyna glanced to the old spear in her hand. "I can."

With every step, her body felt weaker and heavier, draining all reason to keep moving, until she was within sight of Cairsie once more. Her legs nearly gave way, forcing Iyna to use her mother's spear to keep standing as Rioree and Pern rushed to the body with the cart.

Watching the two of them tear the arrow from Cairsie's neck, Iyna's vision blurred and her cheeks dampened. Her mind flooded with memories of Cairsie joyously telling all kinds of tales of what she and her friends had done during and after their training. Her stiff body was lifted into the cart, and Iyna's hands slid down her mother's spear as her knees gave way.

As the cart moved past her, Iyna turned to Cairsie's still face, and a faint whisper left her mouth. "Thank you."

Both Rioree and Pern held their heads low, avoiding her watery eyes as they passed by. Noticing their sorrowful faces, Iyna remembered Vernon helping her last night and was filled with a sense of helplessness. Her hands tensed, tightly regripping her mother's spear, and she pulled herself back to her feet.

Sadness was the only thing Niyaa felt as she walked through the broken green gate and into the grey street. Her parents had tried to put on brave faces and say hopeful words, but as they entered the blackened village grief met each of them.

Before long, they arrived at the village centre where they found it blanketed by grey ash and an eery silence. Niyaa spotted Vernon searching the ashy ground, and a burst of relief overcame her. She sprinted to him and hugged him tightly, tearfully saying, "I'm so happy you're all right."

His hand brushed her hair. "And I'm glad you're safe, too."

Niyaa looked into his eyes. "And Iyna? Is she all right?"

"She is, but…" Vernon glanced towards the offering.

Niyaa turned. Iyna was standing silently near a mound of darkened straw where three people lay.

Vernon stepped back with a worried look. "Cairsie … didn't make it."

Niyaa's eyes widened with disbelief.

"Best to leave her alone for now," Vernon suggested. "It's always difficult when you lose …"

"Oi, Vernon!" Niyaa's dad said. "I want to have *word* with the governor. You know where he is?"

"You speak as though he cares for his family's safety." Vernon's teeth clenched. "I will be the first to have a word with him, Darryam."

Niyaa's mom crossed her arms. "If he hasn't run off, that is."

Vernon's hands tensed into tight fists as he repeated her words. "If he has not run off."

He stormed off but stopped when his sandals hit something in the ash. He smiled and brushed the ash off his favourite book, bringing a little hope to Niyaa.

Darryam turned to his daughter. "Your mom and I are gonna look through our house. Could you find all the tankards for us?"

Niyaa glanced at the smashed glass table and the tankards scattered about. "I will."

"That's my girl." He turned to their wrecked brewery home.

Picking up a dented tankard, Niyaa caught a glimpse of the two moons sitting far above the southern mountains, their grey light shining in the pale blue of the sky. Niyaa wondered why they weren't watching over the village last night.

As Vernon gazed upon his home, the shock nearly caused him to loosen his grip on *The Foundations*. The entire first floor and roof had collapsed, leaving naught but four scorched walls with hollowed upper floor windows. Only the lounge's reinforced windows, though cracked and clouded, seemed intact. Gazing over the warped black iron door, he saw a hallway filled with ash-covered rubble and shattered glass. Nothing of value had survived.

His dirtied sandals stepped onto the dented emblem of Felliet that had been sheared off the black door. Vernon heard shovelling, and his despair turned to rage. Storming across the rubble mounds filling the hallway, he found his father digging through the debris of the study with a broken piece of slate.

"Where were you?" Vernon demanded.

Jornis paused to examine his son and continued to dig. "I see you are unharmed."

Vernon's arms tensed. "No thanks to you."

"I was busy protecting our future." The governor continued sifting through the ash and stone.

"Protecting our future?" Vernon shouted back. "What exactly did you do to protect our future?"

"If you are searching for someone to blame, you should turn your gaze towards Ellity." Jornis paused. "Edenor was pillaged because the Beast Riders desired retaliation from the third expedition that occurred recently."

"A third expedition?" Vernon's eyes widened. "We sent soldiers into the desert?"

"The forces were from Erium, not Felliet. However, what concerns me is not where they hail from but the lack of forewarning." He dug faster. "Only half of their thousand spearmen returned, a fact the border villages only learned twelve nights after the event. Furthermore, the information came from a courier from Vellide, not the capital."

"Why not announce it to the village?" Vernon asked. "You could have warned everyone."

"Every guard was well informed, and each understood the danger. Informing anyone not capable of fighting would have been a pointless act of fearmongering." Jornis scraped away the final pile of ash, clearing a corner of the slate floor. "The only other measure left to me was to repeatedly send letters to the Elite Dictorate, demanding reinforcements." He knelt down. "As expected of those incompetent fools, there was not a single reply."

Vernon tried in vain to come up with arguments against his father. Jornis removed a slate tile from the floor, revealing a concealed hole filled with parchments.

Jornis took various letters from the hole, briefly examining each one. "These papers will allow our family to return to Ellity."

Vernon's eyes widened with baffled anger. "You can't possibly consider returning to that life of backstabbing and greed!"

Jornis didn't react. "Would you rather labour in the fields at the mercy of rightfully vengeful raiders, all while the current members of the Dictorate plunge Felliet closer to collapse?"

Once again, Vernon was left without argument.

Jornis came across a map of Felliet and rolled it flat across the slate he had used to dig.

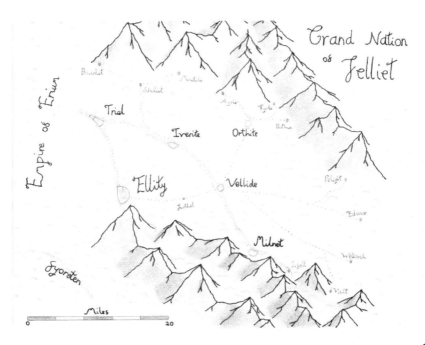

Staring at it, Vernon was reminded of the pitiful condition of this puny country and the maddening reason why it seceded from the great Empire of Erium.

The cart haulers had done well building the pyre; not only did they gather sufficient unburnt straw, but the six bodies had been placed with care, albeit three stacked atop three. With the majority of the villagers gathered to witness, it was time for Jornis to carry out his final duty as Edenor's governor. The pleasant thought lingered in his mind for a short while, and he finally scraped flint against iron, releasing sparks onto the golden strands.

Flames sprouted and flourished in strength, engulfing the bodies in the abundant sound of crackling. With the wretched stench of burning flesh overpowering his nostrils, Jornis stepped away from the fire and faced the crowd. Every expression was either filled with hatred or brimmed with anguish, making it unlikely his words would be logically understood. "The Beast Riders will return." Jornis watched as the crowd turned to him with appalled faces. "They now know the border villages are vulnerable and will continue these raids unless the Elite Dictorate sends troops. Until that happens, every person here needs to leave Edenor."

Most of the crowd moronically glanced at one another while others mumbled their limited options with a handful choosing to ignore his warning and stare at the flames.

Moments later, one of the brewers pushed his way to the front, shouting in a temper. "Our parents founded Edenor, and it has proudly stood for decades! We shouldn't just abandon it!"

The man clearly didn't understand the dire position staying would pose. "Darryam, correct? Let me clarify the current situation for you. We have no fighters among us anymore, no longer any shelter from the rain and no grain left unburnt in the destroyed mill. The Beast Riders know every single one of those facts. Now you would suggest remaining here, undefended, purely because your parents profited from the Eastern Extension?"

Darryam paused. Jornis imagined the man's feeble mind trying to bring up a counterpoint. "We can learn to defend ourselves. We can rebuild our homes and—"

"And what if they return tonight?" Jornis asked.

The brewer fell silent.

Jornis turned his focus to the other disgruntled members of the crowd. "We have no alternative. You all need to leave Edenor. If you know of friends and family living elsewhere in Felliet, then move there; otherwise, I suggest the capital would be an ideal place to find employment, for it remains cripplingly short of labourers."

The other brewer made her way through the crowd to stand by her husband. "I would rather rot on the ground than head to Ellity!" She looked around her. "If we must leave, then I choose somewhere where we'll feel welcome. Edenor's bought cartloads of stone and tools from Pelight, and they've bought cartloads of bread and ale from us. Our family will head there."

Jornis watched as Mysia gave a reassuring smile to her husband as though her plan had any sense or reason to it. He sighed. "Pelight is smaller than Edenor, and its few farms are scarcely able to support itself. This means it lacks adequate space and food to house any newcomers."

Darryam asked, "You think it was easy building *this* village?" He smirked. "Long before you arrived, we had to work hard to scrap together enough coin for new seeds and uproot all the glass shards growing in the fields."

Obviously, this couple would never listen to reason. "Very well," Jornis said. "If you feel able to survive in a village such as Pelight rather than going to one of the towns or Ellity, then you may head there. Be warned, however, their garrison will be just as unlikely to defend against any raids as the guards here."

The girl holding a spear immediately interrupted. "Don't you dare say Cairsie didn't protect us!"

Taken by surprise, Jornis paused to reflect on his words and realised discontent had grown throughout the crowd. "My apologies. I worded that poorly, so I would like to clarify. The five guards of Edenor fought bravely against such overwhelming odds and had they a dozen more similarly exceptional fighters, those monsters would never have been able to enter the village." Using the word *monster* felt both improper and debauched, but at least the description seemed to ease much of the anger from the girl's expression. Jornis swiftly readdressed the crowd. "Gather your belongings, for once the great mother is at her highest, we shall depart Edenor as a single group."

Gradually the villagers dispersed but not without many distrusted glares towards their former governor.

The girl approached him, no doubt wanting to argue. She stomped her spear into the ground. "How do I become a soldier?"

Surprised again by this girl, Jornis briefly hesitated before attempting to dissuade her. "The life of a soldier can be rough. I expect it will become worse very soon. I must ask whether you have thought this through and are not merely acting on sudden emotion."

Her eyes narrowed. "I have."

"You must understand, Felliet has no army. Almost certainly you will be a guardsman in Ellity or one of the towns, merely patrolling the streets, resolving barfights and occasional criminal hunts. The revenge or glory you seek will not manifest going down that path."

"I don't care." She tightened her grip on the spear. "I will become a soldier."

Jornis stared at the girl's fiery expression, realising she could not be persuaded. "Very well. If you believe you can endure the hardship of fighting for your life and those around you, then you may accompany us to Ellity where the Plythiat tower stands nearby. There you can enlist."

Trudging along at the back of the despair-ridden caravan, Vernon thought of the upcoming days he would be spending in that corrupt city, never again feeling the rural breeze against his skin. In the limited time he had, he ignored the beating footsteps along the dirt road, blocked out the occasional sobbing and instead revelled in the delight of nature around him. Effortlessly swooping above, white fanbirds chirped, while the surrounding hills were adorned with bright flowers of blues and yellows filling the midday air with a pleasant aroma. Obscuring much of the landscape ahead of him was a cluster of towering, budding flowers gracefully swaying in the gentle breeze. Vernon had always wondered how such colossal, leafless parasollers kept their giant colourful petals from never so much as tilting away from the sun, even on the windiest days.

Entering the canopy, Vernon's nostrils were overcome by both the sweet aroma thickly coating each stem and the rose-like scent of the pink stalks abundantly flourishing in the shade of these soaring parasollers. He marvelled at the sunrays passing through the giant petals above, for they cast a shifting collage of purples, blues and yellows across the entire foliage of pink stalks. Just like the first time he walked through this beautiful place, he buried his worries in childish delight.

Unfortunately, it wasn't long before the caravan left the canopy, bringing Vernon's wonderous enjoyment to a swift end. He witnessed villagers taking a diverting path with only Jornis and Iyna waiting on the main road to Vellide. Niyaa's family stopped at the crossroads. Darryam, carting their brewing pot, glanced to his wife, and they both turned to Niyaa.

Mysia crouched to her daughter's eye level. "Niyaa, this is where we depart from those heading to Ellity."

Surprised confusion filled Niyaa's expression, and she turned to her friends. She looked back to her mother. "What? No. We can't split up. We … we can't." She desperately turned to her friends. "Why … why don't you come with us?"

Vernon made no attempt to give her a reassuring look. "I'm sorry."

Iyna wordlessly lowered her head.

Niyaa turned to her parents, and her voice croaked. "They can stay with us. We can make room."

Mysia slowly shook her head, and Darryam placed his hand on his daughter's shoulder as her eyes watered. She turned to Iyna and Vernon and sprinted to them, tightly embracing them both in a hug.

Vernon returned the gesture. "It will be all right. You, Iyna and I will be fine wherever we end up."

Though she hesitated, Iyna put her arms around them both, and the three of them held each other for as long as they could. Only when Jornis called for them to hurry did they slowly break apart, and soon after, Niyaa and her parents headed towards Pelight.

Gratifyingly, the two ignorant children uttered no words throughout the long journey; however, their growling stomachs routinely broke Jornis's inner thoughts. As the day turned to night, the lanterns shining from Vellide's brown walls came within sight. Unusually, it seemed as though the town walls were fully manned, and as they approached closer, Jornis observed they were unadorned by climbable ivy and not weakened by deep elaborate carvings.

Nearing the eastern gatehouse, the moat and river had been cleared of any lone parasollers while the wheat and glass fields were placed a good distance away, lest anything act as cover. It was satisfying to know governor Parick was sensible enough to understand the dire situation Felliet was in.

Crossing the stone bridge over the moat, Jornis was further pleasantly surprised by the four spearmen standing guard beneath the town's portcullis, each wearing iron chainmail. He pondered how this town could possibly afford to outfit their garrison with such expense, and a brief smile came to him.

One of the guards spoke. "What business do you—"

Jornis put an end to the questioning. "As the governor of Edenor, I seek an immediate audience with Parick Sepp, and if you continue to obstruct me or my companions, I shall have the four of you empty every cesspit in this town."

The guard flustered. "Erm, right … I'll escort you to his house."

They followed the guard through the smooth stone highway that cut through the town all the while abutted by blue cladded homes and shops. Not only were they taller than his former residence in Edenor, but each were kept in remarkable cleanliness. This further added to the mystery of how a minor town so far from the major trade routes had accrued such notable fortune since he had last ventured through it nine comets ago. The further Jornis pondered the answer, the better an ally Parick seemed.

The guard escorted them into the large, central market square lined at its edges with narrow, brick water channels. Predictably, the stones Jornis trod on still emanated a faint smell of ale while many festive decorations remained strewn on the tiled rooftops around the clearing. Curiously, however, the town centre had no obvious elite residence, leaving as the only distinct structure the glass domed chapel.

Nearing the short, narrow bridge at the other end of the marketplace, the guard pointed to the nearest house on the opposite bank. Had the shield of Felliet not been bolted onto its black iron door, Jornis would have assumed it belonged to a simple commoner.

"This is the governor's house," the guard announced.

Jornis barely glanced at him. "Remain here with these two until I return."

Not waiting for a response, Jornis approached the black door and used its simple knocker. Almost instantly the door opened, revealing a young, pink-haired stewardess wearing a red and white velvet dress, who merely stared at him without uttering a word.

He stepped forward. "I am Jornis Meyorter, governor of Edenor, and I must speak with Parick Sepp."

Without replying, the stewardess stepped to one side, inviting him inside. Setting foot on the red-veined granite floor, Jornis observed only an undecorated iron chandelier furnishing the short hallway. The stewardess bolted the door shut and gestured to an open lounge at the end of the hallway in which Jornis could hear the crackling of a fireplace. She calmly departed through a side door.

Entering the windowless lounge, Jornis was again met by a barely furnished room where only a pair of padded armchairs and a glass serving table stood to fill the bare carpet. However, above the crackling fireplace, which a young blonde stewardess presently fuelled, hung a large portrait of a ginger-bearded elite. He caught the attention of the young stewardess, and she wordlessly departed through one of the two side doors, leaving Jornis alone in this bare room. He could not help but grin at the obvious intention to unease any guest, placing them at a disadvantage when making deals. Therefore, rather than relaxing in one of the armchairs or demanding attention like most other elites, Jornis positioned himself with his back to the fireplace, patiently observing the room.

An excessive while later, the ginger-bearded elite threw open a side door. "Jornis Meyorter." He toured past the armchairs to stand before his guest. "It's quite a pleasure to meet you, even more so in my abode."

The two stewardesses followed, one carrying a brass tray ladened with a bottle of unopened whiskey and a pair of two crystal cut tumblers while the other held an oval plate of assorted cheeses. Without instruction, they set the tray and plate on the table and positioned themselves at the farthest end of the room.

Keeping his eyes fixed on Jornis, Parick gestured to the bottle. "Would you care for a glass? This vintage has been barrelled for eight entire comets."

Though admiring the attempted distraction, Jornis kept his gaze locked on Parick. "I must abstain from such pleasures until we have discussed an urgent matter."

"Oh?" The man's face filled with curiosity as he sat in one of the armchairs and waved at the pink-haired stewardess to come closer. She opened the bottle and filled the two tumblers, placing one in Parick's open palm, and returned to the far end of the plain room. The elite sniffed the drink. "A matter urgent enough for Jornis Meyorter to come visit. How intriguing."

Jornis shifted his gaze to the two stewardesses standing along the back wall and focused on Parick once more.

The elite leaned back in his chair. "You needn't worry about my girls. I have trusted them with many sensitive matters, and they have never dissatisfied me."

"Very well," Jornis said, accepting his conditions. He sat firmly upright in the second armchair and explained, "Beast Riders have crossed the border and reduced the village of Edenor to rubble."

Parick paused for a moment, staring deeply into his whiskey. "I appreciate you informing me of this grave matter, but I can tell you didn't visit me to relay a single message."

Jornis's eyes narrowed. "I understand the Elite Dictorate approved a third expedition without a suitable warning to any border settlement."

Parick stared at Jornis for a long moment and took another sip from his crystal tumbler.

Firmly grasping the second glass, Jornis declared, "I came because I have a proposition."

Chapter three – Arrival

Fourth eclipse, twentieth day

The twinkling blue and green stars had barely left the sky when Niyaa woke, leaving her feeling sleepy for the rest of the walk to Pelight. Finally, the little village nestled at the foot of a mountain was in sight. Relief washed over the group as they neared the grey wall made from stone unlike the brown-veined rocks scattered across the mountain slope. The moat alongside the empty fields was shallow and only a single plume of black smoke rose from one of the chimneys. Even so, seeing a packed bunch of yellow-roofed homes overlooked by a tall house just like Vernon's was a welcome sight for everyone.

As soon as the large group reached the village's unrusty gate, a woman's loud voice brought all the happy relief to a quick end. "Who're you lot?" The female guard had bolted the barred gate shut and was staring out with suspicious eyes.

Darryam stepped forward. "We're from Edenor. It's been attacked by Beast Riders, so we've come asking for your aid."

The guard squinted at the many farmers and craftsmen. "We ain't got nothin' to spare."

Darryam took another step forward, pleading. "All we're askin' is a little shelter and food. In return, you'll realise each one of us is a hard worker who can help grow more crops."

She half closed her eyes. "We don't need you here and we don't want ya, so go back to Edenor."

"We can't!" Darryam shouted.

Mysia quickly stood by him, smirking. "Thankfully, you don't get to decide. Now, tell your governor to meet us here right away."

Niyaa glanced to her parents with a mix of pride and wariness.

"He'll just say the same thing I have." The woman shrugged.

Mysia said, "We'll see."

An uncomfortable tense silence plagued the air between them until the guard stormed away, and Niyaa let out a good long sigh of relief.

A short while later, the guard returned with a slender man in a shiny tunic who climbed atop the small wall and peered across the dry moat beside the gate. "Greetings. My subordinate told me you are all from Edenor which was recently attacked. Which among you is the governor?"

Niyaa's parents glanced to one another, and Darryam explained, "That coward left for the city."

Every bit of sincerity drained from the man's face as he feigned politeness. "That is unfortunate. However, I'm afraid I cannot offer much in the way of shelter."

Darryam responded, "Many of us could sleep in your chapel or in some tents. At least until Edenor's rebuilt."

The governor shook his head. "Afraid we lack many tents and our chapel is rather small. Furthermore, since the festival, we have only enough bread for *our* people."

"We're the best farmers around." Darryam pounded his chest. "Plus we can always scavenge the land for mushrooms and frogs if need be."

Mysia quickly chimed in. "I'm quite sure Jornis Meyorter will be punished for abandoning his people the way he did. However, the one who truly welcomes us will surely be seen as going beyond his duty for the good of Felliet."

The man put his hand to his chin and grinned. "You're right, it would be for the betterment of Felliet that its people are cared for. Therefore, I announce as the governor of Pelight, I, Seveck Heef, shall welcome you all into our walls."

Niyaa sighed in relief.

Darryam turned and crouched in front of his daughter. "This will be our new home for a while, and even though it isn't Edenor, we can make it bright together."

"I know we will." Niyaa nodded.

The gate's bolt slid open. The female guard bit her lip as she stiffly opened the gate for the desperate villagers. A strange uneasiness washed over Niyaa.

Despite spending the previous night in a cushioned bed in Vellide, Vernon had gotten little sleep, for his unending worries had made his thoughts restless and his stomach uneasy. The pewter leather satchel and expensive grey clothes he had been freely given only worsened this feeling. Still, he was thankful Iyna had been given strong sandals to handle the loose stone along the road, as well as for the salted fish last night and the buttered bread this morning. After a full day travelling Felliet's poorly kept road, Ellity's dimly lit wall appeared in the darkening landscape.

Parasollers still wildly flourished along the moat, the grey walls were still riddled with pewter ivy and the city's ramparts remained meagrely supplied with both soldiers and lanterns. Had it not been for the extravagant grey glass shield emblem hanging above the iron portcullis, Vernon would have assumed nothing had changed.

Biting his lip, Vernon followed Jornis and Iyna across the grey bridge, passing a pair of drunken guards boasting about their aim. Neither so much as batted an eye to the three strangers entering the city nor to their tribows, coated in scratches and dirt marks, haphazardly left on the ground.

Setting foot in the city, Vernon gazed down the straight, wide highway that stretched a mile through the commoner area to the inner wall. The entire way along the undecorated street, he saw unpainted stone walls and plain tiled roofs with a smell of horse manure oozing from the cobblestones. Meanwhile, towering from the centre of the extravagant, inner wall were the three glass spires of the Elite Gallery: two grey and one black. Vernon felt his muscles tense at the injustice of this wretched city.

Trudging down the wide, quiet street, Vernon noticed only a few homes shone candlelight from the single-paned windows and realised the shortage of labourers was still ongoing. Memories surfaced of when he had delivered trivial messages from one prosperous elite to another, passing exhausted labourers hauling carts laden with harvested glass or quarried rock. Remembering it was his father who had made him do such jobs in the hopes of forging connections with various debauched elites, Vernon felt his stomachache worsen.

Halfway through the neglected commoner area, Vernon heard joyous laughter emerging from a pair of large windows, flooding the darkening street with bright light, soothing his bitter thoughts. Vernon rushed to peer inside; whereupon, he observed a small merry crowd gathered around an oval bar in the centre of a quaint square room. Pressing his hand against the glass, he felt the pleasant warmth from the ceiling fire bowl, and imagined himself relaxing at one of the many tables around the inviting tavern. He read the sign engraved above its stained stem-woven door: The Welcomerry Band. He turned to the others, only to realise neither Jornis or Iyna had waited, forcing Vernon to prise himself away from the comforting sight and catch up with them.

They approached the second gatehouse which stood in blunt contrast to the outer wall, for not only were its ramparts properly lit but the four guardsmen stood proudly in expensive iron chainmail with shortswords hanging from their belts. Vernon glimpsed their scrutinising eyes from below their iron domed helmets and observed each one staring at Iyna, clearly focusing on her commoner clothing instead of her spear. Yet, for the simple reason she travelled with two people in fine attire, they hardly bothered to question her, and the three of them passed unobstructed beneath the brass-lined portcullis.

Entering the grid-like streets of the inner wall, Vernon's nostrils were bombarded with the abhorrent scent of silver lavender that adorned every windowsill, gardenbed and glass balcony along the extravagant street. He couldn't help but recoil at the once-forgotten stench as he gazed at the polished elevated houses and their dark turquoise roofs. He trudged along the smoothened stonework of the extravagant inner wall with tense arms and resentful breathing.

Reaching the plaza at the heart of the city, Vernon felt his anger rise, for beneath his feet lay the tip of the shield of Felliet depicted across an enormous marble mosaic. This, like the glass emblem above the city's entrance, was new to him, and he realised it would have been paid for by the taxes collected from the neglected commoners. Vernon's gaze drifted to the Elite Gallery towering at the other end of the mosaic. Its absurd frontal grey spires intricately displayed mountain carvings and was showcased by the candlelight shining from within the Gallery's curved glass roof. Yet the central spire, soaring above its grey counterparts from the furthest end of the glass roof, was entirely made of glistening black crystal. It remained as the one undefiled symbol of greatness in Ellity and of Felliet's foolishness.

Approaching its heavily guarded solid brass doors, Jornis glanced at Vernon and Iyna. "Wait for me here."

Neither responded.

Vernon was left to stand in the centre of the shield mosaic, watching his father walk to the guards in polished chainmail, no doubt saying something condescending before entering the detested Elite Gallery. Watching the bronze-lined doors close behind his father, Vernon bit his bottom lip and averted his gaze.

Disappointment greeted Jornis upon entering the Gallery's hall, for he saw that in his absence the elites were allowed far greater autonomy to decorate the long walls with their respective crests. Simple brass-engraved shields had been replaced by elaborate, uncoordinated concoctions of ornaments, flowers, tapestries and stained glass along these ashen walls. Predictably, the most elaborate crests belonged to the eleven members of the Dictorate, hanging above their respective panel seats at the far end of the Gallery. The largest was a needlessly exorbitant bronze shield displayed prominently in the centre and engraved with the family name Zenth. Jornis had once pondered whether Felliet's head family would discontinue its arrogant outlook after so many blunders, so upon seeing their elaborate crest, he felt foolish for thinking so optimistically.

Head held high, Jornis marched his way past the wasteful displays towards the overly guarded judging panel where only three Dictorate members had bothered to handle today's line of commoners. Seeing the inept fanatic Rellorn and the ignorant fool Ovallian slouched in those authoritative seats made Jornis's muscles tense. At least the third elite, sitting upright near the centre of the stand, seemed to pay attention to the commoner's concerns, albeit the ramblings of an elderly stonemason standing before the panel.

"You!" the repulsive Ovallian shouted at Jornis, silencing the frail commoner. "How dare you set foot in these walls!"

Ignoring the buffoon, Jornis kept his gaze on the female elite as he marched past the common people, placing himself before the panel. Noticing her black silk robe, he knew the previous head of the Lawver name had passed and was glad to see Felliet's newest rulemaker was at least attentive. Not bothering to waste his time on the elderly commoner, Jornis promptly said, "Before I share my information with you, I must implore that we speak privately."

The Lawver head paused for a brief moment. "Very well." With a single wave of her hand, several of the swordsmen approached the shocked line, escorting them out.

Keeping his eyes focused on the panel members, Jornis patiently waited for the doors to slam shut on the pointless complaining of the commoners. "I, the head of the Meyorter name, have come before you today with a warning. As of yesterday, Felliet faces threats from *both* its borders, neither of which it can challenge alone."

Rellorn guffawed in his white hood. "Hyperbolic as usual, I see."

Jornis continued, "An organised group of Beast Riders easily overcame the defenders at Edenor and destroyed the village. It is clear the third expedition drove them to retaliate, and as a result they have become a threat to every settlement east of Vellide." Jornis glanced at the religious fool. "I demand to understand why the Elite Dictorate deemed it necessary to allow this to occur."

"You would allow those *things* to continue to roam free under the great mother's warmth?" The hooded fanatic leaned closer. "Each one of them needs to be exterminated as soon as possible!"

"Does your hatred for the Beast Riders exceed your duty to serve and protect Felliet?"

"Destroying them quickly is the best thing for humanity, Felliet included," Rellorn argued.

Taking a deep breath, Jornis said, "Allowing a foreign army to march through *our* lands to fight *our* enemy shows both military and diplomatic weakness. Therefore, your careless actions have demonstrated Felliet is vulnerable to the other eight nations." He turned back to the only sensible member on the panel. "Needless to say, this expedition has not only opened the east to future raids but has shown Felliet is unable to defend itself on the field or at the negotiation table."

Silence gripped the vast Gallery till Ovallian's brass chair creaked as the man leaned back. "I see no reason to be concerned. Those villages serve little purpose to Felliet and our relationship with Erium is sound." He brought his body forward, slamming his chair legs down, and demanded, "What I would like to know is why you would dare show yourself after so disgracefully allowing a bunch of mere bandits to destroy your village."

Refusing to acknowledge the moronic argument, Jornis kept his attention on the Lawver head. "If the settlements east of Vellide no longer believe the Dictorate are willing to protect them, they will eventually secede from Felliet, potentially allying themselves with Erium or even those *bandits*. Ultimately, why *would* they trust you after deliberately ignoring repeated requests for reinforcements that could have avoided Edenor's destruction."

"Don't you dare shift the blame!" the fool spat back. "You forget that you only married into a prestigious name. You hold no authority here nor anywhere else!"

Incensed, Jornis glared at Ovallian, steadfastly keeping any words from leaving his lips.

The Lawver elite turned to the ignorant fool. "Ovallian, speak no more. The further your tongue moves, the further your name is soiled."

Ovallian's face scrunched with sheer rage at her remark. He stormed out of his seat and barged through a black side door.

The Lawver elite returned her attention to Jornis. "What do you suggest?"

"Felliet needs allies." He took a short breath to calm himself. "Send lesser elites westward to build the foundations of trading and military alliances. If successful, this will see our needs are properly addressed in the federation."

She pondered the advice for a long moment and asked, "I assume you are volunteering to be one of people assigned to this task."

A bitter memory of the last day in the great chamber came to Jornis, and he replied, "Can you think of alternative candidates with a greater knowledge of diplomacy? With experience negotiating for the betterment of Felliet within the federation?"

Rellorn smirked. "Such as your decision to bring us into that disaster of the Southern Campaign?"

Jornis felt his arms tense as he half-heartedly shifted his gaze to the uninformed priest. "Erium's armies are vast with men who are far better trained and equipped. Unlike Fyoreten, Felliet does not have a powerful ally to its border, nor does it possess an army. Therefore, had we abstained to send hundreds of guardsmen to that doomed-to-fail war, the emperor of Erium would have had little reason not to conquer Felliet." Jornis turned back to the Lawver elite. "Hence the reason we need allies."

The two elites glanced at each other. "Then as a member of the Dictorate, I, Pryias Lawver, shall grant you permission to build an alliance with a federation nation you deem appropriate. However, I must ask that this matter remain confidential."

"It would be foolish to allow our enemies to discover our plans," Jornis replied.

Rellorn leaned back in his chair and muttered, "At least it means you would be far from our lands."

Pryias asked, "Is there anything you require?"

"An inexpensive but reliable horse," Jornis said. "And for my son to attend the academy."

Standing on the beautiful mosaic pattern, Iyna was in sheer awe at the enormous structure whose stunning glistening towers stretched far towards the stars. Even the blue homes around her were incredible and gave off a nice smell of lavender from their gorgeous balconies and flowerbeds. Her gaze drifted to the guards in polished chainmail, and she wondered whether her mom and Cairsie had ever stood together on this beautiful plaza. Though her mom's face had become blurry in Iyna's mind, she could picture the two of them joking and singing together amidst a bunch of their friends in one of these beautiful city homes. Without realising, a pleasant smile came to her.

She didn't know how long she was staring at her wonderous surroundings, but once she heard the heavy grand doors open, she was brought back to reality. Jornis was leaving the bronze doors, anger in his eyes, and she knew he must also have hated recounting the horrors of that night.

Jornis approached his son and coldly told him, "Tonight you will be lodged in one of Felliet's boarding estates."

Vernon gritted his teeth. "And when am I supposed to join the academy?"

"Tomorrow," Jornis answered and turned to Iyna. "The Plythiat tower is a mile north of the city's walls."

"Thank you." Iyna tightened her grip on her mother's spear. She turned to Vernon, and despite knowing this moment was coming, neither had any words to say, leaving them staring longingly into each other's eyes. In the same moment, they both tightly embraced each other.

Iyna thought of their duels, their reading lessons and the many times they had spent playing in Edenor. She held him tighter, longing to keep this moment lasting.

Jornis placed his hand on his son's shoulder. "It's time to go, Vernon."

The two pulled themselves away with the same saddened look.

"Farewell, Iyna."

"See ya, Vernon."

They turned away from each other, and keeping her chin high, Iyna refused to look back as she marched out of the plaza. Her pace quickened till she was nearly jogging out of the rich-person area, passing the confused guards from the northern inner gatehouse.

Not long after, Iyna ran out of the city, whereupon she gazed across the hilly landscape with its many glass fields mirroring the starry sky. She spotted a wide grey tower standing alongside a dim, blue cladded manor house, and her heart raced as she ran towards it. Heading down the wide dirt track towards the Plythiat tower and posh home, she noticed a third hall-like building that spewed bright candlelight from its many high-up windows.

Arriving at the grassless courtyard sitting between all three buildings, Iyna heard the sound of plentiful joyous conversations from the long building. A small candle shone out of the tower's ajar door. Peering inside, she saw hundreds of metal crates, barrels and cloth sacks filling every foot of an incredibly large circular room. Only by a narrow passage through the clutter could someone find the stairs that curved along the tower's left side. Fast asleep on several of the sacks before the iron door was a man in plain grey clothes who had turned away from the candle that dripped wax onto a nearby barrel.

Iyna took a deep breath and stomped her spear handle against the stone floor. "I would like to become a soldier."

The man groaned as he turned his head slightly.

She raised her voice. "I would like to become a soldier."

He looked directly at her and got up, stretching his arms wide. "Sorry 'bout that. It gets awfully boring doing this job." He reached his arm between the sacks and grasped a small book. "Name and age?"

"Iyna. Seventeen."

"Tribow or sp…" He looked up from his book. "Spear it is."

"Thank you." She glanced outside. "Where do I go now?"

He gestured to the stairs. "Best put that spear of yours with the others at the top."

Iyna stared at the weathered, sharp iron tip and said, "Will it be used by anyone else?"

"Not until everyone finishes their training," he explained.

She brought her mother's spear close to her chest, afraid to agree.

He smirked. "It means something to ya, don't it?"

She nodded.

"Well"—he rubbed the back of his head—"I don't do this often, but I'll keep it safe in 'ere if ya want."

Iyna was overcome with relief. "Thanks."

"Just make sure not to tell anyone, all right?" He held out his hand.

Iyna hesitated as she gave her mother's spear to the stranger. Her discomfort grew as she nervously watched him carry it across the many crates and barrels and hide it at the shadowy end of the circular room.

As he ventured back, she asked, "What's your name?"

"Soart." He lay back down on the nearby sacks. "Now you'll need a full stomach for the morning, so I'd suggest you best head to the dinin' hall before my stew runs empty."

Iyna anxiously glanced to the dark side of the circular room and forced herself to leave the tower and head straight for the long building's wicker door. As she placed her hand on its latch, her mind dug up the fuzzy memory of when Cairsie returned scarred from that battle. A chill raised every hair over her entire body as though she were once again shivering in that white land. Iyna clenched her hands and shook her head, disregarding the nagging fear and pushed the door open.

Her confidence wavered as she gazed across the rows and rows of tables, seating perhaps a hundred chatting people in all kinds of groups, leaving her standing there with little idea of how or who to approach. Yet, strangely, only half the tables were filled, leaving the other half of the hall devoid of life. She glanced at the high table beside the door and disappointedly saw each of the large pots and numerous bowls it held were emptied of food. Not wanting to speak to anyone tonight, she trudged her way alongside the wall to one of the many empty tables and slumped down by herself.

Barely a moment later, a woman called to her. "Hey newcomer! Got a spare bowl here if you want."

Iyna looked over and saw a woman with a beaming smile gesturing to an empty spot next to a grinning, scruffy red-headed boy opposite her. She picked up a bowl of stew from in front of a skinny pale girl who sat next to her and held it up for Iyna to see. Feeling her stomach rumble and seeing the woman's bright smile, Iyna swiftly joined them.

Taking the seat next to the boy, Iyna relaxed as the woman slid the bowl of barely touched stew to her. "Leemia here doesn't eat much at all, so her bowl usually goes to someone else anyway."

The pale girl kept her nervous eyes on the table and whispered, "You … you can … have it."

The woman beamed. "Leemia could barely say a full sentence when she arrived, plus she's looking a lot healthier now."

The pale girl blushed as a slight smile grew on her face. Iyna devoured the cold stew.

The boy scooted closer to her. "Name's Beely. One of the best tribowmen here."

The woman laughed. "I heard it takes you forever to crank your tribow."

"Well, yeah." Beely shrugged. "But if you look at my aim, then I'm just as good as Leemia."

Between spoonfuls, Iyna asked, "So you three are tribowmen then?"

"Not quite." Beely pointed to the woman. "For some reason, Sareesa here thinks a spear is better than a good tribow."

Sareesa folded her arms. "Well in close quarters *your* weapon's pretty much worthless, especially since the moons passing is shorter than how long it takes for *you* to reload."

"I'm not that slow at cranking." Beely turned to Leemia. "Are you gonna back me up on this?"

Her eyes barely met his and darted away. "I … I think both … are good."

"Oh, come on, we're supposed to be on the same side." He looked at Iyna. "So which one do you prefer?"

Iyna smirked. "Without question, the spear." Iyna's happiness faded as she remembered Cairsie's bloodied body. With that horrendous memory brought back to her mind, she looked down into her bowl, unable to eat any more.

Sareesa asked, "What's the matter?"

Iyna took a deep breath and raised her head. "I just … I come from one of the villages that mark the eastern border … and a couple nights ago, the Beast Riders burnt it all down."

Beely raised his voice. "The Beast Riders destroyed your village?"

His voice stunned nearby groups into silence, and the whole hall fell eerily quiet.

Iyna felt isolated and uncomfortable as she looked around the room at the huge mix of curious and worried faces turning to her. All she could do was give a single nod.

Every man and woman in the hall erupted in upsetting talk and questions, leaving silence hanging over only a single table.

Sareesa was the first of them to act, slowly sliding her hand across the table. "I'm sorry to hear that. If there's anything I can—"

"Don't," Iyna snapped back. "I don't wanna be pitied."

Sareesa retracted her hand. "I understand."

Iyna felt the weight of the unbearable silence bearing over the table and felt the need to break it. "So when do I begin my training?"

"Early tomorrow," Sareesa said. "We usually begin with individual duels."

Iyna's eyes lit up, and her mouth smirked slightly. "I look forward to it."

Chapter four – First Step

Fourth eclipse, twenty-first day

At the sound of an irritating handbell, Iyna woke from her cloth hammock. She groaned as her eyes adjusted to the bright sunlight beaming through the glass slits circling the sleeping room. Steadily sitting up, she turned to the twenty other recruits and recalled the constant snoring and fidgeting from them. The worst thing though was the unending creaking of the rope holding up the two circles of hammocks. She was almost grateful only half the room was filled.

Stepping out of the dusty cloth hammock, Iyna felt the sharp coldness of the stone against her feet, fully waking her up to the rush of people getting changed as Soart went upstairs still ringing the handbell. Quickly putting on her grey clothes, she turned to Sareesa, Beely and Leemia, tiredly saying, "Morning."

Already sprung from her hammock, Sareesa slipped on her sandals. "How'd you sleep?"

Iyna stretched her back and lied. "It was all right."

"Good to hear." Sareesa glanced through the nearest window slit. "You and I should head down as soon as we can. Our unit leader hates people who're late."

"Yeah," Beely said. "Wouldn't want to be late on your first day."

Her cheeks reddened. "It wasn't my fault. Had someone told me that night we were going to be getting up so early I wouldn't have stayed up reading."

Beely giggled while Leemia shyly smiled behind him.

"You can read?" Iyna asked.

Sareesa mumbled, "Yeah … well, mostly. I struggle with the long sentences."

Iyna thought back to her own reading lessons and wondered whether Sareesa had a similar literate friend. Iyna shrugged. "Not that we'll need to use that stuff anyway."

"I guess not," Sareesa said.

All four rushed with the other recruits upstairs, passing the two other sleeping rooms and the horrid stench of the latrine before they reached the armoury at the top. Iyna's eyes widened at the sheer number of spears and tribows racked around the huge room, with green chestplates and dome helmets shelved along the long circular wall. In the centre lay enormous stacks of iron, triangle shields, straw spears and bolt quivers, leaving only a narrow path around the armoury.

Following the crowded line, Iyna grabbed one of the surprisingly thin green chestplates and put it on, tightening its side straps over her shirt. She placed one of the domed helmets loosely onto her head, and it covered her forehead, giving her a welcome sense of safety. She confidently tightened its string around her chin. Grasping one of the iron shields, Iyna felt the heavy weight in her left arm and was forced to use its leather shoulder strap before grabbing a training spear.

Iyna and her friends rushed into the courtyard, where six groups of recruits were organising themselves in neat rows before their respective unit leader. Beely and Leemia, with their rattling bolt quivers, hurried to the second group while Iyna followed Sareesa to the furthest from the tower. The three tribow and spear leaders were wearing differing armour from each other: padded cloth, iron platelets, tanned leather, and green and iron chainmail. Only one wore the same thin chestplate and helmet as the recruits, and to Iyna's delight, was the one she and Sareesa were running towards. It was little wonder why he had the most people in his unit.

Standing in the midst of the unit, Iyna stared at her new unit leader as he stood without uttering any words or commands while the other recruits still entered the courtyard. Iyna glanced to the other unit leaders and saw each of them already announcing the day's training to their units even as people were still leaving the tower. The spear unit leader covered in thick padded cloth had even begun the duelling.

The last of the recruits left the tower just in time to see the three tribow units march off to a target range around the other side of the tower. Only when the last recruit joined Iyna's group did their unit leader finally announce, "I notice a new face among us today." He turned directly to Iyna. "Young lady, may I ask for your name."

Her voice soared without hesitation. "Iyna!"

"I am Alexan Brige, and I am always glad to see another soul willing to take up arms, Iyna." He grinned. "However, a shield wall requires everyone working together as a single body and a single goal. Therefore, every man and woman needs to fully understand the purpose of why they fight, for if even a single member loses their will, everyone will fall. As such, I always ask the same question to any person wishing to join my unit. Why are you training to become a soldier?"

The monstrous silhouettes galloping away from the engulfed village sprang to her mind, and she answered, "So I can fight those wanting to hurt the people of Felliet."

"A good answer." He nodded and looked around his unit. "Because I liked that answer, I'll ignore the tardiness of some of those here and skip the cross-country."

Sighs of relief spread across the unit, and the whole group gratefully glanced at Iyna.

"Let's begin today's training," Alexan said. "Everyone pair up and start duelling."

Iyna watched as the whole unit spread out into obvious friend groups and raised their triangle shields and training spears to one another.

She turned to Sareesa. "Do you wanna go?"

She grinned. "Be a waste of a morning not to."

Raising the iron shield, Iyna pointed her straw spear at her friend. "You ready?"

Sareesa readied herself. "Yes."

Iyna leapt forward, jabbing her opponent's shield with her spear, forcing Sareesa to step back and shield her face. The quick attack kept going, till Sareesa finally moved her shield to better see, at which point, Iyna's cushioned spear tip manged to find its way past her opponent's defence, striking at Sareesa's shoulder.

"Yes!" Iyna cheered.

Sareesa lowered her arms and showed a defeated smile. "You've done this bef—"

"Far too aggressive," a man with brown hair interrupted.

Iyna turned towards the man confidently marching to them and shrugged. "I won, didn't I?"

He shook his head. "Overaggression leads to a lack of awareness and often results in your opponent finding an exploitable gap in your defence."

She smirked. "Then why don't *you* show me how it's done then?" She lifted her shield once more.

A small, irritated sigh left his lips, and he raised his shield. "Very well. Come at me when you are ready."

Iyna jumped forward, eagerly thrusting her spear ahead, only for him to simply knock it away with his shield and jut his spear forward. Seeing the straw tip fast approaching, Iyna tried to raise her shield in time, only for his cushioned point to hit her nose.

Recoiling back at the throbbing pain, she clenched her teeth. "Damn." She stared at the man. "Again!"

He lowered his arms. "Do not let your anger or thirst for victory control your actions. Calm yourself and use your head when fighting."

Iyna raised her shield and spear. "Again."

He shook his head and walked away, leaving Iyna seething as she watched him calmly return to duel with his blue-haired friend.

Sareesa put her hand on Iyna's shoulder. "Don't worry about Barcial. He thinks himself better than any of us. Well, except for his mate Darius."

Iyna relaxed her arms as she continued staring at the two men raising their shields to one another. "So what was *his* answer to Alexan's question?"

Sareesa walked in front of Iyna, blocking her view of the other duel. "He said he wanted to return home, whatever that means." She raised her shield. "Let's go again."

Prying her gaze away from Barcial and Darius's cautious duel, Iyna raised her tensed arms. "You ready?"

Sareesa readied herself. "Yes."

Iyna leapt forward once more.

Waking up in a soft bed, Vernon sat up and rubbed his eyes. With little desire to move, he turned to the small coin purse, blank parchments and blue ink feather sitting beside his book on the beside dresser. He dared not ponder what kind of disturbing deal his father had made to arrange his return to the academy and wondered whether he would eventually become an elite.

With reluctant fingers, Vernon buttoned his ashen silk shirt and fastened his black trousers. He turned to the pewter leather satchel hanging on the room's door hook and glanced at *The Foundations*. He would not be separated from that book, no matter how worn its cover became.

Stepping into the lavender-scented streets in the dawning light, Vernon gazed down the smoothened street and saw only a handful of gardeners and merchants. A dreaded realisation came to him that he was alone, isolated from any and all companions or comforts. Vernon's head dropped low, and he forced his legs to march forward.

A long time later, Vernon's sandals tread on the granite path cutting through the academy's square grounds to the gargantuan, castle-like structure. His eyes narrowed at its wide half towers bulging from each of its four corners, knowing them to be the windowless lectoriums. The giant defensive walls between them had only arrow slits for windows, reminding him of the bleak coldness inside. The only bright feature of the monolithic structure was a central glass domed tower that beamed sunlight down into the dark structure. Though it was undoubtably the most protected place in the city, Vernon felt it almost fitting that this bleak eyesore was the primary residence of the Zenth family.

Vernon marched down the granite path towards the academy's black iron door, approaching the two chainmailed swordsmen. "I'm a student who—"

Before he could even finish, one of them banged on the handleless door, and it swung inwards, revealing a dim, low-ceilinged room. The dark room was lavished only with a thick stone desk filled with stacks of notebooks and parchments behind which sat a pair of grey-robed stewards.

One of the guards grunted, and Vernon entered, passing two more guards hidden in shadow who bolted the reinforced door shut, sealing the outside light from the claustrophobic room. Only a single candle flickering from the midst of the desk shone in the darkness of the room, forcing Vernon to wait for his eyes to adjust. This unwelcoming entrance had been lost to Vernon's memories, which made him wonder what other dreary sights he had forgotten.

He ventured towards the two stewards. "I'm here to—"

"Vernon Meyorter?" one of them asked as he continued scribbling across a calendar.

"Yes?"

"Proceed to the second lectorium through the door on your right," the steward replied.

Expecting him to say something further, Vernon stood listening to the ink feathers scribble on the paper and turned his head to the faint outline of an iron side door.

Stepping from the discomfort of the entrance, Vernon walked down an incredibly tall but slim corridor that stretched from one end of the academy to the other. Above, numerous stone walkways connected each of the upper floors, and bright sunlight beamed down through round holes above the furthest ends of the corridor. Vernon remembered the beams of sunlight shone straight into the four lectoriums.

Upon coming to the door, he heard the lecturer within, which dug up the painful, distant memory of his last day in Ellity. His body was overcome with heat as he remembered what his father had uncaringly said on that day. Vernon realised his grip on the door's latch was furiously tight, and he took a long, deep breath to calm himself and opened the door.

Inside was the familiar dark theatre room where the beam of light shone over the stepped granite seating to illuminate a small stage below where a balding man spoke from behind a grey podium. Scattered around the abundant, black seating were barely twenty students, most of whom didn't even bother hiding their disinterest. However, in one of the front rows, a woman with long, braided hair was writing a plethora of detail; at least one person was taking their exclusive rights seriously.

As he traipsed down the steps towards the front row, many curious, judgemental eyes turned to him, creating a gnawing sense of entitlement in the air.

Placing himself three seats away from the earnest student, Vernon took out his ink feather and parchments ready to take notes. However, he found his writing hand too slow to copy every word of the lecturer's unpausing monologue, forcing him to shorten and simplify. The woman had no such problem, effortlessly recording every word, and Vernon smiled at her dedication.

Long after Vernon had realised the lecturer was blatantly exaggerating Felliet's importance to the world, the door swung open, floundering the speaker's words. A man covered in alpine mink fur darted his eyes across the room, stopping on Vernon, and he grinned. The latecomer proceeded to sit on the back row, resting his leather boots on the seats in front of him without an attempt to even feign work.

Vernon turned back around. The woman had also glanced at the latecomer's offensive arrival. A short moment later, the door slammed shut, and without looking, he knew that ego-filled man had not bothered to stay.

A tediously long time later, the lecturer concluded his long, overaggrandising speech, and Vernon sighed in relief as the students packed their satchels and belt bags. He stiffly rose from his hard seat and turned to the woman packing her emerald satchel. "I'm glad to see another person here who's willing to prove themselves."

She made no reaction.

Vernon tried to compose himself. "My name's Vernon. I was wondering if you perhaps…"

Without a hint of emotion, she passed him, walking up the lectorium steps to leave. He threw away the idea of befriending these entitled students and sighed, following them out of the room.

Waking on the hard chapel floor, Niyaa ached all over, and with so many people crowded inside, it had been uncomfortably hot, leaving her without much sleep. The governor sorted out several spare rooms, tents and storehouses for them all to sleep in after that first night, bringing much-needed relief to the weary newcomers.

Niyaa's family had been given the top of the spire mill, and though it seemed like workers would be grinding wheat seeds each day below them, she was happy to get a sheltered place with her mom and dad.

Walking inside Niyaa's ears filled with the constant turning of the mill's green, squeaky beam and the rolling of the stone grinder, and she climbed up the ladder with her dad following close behind. At the top sat a tiny empty room filled with dust, where the only light peeked out of a single shuttered window.

Her dad stepped off the ladder and looked around. He nodded. "This'll work."

He stepped towards the shuttered window and threw it open, bathing the room in bright sunlight. Rushing to it, Niyaa peered out across the amazing green and blue landscape, feeling the gentle breeze against her skin. Along the mountain slope, the greenery gave way to rocks of brown and grey, with a distant canopy beautifully swaying along a stream at the foot of the mountain. A glance down at the depressed faces of the Edenor people as they hauled their few belongings to their new tiny homes faded her excitement.

Her mom called up from the bottom of the mill. "Is there any rope up there?"

Darryam shouted down the ladder. "Afraid not. We'll have to leave the pot down there for now."

"All right," Mysia said. "I'll fetch some straw for us to sleep on."

"I'll give ya a hand." Darryam paused his climb down the ladder and asked his daughter, "So what do you think of this place?"

She glanced out the window once more. "It does have an amazing view."

"Yeah, it really does," he replied. "I spoke with the governor last night while everyone was sleepin'. He says he wants all of us to chip in with the work round here."

An excited thought entered Niyaa's mind. "So you mean you and mom can start brewing again?"

Darryam looked away. "Afraid we're gonna be working in the fields." He forced a smile. "After all, you can't brew without wheat."

Disheartened, Niyaa turned away.

He stepped from the ladder and crouched before her. "It'll only be till next harvest."

"I know, but…" Niyaa pictured herself watching her parents tirelessly farm the crops for an entire comet cycle. She looked up at him. "What … what can I do?"

He put his hand to the back of his head. "Well, apparently, the smither here has been behind on his work." He hesitated. "So … maybe you can give 'im a hand?"

Niyaa nodded. "All right."

Darryam put his hand on her shoulder and gave a reassuring smile. "I know it won't be easy here, but it won't be for long.'"

"Yeah." She forced a smile. "And I'm sure after the comet passes a couple times, we'll be back in Edenor."

"Hopefully," he said. "You never know, you might really like forging stuff."

Niyaa wondered whether she would ever see her real home again. "Could you show me where this forge is?"

"Of course."

After leaving the mill, the two of them walked through the narrow dirt streets, arriving at a large open doorway which exhaled heat. Inside, the roaring brick furnace was melting some pale green thing Niyaa could see through its cloudy glass door. The wide back wall was filled with slate shelves holding all kinds of odd, misshapen and worn green tools with a neatened set of iron hammers and tongs in the far corner. She turned to a grey-bearded middle-aged man grumpily pounding a hammer over and over against a metal green sheet clamped to a thick, iron table.

Darryam stepped towards him. "Scuse me."

The man stopped hammering and looked at him with half-closed eyes. "Was wondering when one of the newcomers would come asking for something made."

"It's not that," Darryam replied. "I'm here cause the governor said you need a hand, and I was thinking my daughter could help out."

The smither turned to the girl and his face reddened. "You think forging and shaping is so easy that anyone could do it?"

Darryam crossed his arms. "She's a fast learner."

"Still means I'll have to train her," the smither replied, flinging his hammer on the iron bench. "So why should I take her on?"

"Because the governor says you're fallin' behind and need a hand, especially now that there's more people here and you'll have a lot more work."

"I'm only behind cause the damn gov won't fund me new agron." The smither pointed to the messy shelves of broken green tools. "I've been having to rely on melting down old scrap for the metal."

"Then it won't hurt to have someone lending a hand."

A long uncomfortable moment endured between the two of them, leaving only the sound of the roaring furnace filling the air, and the smither leaned against his iron bench, mumbling, "She can start by sorting those shelves."

"Thanks." Darryam uncrossed his arms and turned to Niyaa. "I'm gonna go help your mom move some stuff, but if anything happens, you come right back, you understand?"

She nodded. "All right."

As soon as he left, the smither grabbed a bent green pipe from one of the shelves. "What do you know about shaping agron?"

"Well I…" Niyaa thought hard about it and remembered the guard's armour and Edenor's gate. "I know it's used to shape a lot of stuff."

He sighed. "So explain *why* it is used in a lot of stuff?"

Niyaa looked away. "I don't know."

"Because it's far cheaper than iron and can be easily repaired or reformed though losing some of its strength in the process. As such there really is nothin better for tool handles, floor supports, shelf brackets, casks, barrels and all kinds of other things." He dropped the bent pipe back on the slate shelf. "This lot needs sorting into pieces we can use and pieces we can't. Grab a scrubbing brush and see if any flakes peel off or not."

Niyaa glanced to the iron tools in the corner and spotted a pair of wire brushes. She turned back to the man. "What's … your name?"

His face filled with surprise and he mumbled, "Erger." He paused. "And yours?"

"Niyaa."

"Well, Niyaa, best you start right away, as I've just had a pair of stone cutters asking for some new chisels." Erger turned back to his hammering bench.

Walking past the man to the tool corner, Niyaa could almost feel his bitter frustration, and a daunting thought crept into her mind. She would end up working the rest of her life in this village, ending up just as grumpy as this man. She picked up the brush and began working.

Unexpectedly spending much time waiting in the pungent air of Ellity's stable, Jornis observed the majority of the well-bred steeds still residing in their pens. Clearly, the Dictorate saw little need to travel to the rest of Felliet nor even send any courteous messengers. Jornis was once again left to ponder how this blatant disregard had not already led to the Dictorate's downfall.

The stable master returned, gripping the reins of a crimson horse with a suitably inconspicuous commoner saddle. Beside his horse walked a black mare adorned with a similar saddle and proudly steered by a white-haired boy wearing silk ashen attire.

Jornis examined the boy and turned to the stable master. "What is the meaning of this?"

"Orders from those I cannot question," the man answered, holding the crimson horse's reins for Jornis to grab before retreating further into the stables.

The boy led his horse alongside the other steed. "My name is Copias, and following a request by the Elite Dictorate, I was assigned to accompany you in this task and assist where needed."

This was Pryias Lawver's method of keeping an eye on Jornis's movements. "Return to your employer, for I have no need of an assistant, Copias."

Stunned surprise filled the boy's expression, and he placed his foot through his mare's stirrup, pulling himself into the saddle. "She told me that unless I accompanied you, the Dictorate would not endorse your mission."

Jornis felt a headache emerging as he considered any potential excuses he could argue. Irritated, he agreed. "So long as you do not interfere with any of my duties then you may accompany me."

"You needn't worry." The child unashamedly grinned. "I am only here to report the situation and nothing more."

Feeling his headache worsen, Jornis wordlessly climbed his horse and departed for Erium's capital.

As the sun began to set, a mentally drained Vernon left the bleak academy with only a singular thought residing in his mind. With a determined step, he marched down the granite path and onto the smoothened streets of the inner wall, heading towards the commoner area.

Leaving the scent of lavender behind, Vernon stared up at the vast array of stars beginning to fill the darkening sky. The narrow, winding streets diverting from the main road were bathed in shadow, and he remembered the full coin purse he had left within his satchel. He sighed at his incredible foolishness, especially since he knew hardly a single guard patrolled this huge impoverished area. Despite this, the commoner area felt strangely inviting and pleasant as he strolled down the street, arriving at the Welcomerry Band.

Peering through the tavern's large windows revealed a near identical image from the night before, especially since many of the joyous drinkers crowding the oval bar remained the same. An excited smile crossed Vernon's face as he pushed the door open.

Revelling in the rhythm of the drinkers and the inviting warmth of the crackling fire bowl, Vernon took a long breath and relaxed. His gaze was drawn to the two bartenders cheerfully serving tankards from the various casks. The first was a bold, behemoth of a man who outmatched any of the glass cutters, stonemasons and cart haulers in the tavern. The other was a woman whose long, ear-obscuring silvery hair was pinned down with a large black hairband.

Preferring not to push his way through the middle of the cluster of drinkers, Vernon went to the leftmost edge of the small crowd.

The barwoman smiled at him. "What can I get ya?"

He looked at the many casks, trying to read each one. "I'll go for the … Red Lagoon, please."

As he reached inside the satchel for his coin purse, two brass coins were placed on the bar next to him. The man beside Vernon was dressed in worn brown cloth with a large grey sack strapped to his back.

He grinned. "I'll buy this one, stranger." He downed the rest of his tankard and put a couple more coins down. "Fact, I'll have the same."

Vernon's mouth gaped open at the unexpected kindness. "Thank you."

Taking the coins, the barwoman filled two tankards, asking over her shoulder, "So where you from?"

Vernon averted his gaze. "I … recently moved from the countryside." Trying to keep the atmosphere, he asked, "What about you two?"

The barwoman turned back to the filling tankard. "I've lived here all my life but Orfain 'ere moved from Erium a few comets back."

"Easier doin' business here." Orfain shrugged. "Plus fewer rivals on the trade roads."

The barwoman set the two tankards in front of them. "'ere you are."

"Thanks." Vernon sipped the ale for a quick taste and took a large gulp. "That's *really* nice."

"You bet it is." She grinned. "We got the best ales in Ellity." She pointed her thumb at the other bartender. "Me and Grayfern, we only pour the best."

"I can tell." Vernon glanced to the imposing man who stood wiping down the right end of the bar and turned back to the barwoman. "So what's your name then?"

She smiled and leaned against the bar. "Hazel."

Vernon took another large mouthful. "Well, Hazel, I hope you won't mind if I come here more often."

"Not at all." She darted her eyes at Orfain. "In fact, this one loves to tell all kinds of tales of his travels, don't you?"

Orfain raised his tankard to the barwoman. "Hardly a better way to spend an evening."

Vernon copied, raising his own tankard. "I would love to hear them."

The two tankards clinked against each other, and the two men took a hearty swig of red ale.

Chapter five – Observations

Fourth eclipse, thirty-second day

Running alongside red barley fields laden with fresh, potent manure, Iyna grinned. After the cross-country run, she was going to take part in a shield wall clash. When Sareesa had told her Barcial always volunteered to lead one side, Iyna jumped with joy as it meant she could volunteer to lead the other side and beat him. Just a shame no one else shared her eagerness in the early light of the morning.

With the Plythiat tower back in sight, Iyna turned to Sareesa, who was wearily running with her. "Not long now."

Sareesa glanced back with half-closed eyes, huffing. "Can't … believe you have … the strength to talk and run."

"Ah, this is nothing." Iyna smirked and glanced back to see the tired looks on the other recruits, their shields weighing heavily on their backs. She wondered whether any of them had even done a proper run before joining. "I'm gonna be the best spearmen here for sure."

"I hope … so," Sareesa replied.

The recruits trickled back into the courtyard past Alexan, patiently waiting ahead of them. He seemed disappointed at the sight of his exhausted unit.

Entering the courtyard, Sareesa clutched her legs, panting heavily.

"You all right?" Iyna asked.

Sareesa nodded. "Would've … thought it become … easier over time.

"It will. Even in the eleven days I've been here, I've noticed everyone's pace has improved." Iyna saw Barcial and Darius returning, their breathing calm and their pace steady.

Sareesa smiled between her deep pants. "Well, you don't … seem to need much improvement."

Iyna thought about the many runs she had done with Cairsie, leaving her unable to reply.

Sareesa straightened up and stretched her lower back, letting out a deep sigh. "We have to do a wall clash now … don't we."

"Yeah, I can't wait." Iyna gripped her training spear tighter.

"Just wait till you're in it." Sareesa smirked.

As soon as the last recruit trudged back, Alexan raised his voice. "That was a good run. Now I would like two volunteers to lead the shield walls."

Barcial confidently stepped forward, and Iyna copied, standing next to him with a determined smirk.

Alexan looked at her with interest. "Very well, Iyna and Barcial, choose your team and we shall begin."

Iyna realised she knew only a single name in her entire unit.

"Darius," Barcial said.

"Sareesa." Iyna let out an embarrassed sigh.

"Urksman," Barcial said, looking at a tall young man.

Staring at the quiet group, Iyna pointed to a fairly large man. "You."

After awkwardly pointing to each person in her team while Barcial knew every name, the sides were assembled. Alexan explained, "This will be done the same way as the last lunar eclipse. I want two rows of shields, and if you're hit, even in the hand or foot, then you're out. Anyone I find cheating will run the cross-country course three times over." His gaze rested on the two practising unit leaders, lingering on Iyna. "Your role is to create a strategy to defeat your opponent with as few losses on your side as possible." He stepped back and raised his voice. "Now organise your teams into position."

Instinctively, Iyna's group formed two close lines, facing Barcial's team as Iyna rushed to follow while whispering to Sareesa, "Where do I stand?"

"Centre rear."

The two rows of shields formed; the first hunched down with their shields guarding everyone's legs and stomachs overlapped by the second row, shielding everyone's torsos and heads. Poking through the small gaps between the overlapped triangle shields were both rows of straw spears.

While Iyna could cope with the tightly packed lines of people and the weight of her shield over Sareesa's crouched head, she was frustrated at barely seeing out of the single, tiny gap in front of her, especially as it grew and shank as everyone's shield arms wobbled slightly, worsening her slim view of Barcial's shield wall ahead.

Without turning back, Sareesa asked, "What's your plan?"

A wide grin crossed Iyna's face. "We'll rush 'em."

Sareesa whispered to the person next to her, "Fast advance forward."

Iyna copied her, whispering the same order the other direction.

A short moment later, Alexan bellowed, "Begin!"

Iyna's side lifted their shields and fast walked towards Barcial's stationary side. Iyna glanced through the swaying shields that Barcial's side had retracted their spears and overlapped their shields further, closing every opening. Knowing he wouldn't be able to see anything, Iyna smirked and tightened her grip on her straw spear.

Iyna's team harried Barcial's shields, repeatedly jabbing them and pushing as hard as they could.

Barcial's shield wall slowly moved back, and Iyna confidently yelled, "Keep pushing!"

Her side picked up the pace, putting more pressure on their opponent's shields, and a divide formed in front of her. She cheered, "We got this, just keep pushing!"

As the gap in Barcial's shield wall widened, Iyna saw the two ends of her wall hadn't advanced at all; instead, only her middle bit had pushed forward. Confused, she returned her gaze ahead and saw Barcial's team had entirely split in two. He had half surrounded her.

Before she could say anything, Barcial's voice rang out, "Attack now!"

His shield wall opened and out sprung their spears, surprising her side entirely. Several of her side walked away, so she shouted, "Back!"

It made little difference, for Barcial's side was pressing, unyielding any ground between them. The tightness in her rows eased as more people were struck, forcing her to keep jabbing her spear and hoping she would hit anyone.

A straw spear came through the gap in front of her and smacked Sareesa's helmet. She sighed and turned to Iyna. "Looks like we've lost this one."

Watching Sareesa push her way out, Iyna realised her legs were exposed. She lowered her shield, trying in vain to defend her whole body while shifting her feet to avoid the oncoming spears. A moment later her shin was hit, and she stomped away.

Her team had collapsed entirely, with everyone struck.

A slight smile crossed Barcial's face as his side victoriously lowered their shields. Iyna clenched her teeth in utter hatred. Alexan applauded. "Well done, everyone. It's vital to any soldier to follow the orders of their leader, and you all performed in an exemplary manner. I believe you each earned a poached egg and buttered bread."

Iyna's anger turned to bewilderment as *everyone* cheered.

Alexan added, "Now go get some of Soart's finest breakfast while I talk to these two."

The rest of the unit rushed to the cafeteria with only Sareesa and Darius looking back, and Iyna and Barcial stepped before their unit leader

Once the rest of the unit had gone inside, Alexan took a deep breath. "Unfortunately, while *they* performed well, the both of you had fundamental flaws in your tactics." He turned to Iyna. "Very few times should one carelessly charge ahead as it will almost certainly lead to defeat. You also must be fully aware of your surroundings at all times and what positions those you lead are in. Otherwise, you risk being caught off guard as you were today."

Iyna averted her gaze.

Alexan turned to Barcial. "Do you understand the failure in *your* strategy?"

"I do not."

"Having your troops remain stationary while constantly under attack is poor for morale even in the best of circumstances. Furthermore, dividing your force may allow your side to surround the other, but it leaves you unable to communicate with the whole of your force. If anything went wrong, you would have no method of properly redirecting either of your divided groups." He sighed. "I expect more from the both of you in the last four eclipses of your training."

Staring through the cloudy furnace door, Niyaa watched as the bent spade head melted gooey green agron into the wide stone bowl. The heat of the charcoal fire was excruciating, drawing plentiful sweat onto her brow, yet she continued watching, determined to get it right this time. Erger had told her several times to wait for it *all* to melt without letting it bubble, instructions she had yet to succeed in. Unlike the other times she had tried, he was carefully observing this attempt, making her even more nervous.

The spade head paled in colour and fully draped into the bowl, so Niyaa reached for the iron tongs.

Erger said, "Give it a little longer."

She retracted her arm and stared through the cloudy furnace door, fidgeting as she waited for Erger to say when to stop.

After a long moment, the agron spade head was a puddle in the stone bowl, and she turned to Erger, who asked, "Do *you* believe it's ready to take out?"

Niyaa hesitated. "Yes?"

"Good," he said to her relief. "You can be the one to pour it into the mould."

Grasping the tongs, she opened the door and carefully pinched the stone bowl with the curved iron ends. She steadily carried the heavy bowl to an open iron mould with dozens of nail-sized indents.

"Now this is the tricky bit," Erger cautioned. "You must gently pour it across the mould without spilling any on the floor."

The bowl felt even heavier in the tongs. Biting her bottom lip, Niyaa carefully knelt down. She tilted the stone bowl and poured the molten agron in the iron mould, hearing the thick goo sizzle as it flowed across each nail hole.

When the whole mould was covered, Niyaa breathed in relief and moved the bowl to set it on the floor.

"Don't let it touch the ground!" Erger raised his voice.

Niyaa nearly let go of it in her panic.

"It's a nightmare to scrap agron off stone." Erger pointed to the furnace. "Always keep the crucible in there."

She placed the stone bowl back in the hot furnace. Erger had put gloves on and was making his way to the mould.

"I'll finish up here." He gestured to the mattock head resting on the hammering bench. "Could you take that to Fohorn? He'll be digging in the field on the other side of Pelight." He grabbed the mould lid and mumbled, "The man's been nagging me for several days about it now."

Picking up the mattock head, Niyaa left the dimly lit forge. The bright midday sun pounded her eyes, forcing her head low as she walked. After her eyes adjusted, she found herself in an empty, dirt street, and for the first time since coming here, she felt truly alone. This village had no one even close to her age, and aside from Erger and her parents, Niyaa didn't speak to anyone, let alone have someone to play games with. Unable to do anything about it, she sighed and made her way along the quiet, narrow streets to the gate.

When she got there, she found the barred gate closed with that grumpy female guard standing by. "What're you doin' then?"

Niyaa held up the mattock head. "I … erm … need to deliver this."

"Isn't surprising you lot get the easy jobs." The guard rolled her eyes. "You know what, my spear is getting pretty old and needs tendin' to. Since you wanna stay here, I suggest you have Erger look at it right away." She held the spear out.

Niyaa stared at the guard for a long moment. "But I have to deliver this."

The bitterness grew in the guard's voice. "I don't like waiting."

The spear dropped into Niyaa's arms, weighing her down. She turned around and trudged back the way she had come. At the forge, the smither had firmly clamped the iron mould shut.

Erger looked at the mattock and spear in her arms. "How come you're carrying that?"

Niyaa darted her eyes away. "The guard at the gate told me to get you to repair it."

He grunted. "That will be Kivy then." He pointed to the hammering table. "All right, place it there. We'll just do a basic recoating on it."

Erger grabbed one of the wire brushes and casually tossed it to her. "Start by scraping the handle to remove dirt and flakes." He grabbed a bent door knocker and placed it in the furnace bowl, muttering to himself, "Easily could've lasted many more eclipses."

Niyaa obeyed, rubbing the wire brush up and down the green spear handle as she thought about the happier days like the times she would show off her drawings to her friends or the days she gleefully watched her parent's cask one of their ales.

In the break between lectures, Vernon yet again was forced to turn his attention to the plentiful array of books filling the vast walls of the academy breakroom. Once more, he was the only student preferring the comfort of books to the personalised dishes crafted and delivered by the academy's esteemed chefs. These past eleven days had repeated the same routine without a single hope the others would change their egotistical outlook.

As usual his gaze drifted across the artwork symbolising the subject of each bookshelf. Ignoring the portrait of sunbeams raising foliage from the soil and passing the mural of clashing shield walls, Vernon once again paused on the half world map. It was undoubtedly his favourite art piece in the large room, for despite it centrally placing Felliet, it accurately demonstrated the superiority of the Empire of Erium.

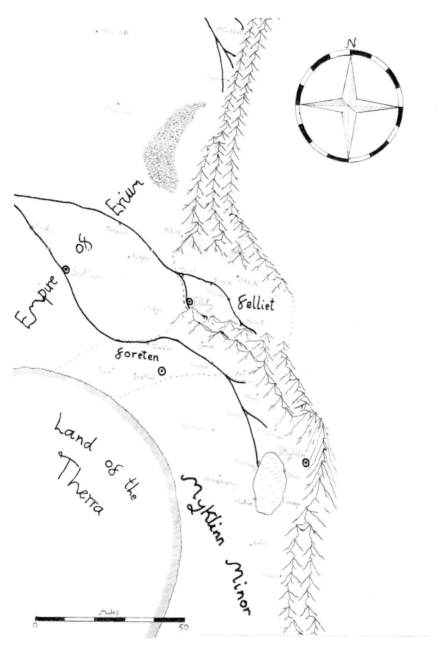

Staring at the vital trade roads connecting the iron, agron and
copper, Vernon imagined the horrified look the first emperor would have

had upon seeing his world torn like this. Perhaps Rochious Imerial would have rightfully refused to allow the idea of the federation to come to pass and instead chosen to bring an everlasting peace under his direct rule. Shame.

Ascending the crystal white stairs towards the observers stand, Jornis was displeased the boy would be accompanying him inside the great chamber. His displeasure worsened as the boy moronically gazed up at the elaborate crystal roof with his mouth gaping open. The fact Jornis's return to these walls, filled with the world's best diplomats, merchants, nobles and scholars, would be alongside such an imbecile was infuriating. He considered whether the boy's inclusion was actually some insult from Pryias or the rest of the Dictorate.

Taking his seat in the bronze-lined observers stand, Jornis gazed down at the chamber below and smiled. He had almost expected the eight representative chairs turned to face the emperor's seated position but was pleased to see they still continued to face each other. The Federal Throne maintained its simple yet perfect design. A thick bronze seat was supported by four thick symbols of the founding four nations: black crystal, cast iron, brown limestone and bright sapphire. Bound around these legs were threads of silver skyline, yellow silk, agron chain, grey glass and Therran wheat, clear symbols of the other five nations. Engraved above at the pinnacle of the grand throne for all to see were the words *where integrity prospers.* The unquestionable symbol of unity remained unaltered. In fact, the only element in the entire great chamber reflecting Erium's authority was the white crystal sword sheathed in the centre of the pearl floor.

Noticing the awed expression on the boy, Jornis murmured, "Continue your childish behaviour, and I will ensure whichever name you and your family hold shall fade into obscurity."

The boy sat up straight, yet an abrupt smirk crossed the young face. Perhaps it was an act of further adolescence or merely an abandoned retort; either way, Jornis took out his notebook and returned his full attention to the chamber below.

Long after the observers took their seats, the grand doors underneath opened, quieting the chamber to the sound of footsteps along the polished floor. Adorned in unjewelled white silk Emperor Anisious Imerial, first son of Cloresious Imerial, marched to the Federal Throne. Zealously following was Erium's minister of scales and the delegate of citizens, two positions Jornis had experienced frequent unpleasant meetings with. Thankfully, however, he recognised neither. Brazenly strutting many paces behind came Erium's fresh-faced supreme commander in his glistening black armour. The last of the emperor's advisors shuffled his bronze-lined sandals towards the grand bishop's seat, which unlike the other simple bronze advisory seats was tastelessly covered in orange and yellow jewels. The frail grand bishop took a long while to traverse the pearl floor, giving Jornis time to note the casual manner in how the supreme commander sat, confirming his suspicion each of them had been chosen based on relationships and deal making rather than merit.

The representatives trickled in, beginning with a man covered in layers of yellow silk, whose fingers and neck were covered in bronze and citrine quartz, unmistakably hailing from the prosperous coastlines of Gildren. The next two representatives entered together, one proudly displaying the iron woven furs of Myklinn's royalty while the second adorned herself in the brown cloth of Artor's feminine court. Jornis had long considered a potential alliance between these nations, but witnessing the representatives so blatantly close caused a strong unease to creep over him. He wondered just how long this act had been happening in the great chamber and whether this dangerous alliance would come to fruition. The pair exchanged sour glances with the man in yellow.

The Therran's entrance drew everyone's gaze to the orange glow of its bulbous, pupilless eyes. The chamber fell eerily quiet as the Therran's wheat-skinned, genitalless body silently approached its seat without a single flinch or deviation from its mouthless, earless head. The sight of that abomination taking its place alongside the man in yellow made every minute hair on Jornis's body raise, basking him in a sudden disgusted chill.

The representative entered, wrapped in a silver embroidered woollen robe, and never took his gaze away from his rival, the man in iron furs. Closely following was a man covered in agron chainmail, the armour famously worn by Fyoreten soldiers, who predictably glared at the emperor of Erium as he sat beside the man in silver wool. The next arrived in a violet robe fashioned from the sapphire lilies that flourished in the waterways of the Riverveins, the only nation that could reliably and realistically survive without external trade and security. Jornis needn't bother making notes on their representative. Last and without question least, the final representative limped on his cane the entire distance to his seat. Jornis's arms tensed, nearly breaking the ink feather in his hand, as his replacement slowly hobbled to Felliet's representative seat.

Once the pathetic excuse for an elite finally slumped his decrepit body in the chair, the emperor addressed the chamber in a booming voice. "This session shall now begin. We shall first address the matter of Iorden." He turned to the Fyoreten representative in his green chainmail. "What is your claim to the town?"

The armoured man stood. "The border was firmly established thirty-nine cycles ago. On that day, your father acknowledged Fyoreten as independent from Erium. Iorden lies well within our territory, and further, if you were to ask any of its residents, you would find each one a proud Fyoreten citizen who cheers at the anniversary of our victorious founding. It is undeniably ours."

The minister of scales swiftly argued, "While these citizens might tell someone such as yourself they are happy to be Fyoreten, their actions appear to signify the opposite." The advisor crossed his legs. "A majority of the border follows the Princilton river does it not?"

The armoured man glared at the advisor. "As was defined by Emperor Cloresious."

The minister shrugged. "Well, it appears the residents of Iorden do not abide by this definition, for they understandably desire the prosperity Erium provides. Many of them hunt and fish in Erium land while others even build homes along said river, travelling across it freely." The minister glanced victoriously at the other representatives. "Perhaps the town's residents do join in the occasional festivities, but it appears they continue to see themselves as people of Erium."

"This is absurd!" the man in agron chainmail barked back. "We have never violated the agreement made. We have never built walls around the northern towns and villages nor have our people trespassed in your land. Perhaps your mind is so demented that you think a few fishermen could allow you to illegally claim our town."

A wide grin crossed the advisor's face as he turned to the emperor.

"I have heard quite enough." Emperor Anisious loudly addressed the observers stand. "It is unfortunate that many citizens living in the Fyoreten region still believe themselves part of Erium. Perhaps past bloodshed could have been avoided." He turned to the stunned man in chainmail. "You have until the next gathering to relinquish the town of Iorden."

Jornis knew all too well Erium would one day retake the uncooperative nation of Fyoreten but pondered why Myklinn Minor's representative didn't immediately object.

"With that settled, we shall move onto the next agenda." The emperor turned to the grand bishop. "I believe the priesthood wishes to raise an issue."

The frail man slowly rose from his jewelled chair and stared distantly at the observers stand. "At the start of all things, there was only dark, desolate plains, where life could not grow. But from this darkness rose the great mother and with her warmth and grace birthed all manners of creatures and plants upon the world. After crafting this paradise, she birthed the purest creatures of all so that they may admire—"

"Get to the point," Emperor Anisious interrupted.

"Well … well, my point is that there are people who dare place the two sons on the same level as the almighty mother." The grand bishop's voice grew in both volume and fluster. "These moon worshippers are an outrage! After all, it was due to her guidance and care that her two sons even had the power to—"

"What do you recommend?" the emperor asked, preventing another speech.

"Well, I recommend … I recommend!" The elderly man turned once again to the observers stand. "I recommend that these people be destroyed."

A hail of insults and objections erupted from the stand, echoing across the white walls of the chamber. Jornis turned to the boy next to him and, seeing his expression, subtlety waved his ink feather within the boy's line of vision, preventing him from raising his own voice.

"Silence!" the emperor shouted, quietening the hall. "There will *never* be another culling." He turned to the grand bishop. "The priesthood has spread to every corner of the world. Every citizen of every nation knows of the great mother's warm guidance. It is far too strong to be destroyed by these *moon worshippers*."

The elderly advisor's face grew red with anger, and he slumped down onto his jewelled seat.

Emperor Anisious sighed and turned to the man in yellow silk. "Next agenda, the expansion efforts of the Radiant Republic."

The man of Gildren put a hand to his chest. "It pains me to speak of such abhorrent matters, but it appears three eclipses ago the insolent savages of the Radiant Republic attempted to establish a settlement on a barren island, far to the west. Fortunately, their pitiful fleet were unable to provide enough supplies and their venture failed. However, I believe it is in the interests of the federation these lands be taken, lest they eventually fall into enemy hands."

The woman in Artor's brown cloth folded her arms. "And who will control these islands?"

The Gildren representative refused to turn his gaze from the emperor. "It would be unwise to create a new country whose lands consist only of a few islands far from the mainland. As for *who* controls them, Gildren is the closest nation and already houses Erium's warships as well as our own extensive trading fleet. Therefore, I recognise no other alternative than to place these new lands in the care of Gildren's council."

The Artor representative, with her arms still folded, turned to the emperor. "The siloins of Gildren already dominate the eastern trade network. Any further expansion to their wealth and land should be disallowed entirely."

The man in yellow shrugged. "Would you rather the Radiant Republic, the closest to a rival the federation has ever had in its long history, expand *its* wealth and land?"

"They are no more than a collection of traitors, peasants and criminals," she said. "They pose far less a threat to the federation than your nation's unrelenting greed."

The emperor interjected. "While I agree the Republic's army and navy are far outmatched by all nations of the federation, any endeavour they undertake cannot be allowed to blossom. Therefore, I agree with the proposal put forward by Gildren's council. These western islands shall be placed in their care." The emperor paused, turning his gaze to the observers stand. "However, since this endeavour is for the benefit of the entire federation, the resources mined and grown shall be sold at cost."

"A wise decision," the man in yellow silk replied. "The supplies and ships will be ready before the comet shower."

Jornis surmised that of the eight siloins of Gildren, only a select few would benefit from this expansion with the one land locked likely to economically suffer. He grinned as he realised this endeavour could be used to form a trade deal with that siloin; from there, a full alliance between himself and the siloin could be arranged. However, he would need to first establish communications, so he jotted down ideas.

"Very well." The emperor turned his attention to the observers stand. "In the remaining eight lunar eclipses, both Erium and Gildren shall prepare their fleets for departure. Now, next agenda…"

Upon opening the tavern door, Vernon was met with an unfamiliar hooded man brazenly pushing past him as though he'd lost a drunken argument. The Welcomerry Band had only a handful of the regular drinkers, with a much calmer atmosphere in the room. Predictably, however, Orfain was still there, casually chatting to Hazel and Grayfern with his large, full sack resting on the oval bar.

Approaching them, Vernon relaxed and breathed out. "Evening."

Hazel smiled. "Another bad day, huh?"

"I simply do not understand those spoiled people." Vernon sighed. "They are so indulged in their own wealth and status that they completely ignore everything around them."

Clearly having no interest in the conversation, Grayfern grabbed a cloth and started wiping the right end of the bar.

"I wouldn't fret about it." Orfain shrugged. "Those kinds of people are in every corner of the world."

Vernon brought out two brass coins. "I know, but Felliet, and especially the academy, seem to be full of them."

Taking the coins, Hazel smiled. "Well, I'm glad you're not among 'em."

He nodded. "I am as well."

As Hazel poured Vernon's usual ale, Orfain turned to Vernon. "Nearly forgot. Did you hear the rumour today?"

Vernon couldn't help but smirk under his half-closed eyes. "I've been in a dimly lit room all day, surrounded by people who prefer to talk as little as possible."

"Well, it's spread all over the city," Orfain said. "Apparently a bunch of Beast Riders were caught at Milnet."

Vernon sprang awake. "Are you sure?"

"It's just a rumour." Orfain swigged his ale. "But supposedly they were caught trying to sneak into the town. Don't know much more than that though."

"What do you think will happen to them?" Vernon asked.

"Well, I doubt they'll be sent to the choppin' block," Orfain said. "More money taking 'em to the Atimah."

Descriptions of those hive-like tunnels and the enormous four-legged creatures which made them was thrust to the forefront of Vernon's mind, sending a chill rippling throughout his body.

Hazel placed Vernon's drink lightly against the bar and turned to Grayfern. "Just gonna get more cubes for the fire."

Grayfern softly replied in his deep voice, "Take your time."

She left the bar without another word, climbing the ladder in the corner of the room and disappearing through an upstairs hatch. Vernon glanced at the fire bowl hanging above them which was burning normally. Clearly, she must also feel pity for the Beast Riders and the culling they endured.

Chapter six – Reflection

Fifth eclipse, first day

Last night, Niyaa had gazed up at the thin, silvery ring of the larger moon as its younger brother eclipsed most of him. The sight of the lunar eclipse lingered in her thoughts as it worsened the upsetting idea that she'd be spending the rest of her life in this miserable place. Everyone was unhappy there, that guard Kivy especially. Even her parents, though they tried to hide it, were exhausted working every day in the fields. It all left Niyaa desperately wanting to improve the mood, and she wondered whether it'd make everyone's lives a little easier if she worked harder.

Therefore as soon as morning broke, she crept down the mill's ladder and made her way through the dirt streets. Just before she stepped inside the forge, she heard angry mutterings within, so she hid on the side of the doorway, ears warily open.

She recognised Erger's voice. "…won't do it."

"It's a simple request," the other man coldly replied.

"How can you even call yourself an elite?" Erger asked.

"Quite easily." The second voice belonged to Governor Seveck. "My family earned a family name. Later, I was bestowed the right of ownership of Pelight and its people to do whatever I see fit."

Erger's voice grew louder and more bitter. "You don't own Pelight *or* its people."

"I think you'll find I do," the governor replied. "Every village and town has … *needs* someone to control and rule, lest the disorderly commoners start running amuck. As such, the Elite Dictorate in their wisdom chose the Heef family to keep the village of Pelight in order and to ensure it prospers."

"You mean to ensure *you* prosper," Erger argued back.

The governor huffed. "The intentions do not matter so long as Pelight flourishes. But if you obstruct me, I will *ensure* you will never use your furnace again." A long silence hung between them until the elite added, "I will see you at sunrise tomorrow."

Footsteps approached the entranceway, and Niyaa dashed away, hiding around the corner of the forge just before the governor stepped outside. Waiting till his footsteps became distant, she tiptoed towards the doorway, thinking of what she should say. Something metal slammed against the items on the shelves, clattering many things, and she quickly ran inside.

Erger was furiously seething near the bent agron sheet clamped to his hammering table with his hammer lying across the scattered broken agron pieces.

He glared at her. "Early today, aren't we?"

Niyaa looked down at her sandals. "I-I overheard some of it."

"Doesn't matter anyway." Erger scowled and grabbed his hammer. "Did I show you how to shape agron into a barrel?"

She shook her head.

"I'll show you then." Erger stiffly returned to the table and gently hammered the green sheet while gradually bending it with his free hand. "The most important rule about shaping barrels is to do it as slowly as possible."

She stepped towards him, unable to say a word.

A few pounding strokes later, Erger stopped, hovering his hammer above the metal sheet.

Niyaa asked, "Erger?"

His hammer fell, clattering against the metal sheet and leaning his hands on the table's edge. Staring distantly away, he asked, "Have you ever been to Ellity?"

"No."

A proud grin crossed the man's face. "I lived there most of my life, made quite the reputation there too. In fact, I was among the best." His smile faded as he turned his distant stare blankly to the sheet of agron. "Yet when the culling happened, I only had orders for weapons, none of which I could add my personal touches to. When Felliet became its own country, many of the city's smithers left for Erium, and my work practically doubled." He clenched his hands into fists. "It was then that the … *underside* of that city grew more and more."

He fell silent.

Seeing his sadness, Niyaa rushed to him, placing her hand on his. He jumped at her touch, but she refused to let go.

He gently brushed his free, hefty hand across her hair, giving her a grateful smile. "You know, I reckon someone like you could make a fine smither."

She stared at him, wondering whether he was being sarcastic.

He turned to the tool corner and nodded. "I think I might have something you might like." He strode across the room and grasped a little tool from the far end of the shelf.

Niyaa watched as he brushed the dust off its small quartz handle with a curvy, iron nail sticking out. She wondered what such a cute tool would be used for in a forge.

Randomly grabbing a warped agron platter, Erger unclamped the yet-to-be barrel, letting the large sheet clang onto the floor. He placed the scrap metal on the table. "Engraving always weakens the metal wherever it's placed, which is why most amateur smithers are sensible enough to avoid it. However"—Erger proudly smirked—"if you're skilled enough in the art then it'd be foolish not to add your symbol to it." He held the shiny tool out for her. "Start by making some light scratches. Later, I'll show you how to properly curve 'em."

Niyaa beamed with excitement, and her thoughts raced with all kinds of drawings and pictures. She eagerly took the little quartz engraver.

Iyna's feet pounded against the dirt cross-country track as her mind lingered on the humiliating shield wall clash. For the rest of the day and night, she could think of nothing else; after all, if she could so easily be beaten, how could she ever stand up to those merciless creatures?

Sareesa spoke through deep breaths as they jogged together. "Still thinking … about it?"

Snapped out of her deep thoughts, Iyna shook her head. "Got to get better."

"Shouldn't treat it like … a competition," Sareesa wearily replied. "Doubt any of us … will do any real fighting."

Wide eyed, Iyna turned to her friends, and her hands clenched into fists. "Someone's got to face those monsters before they attack again." Only the sound of sandals treading against the dirt was left to fill the air as Iyna wondered how she could possibly fight them. Hesitantly, she asked, "How do I make myself stronger?"

Sareesa chuckled, slowing her step. "It's nothing … to do with strength."

Iyna stared at her friend and slowed her pace to match. "What'd you mean?"

"You're fitter than … most of us." She puffed. "Plus you're … really good with the spear."

"Then what am I lacking?" Iyna asked.

Sareesa patted her friend on the back. "You just need … to use that head of yours … when fighting."

Those words reminded Iyna of that irritating duel, and she bitterly turned ahead. "Pretty much what Barcial said."

"Well, there's a reason he's … the best in the unit…" Sareesa wiped sweat from her forehead. "Why don't you ask him for … advice?"

"Definitely not!" Iyna answered and realised in both the duel and shield wall clash, he had anticipated her eagerness, easily giving him victory both times. She grinned. "I won't lose next time."

Sareesa giggled. "Thought you … didn't like him."

Guffawing, Iyna gave Sareesa a friendly shove. "Shut up."

"All right, but if you want … relationship advice … then come to me whenever … you want," Sareesa joked.

Iyna smirked. "Only if you can beat me back to the courtyard."

"Oh … I hate you." Sareesa exhaled. "All right … you're on."

The two of them broke into a sprint.

In the dim light of Sidium's vast records crypt, Jornis meticulously examined the recent trades between Erium and Gildren. Unfortunately for him, practicality was far from the design of this vast underground hall, for not only were the silver wall-lined desks few in number, but each lacked space to copy details. Furthermore, the arduous process was made worse by the improper organisation of the books, scrolls and bronze tablets shelved onto the colossal stone racking. This all meant Jornis would have to endure the stifling underground air for the next several days as he searched for details on the deals made between the land-locked siloin and Erium nobles. It truly was the only effective method that would not raise suspicion, but if successful, he would have the precise location of the land-locked siloin base within the Empire of Erium. From there, he could meet with that siloin's official and convince him or her to arrange a meeting with the head of the Marble Wheels.

After exhaustively combing artwork commissions from the previous two eclipses, Jornis felt the presence of that boy standing next to him. He remembered tasking him with a list of random insignificant books to find that would have distracted him long enough. Keeping his attention on his task, Jornis asked, "Have you found what I asked for?"

"I found the first one," the boy replied.

Jornis glanced up and saw a record of supplies sent to the priesthood sanctuary. "Time waits for no man. Keep at it until you find them all."

"I have a question." The boy glanced at one of the palace guards standing beside the walls. He lowered his head and whispered, "Do you believe Felliet could be threatened in the same manner Fyoreten was yesterday?"

"A mere glance at any world map will answer your question," Jornis replied, attempting to return to his records.

"But there shouldn't be a reason for it." The boy quietened his voice further. "Felliet maintains a positive relationship with Erium. There should not be a single reason why they would threaten us, correct?"

Unimpressed, Jornis turned half-closed eyes to the boy. "By questioning it, you know that to be false." He sighed. "There are two reasons why Felliet has not already been *threatened.* The first is simply that Erium needed to rebuild and strengthen its armies after the culling. The second is, quite simply, too little to gain from occupying Felliet." Jornis went back to the records and turned the next page. "If you truly want to avoid such a scenario, I suggest you do as I command."

The boy hesitantly placed the book atop the useful text, disrupting Jornis's work. "I am under the command of Pryias Lawver and no other."

Jornis watched Copias return to the colossal racking as he pondered whether the boy's loyalties for Felliet and its debauched Dictorate were genuine. He prised such distractions from his thoughts and returned to his gruelling work.

Standing beside one of the tavern's large windows with Orfain, Vernon felt unnerved by the crowds of people awaiting the parade along the main street. It was certainly ideal for Hazel and Grayfern as the Welcomerry Band was full to the brim with customers, though the usual cheery atmosphere had become an unsettling concoction of emotions. A bunch of patrons were cruelly excited, many were impatiently ignorant, and some debated while most remained uncomfortably sombre about the parade of captured Beast Riders.

Hearing those differing thoughts radiate across the small room amplified the many unanswerable questions plaguing Vernon's mind since leaving Edenor.

"Somethin' bothering you?" Orfain asked, snapping Vernon out of his deep thoughts.

"Oh, it's nothing." Vernon faked a smile and sipped his barely touched tankard. "Guess I was daydreaming a little."

"Daydreaming, huh?" he asked. "And I guess the Beast Riders have nothin' to do with it?" Vernon averted his gaze, and Orfain chuckled. "Don't worry. They wouldn't be able to harm anyone 'ere."

Vernon shook his head. "Course I know that. It's just…" He took a large swig of ale. "It's just I don't know what to make of them."

"Yeah, I can understand." Orfain's nonchalant attitude faded as he leaned his back against the large window. "Never met one meself, but my old man did once. A couple of 'em broke into his home one time tryin' to nick some clothes, though when they saw him and his club, they quickly ran off."

"They were just after clothes?" Vernon asked.

"Yeah." Orfain shrugged. "Guess they wanted a disguise and figured my old man's supplies would work."

Vernon felt his shoulders sink. "So they were two Beast Riders desperately trying to hide, who rather than fighting, ran from your father, who I imagine was alone?"

Orfain awkwardly looked away. "I ... guess you could put it like that."

Disheartened, Vernon stared into his tankard until a glass cutter burst through the tavern doors. "They're here!"

A frenzy ensued with nearly everyone rushing out while Hazel practically vaulted over the bar to be among the first outside. Orfain simply stood on a chair, peering over the crowd through the window, and Vernon copied him.

Quiet crowds lined both sides of the main street. Distant shouts and taunts grew louder. Vernon glimpsed an approaching rider whose saddle pulled a chain, and his eyes widened with horror.

The unrelenting chain was attached to iron muzzles strapped over the faces of six fully naked prisoners. Vernon covered his mouth in disgust as he observed heavy bruises across their skin, with each of their animal parts badly broken, all with hands bound. They were beset by cruel shouts from the passing crowd.

Mouth aghast, Orfain spoke. "Those two at the back, they … they aren't Beast Riders."

Vernon took a closer look, and he was right. Unlike the other four, they lacked any abnormal limb, yet they were pulled through the same relentless crowd. An ache swiftly inflamed his stomach at the senseless treatment.

Hazel, at the front of the crowd, was furiously screaming at the six prisoners, and as the lead prisoner passed, she threw a rock. It slammed against his muzzle, staggering his steps as he was hauled forward.

Vernon was in utter disbelief. Hazel was always calm and friendly. Never once had she even hinted at hating anything or anyone. He turned to Orfain for answers, only to see his expression equally as stunned.

The Beast Riders were led further along the street, dispersing the crowd in their wake, many of whom simply re-entered the tavern. Hazel, however, was fixed in place staring red faced at the departing Beast Riders.

Orfain leapt off his chair and pushed his way outside with Vernon closely following until they were both standing before their friend. Despite her hands tightly clenched into fists and her breath madly seething, her narrowed eyes were tearful.

Orfain stepped in her line of vision. "You all right?"

She closed her eyes, took a deep breath and placed her hand onto her black hairband. "I'm fine." Hazel retreated inside and disappeared up the ladder in the corner of the tavern.

Vernon and Orfain turned to each other, unsure of what to say or do, and they stepped back inside, catching Grayfern's concerned glance.

The two of them approached him, and the huge barman placed two full tankards on the crowded bar in front of them, whispering, "Best not to ask about her dislike of them."

Grayfern went to serve the people swarming the bar, leaving Vernon staring into the drink before him.

A moment passed, and Orfain took a hearty gulp of his ale. "Grayfern's right, best not ask 'bout it." He faked a relaxed shrug. "Besides, if it affects the business in any way then I'm sure she'll let us know."

Vernon watched as Orfain's hopeful expression turned worrisome, and he too drank a large mouthful of ale, knowing she held a pain he couldn't mend.

Chapter seven – Westward

Sixth eclipse, fourth day

With a grey blanket covering the sky, Iyna emerged from the tower yawning and found iron chainmailed guards standing in place of the unit leaders. She turned to her friends for answers but found them just as confused.

Beely pointed his uncranked tribow. "What's with the horses?"

Several well-groomed steeds were tied near the rich manor house as well as alongside an empty horse-drawn wagon.

Leomia stuttered, "Is-Is someone...someone coming to-to-to visit?"

Sareesa tightened her grip on her straw training spear. "I don't think so."

Anxiously staring at the supply cart, Iyna nudged Sareesa's back-held shield. "Leemia's probably right. Just some rich person coming to visit and see the unit leaders." Perhaps they'd all be sent to attack the Beast Riders. She grinned in excitement.

Beely smirked. "Never know, they might be sending some of us to garrison one of the towns."

"I hope so," Sareesa said, and the group split off to their units.

With only half the recruits still leaving the tower, the closest chainmailed guard loudly announced, "Your unit leaders are discussing important matters! Until they return, no one is allowed to leave the courtyard! Spearmen shall duel one another while the tribowmen practice their cranking speed."

An awkward silence descended over the yard, and the recruits glanced at one another as they awaited further instruction. The stillness broke only when Barcial, predictably standing at the front, turned to the rest of his unit. "All right, everyone, pair up and begin duelling."

The three spear units quickly paired up with their usual partners, except for Iyna who stared at Barcial as he paced up and down their unit judgementally observing the duels, as if he were in charge.

"You ready?" Sareesa asked, raising her shield.

Iyna didn't respond or even look at her friend. Instead, she marched toward Barcial with a firm grip on her shield and straw spear.

Only when she was right before him did he notice her. He shook his head. "Not today."

"Why?" Iyna smirked, raising her shield. "Afraid you'll lose this time?"

He glared at her and, without saying a word, raised his shield ready to duel.

Iyna held back her eagerness to lunge forward and carefully watched his stance, her mind racing with possible strategies. Perhaps she could pretend to strike at his right side only to go over his shield or maybe she could sidestep left and go for his face.

He sprang forth, repeatedly striking her shield with a grim look on his face. Iyna was forced back, thrusting randomly to keep the distance. He crouched and struck her ankles.

Realising his initial jabs were a distraction, she felt her body weaken but his red-faced scowl made her wonder whether it really was a planned strategy all along. Without uttering a word, he stiffly turned away and continued marching down the line of duels, watching the other recruits.

Iyna glanced at his friend Darius, staring distantly to the sky above. He hadn't even taken his shield off his back.

Sareesa tapped Iyna's shield with her spear hand. "Good attempt."

Iyna's deep thoughts vanished, and she renewed her grip on her shield and straw spear.

"Don't worry about it." Sareesa smiled. "You're sure to beat him soon enough." She raised her shield.

A strange grin crossed Iyna's face, and she too readied to duel. "I'll just have to work harder."

Just as Iyna's training spear carefully prodded her friend's shield, the people in iron chainmail shouted one after another, "Form ranks!"

After a brief moment of hesitant confusion, all the recruits rushed back into formation as their unit leaders emerged from the grand house. Each of the unit leaders looked grim and resentful as they followed a large man covered in a brass-lined grey robe and plentiful bronze.

"Your training is over." The wealthy man raised his voice. "The emperor of Erium has declared war against the nation of Fyoreten and intends it to be a joint coalition of all federation members. Therefore, the Dictorate has deemed it necessary to raise an army to represent Felliet in this conflict with me as its commander. You now have the greatest honour of representing our proud nation on the battlefield. As such, you all will need to demonstrate unyielding courage and utmost…"

His words grew distant to Iyna's ears at the realisation of the stunning news. Her muscles weakened and her vision blurred as the absurd idea of marching *away* from the desert consumed her mind.

Only when Alexan spoke could she listen. "Grab your spears, armour and hammocks. We are to set off immediately when you return."

Iyna half-heartedly glanced at Sareesa, whose hands trembled with fear and shock, as she stiffly followed the other recruits to the tower's armoury. The iron chainmailed people escorted the commander to the horses. Darius was comforting Barcial, neither of whom had budged.

Alexan calmly walked to them, softly saying, "I understand this must be difficult for the two of you. Honestly, I prayed to the great mother this wouldn't happen." Guilt in his eyes, he put his hand on Barcial's shoulder. "You have to keep putting your foot in front of the other, no matter how painful the journey may be."

Barcial shook his head. "I can't … I-I mustn't."

"You can and must," Alexan replied. "You now have a duty to protect the rest of your unit and the people of Felliet." The unit leader took his hand away. "I know you to be strong enough to endure."

Iyna raised her head as she watched droplets fall from Barcial's cheeks.

Alexan's voice softened. "These days will pass."

Darius placed his hand on Barcial's chest. "He's right. This nightmare will be a distant memory one day. We just have to endure it for a while longer."

Barcial gloomily turned to his close friend and placed his hand on his own chest. Without further words, the two of them approached the tower.

Alexan noticed Iyna standing still and raised his voice. "Why are *you* still here?"

Outraged, Iyna furiously argued, "The real enemy are the Beast Riders, not Fyoreten." Alexan advanced towards her as her voice grew louder. "We should be marching to the desert, finishing those monsters off before they attack again. We shouldn't—"

Alexan slapped her hard across her the face, silencing her words. "The Elite Dictorate have a much greater understanding of the threats to Felliet than either of us. If you truly intend to protect this nation's people instead of seeking revenge, then follow the orders you've been given."

All anger faded from Iyna's thoughts as several hard questions struck her all at once.

"Do you understand?" Alexan demanded.

She realised she had no other option and reluctantly muttered, "Yes."

"Good." He pointed to the tower. "Now get your equipment."

Disheartened, Iyna obeyed, trudging away as she questioned what she wanted.

"I want to see you lift your legs, Iyna!" he shouted.

Her mind emptied, and she sprang into a sprint towards the crowded tower's iron door.

In the midst of the pushing crowd along the narrow path through the vast crates and barrels in the large storage room, Iyna looked around for Soart. Not spotting him, she climbed atop the crates and barrels and ventured across to the shadowy edge. Coming to the hidden gap between stacks of crates, she found her mother's spear.

Eagerly grabbing its worn handle, Iyna remembered the one and only time Cairsie had talked about the disastrous campaign that took so many brave lives. All unease and heartfelt questions Iyna had faded to a strange resolve as she thought about her own survival.

Even after a full lunar eclipse had passed, Vernon's thoughts were still engulfed by the picture of those horribly beaten prisoners and the sounds of the relentless crowds. His imagination kept conjuring increasingly worse thoughts of their treatment under the Atimah, taking his attention away from both the lecturer's speech and his own notetaking.

"Vernon," the lecturer asked, surprising every student back to the present. "Could you explain what purpose the tributary system serves?"

Never before had the lecturer even asked a question in the lectorium, not even rhetorically, yet he directed all his focus on a singular student. Vernon stood and confidently answered, "To provide the needed coin to fund Erium's army so it can stop internal wars and prevent the federation from shattering."

The lecturer glanced at the handful of other students, who suddenly seemed more attentive. "Partially. However, the majority of the tributary coin goes towards laying new roads and digging new mines, with not an insignificant amount used to maintain the southern forts and Erium's navy."

"You mean to protect against the Radiant Republic?" Vernon blurted out. "But it simply cannot hope to ever threaten our borders."

Disbelief filled the lecturer's expression, no doubt because his foolish argument had been challenged by a student. Before he could respond, however, a laugh near the entrance drew everyone's attention.

Unsurprisingly, it came from that smug latecomer ogling down at Vernon from the back of the dark room. "*Our* borders? You imply our lands belong to the federation."

"Does it not?" Vernon narrowed his eyes. "If you believe Felliet has the strength to stand on its own, to compete with other nations militarily or economically, then you are without question an ignorant fool."

The latecomer spat back, "I will not have your pitiful name insult the greatest of nations."

"It would first have to be the greatest nation for my words to be an insult and not a fact," Vernon replied. "Felliet hardly has any land or population with no army to speak of. Again, only an ignorant fool would think it was a strong nation, let alone great."

The latecomer gritted his teeth before suddenly relaxing. "I think your theory should be assessed." He stood with a sly grin on his face and strutted out of the lectorium, leaving the door wide open.

Vernon sighed and returned his gaze to the stunned lecturer who fumbled his words and resumed his monologue. Vernon wondered whether anyone would ever listen to such a smug moron and remembered that practically all the elites were of a similar nature. He sighed and pondered what kind of scolding he'd receive.

It was not long before his prediction came true. A grey-robed steward entered, quietening the lecture. He promptly announced, "Could Vernon Meyorter, Iyessa Synthion and Buckley Cendion follow me?"

An unusual mix of guilt and satisfaction swept over Vernon as he watched that attentive, cold woman on the front row pack her belongings. A young boy far to the other side of the lectorium was also standing. Perhaps these other two students were also to be told off for a unconforming statement they had made.

All three students followed the steward through the narrow corridor, arriving at a slim, reinforced door which led to an even narrower set of granite stairs. Once the steward locked the door behind them, the steep staircase was bathed in almost complete darkness, for not a single lantern hung along its stone walls. Only the slim light peeking through the other floor's doors illuminated the black steps, forcing each of the students to carefully watch their footing on the ascent.

Arriving at a black iron door, the steward used its heavy knocker four successive times, and the door gradually cranked open. Vernon's eyes were pounded by bright lanternlight shining behind a pair of stern chainmailed swordsmen.

The steward told the closest guard, "These three are to have an audience with Reethial Zenth."

With a rustle of their heavy armour, the swordsmen stepped aside, and the students walked down the middle of a short, bronze-carpeted hallway lined with portraits and engraved doors. A far grander entrance at one end made Vernon's arm tense. The other end had an elaborate bronze-lined black iron door, guarded by another pair of swordsmen. Vernon sighed as he followed the steward to the unmistakable room for the master of the academy, Reethial Zenth.

The reinforced entrance cranked shut, and the steward approached the opulent door with the students following closely behind. The female student had a similar look of disdain while the young boy seemed only anxious. Vernon grimaced as his nose picked up the familiar, sharp scent of expensive oils used in those abhorrent portraits.

The two guards opened the bronze-lined door to the approaching group, revealing an orange flickering glow of a well-stocked fireplace. Directly ahead lay an overly large, grey marble desk behind which sat a pale elite in full black silk. The elite hardly bothered to turn his embittered gaze away from his letters when he spoke. "What is it?"

"The students you called for have arrived." The steward stepped aside.

A quiet pause followed, and Reethial set down his black ink feather and looked at the three students. "Send them in."

Vernon's nostrils were overwhelmed by a wall of oil stench, and he noticed a black-robed painter alongside the simmering fireplace. Glimpsing a part of the unfinished portrait, Vernon rolled his eyes at its bright, vibrant colours standing blatantly in contrast to this grim, shuttered room with such a detestable figure at its centre.

Without introduction or greeting, Reethial leaned back into his grand padded chair. "The wretched scum of Fyoreten refused to hand over the town of Iorden to Erium, so the two nations are now at war."

Vernon's eyes widened.

"While Erium's armies could easily crush Fyoreten, the emperor in his passion for unity, has expressed that every nation should send an army to this conflict. In light of this, the Elite Dictorate has wisely selected me to replace my ageing uncle as the new representative in the great chamber." The elite darted his disapproving gaze from one student to the other. "On separate occasions, my son has advised you three be removed not only from these walls but from Ellity altogether. However, I believe what is most befitting for your inferior names is to assist in my upcoming work in Sidium."

Iyessa said, "We are students of this academy, and were we to travel to Sidium we will not be able to fulfil our teachings here."

The elite picked up his ink feather and dipped it in ink. "It is a great honour to have the opportunity to assist members of the Zenth name, especially one such as I. This privilege is certainly far greater than *your* name deserves."

She stepped forward. "I have a duty to finish my lessons here."

"Your duty?" The elite narrowed his eyes at her. "Your duty is to serve Felliet as the Zenth family sees fit. Ignore my command and I shall have your pitiful, foreign name finally eradicated."

Though she kept her tongue still, her eyes grew furious.

"I expect all three of you to be outside the Gallery's doors at midday tomorrow." Reethial turned to his letters and continued writing. "Now leave."

Iyessa raised her chin, took a deep breath and swiftly left before Vernon and Buckley. Once the door shut to Reethial's quarters, her pace grew faster towards the lesser entranceway.

Buckling muttered, "Yes." An overjoyed smile crossed his face as he practically skipped down the bronze carpet to the slim entranceway.

Vernon, meanwhile, was stunned as he tried to unravel the situation. On one hand it provided an opportunity to travel to the black city and witness the glory of the great chamber. However, it would be done in service of not just any elite but the brother of the Zenth family's head. He needed to think.

Jornis was pleased to be reminded the famed black crystal walls of Sidium did not darken the rooms they housed, instead reflecting the candlelight off their metallic surfaces. Furthermore, the thick hexagonal blocks of his lodging sufficiently quietened the outside rain and confined any interior sound to his lone ears. This allowed him much-needed time to organise his plentiful notes from the comfort of the room's glass desk.

With the downpour of rain soundlessly beating against the curtained window, Jornis re-examined his notes, confident he knew the location of the Marble Wheels operating base within Erium. He questioned the trade deal he could offer the land-locked siloin, specifically whether he should offer simple agron and iron or Felliet's farmed glass. Jornis knew he wouldn't be able to offer both as it would appear desperate, but he knew it would need to be greatly sought after for the deal to become the founding of an alliance.

A knock at the door broke his concentration, and before answering, Jornis slid the notes within a stack of extensive transcripts derived from insignificant random records.

"Enter," he said. The door opened, revealing the boy. Jornis turned his attention back to his desk. "It is certainly uncouth to merely stand in a doorway after being instructed to enter." Only when Jornis heard the door shut did he retake his notes from the other records. "What do you have to report?" Jornis begrudgingly turned and saw the boy bitterly scowling.

"Why are our horses saddled?"

"They are saddled because we will soon depart Sidium." Jornis reached for the soon-to-be-outdated map he had bought for a mere four bronze.

"And for what reason was I not informed?"

"The task *I* have been assigned is to remain secret from all potential enemies, and as such it is unnecessary to pointlessly babble each detail." Hearing no immediate counterargument, Jornis unrolled the city and town map and waved him closer. "We shall depart for Rubium tonight."

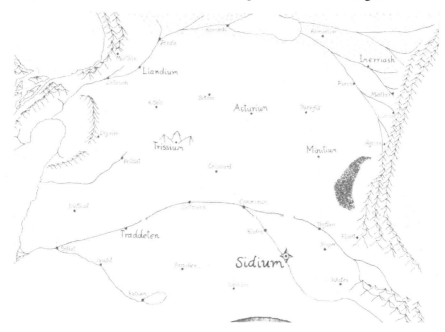

"Why?" the boy asked. "Surely we would be more likely to find persons of interest in the capital."

Jornis turned to him. "While that is indeed the case, Copias, the likelihood of establishing an informative and successful meeting is low."

"So what makes the city of Rubium different?"

"We shall discuss this further on the road." Jornis rolled up the map. "Send not a word to the Dictorate, for we must ensure complete secrecy in this endeavour." He rose to his feet, staring into the boy's eyes. "Do you understand?"

"I do," Copias replied.

"Good, have your belongings packed by tonight."

"I had them packed when I saw the saddles," the boy said. "Shall I send someone to pack *your* things?"

"Did I not say we must ensure complete secrecy?"

Copias folded his arms. "It would be more suspicious if an elite didn't send someone to pack his belongings."

Annoyingly, Jornis couldn't fault the boy's reasoning. "Very well, send someone up."

Without a reply, Copias nodded and marched out. Jornis sighed and hid the crucial notes within an arbitrary list of priesthood supplies and expenses as he briefly pondered what kind of elite Copias would eventually become. That is, if Felliet survived.

Sitting cross-legged atop her straw sleeping mound, Niyaa couldn't stop fidgeting as she was so excited to show off her engravings to her mom and dad. The smell of the herbs and mushrooms fluttering from her mom's cooking pot near the open window made her even more impatient for her dad to finish his talk with the governor.

Hearing her mom scoop one of three clay bowls into the brownish green soup, she said, "But Dad isn't home yet."

Mysia turned her tired eyes to her daughter and tipped the contents of the bowl back in the bubbly pot. "Sorry, I must've done it out of habit." She continued stirring with the spindly clay spoon. "So what did you bring back from the forge?"

"It's a surprise," Niyaa said. "I want to show you and Dad at the same time."

"Now you've got me excited." Mysia smiled over her shoulder. "Also, we finally got the glass out of the new fields, and soon we'll start ploughing."

Hope filled Niyaa. "So ... does that mean you and Dad can start making ale again?"

"Only when the wheat is ready to harvest."

Disappointed, Niyaa lowered her head. "When will that be?"

Mysia stopped stirring and quickly bent down to her daughter's eye level. "I know it's hard living here, but there are only three more eclipses before the comet arrives. When that happens, all the wheat and barley seeds will have long been planted. So, on that day, me, your dad and you will make the greatest ale Felliet has ever seen."

Niyaa's face lit up. "I can help make it this time!"

"I wouldn't want anything more." Mysia's smile grew. "You can even taste the first tankard."

"Really?"

"The cycle will end before you even realise. What's more..." The sound of someone climbing the ladder drew their attention. "What's more, the flowers will be in full bloom by then, allowing for all kinds of new flavours."

Darryam stepped off the ladder and sighed, slumping down on the huge straw heap opposite the window.

Niyaa looked at her dad and turned back to her mom. "Can I pick the flowers to add?"

Mysia stood up straight. "We'll do it together."

Niyaa's giddiness grew as her imagination pictured all kinds of coloured drinks she could help make. Perhaps she could use sweet gingergrass or lilac buttercups.

Mysia turned to her husband, her smile vanishing. "What'd he say?"

Darryam shook his head. "He's leaving the village and will only come back after the next harvest."

"He's gonna abandon us like Jornis did?" Mysia raised her voice in disgust.

Niyaa's excitement faded.

"The coward didn't even listen to a word I said, just told me to inform the other *newcomers*." His eyes narrowed and voice quietened. "Honestly, I'm not sure if he'll even return."

"But we'll need *someone* to lead this place," Mysia said.

Darryam nestled his forehead in his hand. "I can have a word with the priest to see who can take over."

Niyaa looked at her dad with confused eyes. "Why not you?"

"Me?" Darryam sat up straight. He relaxed back against the straw mound, shaking his head. "I won't be able to take over."

"You absolutely could," Niyaa said. "You'd be the perfect choice."

He smiled. "And why's that?"

"Well…" Niyaa thought for a moment. "You were the one who spoke back to that grumpy governor at Edenor."

Mysia shrugged. "She does have a point."

Darryam sat up again. "You can't be serious. I could never, I mean … I don't have the skills."

Niyaa shook her head. "You'll be the best governor ever."

He darted his eyes to his wife and relaxed. "I'm afraid I can't, Niyaa."

Mysia folded her arms. "And you think you'll do a worse job than Jornis or Seveck? Two men who've both shown they'll abandon their people without a moment's notice when met with the slightest of problems?"

Darryam went silent.

Mysia turned to her daughter. "Show him what you made."

Niyaa nodded and rushed back to her sleeping mound, slid her arm through the straw and grabbed the square agron piece. Pulling it from the mound, she proudly showed off the stick figures of her family standing behind their old table in front of their brewery.

Staring at the crude picture, Darryam beamed with delight and turned to his daughter. "It looks wonderful."

"Thanks." Niyaa smiled and thought of other drawings she could make.

He turned to his wife. "That's unfair."

She shrugged.

Darryam sighed, rose from his straw mound and smiled. "All right, I'll see what I can do."

Dark evening clouds blanketed the sky, and Vernon was still contemplating his confusing situation as he strolled along the quiet main street, satchel at his side. Flicking through *The Foundations*, wondering what Emperor Rochious would do in his stead, yielded no obvious answer. The tough choice left a ceaseless headache plaguing his mind which he hoped could be eased by the friendly atmosphere of the Welcomerry Band.

Inside, however, he found the tavern lacking the regular bustle of joyous labourers; instead only a small handful of drinkers sat at the bar with a strange uneasiness lingering in the air. Likewise, only two tables were occupied, one beside the corner ladder filled with unusually quiet regulars and the other at the far end which seated three tribowmen. The latter unnervingly had tribows resting between their tankards, but thankfully Grayfern kept a watchful eye on them from the right end of the bar. Hazel was cleaning a tankard.

Vernon asked, "So how is it so quiet in here all of a sudden?"

"Didn't you hear?" she asked. "There's a rumour goin' around that Felliet's creating an army and will soon be joining a war with Fyoreten." Hazel glanced at her other customers. "Got everyone all worked up, especially the soldiers and merchants."

Vernon leaned against the bar. "Wish I could say it wasn't true."

Her eyes widened. "Someone high up tell ya then?"

"Reethial Zenth," Vernon said. "And apparently he will become Felliet's new representative in the great chamber."

Hazel turned to fill the tankard from his usual cask, quietly asking over her shoulder, "So how come the brother to the head Zenth told you this?"

Vernon sighed. "He demands I travel with him to Sidium to become one of his personal assistants."

"Isn't that a good thing?" she asked.

"In one way." Vernon reached inside his satchel, taking a couple of coins and placing them on the bar. He felt a sudden urge to explain his dilemma. "But I absolutely despise the idea of being a steward to those uncaring elites. Worse still, it'll be under one with the Zenth name ... and yet."

"And yet?" Hazel placed the full tankard down.

He smiled. "And yet the idea of going to Erium, seeing the black capital for the first time and physically standing inside the great chamber is something beyond my greatest desire."

She folded her arms. "Is that *really* something you desire?"

"How could it not be?" Passages he had read came to him, bringing a passionate smile. "To actually have the chance to stand inside the great chamber and see the white crystal sword sheathed in its floor would be astonishing."

Hazel leaned closer to Vernon. "So what if it means you'll be working for an elite? You get to do something you really want."

"Because…" Vernon stopped his rebuke and averted his gaze. He quietened his voice. "Because I feel that if I were to go, then I would truly become one of them."

She scoffed. "When you first entered 'ere, I honestly thought you were one."

Vernon stared back. "I am *not* one of them."

Hazel's cheerful demeanour faded as she leaned closer to Vernon with unflinching, serious eyes. "You choose who you are and who you'll become. It matters not what you're assigned at birth or what others think of you. *You* choose who you are." She stepped back with a grim and tense expression and filled a second tankard.

Vernon pondered her words for a long while. "I think I really needed to hear that."

She stopped the cask tap, gulped a hefty mouthful and whispered back, "Happy to help."

Taking a similar mouthful of ale, Vernon saw Grayfern, who had evidently listened to the whole conversation, giving him a single nod of approval and returning his attention to the three drinking guards.

Another refreshing tankard later, Orfain finally entered, carrying a hefty sack, and stood alongside Vernon with a forehead covered in sweat.

"Been working?" Vernon asked.

"Yeah," Orfain said. "Once I heard a war's comin', I knew there'd be a rush to buy stock before the prices rise. Thankfully, I managed to beat most of the competition just in time."

Hazel remarked, "I'm glad your business is doin' well."

"No worries there," he said. "Got everything stored nice and safe."

"Good to hear." Hazel put her hand on a cask. "The usual?"

"If you could." Orfain placed two brass coins on the bar and turned to Vernon. "So how's your day been?"

Vernon wondered how he should explain. "Well…"

"He's leaving for Sidium," Hazel said.

Orfain's eyes widened. "You're headed to Erium! When you supposed to set off?"

"Early tomorrow." Vernon stared longingly into his drink. "And I'm unsure when I'll return." Thinking on his own words, Vernon realised he wouldn't have to return to this debauched nation ever again. He could remain in Felliet's embassy and make a new life in Sidium. He glanced at his friends and hid his optimism. "I'm almost certain I won't be able to visit."

Orfain heartedly placed several coins down, saying, "Well, since it's your last night here, we better celebrate as though the comet were passing overhead." He turned to Hazel. "Bring another for Vernon."

She finished her tankard. "Will do."

Seeing Hazel filling another tankard with half of one still in his hands brought a good chuckle out of Vernon.

Orfain drank a huge gulp of his ale. "Suppose you never been to Erium before, have ya?"

"Well, I know *you* have."

"Well, I bet you didn't know I've travelled to every city and town across the whole of Erium. But the city of black crystal, now that's a place I've been to so many times you could say it was my old home."

"All right." Vernon relaxed. "So tell me, what should I expect in Sidium?"

Orfain grinned with pride as he proceeded to speak of his travels through the city of black crystal.

Another pint later, Orfain was discussing Sidium's vast stables. "...and they were as long as a large field and housed all kinds of horses. From the fittest mares for those messenger types to the steadfast army ones and the many rugged cart pullers. I even saw a baby reed cutter in one of the pens."

"A reed cutter?" Vernon asked. "What kind of lunatic would bring one into a city?"

"Some rich bloke showing off, no doubt, or some worker from the Marsh Basin bringing a pet." Orfain shrugged. "Anyway, I've no idea how they even managed to haul the damn thing into the stables."

Vernon raised his eyebrows. "Didn't you say it was just a baby?"

"Yeah, but it was still bloody massive. They had to put it in one of their double pens, and even then, it bashed the brick walls trying to get out. Nearly scared my Princess to death."

"Princess?" Vernon wondered why he never heard that name before.

"Ah, Princess." Orfain held up his tankard with a fond look. "She was the first pony I ever owned, small sickly thing whose coat was covered in grey patches. She had even lost the sight in her left eye a couple cycles after I bought her." He took a small sip of ale. "Yet despite all that, she lived a long happy life with me, pulling my old cart. She and I travelled along pretty much every road in Erium, and even when she became skinnier in her final days, she still happily trotted along." Orfain stared into the distance.

Unsure of how to continue the conversation, Vernon hesitated.

Orfain turned to him. "You know, you need to be more impulsive."

"I'm sorry?"

"Listen." Orfain finished his drink. "If you want to explore Sidium and do whatever *you* want to do, you need to be more … out there."

Vernon wondered if it was the ale talking. "Afraid I'm still struggling to grasp what you're trying to say."

"I bought Princess with all the money I scrapped together on a random whim, and I've never regretted it, not once. You on the other hand are always thinkin'. Never have I seen you do something in a sudden spur of the moment."

Hazel crossed her arms. "I don't think that's a bad thing."

"Course it is," Orfain argued. "Without taking risks or following your gut, you'll just end up following orders from higher ups the rest of your life." He turned to Vernon. "Tonight I want you to turn off your brain and do something bold."

Vernon leaned against the bar and thought about the terrifying idea of merely becoming a puppet, following the whims and commands of the elites.

"Could be anything," Orfain continued. "Anything at all."

"Very well." Vernon smiled. "I'll take you up on the offer."

The two of them raised their tankards, clinking them together and finishing their ales.

Orfain brought his emptied tankard against the bar. "That calls for another."

"Coming right up." Hazel took his tankard and turned to refill.

Watching Hazel open the cask tap with her back to Vernon, a cheeky idea came to him, and he whispered to Orfain, "I'll show you how bold I can be." He stared at the large black hairband holding down Hazel's thick, silvery hair and placed his left palm on the bar, subtlety raising himself up.

Orfain muttered to himself, "This'll be good."

With most of his weight on his left arm, Vernon stretched out his right hand towards the hairband.

Grayfern shouted in the same instant Vernon plucked the hairband from Hazel's hair, and out sprang two brown spirals where her ears should have been, as wide as her hands and covered in tiny pink hairs that followed the spiral down into small ear holes at their centre. Vernon's eyes were wide with shock and fear. Hazel was a Beast Rider.

She immediately gripped her ear spirals tightly with both hands, letting the half-filled tankard clatter to the stone floor and drawing the attention of everyone in the room. Not a word left anyone's lips, leaving only the sound of ale freely pouring from the open tap to fill the void.

Trembling with terror, Hazel slowly turned to face Vernon, who was stiffly frozen in place without a thought entering his mind.

She quickly snatched the hairband from his loose grip, briefly reshowing one of her ear spirals to the stunned onlookers and placed it back on her head once more. After flattening the ear spirals against her temples, Hazel's shaking hands closed the tap, bringing the whole tavern to a dreaded silence.

Vernon steadily stepped off the bar and slowly turned his gaze to the many bewildered faces around the tavern, fixing his eyes on the three guards.

One of them rose, scraping his chair against the floor, drawing everyone's anxious gaze. The man glanced down at the tribow resting on their table just as Grayfern reached for something under the bar.

Orfain swiftly brought out a small coin purse from his sack and shook it in the air. "How's about we all forget this?"

His futile words echoed off the stone walls without an answer.

The two other guards stood, one tightly grasping his nearly empty tankard while the second plucked out a tribow bolt from her quiver, gripping it like a dagger.

A man on the other side of the bar with the thick gloves of a glass cutter angrily broke the silence. "To think a damn Beast Fucker was serving me drinks."

Grayfern glared at the man and revealed a thick iron club which had been secretly stashed beneath the right end of the bar, resting it on his hefty shoulder and returning his attention to the guards. The other people sitting near the ladder were rising from their seats, their eyes glancing to the exit.

Orfain climbed atop the oval bar, his voice becoming louder. "Three bronze for every man here."

Hardly anyone in the room paid him any mind, despite the astonishing offer.

The first guard placed his palm on his tribow handle, exchanging a threatening glare with Grayfern. "Give yourselves up and there won't be a need for trouble."

The female guard holding the bolt spoke up. "You'll be awarded handsomely if you help bring her in."

Upon those words, Grayfern leapt over the bar, his legs pounding the floor, and grunted over his shoulder. "Orfain. Shut the door."

Heart racing, Vernon darted his eyes from one face to the next. Then Hazel sprinted to the ladder, springing everyone into action.

The closest guard picked up the tribow and shouted for her to halt, only for Grayfern to charge, madly bringing his club down upon the weapon, smacking it from his hands. A moment later, Hazel reached the ladder, scattering the other drinkers towards the exit.

Orfain quickly leapt from the bar toward the door while shouting to Vernon, "Stay with her!"

Vernon gave chase as he watched Hazel desperately flinging herself up the ladder. Upon reaching the first rung, Vernon glanced back and witnessed the glass cutter clumsily tackling Orfain to the ground, allowing the handful of bystanders to flee into the darkened street. Grayfern battered away the female guard's bolt hand and ruthlessly drove his club into her stomach, bringing her wheezing to the ground.

Vernon heard the hatch above lock shut, and he hurriedly climbed the ladder with the brawling carnage behind him. Futility trying to push the hatch open, he desperately called out, "Hazel! Hazel!"

A tankard bounced off Grayfern's head as he cracked his club into the first guard's arm, sending a pain-filled shriek into the air. The glass cutter wrestled himself atop Orfain, forcing his thick gloves around his throat. Vernon instinctively leapt from the ladder. Landing on the stone floor, Vernon charged at the attacker and swung his full satchel into the man's head, forcing him off.

Orfain let out dry coughs as he regained his breath while the glass cutter got to his feet and sprinted through the door. Grayfern meanwhile had stepped over the two downed guards and cornered the third who desperately tried to shield himself with the discarded tribow. Vernon spotted Hazel through the opposite window climbing down onto the back winding street and running away.

Grayfern was ruthlessly striking at the cornered guard's defence, forcing him to shield himself on the floor.

Vernon turned to Orfain and held out his hand to pull his friend to his feet.

Breathing heavily, Orfain called out to Grayfern, "I'll get … the Blue Excen to the safe place … you safekeep the other supplies."

The huge man ceased his maddening attack and marched towards the door, leaving the guards too terrified and injured to move. Still grasping the iron club, Grayfern narrowed his eyes at Vernon and wordlessly stormed out.

Orfain ambled to the bar and climbed over, taking a small green cask engraved *The Blue Excen*.

Without an idea of what to do, Vernon said, "Hazel ran away somewhere."

Orfain fast marched to the door. "I know where she's headed."

Without another word, Vernon followed Orfain out of the Tavern and into the dark main street. Rushing into the opposing alleyway, Vernon glanced up and thankfully saw no break in the cloud cover, realising the garrison would soon be hunting them in force. He glanced to the few flickers of candlelight shining from the nearby windows and lowered his face.

After checking around the corner, Orfain darted out of the alley's opposite end, and the two of them ran along a narrow serpentine street with their sandals echoing across the loose cobblestones. Behind them came a growing commotion from the tavern, and their pace quickened.

The further they fled from the main street, the narrower and more rancid the streets became till the pair were treading across brown puddles and moss-covered dirt.

Vernon whispered, "Where are we going?"

"Somewhere safe," Orfain answered without a glance.

The pair passed a dilapidated well, and bells sounded from the outer gatehouse. They quickened their pace as the sound duplicated along the walls, surrounding the entire city in a cacophony of ringing alarms.

Awoken homeowners let candlelight pour from their windows, brightening the neglected street they ran down. Vernon glanced down the adjoining avenues, glimpsing people stepping outside and hearing the rhythm of soldiers boots distantly behind them.

He turned to Orfain. "We shouldn't be running like this."

"Not too far now," he muttered back.

Vernon saw a door further ahead open, basking the upcoming route in a flickering spotlight, and he grabbed Orfain's collar, bringing them both to a standstill.

He stared wide eyed back. "What're you…"

Vernon pointed ahead just as a man and wife stepped out. "We need to tread with caution."

"I ain't gonna waste time," Orfain argued.

"You won't be." Vernon glimpsed torchlight brightening distant rooftops. "Getting caught here will only worsen her situation."

"They won't be looking for us."

"They will if we run." Vernon placed his hand on the small cask. "Especially if we appear like thieves."

Orfain bit his lip. "Fine, but I take the lead."

Closely following Orfain's fast walking pace, Vernon darted his eyes to the candlelit windows around them as he despairingly wondered what would happen if they were caught. As they passed the open door, Vernon waved to the curious couple, forcing a smile.

The man asked, "Do you know what's going on?"

Still walking, Vernon shrugged. "Not a clue." He pointed to the oncoming torchlight shining off the rooftops. "I'm sure the garrison will be here soon, so you can ask them."

"Thanks anyway." The man and his wife retreated inside.

Orfain's pace increased as they passed deeper into the commoner area.

"Don't alert attention," Vernon said.

Orfain's grip on the cask tightened, and he returned to his quick march.

The two of them reached an uneven street going downwards that ended at a darkened section of the outer wall. Not one of the buildings nor the wall itself shone any kind of light, leaving this abandoned place in pitch darkness.

"The guards never bother patrolling here," Orfain said. "Just make sure not to lose your step."

Vernon followed Orfain into the black shadows of the disused street with only the sound of his steps and the faint outline of the darkened buildings as a guide. Nearly tripping over a loose stone, Vernon picked up his feet and glanced back to the sliver of light from the originating street. He wondered why Orfain, Grayfern and Hazel would even need a hiding place such as this. What *other supplies* was Grayfern protecting, and what kind of business were the three of them in? Vernon shook his head and returned his gaze to the unseen steps of his friend.

The pair arrived at a warped ajar door of a dilapidated building abutting the wall which Orfain heaved open. Once again, he looked around for pursuers and breathed a sigh of relief. Vernon glanced at the empty ramparts above and couldn't help but smile at the ironic incompetence of the elites; their understaffed garrison had actually aided him.

Setting foot on the cracked floor inside, Vernon squinted his eyes at the dark outlines of the large eating room, and Orfain carefully set the door back ajar. Dust was as thick in the air as it was coated on every dilapidated surface. The only wall lacking any kind of damp was the outer wall with nary a single piece of straw left in the large deep fireplace it housed. Even the small window beside the door was cracked and clouded, allowing only the faintest of light to enter.

"Would Hazel actually be here?" Vernon asked.

Orfain went to the clouded window and peered out. He muttered, "Why here? They can't be that determined."

"What is it?" Vernon whispered.

Orfain stepped away from the window, cask in hand. "They're coming."

Vernon gazed at the ajar door but resisted the urge to peer out. "So where do we…" All words left him as Orfain crouched inside the empty fireplace, set the cask down and climbed up.

Seeing Orfain's feet disappear up the chimney, Vernon rushed to gaze inside. Orfain was climbing up subtle grooves in the grey brickwork of the outer wall.

Reaching a first-floor height, he whispered down, "Wait till I lower the rope before you climb up."

No longer was Vernon in any doubt that his friends were on the unlawful side, and he glanced at the ajar door. The sound of the approaching guards grew, and instinctively, he turned back and crawled inside the fireplace.

High into the chimney, Orfain slid open a camouflaged door, revealing a faint flickering glow, and clambered inside. He lowered a hooked rope, whispering, "Attach this to the Blue Excen."

Attaching the hook to the cask's study handle, Vernon heard a neighbouring door bash open, and he whispered, "Pull it up now."

Orfain winched the cask up, and Vernon set his hands into the first of the brickwork grooves and pulled himself up. With his fingers gripping the dusty grooves, his sandaled feet finding the gaps and his satchel dangling from his neck, Vernon climbed up.

Halfway up the chimney, the warped door smashed open. Both he and Orfain froze in place, their eyes locked on one another as the guards stomped across the cracked floor. Trying to keep his body as still as possible, Vernon's legs started quaking. Biting his bottom lip at the frantic footsteps and tossed furniture, Vernon hoped none of the guards examined the fireplace.

Almost as quickly as they burst in, the sounds vanished, so Vernon reached for the next rung as Orfain slowly continued winching the heavy cask up, setting it inside the opening. He took Vernon's hand and pulled him inside.

As Orfain replaced the painted cover, Vernon breathed a long sigh of relief and exhaustion. Looking at his surroundings, his eyes widened, and he wearily got to his feet, completely stunned.

Before him lay an incredibly long room inside the wall itself filled to the ceiling with multitudes of finely stitched sacks, jewellery chests, miniature whiskey crates and other luxuries. In fact, the only place devoid of treasure was a single straight passageway to the other end where a single candle flickered from an ornate brass stand.

Vernon's eyes drifted across the expensive array of goods. "What … is all this?"

Orfain picked up the small, heavy cask and moved past Vernon towards the light. "A place you weren't meant to see."

Following him along the narrow divide, Vernon was completely bewildered.

Hazel revealed herself from behind a stack of crates next to the candle stand, with narrowed watery eyes. "Why did you follow me?"

Orfain spoke back as though an insult had been thrown at him. "After everything you've done, you think I would just give up cause you're…" He stopped himself and gently set the cask down. "I don't care that you're … a Beast Ride—"

"I'm not one of them!" Hazel yelled. "Those disgusting things only spread misery wherever they go. I am *nothing* like them!" A long pause hovered between them, and she turned her gaze away. "What will you do?"

Orfain stepped forward and placed his hand on his chest. "Whatever you want me to."

Hazel spun to look at him.

"You've given me everything I own," Orfain said. "No matter what, I am yours."

Hazel smiled briefly. "Thank you." Her eyes met Vernon's and all joy or relief faded from her expression.

He stepped forward, apologising, "I am so deeply sorry about what I did."

"Don't." Hazel turned away.

"I had no idea, if there's—"

Orfain grabbed him by the shirt collar, stopping another word.

An uncomfortable silence sat among the three of them. Hazel finally spoke. "Thanks for coming after me."

"Nothing else met my mind." Orfain grinned.

Hazel glanced to the small cask. "And I'm glad to see you saved the Blue Excen."

"Grayfern's safeguarding our other supplies," he said. "We should be fine to lie idle in the shadows for the next few eclipses now."

She shook her head. "If you think they'll forget about us as quickly as they do a common robber then you're a fool."

Orfain leaned his back against a stack of miniature barrels. "We don't have any other choice. The sketchers will have drawn dozens of handouts by tomorrow, and the entire garrison will be out looking for us. No doubt the people who saw the whole thing will be placed at each city exit." He folded his arms. "Best thing we can do is just wait in the shadows."

"The priesthood are relentless." Her words slowed. "Once they hear … of me, their trackers will use every method they can until I'm caught. They will search every home and storehouse, triple the number of patrols and interrogate everyone we know and don't know." She half closed her eyes. "We wouldn't be able to poke our heads out even for scraps of food and water."

Orfain shook his head. "But escaping now will be suicide."

"We have no other choice," Hazel replied. "We should gather what we can and head for the river grate."

He stomped toward her, raising his voice. "If you try to leave through there, you'll drown."

Her gaze darted away. "We can make it if the current isn't too strong."

Vernon leaned against a nearby pile of clothing sacks and pondered a solution.

"We can't risk it." Orfain scratched his head. "If we're gonna leave, it should be in my cart."

"They'll be searching every one of them now," Hazel replied. "And I bet they'll be looking for you as well."

Vernon imagined the gatehouse and the guards searching the poorer traders before a moment of realisation came to him. "Not if it belongs to an elite."

Hazel and Orfain both turned to him, awaiting his suggestion.

"Since I'm travelling with Reethial Zenth in the morning, why not accompany his carriage train?" Vernon pointed to Orfain. "You know every road in Erium and would be sure to know any shortcuts from here to Sidium."

He grinned. "There's only one way from here to Sidium, and that's along the Ciclet highway, the one you can't avoid."

Vernon felt a wave of defeat wash over him.

A moment later Hazel nodded and approached the cask, turning its tap upside down and opening the valve. Vernon stared in awe as the top sprang open, revealing a padded inside filled with bronze coins, brass necklaces, jewelled rings and glistening pink sapphires. Hazel sifted her hands through the treasure, clearly searching for a specific item.

Orfain turned to Vernon with a sly grin. "We prepared a small deposit for hard times."

Seeing the incredible wealth before him, a dreaded question left Vernon's lips. "Did you steal this?"

"Course not." Orfain patted Vernon's shoulder. "The Blue Excen is what we made by carting and safekeeping the supplies around you."

Confused, Vernon turned to the surrounding luxury-filled crates, sacks and barrels. "I don't understand."

He smiled. "Hazel, Grayfern and I are partners. They provide me a safe place and I deliver the goods."

"Goods I'm guessing avoid inspections?" Vernon felt a strange disdain rise within him.

Hazel smirked. "Only because it's *this* city."

"And why only Ellity?" Vernon asked.

Orfain shrugged. "Ever try trading outside goods to this place? It's a nightmare of tax duty."

Vernon pondered the words, and his body relaxed. "So you circumvent the garrison to sell these things to the elites."

"Not just the elites. We supply all kinds of rich and poor shopkeeps across the whole city." Orfain patted his chest. "Cause of us, Ellity's people can actually afford these wares."

"*Everyone* wins," Hazel added, carefully taking out a silver necklace cord that dangled a thin black kite piece, bringing a delighted smile to her face. "Here it is."

Vernon stared closely at the necklace. It glistened in the candlelight, and his eyes widened. "That's not black crystal, is it?"

Hazel grinned as she tied it around her neck. "The Zenth family consider themselves at the top of all other elites, correct?"

Vernon nodded.

"Well, there's only one name they cannot even pretend to be equals to, let alone superior." She rubbed her thumb against the black crystal's metallic surface. "I'm more than willing to bet they greatly desire the symbol of the Imerial family." Her smile faded as her demeanour became serious. "If you introduce me to Reethial Zenth, I can make an offer to sell pieces of black crystal to him when we arrive at Sidium."

Vernon pondered the idea for a good, long while and asked, "Do you think you can convince him?"

"I wouldn't say otherwise," Hazel answered. "Now you two should get some sleep, for we need to be fully awake and aware at sunrise."

Chapter eight – Reddened Crossroad

Sixth eclipse, fifth day

With nothing but a hardened sack of dye powder as his pillow, it had been a restless, dreaded night on the cold floor. At the shimmer of orange sunlight beaming through the opened chimney entrance, Vernon sat up. Turning to Hazel and the ornate mirror she used, he was in awe, for her thick silvery hair had become golden with brass-ringed braids along her temples perfectly hiding her unique ears. Adorning her body was a silk violet dress that served to exemplify the single piece of jewellery she wore. Undoubtedly, she could pass through the lavender-reeking streets of the inner city without attracting pompous attention.

Vernon lifted his weakened body, feeling all the aches through his stiffened muscles and glanced at Orfain, somehow sleeping soundly. He stepped towards Hazel. "Where did you learn to make your hair like that?"

She kept her gaze fixed on her reflection. "This isn't the first time I've had to change my identity. Also, you should call me Lysia from now on."

Vernon's throat ached with guilt, yet he steadied his tongue, for any words spoken would only further worsen the mood; instead, he chose to wake Orfain.

He awoke slowly to Vernon's touch, no doubt feeling the same aches, but he promptly got to his feet. He approached Hazel. "I see you got Erium's hairstyle pretty much spot on."

She smiled quickly and pointed to an opened crate brimming with fine clothes. "You two better get changed lest you attract attention. Oh, and Orfain, I am Lysia from now on."

"You mean until we get to Sidium, right?" He frowned.

"I cannot be referred to as Hazel anymore." She turned back to the mirror. "Now, you better change. We have a lot of work to do before the morning rush of shoppers appears."

Orfain stood there motionless, his hands becoming tight fists, yet no argument left his mouth; instead, he reluctantly moved to the crate and chose a brass-buttoned black waistcoat.

Vernon followed Orfain to the open crate and stared at the expensive outfits. Shame washed over him. "Are you sure it's all right for me to have one of these?"

She didn't look away from the mirror. "We are going to be offering black crystal to one of the most prestigious people in Felliet. You need to wear your best outfit."

Left without argument, Vernon's body weakened as he plunged his hands into the clothes chest. Rummaging through the finely stitched clothes, searching for the cheapest set, he came upon a modest pale blue collared shirt and a pair of black corded trousers.

Orfain changed into his new attire. "So how do I look, Ly … sia?"

She smiled and approached him, taking his hand. "You look quite dashing."

He returned the smile.

Lysia turned her attention to Vernon, almost scanning him. "I suppose that'll work, but you'll need a new satchel." She wandered to the far side of the warehouse and opened a wide chest. She returned to Vernon with a pristine pearl satchel with a thick, silk-threaded shoulder strap.

"This one has a false pocket for storing secret parchments. It'll do you proud."

Thinking it to be a joke, Vernon shrugged and forced a smile. "Don't think I'll need a secret pocket."

She held the satchel out to him without another word.

Embarrassed, he swiftly accepted it and took *The Foundations* out of his old grey bag.

Lysia asked, "What kind of book is that?"

"A historical one," Vernon answered, relieved the subject had changed. "It's all about the founding of Erium by the great Emperor Rochious."

Lysia was quiet for a brief moment. "I think it might make for a good read." She walked to Orfain. "Take the Blue Excen, load your cart and wait for us at the southeastern inner gate."

"I'll see you there." Orfain lowered the cask down the chimney hatch and climbed down, out of sight.

Lysia stood there silently, her gaze fixed on the open hatch for a long while. She turned to Vernon. "Let's not keep Reethial waiting."

Leaving the dilapidated house, they walked along the same abandoned street Vernon had fled down. With every step, he darted his eyes to the surrounding broken windows and worn doorways, anxiously wondering if anyone was watching.

"Relax," Lysia said. "Revealing your nerves only draws attention."

"Afraid I don't know how to hide them," Vernon muttered back.

"You realise only a handful of people in this entire city know where you were last night, and fewer even knows your name."

"I suppose."

They entered the adjoining street, and Vernon stiffened at the sight of several labourers and craftsmen taking in the morning air.

Retreading along the loose cobblestones, they passed the same door he had walked by the previous night. Vernon's breath further deepened as he imagined the same couple stepping outside. The longer they walked, the livelier the impoverished streets became, and the more Vernon overheard confused, gossiping chatter about last night's bells. Gradually his wide gaze lowered until he was only looking at the cobbles before him as they travelled further through the commoner area.

The surroundings became darker, and Vernon raised his eyes. They were walking in the long morning shadow of the inner wall. Lysia had led him along a completely indirect route through the poor homes and workshops, avoiding the main street entirely.

Without warning, she stopped and reached her palm to him. "Could you hand me your book, please?"

Vernon hesitated at the strange request but placed *The Foundations* in her hand. They were nearing the inner gatehouse, and his legs stiffened.

She opened the book to a random page. "Keep your chin high and your body relaxed," Lysia instructed, darting her eyes across the words as they continued walking.

Under the iron portcullis of the inner gatehouse, eight chainmailed guards stood, double the previous number, all of whom were sternly watching every passerby. A pair of silver-haired women stood next to the stone wall with bitter, confused faces. Clearly the guards were rounding up anyone who remotely resembled Lysia, and his heart raced faster.

Vernon glanced to Lysia, who somehow remained composed as she read the book. Her pace slowed, bringing Vernon ahead of her. Taking the lead, he anxiously turned to the guards, forcing a smile.

One of the guards asked, "Young man, did you notice anything last night?"

Vernon stopped, forcing a shrug. "You mean other than the bells?" Getting no response to his words, he stuttered, "No … we didn't see anything."

The guard darted his eyes to Lysia. "The criminal was apparently a common barwoman with silver hair." Vernon watched the man's eyes squint at the book and relax. "If you hear anything, let us know."

Stiffly moving his body past them, Vernon breathed in the abundant stench of lavender and exhaled in relief once they were a fair distance along the smoothened street.

Lysia closed the book and handed it back. "Thank you for that."

Vernon opened his new pearl satchel and dropped the book inside. "I don't wish to do that again."

"Nor do I." Lysia let out her own relieved breath.

Stepping on the shield mosaic, Vernon knew the elaborate bronze-framed black carriage would seat Reethial along the journey. In blatant contrast, the other carriage of his procession was made of simple grey cloth with the shield of Felliet embodied on either side. Encircling both were a dozen riders in polished iron chainmail whose swords were nestled in engraved brass sheathes. Only one was given permission to dismount, his grey ringed brooch marking him as the head bodyguard.

Dutifully approaching him, Vernon took in a deep breath and asked, "May I have a word with Reethial?"

The guard disinterestedly turned at him and replied with a tiredness in his voice, "You're one of the students, aren't you?" He pointed his thumb to the third carriage. "Get in and wait."

Undeterred, Vernon continued, "It's just that I have someone here who wishes to speak to him."

The man's eyes narrowed. "I don't care who it is, I have my orders. Now get in the damn wagon."

Before Vernon could think of an argument, Lysia waltzed up to the armoured man. "Excuse me, but could you do me the courtesy of providing an audience with your noble?"

The guard looked at her suspiciously. "Noble?"

"Apologies," she replied. "I come from Erium and I forgot you refer to them differently. As for why I seek an audience with your elite"—She rubbed her thumb across the black crystal necklace—"I have a certain offer he would find … valuable."

The guard stared blankly at the necklace for a while, and his eyes widened. He turned his gaze to the black spire towering over the back end of the Gallery and quietly asked, "That isn't black crystal, is it?"

She grinned.

"All right, you can speak to him when he leaves the Gallery." He glanced at the extravagant doors. "He shouldn't be too long now."

"Thank you."

The guard's eyes turned back to Vernon. Without a word spoken, he knew his presence would only hinder Lysia, so he swiftly left for the rear of the plain wagon.

Beneath the grey cloth, the wagon was half filled with numerous chests and barrels with only hard benches near its entrance. Buckley was already seated, happily reading a small playbook. Reluctantly climbing inside, Vernon placed himself next to the open rear end and stared out at the obtuse wealthy of Ellity trekking across the plaza. He beamed as he thought of his upcoming departure.

Iyessa arrived at the wagon. Predictably, she kept her chin high and satchel still as she climbed aboard and narrowed her eyes at Vernon. She turned her gaze away and silently took a seat near Reethial's belongings.

Frustration overwhelmed Vernon, and he finally asked, "What gives you the impression you're superior to me?"

A momentary twitch appeared on her lips before she took out a small book from her emerald satchel and began reading.

"Fine then," Vernon responded.

The mood became sour and the quiet wait insufferable. Vernon heard the Gallery doors open but couldn't see them from where he sat. The sound of a single set of sandals approached the egotistical black carriage and Reethial's voice said, "Who is she?"

"My name is Lysia." Her relaxed tone endured. "But to get to the point, I possess certain items that may interest you."

After a long, uncomfortable pause, Reethial said, "Such items would be of interest. However…"

Another pause plagued at Vernon's nerves.

"...I highly doubt the emperor would give permission of such items to someone without a family name."

Lysia sounded unfazed. "His greatness believes only a select few should be given permission to trade such wares and not an entire family. Consequently, such a trade is to be kept hidden to avoid preying eyes and thieving hands."

"Hmmm." Reethial seemed optimistic. "I can understand but if you are truly who you say you are, why approach me and not one of Erium's nobles?"

"Quite simply, I believe the glorious symbol of the Imerial name should be worn by the most prestigious of individuals. And who better than Reethial Zenth, head of Ellity's academy and the new representative of Felliet?"

"I would agree none are better." His voice became celebratory. "Could I interest you in a private dinner so we may discuss this further?"

"I am in fact to depart for Sidium today," she lied. "But I must say I am quite tired of travelling in my helper's cart along these rough roads."

"You need suffer no such indignity," Reethial replied. "It would be a pleasure if you would accompany my wife and I to Sidium."

"The pleasure would be all mine." Lysia paused. "Oh, could you allow my helper to follow us? He has all of my belongings in his cart and is waiting by the westerly gatehouse."

"It shan't be a problem."

As soon as Vernon heard the first carriage's door shut, he sighed in relief knowing his friends were safe. He sat back and amusingly pictured the guards and sketchers having to step aside for Reethial's procession with their targets inside. A moment later, the carriages began moving, and with a joyous face, Vernon watched the Gallery gradually become distant.

The forge was strangely quiet. Not only was the furnace cold but the hammering table was completely bare. She stood in the middle of the room for a long while waiting for Erger but remembered the conversation she had overheard. In an instant, she sprinted outside.

Running along the dirt street, she hoped to find Erger chatting to a guard, farmer or stonemason about repairs. She found no sign of him anywhere in the small village, so she rushed to the gate hoping he was talking to someone in the fields outside instead of leaving with the governor.

Kivy shouted down to her from atop the wall beside the closed gate. "Where *you* thinkin of goin?"

Niyaa nervously looked away. "I … need to find Erger."

"He left with the gov at sunrise." Kivy glanced at the westerly landscape, angrily muttering, "Bloody good for nothins."

Niyaa put her hands on the gate's greens bars and wondered what she should do.

"So why you still 'ere?" Kivy asked, walking to the edge of the wall. "Get back to the forge."

Niyaa looked at her in bewildered disbelief. "I can't work the forge alone."

"Then what good are you to us?" Kivy's face reddened, and she slowly bent her knees, keeping her eyes staring down at Niyaa. "It's thanks to you lot that us folk livin' here hardly has any food left. Yet you have the nerve to ask for one of the people working their backs swollen to give you a hand?" She pointed her spear back to the village. "Get back to the forge before I carry you there."

Niyaa felt her hands tighten around the bars of the gate.

"Well?" Kivy asked.

Without a word or glance towards the guard, Niyaa bit her bottom lip and trudged back along the dirt street. The closer she got to the forge, the heavier her body seemed.

Stepping inside the coldness of the forge, she was unable to move as the loneliness consumed her mind. Only when her stomach growled did she wake from her trance and reluctantly look around the room. The unfinished agron barrel had been left on the cold floor. She ambled over to it and placed it on the hammering bench, ready to finish it.

Half a day listening to only the wagon wheels and horses' hooves along the stone highway had done little to persuade the other two students to make conversation. This left Vernon with only a couple of options to pass the time, either reread *The Foundations* or stare at the moving scenery of green, yellow and blue hills. He had expected the vibrant colours that flourished west of the mountains to be awe inspiring, but in the company of the silent self-indulgent, he couldn't enjoy the passing landscape. At least he could take solace the sky remained clear and Orfain seemed content at the back of the procession. Furthermore, it would not be long before they would be comfortably resting in the small town of Wisten. He wondered whether the Erium people would act welcoming or unfazed by the arrival of Felliet's new representative.

The procession came to an abrupt halt, startling all inside the cloth wagon.

Reethial swiftly opened his carriage window, demanding, "Why have we stopped?"

Vernon peered out and saw the bodyguard sent to secure lodging in the upcoming town returning at a full gallop. Vernon wondered if there was some problem with the rooms, but the rider's quickened pace meant something was seriously wrong.

The man yanked the reins of his sweating horse just before the first carriage. "Fyoreten horsemen … have been spotted up ahead."

Vernon's gaze widened.

The head bodyguard asked, "Whereabouts?"

"I checked with the local traders." The man paused to catch his breath. "They passed close to Wisten … but didn't go for the town itself."

"They must be targeting travellers along the roads for bronze and information." The head bodyguard turned to Reethial. "We should return to Ellity at once and wait till the road to Sidium is free from danger."

"How dare such commoners obstruct the road to Felliet!" Reethial furiously spat. "I'll be glad to hear Erium's armies crushing them into the dirt."

Dread overcame Vernon, for returning to Ellity would guarantee Lysia's and Orfain's capture. He glanced back to his friend listening to the entire thing in his cart with a similar fearful expression.

Lysia interjected, "Would not travelling back the way we came be more dangerous? If Fyoreten's men were targeting travellers or the wealthy that is."

The head bodyguard turned to her. "It would be a far greater risk to continue on. Our only option is to turn back."

"Not necessarily," she replied. "Could we not head north? Avoiding the highway entirely?"

The armoured man shook his head. "The carriages are much too heavy to go off the road."

"The grass is dry enough," Lysia said. "Not to mention it would be a rather short journey with my helper leading the way."

He glanced dismissively at Orfain. "How so?"

"He is a man well versed in the routes across Erium," she explained. "He will know how to reach the nearest road north of here." The head bodyguard seemed unconvinced, so Lysia directed her attention to Reethial. "If you prefer the safety of Felliet, I'm afraid we must part ways, for I have important matters that I need to address in Sidium."

"Don't you fret," Reethial said, waving his hand to the head bodyguard. "See to it my procession heads north with this beauty's helper guiding the way."

Begrudgingly, the armoured rider nodded and trotted towards Orfain.

Vernon breathed a sigh of relief and sat back down. Only then did he notice Iyessa's hands were tense, almost bending the book in her tight grip.

Finding little sleep in the cramped, communal tent, Iyna had marched nonstop with her unit across countless colourful hills without knowing if or when they might see battle. Annoyingly, all that any of them were told was they were to meet with Erium soldiers. Not a single word came from anyone's lips, leaving only the sound of clunking movement of thin armour and shouldered shields from the three marching spear units. Following closely behind came the rustling of bolt-filled quivers of the three tribow units and the squeaking wheels of the supply cart driven by Soart.

Iyna stared up at the blue sky, hoping clouds would gather and quench her thirst as the commander riding with his bodyguards far behind his army had disallowed more than a mouthful of water per person.

As the great mother reached its highest in the clear sky, Alexan shouted, "Halt! Form a shield wall, now!"

Iyna's unit paused in a moment of collective hesitation and rushed to the front row to form the practiced two lines and lock their shields. Iyna stood in the back row in her cramped shield wall next to the gap where Alexan would stand.

Alexan shouted to the other two spear unit leaders, "Fyoreten's emblem ahead."

Iyna squinted through the tiny gap in the overlapped shields and saw atop a faraway blue hill several brown tents with something green perched atop a pole. All feeling of tiredness turned to resolve, and she regripped her shield and mother's spear.

The other two spear units had hastily formed their walls on either side of her unit while the tribow units cranked their weapons, ready to rain bolts upon the enemy. The commander trotted through his army and stopped his horse before Alexan. "How dare you give orders without my consent!"

Alexan pointed at the blue hill. "The enemy is directly ahead. Had we continued to march, we would be in range of their bolts."

The commander glanced ahead and scoffed. "They don't stand a chance against us." He turned to the other unit leaders. "Forward march!"

"We should wait for our allies—"

"I will not have the first army Felliet has formed pathetically wait for help." The commander huffed. "Now order your men forward."

Alexan clenched his hands, and the commander turned his horse and trotted back to the rear. The right shield wall, followed by the left, steadily marched forward.

Alexan positioned himself inside his unit's shield wall, standing next to Iyna. "No matter what happens, keep the shields tight." He paused. "Slow march forward."

Step by step, Iyna's shield wall marched towards the hill she could barely see through the gently swaying shields. The only sounds were the nervous panting of the soldiers around her and several of their spears quivering against the shields.

Alexan spoke softly, "Calm yourselves."

His words hardly seemed to make a difference, and they arrived at the blue lilies covering the hill. Glimpsing a bunch of crossbowmen hurrying along a dirt wall through the tiny gap in the shields, Iyna's heart pounded in her chest.

A distant shout came from the commander. "Spears halt."

"Halt!" Alexan repeated, stopping his unit at nearly the same time as the left, leaving their shield walls at the base of the slope. The right spear unit marched further up the blue ground before finally stopping.

Standing still, Iyna's shoulder and arm ached from holding her iron triangle shield over Sareesa, and she wondered just how long any of them could maintain the shield wall.

Alexan calmly spoke, "So long as all you remember your training and keep the shields tight, we *will* see tomorrow's sunrise."

Iyna glanced to either side of her and saw in the two hot, cramped rows the same dread and anguish on each face.

The commander's distant voice shouted again. "Tribowmen! Unleash a volley!"

Hearing the tribow unit leaders loudly order their units to aim, Iyna glanced back and saw the three units had spread out. Beely and Leemia were in the midst of the central unit. Terror showed on their faces as they lifted their tribows, aiming them at the hilltop. Many green kettle helmets poked above the dirt wall.

The three tribow leaders shouted, "Release."

Over a hundred tribows snapped their strings with a jaw-dropping sound as their bolts pierced the air but thudded into the ground short of the dirt wall. Iyna's breath quickened as she reaffirmed her grip on her spear.

"Crank!" the tribow leaders demanded.

The Fyoreten men responded, unleashing their bolts onto the shield walls. Bolts battered against Iyna's shield wall, and her unit hurriedly closed the gaps in the wall, pinching the spears in place. The volley ended just as quickly as it had begun. Iyna smirked in relief that the shields held.

"Everyone all right?" Alexan asked. No reply. "Good, no one's been hit. Keep it up and each one of us will all make it back safely."

The distant commander shouted, "Spears advance!"

Already ahead, the right unit leader ordered his shield wall to march forth, ending any respite the spearmen had.

"Remain calm and keep the shields tight," Alexan repeated and loudly ordered, "Slow march forward!"

Every breath was heavy and every face bleak as Iyna's shield wall marched up the hill of blue lilies.

The sound of Fyoreten crossbows rang out again. Iyna's teeth clenched as several of the bolts pelted her shield. The barrage ended abruptly again, and the heavy march continued.

Long after, the tribow unit leaders once more shouted, "Take aim!"

"Release!"

The bolts thundered far lounder through the air above the spearmen, and painfilled screams sounded from the dirt wall. Iyna steadied her spear as her shield wall marched determinedly on into another Fyoreten response.

Iyna gritted her teeth at the oncoming pelting, but the bolts sailed over them, raining down on the spread out tribowmen and sending a half dozen bleeding to the ground.

"Keep your eyes ahead!" Alexan demanded.

Iyna pried her gaze away from the agonising screams and faced the sliver of light through her shields. She whispered to Sareesa, "They're still alive, just keep facing forward." Iyna's heart raced, and she repeated, "Just keep facing forward."

Hesitantly, Sareesa obeyed, steadying her shield.

Halfway up the hill, another Fyoreten barrage flew overhead, and more screams followed. Iyna bit her bottom lip, forcing herself from looking back. A loud horn bellowed from within the camp, its long-lasting blast echoing across the vibrant landscape. Iyna's arms tensed harder as she braced for a Fyoreten charge, yet the three shield walls continued their slow march unchallenged, leaving a strange uneasiness in the air.

Soon after, Fyoreten bolts struck the right shield wall, ruthlessly hammering their side. A man cried out in agony. The unit leader ordered his wall to keep advancing as a spearman with a bolt in his shin tried to stumble back to them.

On the other side of Alexan, Barcial yelled, "Horsemen on the left flank!"

The shield walls came to an abrupt halt as every pair of eyes turned southward. A dreaded chill washed over Iyna at the sight of fifty axe-wielding horsemen bearing down on the undefended tribowmen.

The tribow leader closest to the oncoming horsemen shouted an order. "Aim … aim at the riders!"

The other tribow leaders followed suit, but their panicked soldiers rushed, releasing their bolts in an uncoordinated effort. The scattered bolts fell short and wide of the oncoming horsemen.

Fyoreten bolts struck the right shield wall again, bringing down the lone man and striking two more.

An order from the left spear unit drew everyone's attention. "Slow march back!"

Iyna heard Alexan furiously mutter to himself before he repeated the retreat. "Slow march back!"

A moment later the right followed the command.

Keeping their shields facing the camp, the shield walls stepped down the slope. The terrified voices from the tribowmen grew in number. Iyna tried not to look back, her shield growing heavier as the fear of the tribowmen settled on her. The pace of the spearmen quickened.

The sound of hooves beating the ground finally forced Iyna to turn and watch. The horsemen smashed through the tribowmen, butchering them as they tried desperately to flee, littering the ground with trampled bodies.

Leemia stood her ground, raising her tribow at the charging horde as the soldiers around her descended into a maddening scramble for safety. In her small pale hands, the tribow shook, and she aimed at the closest rider, fiercely waving his shortaxe. Yet Leemia didn't pull the trigger and instead just stood there, unmoving, until the axe blade smashed into her forehead, throwing her lifeless body to the ground.

Another barrage of Fyoreten bolts followed, pelting against Iyna's shield and forcing her gaze forward. A woman at the edge of the wall was struck down. Further screams sounded from the other walls, and the backwards pace quickened to nearly a jog, swaying the shields and widening the gaps between them.

"Slow!" Alexan shouted. "Slow!"

None obeyed.

Terror had fully grasped the spearmen, everyone's shields swayed in their backwards retreat down the slope. The commander and his bodyguards were galloping away from a handful of pursuing riders while the rest of the enemy horsemen chased down the remaining tribowmen.

The Fyoreten bolts came down once more upon the right shield wall and brought many screaming to the ground. The unit scattered into a desperate sprint and people in Iyna's shield wall followed suit, running with shields against the backs of their heads.

All command vanished as the panicked spearmen raced down the blue hill. Iyna ran in the midst of the chaotic retreat, not daring to look back at the camp.

The Fyoreten bolts rained down one after another, pelting the back-held shields and sending further wounded cries into the air. None dared slow, and before long, they had reached the bloodied base of the hill.

The horsemen turned towards them, bringing every spearman to a dreaded, hopeless halt.

Rage engulfed Iyna, and she surged ahead of the rest, hunching down with the shield on her back, planting her spear forward and yelling as loudly as she could, "Come at me!"

Alexan rushed to join her, shouting back to the spearmen, "Shields behind! Spears in front!"

Felliet soldiers across all three units copied them, forming a long line of forward spears and backward shields. Although they looked terrified, none of them fled, not even as the bolts continued striking their awkwardly held shields. Every spear was held firm toward the oncoming horde.

The ground trembled from the charging hooves, sunlight shimmered off shortaxes, and frenzied battle cries filled the air. Teeth clenched, Iyna gripped her spear tighter.

The lead rider yanked back the reins of his horse, yelling to the others to stop and slowing the charge just before it slammed into the spears. Horse squeals and confused shouts filled the air. Iyna was forcibly pushed across the dirt with her spear piercing the lead rider's steed. The creature shrieked with pain as it tried to pull away from three spearpoints. Its rider, beset by a wall of spears, wildly swung his shortaxe at them.

The other horsemen had pushed the lead riders against the spears, leaving them no room for escape. The panic-stricken horse pulled against the spears, so Iyna yanked hers from the creature's neck. Alexan thrust his spear into the creature's forehead, bringing both horse and rider to the ground. The Fyoreten man raised his shortaxe and miniature round shield.

With a burst of energy, Iyna thrust her spear forward, stabbing below his green chainmail into his lower gut. The axe fell from his hand, and Sareesa struck his neck. Blood spurted from his mouth, and he collapsed to the ground.

The other Fyoreten men frantically yelled to one another as the bloodied line of collapsed horses and wailing riders were silenced.

Sareesa's spear fell from her shaking hand. The other riders dismounted and approached the spearmen.

Alexan loudly cried, "Hold your ground!"

A Fyoreten man stopped just before the line of corpses, slightly out of her spear reach. He grinned and knocked her spear away with his shortaxe, but Alexan's spearpoint stopped any advance.

The other Fyoretens copied, smacking the spears, trying to make an opening in the unmoving line of spearmen. With every bash, tremors ran down Iyna's spear arm and she gritted her teeth, desperately trying to keep all gaps closed.

Barcial shouted, "The crossbowmen are advancing!"

Alexan ordered, "All advance!" He marched forward, striking the leading Fyoreten's miniature shield. Iyna followed, leaping atop the horse's body and thrusting her spear into the man's eye.

The line of spearmen rallied, overwhelming the Fyoreten's pathetic shields. One after another, spears brought the Fyoreten down till only a handful remained. They fled to their saddles.

"Turn the spears back!" Alexan shouted.

Iyna turned her body away from those cowardly butchers and brought her spear through the gap in the renewed shield wall. Forty or so scattered crossbowmen stopped in their charge, dagger-wielding hands falling to their sides.

Alexan grinned. "All charge!"

The spearmen charged forth, sprinting without formation or strategy, just a vicious, eager desire to run the enemy down. The Fyoreten fled back to their camp, but the crazed spearmen caught up to them.

Iyna pushed her exhausted body further and faster. She plunged her spear into the back of the throat of a fleeing crossbowman, who collapsed onto the blue lilies. She yanked her spear from the body and kept going.

She chased the last dozen Fyoreten over their dirt wall into their camp. She kept running with the other soldiers, pursuing the last few Fyoreten through the brown tents.

"All halt!" Alexan shouted. "No need to prolong this battle!"

Iyna stopped with the other pursuing spearmen, letting the tiny handful of Fyoreten escape the camp.

Alexan raised his spear to the sky. "The day is ours!"

Relief exploded within Iyna, bringing all the weariness she had ignored flooding back to her body as she joyously felt her knees give way in the midst of her cheering comrades.

The trotting hooves echoed along the red brickwork of the long, dim tunnel, breaking the silence Jornis and Copias had shared throughout the journey from Sidium. Despite the evening sun still shining in the clear sky, the ancient outer wall was so needlessly thick it shrouded its eastern tunnel entrance in complete darkness. Rust had settled on the many portcullises and murder holes above them, and chalked graffiti littered both sides of the ancient brick walls. The city's commoner garrison had neglected this structure much as Rubium itself had been neglected.

Upon leaving the tunnel, Jornis narrowed his eyes. No widened street lay before them; instead, they were met with an odd maze-like layout through a haphazardly uncoordinated city of brick, stem, straw and stone. Before either of them could move their horse towards the cloth-forged stables to their right, the pungent smell of the air struck his nostrils and he winced.

A drunken half-dressed guard, lazily leaning near the entrance, chuckled. "You rich folk enjoying the smell?"

Jornis turned his horse to the stables, but Copias addressed the guard. "It certainly reflects the pitiful state of Rubium and its people quite perfectly."

"What'd you say?"

Jornis turned to the boy. "Rein your horse without complaint."

Copias looked confused but obliged. At the stable pens, he whispered, "Why did you not put that commoner in his place?"

"Why did we travel to Rubium?" Jornis dismounted onto the weed-covered floor.

"To meet with an official working for the Marble Wheels."

Jornis's grip on his reins tightened. "And why would a siloin choose a city such as this for their base in Erium?" Seeing the boy's hesitation, Jornis asked, "Do you feel a presence of prosperity in this city?"

The boy climbed down from his saddle. "The emperor, or any noble for that matter, would not dare invest in the old capital."

"No named person would know of what goes on here." Jornis quietened his voice. "Your little transgression just now may have alerted the Marble Wheels to our presence. Or worse, given them a disapproving opinion of us." He stepped towards the boy. "Keep your foolish tongue still."

"I apologise," Copias said. "It was an error of judgement."

Steering his horse into the pen, Jornis said, "So long as it does not reoccur."

"It will not." Copias led his horse into the pen. "Shall we go to the base now?"

Jornis shook his head. "There is no rush. After all, we must be fully presentable if we are to approach a siloin trading post unannounced."

The celebrations gave way to grief as the soldiers piled the corpses at the bottom of the hill. The injured groaned and sobbed. Tending to them was a mere handful of people, with Barcial and Darius treating the wounded Fyoreten. Iyna, trying to avoid the growing body pile, had volunteered to gather the fallen crossbows, piling them near the largest brown tent. When she finished, she stood motionless in the middle of the foreign camp.

Barcial was struggling to hold down a Fyoreten woman with a bolt lodged in her thigh, and Darius was heating his spear point in a makeshift campfire. Iyna rushed over and forcefully pressed the panicked woman to the ground, steadying the wounded leg. Barcial looked at Iyna with gratitude.

Darius glanced over his shoulder as the iron speartip turned red. "Have her bite down on a piece of cloth."

The woman wiggled, trying to escape as Barcial tried to shove a torn shirt into her mouth, only for her to face away. Darius crouched beside her and carefully pulled the bolt from the woman's flesh. She gave an agonising cry as blood gushed out, and Darius pressed the reddened metal flat against the wound with a haunting sizzling sound. She cried out a thunderous scream as her muscles tensed against Iyna's and Barcial's firm grip. Darius lifted the spearpoint away from the thigh and examined the scorched wound as the woman seemed to exhaustively calm. He wrapped the torn shirt around the wound, and Iyna and Barcial finally released their grip.

Darius then examined an injured Fyoreten man who tried to make excuses about the bolt through his forearm. Barcial walked over to help. Iyna wondered why they so readily helped the Fyoretens. Remembering Leemia's death brought rage coursing through Iyna at the sheer pointlessness of this war. Had her mother felt the same way about the Southern Campaign? Why did either have to happen?

Hearing more excuses from the Fyoreten man, Iyna glanced at her spear and at the small campfire. She placed the iron spearpoint in the flames.

A pair of horses galloped up the hill. The commander and one bodyguard leapt over the dirt wall with bitter scowls on their faces. The commander's fancy grey robe was gone, replaced with his plain white undershirt stained with a large crimson patch across his gut.

The bodyguard dismounted and steered the commander's horse to the large tent as the injured commander demanded, "Where's my damn subordinates!"

Alexan and Orbert, the only unit leaders to have survived, emerged from the tent, still wearing their agron chestplates and iron platelet armour.

The commander yelled at them, "What are you standing there for? Tend to me now!"

Alexan looked around till his eyes met the people tending the injured. "Barcial! Help your commander from his horse and see to his wound."

Barcial pulled himself from the injured Fyoreten crossbowmen and trudged to the commander's horse. He held his palms out to accept the large rider's mud-covered boot as he climbed down from his saddle.

Alexan turned to the bodyguard. "You did well to spot our emblem."

Iyna glanced up at the sideways facing iron shield atop the pole that had hung Fyoreten's emblem: a green greataxe crossed beneath a miniature round shield with a pitchfork. She wondered how she had missed it being taken down.

"The great mother guided her light off our shield for all to see," the bodyguard replied.

"Enough of this pointlessness," the commander spat back.

Alexan gestured to the large tent. "If you would follow us inside, I'll have Barcial treat your wound."

The commander examined Barcial with disgust. "I won't have some commoner treat me."

"He is well practiced in the art," Alexan explained.

"As a prestigious member of the Lawver name, I shall not have some common fool tend to my wound, Brige!"

A tense silence sat between them for a brief moment till Alexan directed his hand to Barcial. "This is Barcial of the name Synthion. I assure you he is no commoner and, furthermore, has extensive experience tending to injuries."

"Synthion huh?" A wide grin appeared on the commander's face as he smugly looked Barcial up and down. "Hasn't *your* family fallen far."

Barcial's hands were clenched in fists of rage behind his back.

The commander guffawed and turned back to the unit leader. "I accept your offer and will let this lowlife treat me."

"If you would follow me," Alexan said as the commander strutted past him into the tent.

Orbert exchanged a concerned glance with Alexan before following the commander inside.

Alexan turned to the bodyguard. "Make sure no one enters." He and Barcial entered the tent, closing the thick curtains behind them.

Iyna returned to her spearpoint and watched it glow red. She nodded to Darius as he gave some of his water to the injured Fyoreten man. She thought about the name Synthion and the strange familiarity it brought and wondered what Alexan had meant when he sympathetically spoke to them back in the courtyard.

She took her reddened spear over to Darius and tightly grabbed the frightened man's arm.

"Thank you," Darius had the man bite down on a cloth shirt and carefully pulled the bolt from his arm before scorching the wound. The injured crossbowmen let out a muffled scream, his arm went limp and his eyes closed.

With the flesh still sizzling, Darius reassured her, "It's quite common for people to pass out when experiencing great pain."

Iyna breathed in relief and turned to him, whispering, "You and Barcial are Fyoreten, aren't you?"

His eyes widened, but he gave a hesitant nod.

Iyna turned back at the injured man and quietly asked, "How'd you even end up on our side?"

Darius carefully took the hot spearpoint away from the arm and examined the scorched wound. "Through unavoidable decisions." He shook his head and returned her spear. "I don't want to talk about it right now."

Grasping her spear, Iyna turned to the rows of wounded Fyoreten and Felliet, noticing hardly a difference between them without their armour.

Darius sighed. "I will take care of matters here. You need to see Sareesa."

"Sareesa?" Iyna looked at him in confusion.

"I supposed you haven't noticed, but she has yet to move from the base of the hill." He walked to another injured Fyoreten.

Iyna felt a wave of guilt wash over her, and she marched over the dirt wall.

Gazing down the hill whose blue lilies were scattered with red patches, Iyna was consumed with dread at the sight of the growing mound of horses and bodies. Sareesa sat before a pool of blood that belonged to the Fyoreten rider they had killed. Iyna forced her weary body down the slope.

She heard the commander yell in pain, bringing her a brief smile as she pictured hot metal pressing against the coward's wound. The moment passed when she noticed the supply cart beyond the horrific pile had been ransacked and Soart's mangled body lay underneath. Iyna looked down and slowed her pace till she was sitting beside her friend. She had no words to say.

Sareesa pointed at the bottom corner of the pile. "Beely fell."

Iyna darted her eyes to the pile and stared at each gaping face till she saw Beely's. His neck had been split in half.

Seeing the unmoving terror in his expression drained the last speck of energy from Iyna's body.

"What's the point in this?" Sareesa asked as she tucked her knees close to her teary eyes.

"I don't know." Iyna's mind went blank as she watched yet another body be tossed onto the heap. "I don't know."

Chapter nine – Leadership

Sixth eclipse, eighth day

Hearing the ringing of a handbell, Iyna woke in the brief hope it was Soart waking them up, only to feel disappointed at the sight of Orbert ringing from the brown tent's entrance. Head aching, she wearily got out of her hammock and felt the dry, trampled lilies beneath her bare feet. Everyone else seemed just as weary putting on their thin chestplates and helmets. Sareesa barely lifted her head as she followed the soldiers out of the sleeping tent. Iyna and Darius stuck by her side as they emerged into the clouded sunrisen light.

The commander's bodyguard galloped at full pace out of the camp, fully awakening the confused soldiers.

Orbert stopped ringing the handbell. "Present yourselves."

The soldiers gathered in their separate units before the main tent. All three numbered depressingly fewer than when they had left Felliet. Alexan and Barcial stepped from the large tent's curtain and stood beside Orbert with grave faces.

Alexan addressed the spearmen. "The commander sustained a deep stab wound to his lower stomach in the battle. Unfortunately, rot spread deep and could not be stopped. In light of his passing, we have agreed *I* will take command of this army."

Iyna regretted her brief happiness at hearing the cauterising scream.

"Our objective was to rendezvous with our Erium allies before marching on Fyoreten. That has not changed. I have sent a message to the Elite Dictorate informing them of the situation with a request for reinforcements." He motioned Barcial forward. "Sadly, we lost a lot of good people in the battle and now only have enough to support two spear units. As such the third will merge with the other two. They will be under the leadership of Orbert Cendion and, replacing me as unit leader, Barcial Synthion."

Iyna turned her widened gaze to Barcial. Her surprise vanished quickly. He was by far the best choice. Her mind compared herself to him, worsening her headache.

Alexan approached the third leaderless unit and divided the spearmen into the other spear groups. Iyna realised Barcial would be personally leading soldiers in an invasion of his own country. She glanced to Darius's lowered gaze and felt shame that Felliet was wrongfully submitting to Erium's conquest.

It had been a nightmarish three days of travel, for aside from Reethial's obnoxious complaining, no words had left anyone's mouth throughout the arduous journey. Furthermore, the overindulgent carriage constantly got stuck in soft countryside patches, forcing the bodyguards to haul it out to the tune of the elite's impatient shouts. Even the weather seemed against them, frequently drizzling rain and bringing stiff winds. Vernon had rejoiced when the procession finally made it to the town of Risper on the second day, for it meant spending a night in a warm room and eating hot food. After that, it became a smooth ride to Sidium.

As day neared its midpoint, Vernon leaned out of the wagon, his heart racing as he stared at the approaching black city. Though greyish clouds scattered across the blue sky, the towering black crystal wall glistened as brightly as the sparkling river flowing alongside. Vernon darted his eyes to each of the ballista towers soaring above the extensive outer wall, for not only were its lofty ramparts lined with bronze, but each held aloft a bronze-tipped hexagonal black crystal obelisk. The great emblem of the Empire of Erium.

Sounds of cheer and merriment brought his attention to the black iron gate opened beyond a granite bridge where he observed a multitude of joyous crowds lining the spotless street. A column of four hundred horsemen proudly trotted out, their iron chainmailed riders holding their lances high. The lead rider in full, polished black chainmail waved to the cheering onlookers with his dark helmet resting on his lap.

As the Erium horsemen passed Reethial's carriage, the lead rider stared through its windows with a smug grin. Vernon also grinned, his eyes met the Erium commander's and the student graciously waved. The man returned a single cheerful wave before leading his army on.

Vernon stared past Orfain's cart in complete awe of the riders as they went to reobtain what Erium had lost.

The horse's hooves trotted along the smooth granite tiles of the widened street, passing all kinds of tall, beautiful buildings of glistening, metallic black. Vernon breathed in the magnificent scents of bakeries, florists and perfume parlours as the procession passed ornate drinking fountains and elegant street performers. It was little wonder the finely dressed traders, shoppers and families walking along the immaculate pavements seemed devoid of any sorrow. Indeed there was nary a shred of poverty or anguish.

A shimmer caught Vernon's eyes, directing his gaze beyond the metallic black rooftops to the gargantuan hexagonal palace towering from the heart of the city. The gleaming bronze crowning the black crystal structure shimmered in the midday sun for all in Sidium to witness the prosperity and glory of the empire.

Vernon savoured every wonderous moment through the glistening city. A long, glorious ride, the procession arrived at a grey terraced manor along a diverting street set just before the inner gatehouse. His merriment faded as he sighted the shield of Felliet boldly displayed on the building's slated roof, and he retreated onto the hard seat of the wagon.

The bodyguards dismounted as several grey-robed stewards trickled out of the manor's doors. Iyessa and Buckley climbed outside the wagon. Vernon sighed and followed suit.

The head bodyguard opened the black carriage door for Reethial to strut out. The elite held out a hand to Lysia who smiled as she accepted it. A woman who must have been Reethial's wife moved past them both without a second glance. She calmly walked to the manor's doors.

Almost unsurprisingly, Reethial kept his full attention on Lysia. "So when can I expect it?"

She calmly said, "A handful of errands require my immediate attention, but you may rest assured I will be ready to collect the measurements in a few days' time."

A wide grin crossed the opulent man's face. "I yearn to see it."

"As do I," Lysia replied, and she left his presence for Orfain's cart.

Reethial stood there watching her for a long, uncomfortable moment before he marched after his wife.

Lysia walked past Vernon, and as their eyes met, she smiled slyly. An uncomfortable dread sprouted in Vernon's mind as he pondered the deal she and Reethial had sowed.

Following the directions, copied from the records crypt, Jornis and Copias trekked through the decrepit maze of Rubium and arrived at the Marble Wheels operating base. Its cracked, dull walls resembled much of the impoverished city; however, the narrow street it lay in was remarkable quiet for a city of commoners. A single thread of golden silk was tied to the door's agron knocker.

Upon announcing their presence, the two had to wait for an extended time, clearly a way to further uphold the disguise. The door creaked open, revealing a commoner dressed, frail man leaning on a warped agron cane.

"We have arrived to speak to the owner of this establishment," Jornis said.

The elderly man examined Copias and Jornis. "I'm the owner."

"The real owner," Jornis replied.

"Very well." The frail man paused. "Come on in."

Jornis and Copias entered a plain, poorly furnished drawing room and patiently watched the elderly man hobble into the next room. Jornis should not have been surprised to see this façade continue, for a siloin to individually establish a base of operations to privately trade with Erium nobles was greatly frowned upon in Gildren's council. This was despite the obvious fact each of the eight siloins followed this practice while hypocritically praising Gildren's unity.

The frail man returned. "If you two would follow me."

Jornis noted the undecorated hallway and staircase were an immaculate yellow before he caught the abhorrent stench of decaying fish. He recoiled with every step as the powerful stench grew the closer they got to a door on the second story. Jornis theorised it was a simple yet bold test to ascertain a guest's commitment to a deal while retaining the façade of common Rubium poverty.

Without any announcement, the elderly man opened the door, releasing a torrent of the rotten stench and bringing an unavoidable grimace to Jornis and Copias, confirming the theory.

A bowl of rotten fish sat above the fireplace mantle, and the siloin director stood calmly writing at a corner dresser. A glass side cabinet held an assortment of whiskey bottles and serving tumblers. Jornis positioned himself near the cushioned, yellow sofas placed in the centre of the orange carpet without sitting, as he awaited the director's attention. Copias also avoided the bait of the soft sofas and remained at Jornis's side, though his expression still held the unpleasant grimace.

After a prolonged while, the man set down his beige ink feather and turned to greet his guests. "It is a pleasure to make your acquaintance. As you can see, I am the director of this humble establishment. Unfortunately, your identities remain unknown to me as of yet."

"Allow me to introduce myself." Jornis kept his firm posture. "I am Jornis Meyorter, former representative to Felliet. I have come to arrange a deal between my country and the Marble Wheels."

The siloin director raised an eyebrow. "Curious your Elite Dictorate would send *you* of all people to arrange a deal."

"Why is that?" Jornis asked.

"I mean not to be rude, but your reputation does you no justice."

"I care not for personal glory. My only concern is the prosperity of the federation."

"Not Felliet?"

Jornis glanced at the simmering fire. "Believing one's country is isolated from the affairs of the world is a foolish notion." He returned his gaze to the director. "I believe it is in our mutual interest that Felliet and the Marble Wheels form a trading agreement. After which a full alliance can be established."

The director crossed his arms.

"Your land has no access to the sea and will see not a coin of profit from Gildren's expansion to those western islands. Once Fyoreten falls, trade will be further diverted through Myklinn Minor. In the upcoming cycles, your lands will fall behind the other siloins."

"I have yet to hear specific details."

"Gildren currently lacks mines of any ore; however, if the Bronze sails discover iron, copper or even agron deposits, there will no longer be a need to waste coin importing such metals. In short, they will dominate the whole of Gildren." Jornis took a breath. "Felliet has one iron and several agron mines, so if you accept, we will freely send dozens of wagons every comet cycle."

The man shrugged. "I'm afraid no siloin can form alliances independent of Gildren."

"In the same manner siloins cannot independently establish trading bases in other countries?"

"What you are suggesting goes far beyond trading with a handful of nobles."

"In the eyes of Gildren's skilful merchants, Felliet is an irrelevant footnote in the federation." Jornis caught Copias's scornful glance. "Wagons from such a nation would go unnoticed, especially if it is timed with the tributary procession."

The director put his hand to his chin. "And what would Felliet gain from such a deal?"

"Information," Jornis answered. "Specifically the political climate of Erium and Myklinn Minor."

The man hesitated. "I will draft a letter to Innill, giving you permission to speak with the head of the Marble Wheels." He leaned against his desk, folding his arms. "Now that concludes your business."

"Then we shall take our leave." Jornis left the pungent stench behind.

Niyaa stared up at the rain pitter pattering against the chapel's glass roof as she stood in the middle of the crowd of complaining villagers. With everyone crammed together, the small room became hot and stuffy, leaving them all miserable as they waited for Darryam and the priest to stop talking.

What felt like ages later, the white-robed priest finally turned to the talkative crowd and raised his voice. "Quiet. Quiet down." The chapel calmed. "As many of you are aware, Seveck Heef has left Pelight for an unknown period. I have gathered you all here to determine who will take over the responsibilities as governor in his stead." He pointed at Niyaa's dad. "Darryam here has already volunteered to fill that role. Is there anyone in this room willing to challenge him?"

The room filled with mutters and whispers as everyone looked at one another. Kivy's voice came over them all. "Why should we entrust our village to an outsider?" She pushed her way to the front.

The priest asked, "Do you wish to take over the governor's role?"

"If it means we won't have another outsider taking charge, then absolutely." She stepped to the other side of the priest. "I was born and raised here. I understand this place better than anyone."

Darryam scornfully turned to her. "Do you have some grudge against us?"

"I do," she replied. "Since your lot arrived, we've hardly any food and space to keep us goin'."

He raised his voice. "And had our roles been reversed, what would you have done?"

"I would've damn well stayed where I belonged or at least headed to the towns." Kivy gritted her teeth. "I would never leach off neighbouring folk."

Niyaa's hands tightened into fists.

"Leach off you? We work as hard as any of you in those damn fields," Darryam furiously spat back.

"And why do ya think we've had to sow more of those fields?"

The priest interjected, "Calm yourselves. Kivy, for better or for ill, those from Edenor are here to stay."

"I know." Kivy turned to the crowd. "But 'cause of that we need to act now to think up a plan to feed everyone."

"It's simple," Darryam explained. "Once the harvest comes, we'll have plentiful food, enough for every person 'ere."

Still facing the crowd, she smirked. "And until then?"

"Rabbits, wild mushrooms, stem toads, anything we can gather and hunt." He turned to the crowd. "If we limit and share our food, we'll have enough for everyone to last a full cycle."

Niyaa heard disagreeing whispers in the crowd.

"I know a way to fill our stomachs and keep them full long after the comet." Kivy's voice grew louder. "The gov's house is still filled with all kinds of expensive stuff. We just sell that, and we'll be set."

Darryam eyes widened. "Don't be dumb. When he returns and finds his things stolen, he will tell the elites and punish us all."

"You mean *if* he returns." She grunted. "Besides it's not like he lacks the coin to replace any of it."

The gentle patter of rain became the only sound as the anxious crowd glanced at one another.

"Listen to me!" Darryam demanded of the crowd. "We must not resort to thievery."

"It's the governor's job to safeguard this place, isn't it?" Kivy asked. "So by sellin his stuff, he fulfils his role. *Or* we can slowly starve and let the governor keep his shiny things." She glanced at the priest. "That's all I have to say."

Darryam took a deep breath. "I know her plan sounds easy, but it will only cause more harm. It won't be long now till the seeds are sowed. Then all of us can gather and hunt plenty of food. We just need to wait it out." He paused for a long moment as the rain tapping against the glass roof echoed throughout the silent room. He finally nodded to the priest.

The white-robed priest asked the crowd. "Those who wish Darryam to lead us, raise your hand."

Niyaa and her mom quickly shot their arms up. Only a couple other hands followed.

The priest said, "And those for Kivy."

Almost every hand went up.

"Kivy has the majority," the priest announced. "She will thus take over the governor's responsibilities till his return."

Niyaa spotted a cruel grin on the guard's face.

As the day dwindled to a close, Iyna's mind was still plagued by her powerlessness. Her muscles tensed as she gazed across the clouded, southern landscape. She questioned the point of the war and her helplessness in the face of it, leaving her wearily looking out at the clouded landscape, staring at nothing in particular.

As the sun neared the horizon, a man shouted from the other side of the camp. "Erium horsemen are here!"

Her harrowing thoughts briefly vanished as everyone rushed to the northern part of the small camp.

Alexan emerged from the command tent. "All soldiers, form ranks."

Barcial placed himself at the head of her unit in the same way Orbert stood in front of the other. Alexan placed himself ahead of both, with a calm and alert look as hundreds of horsemen in shiny iron chainmail galloped toward the hill of blue lilies.

Feeling the many horses beating against the ground, Iyna remembered the Fyoreten charge, and a sense of dread and unease washed over her. Would Felliet even need to participate in this wrongful war anymore? After all, it was Erium's conquest of their land.

It didn't take long for the Erium riders to reach and dismount at the base of the hill; their few rear riders were already unpacking tents and food sacks. Only their black-armoured leader galloped up the blue ground towards the camp.

The Erium commander halted just before the mud wall, his smug gaze looking up and down at Alexan. "It's quite amusing to see a commander wearing a simpleton's armour. Perhaps I overestimated Felliet to provide sufficient protection for their commanders." He scoffed. "Apologises, I mean comman*der*."

Visibly unimpressed by this rider, Alexan replied, "And I expected Erium to send a pitiful fool, yet it seems you *exceeded* my expectations."

The commander guffawed. "You should be a little more grateful that I would arrive, considering the pitiful state of your men … apologies again, I mean men *and* women." His gaze peered over Alexan to the Felliet soldiers. "I doubt they will see many sunrises when wearing such pitiful agron armour."

"Using iron for anything other than shields and spear tips would be a waste. But I concede that concept would be foreign to Erium, considering it values aesthetics rather than effectiveness."

The Erium rider leaned across his horse, his eyes half closed. "You speak as though your force even realises what effectiveness means." He glanced again at the soldiers. "Is this all Felliet could muster for its first ever army?"

Alexan waited for the rider to look back at him. "Felliet provides the exact number of soldiers to handle any given situation."

"And you believe this handful of men … handful of *townsfolk* could handle Fyoreten alone?"

"We never expected we had to," Alexan replied. "At least until we discovered Erium was foolish enough to allow the enemy to establish a camp *deep* within its lands."

The rider's smirk vanished. "It's not as though their army would have posed much of a threat."

A slight grin emerged on Alexan's face. "You should be more grateful we dealt with this Fyoreten camp *before* it became a threat."

An incensed look crossed the Erium commander's face, and he steered his horse away, offhandedly saying, "With the main force still gathering at Garhurn, we will set off as an advance force once the Therra arrive."

"The Therra are fighting with us?" Alexan asked in astonishment.

The Erium commander trotted away as if he hadn't heard the question. Alexan's eyes were wide with fear, and Iyna wondered how true Cairsie's tales of those creatures were.

Trotting his horse under the astonishingly thick, downwards swinging gate, Jornis emerged from Rubium onto the lengthened bridge across Lake Scarlen. The boy was staring at the symbol of Erium's absolute authority hanging from black crystal chains above the western gate.

Jornis tugged at the reins of his horse. "We have little time to waste."

The boy frowned. "I wanted to have a look at him."

"I imagine because you fear Felliet will go the way of the Royals." Hearing no response, Jornis sighed. "If you want Felliet to exist more than *Ellity's* outer wall, then continue your task."

The boy nodded and steered his horse away from the skeletal remains of the last captain of the Royals.

They began their journey for Gildren.

Chapter ten – Tentative Partnerships

Sixth eclipse, twelfth day

For four days, Vernon had anxiously awaited Lysia's return to the Felliet embassy. She was downstairs, soon to be led into Reethial's study, and his muscles nervously stiffened. Standing alongside Iyessa and Buckley in the discomforting warmth of the elite's study, Vernon struggled to maintain a calm, unsuspicious expression. Worsening his nerves, the only sound came from Reethial's grey ink feather scribbling against parchment across his wide slate desk with the fireplace silent in the right side of the lavish room.

The door opened and Lysia, wearing a silk cyan dress with accompanying purse, calmly approached Reethial's desk. Vernon's eyes widened and his heart raced. With a confident grin, Orfain stood beside Vernon.

The elite set his feather down. "Are you ready to carry out my request?"

Lysia smiled. "As soon as I have the measurements."

The elite reached for a book on his desk and took a hidden, folded parchment from within. Vernon felt Orfain's hand push a small piece of cloth into his palm. Vernon's hand quickly closed around it and he nervously turned to Orfain who kept his attention solely on the exchange before them.

Lysia took the parchment. "Thank you." The room fell tensely silent as she read. She refolded the paper. "I had not expected such a striking design."

Reethial leant back in his chair. "Did you expect a person of my stature to wear anything less?"

"I wouldn't dare presume such a thing," Lysia replied. "But you should be aware this request will take plentiful time and coin to complete."

Frustration crossed the elite's face. "How long?"

"Difficult to say," Lysia said. "But it certainly will be completed long before your arrival in the great chamber."

Reethial relaxed. "Good."

"For now we should discuss payment." She placed the folded paper into her purse.

The excitement faded from the elite's expression, and they stared at one another for a long moment. "Eighty bronze."

Vernon's mouth gaped at the staggering price.

Lysia shook her head. "I'm afraid I must ask for a minimum of a hundred."

"Out of the question," Reethial snapped back.

"There is plentiful work to be done to cut and shape the black crystal, and if done improperly, the results will appear crude." She paused. "Although, if you wish less black crystal in the design, then you may indeed have it for eighty."

Reethial slouched forward. "Fine then. But expect to be paid only when I am wearing it."

"Of course," she replied with a satisfied glance at Orfain. "I shall see work begin immediately."

The two of them left the study without a word of farewell passing anyone's lips, and Vernon sighed in relief.

Golden ivy clung to every surface of the orange-veined marble that made Innill's short walls, yet their ramparts were well garrisoned and the accompanying moat was devoid of any debris and muck. Even the six defensive towers surrounding the city outside the walls were made of the same polished marble adorned with gilded carvings. Undoubtedly this was to impress the numerous trading wagons flowing to the city while demonstrating the siloin's wealth to immigrants and investors.

Following the stream of unsearched wagons and carts through the brass-lined, marble gatehouse, Jornis and Copias trotted inside. Down the smoothened highway, an abundance of gilded statues were bound to the sandstone buildings as well as a number of spotless glass balconies. Jornis breathed in the smell of freshly spiced food and other scents coming from the restaurants, inns and perfumed tailers stretched along the entire street, each displaying an esteemed service to the passing traders.

After stabling the horses, Jornis and Copias marched down the bustling street, heading for the city centre.

Copias asked, "Are we not going to find lodging first?"

Jornis kept his gaze ahead. "The person we met in Rubium would have sent a messenger of our arrival as soon as we left his building. We cannot afford to give the head of the Marble Wheels further time to prepare."

"But you would save only a few moments." the boy said. "It doesn't seem that necessary."

Jornis sighed. "It's common knowledge each of the siloins of Gildren maintains a firm grasp on their lands, especially the people entering their capital."

Copias paused for a moment. "Does that mean they employ spies in their cities and towns?"

Jornis nodded.

Without further discussion, they reached the heart of the city where an overly large accounting house stood. Crowds of merchants and traders poured through its many glass doors, and Jornis dismissed the idea of pushing his way through. Thankfully, someone called to him from the opposing side of the street.

Three men robed in yellow silk approached, and Jornis pondered whether the director at Rubium had calculated the specific date they would arrive in Innill.

One of them said, "If you two would follow us."

"With pleasure," Jornis replied.

Following the men in yellow robes away from the service house, they walked down plain streets filled with simple beige homes. Despite the lack of gilded carvings and ornate restaurants, these grid-like streets were kept remarkably clean and functional.

The men in yellow robes halted before a towering building of orange marble, and the same man spoke. "You may enter."

They ventured back the way they came, leaving Jornis and Copias to approach the unguarded orange door. They entered into a warm library-like lounge with an unmissable scent of lavender in the air. Jornis pondered the amount of preparation the head of the Marble Wheels had given this meeting. The surrounding titles on the shelves were of plays, stories and other fictions. Further adorning the bookshelves were planters filled with yellow elastic arches, plants Jornis assumed had become extinct in the culling.

Copias closed the door and investigated the books.

"We did not come here to waste time reading irrelevant stories," Jornis said.

The boy smirked. "Could they not reveal a person's tastes?"

"You believe they were set in this greeting room to reflect the reading habits of the Marble Wheels head?"

Copias slouched.

"Keep your posture, boy, lest you appear like a common fool."

The boy averted his gaze and straightened up.

A mere moment passed and a woman in practical, expensive men's clothes entered, placing herself dismissively before her guests. "I understand you wish to form a trade agreement with my siloin."

Hiding his surprise that the head of the Marble Wheels would meet them so swiftly, Jornis replied, "It would be beneficial for Felliet and the Marble Wheels."

"Would it?" She folded her arms. "From what I understand, you wish for my siloin to act against the interests of all of Gildren."

Jornis remained composed. "I fail to see how my offer negatively impacts the other siloins. All it does is provide your lands with ore that your neighbours will soon obtain themselves. Would it not balance your nation of nations?"

"Clearly you fail to understand," she scoffed. "Gildren functions by the close cooperation and integrity of all eight siloins."

"Does my offer exclude the Marble Wheels from trading or even gifting Felliet's ore to the other seven?" Jornis asked. "Does it greatly advantage the Marble Wheels, or does it simply create a level playing field?"

She raised her eyebrows. "You believe we are competing with one another?"

"I think you are cooperating closely with one another to ensure Gildren remains the most prosperous nation in the world." He paused to reflect on his words. "However, with this upcoming western expansion, the Marble Wheels will be able to do little to contribute to that prosperity."

A stillness hung in the air for a long while, and she turned her gaze to the boy. "And what is *your* opinion of this, Copias Lawver?"

Though he'd had suspicions, Jornis was still surprised to hear this boy was related to one of the Dictorate members.

Copias didn't flounder. "I don't believe there are many ways the Marble Wheels can catch up to its neighbours."

Jornis added, "There are even fewer options left for Felliet regarding *its* neighbours."

She paused for a moment, relaxing her stern expression. "I will think on this. In the meantime, please enjoy your time within my city." She turned and left the room.

Copias asked, "So does that mean it went well?"

Hardly turning to him, Jornis replied, "It means she will think on it."

Niyaa pounded at the spade head, trying to flatten its bent edge. Tingles went through her tired hands, worsening with every whack. Glancing up at the messy shelves, she saw several other bent and broken tools waiting to be fixed. Someone stepped into the forge. She sighed and turned to look. Relief and happiness overcame her as Erger walked back into his forge.

She dropped the hammer and rushed to him. "You're back!"

His eyes examined the forge with a stunned look. "This place looks as messy as a Myklinn hunting lodge. Have you not…" He looked at Niyaa's face. "You've been working hard, haven't you?"

Niyaa's relief ended. "Kivy wanted the forge to be running without stop and told me to redo every tool I made till they were right."

"Why would Kivy be telling you what to do?"

She clenched her hands and narrowed her eyes. "Cause she's the new governor."

Erger's jaw dropped.

"She broke into Seveck's house and took all his books, ornaments and stuff."

"You're not mistaken, are you?" Erger asked.

She shook her head. "She sent a couple of guards to sell them in town but yelled at them in front of everyone when they returned with only a couple of bronze."

He moved to the hammering bench and leaned on his palms, taking a deep, frustrated breath. Erger examined the spade head. "Your hammer strokes are too hard. You need to make careful small taps to keep a good edge."

Niyaa glanced at the other bent tools and looked down at her sandals. "Sorry."

"Everyone's craft is poor when they start." Erger lightly hammered the spade edge. "Back when I started as an apprentice, I wrecked many, many more tools than you have."

"Really?"

"Of course." He smiled. "But like most smithers, I learned from my mistakes and slowly mastered my craft." His smile vanished and he set down his hammer. "Thought I would hate going back to Ellity, but walking down those streets again, seeing the other forger's wares … it was incredible."

Seeing his sadness, Niyaa had no words to say.

He picked up the hammer. "In any case, watch carefully how to shape an edge."

Niyaa walked to his side and watched.

"Back in the day I was known throughout the whole city." His hammer strokes grew harder. "Every morning on my way to my forge, people would commission work while complimenting my skills."

Niyaa saw his strokes relentlessly pounding the spade head. "Erger…"

"You know, even the other smithers would ask me for—" The spade head broke apart, its pieces scatting across the bench. Erger stared red faced at the wrecked tool and tossed his hammer down.

"Erger, are you okay?"

"Just…" He put his hand to his forehead. "Just leave me be for today."

His arms and breathing relaxed, and Niyaa placed a scrap piece of agron in the furnace's stone bowl.

As she struck flint against iron, Erger turned from the bench and softly asked, "What're you doing?"

"Melting agron so we can forge a new spade head," Niyaa explained, managing to light the furnace's straw-covered charcoal. She rose to her feet and turned to him. "You're not the only one who hates this place."

He shook his head. "I don't hate Pelight. I just…" He stared distantly at the open door, mummering, "What *am* I doing here?"

"The same reason I'm here." Niyaa walked up to him. "Because we didn't have a choice."

Erger shrugged. "Perhaps you're right."

Niyaa smiled. "But I'm sure there will be a day when we both can leave this place, never to come back."

He ruffled her hair. "Can't say that day won't come." He turned to the warming furnace. "Now you keep an eye on this, while I prepare the mould."

"All right." Niyaa rushed to the furnace door.

Days of waiting for those creatures had filled the soldiers with a sense of dread and unease, especially as their arrival marked their invasion of Fyoreten. The spearmen in their ranks along the slope of the blue hill watched the daunting reinforcements approach, every face grim.

With her shield weighing on her back, Iyna glanced back to the empty camp and thought of the handful of prisoners that the Erium soldiers had led away and wondered what kind of cruel punishment they would receive under their conquerors. The Erium horsemen rushed to strap on their chainmail and saddle their horses. Each of them seemed excited, even as the horrifying Therra silently came closer.

Over ninety brownish-yellow bodies marched in perfect silent unison without a leader or any kind of expression on their wheat-skinned, mouthless faces. Each held upright a huge, red glowing spiral with an extruding thin blackened pipe. Once again, Cairsie's tales paled in comparison to reality.

Alexan commanded, "Slow march forward!"

In a single moment, each soldier took in a long, anxious breath and trudged down the blue lilies towards the assembling Erium horsemen. The riders grabbed their lances, and Iyna narrowed her eyes as she pictured them running down the Fyoreten soldiers.

The Erium commander cantered to the Therra, loudly demanding, "I wish to speak to your leader."

The Therra simultaneously halted, standing motionless without a word.

The Erium commander grew flustered. "Are you fit to march on Iorden?"

The three armies silently waited for the response. A singular voice echoed from the midst of the strange force. "We shall lead the assault." The Therran army turned in unison and marched south.

The Erium commander darted his gaze around like a confused child before raising his lance to his men. "We go now to ensure Fyoreten pay dearly for invading our lands. All men, march forth!"

Vernon followed the directions on the cloth through the black city, which shimmered in the moons' light, to a street opposing the inner wall where a narrow building stood between several regular-looking homes. He pushed the sapphire-windowed door open and walked into a long, tavern room with a short bar to one side and a small simmering fireplace to the other, where Orfain stood adding straw cubes. As the two of them made eye contact, Vernon relaxed and spotted Lysia sitting at the far end of the room in far humbler attire. He approached Orfain, holding the cloth in his hands. "I wasn't able to say earlier, but I'm glad all of us made it to Sidium."

Orfain grabbed his full tankard resting on the mantelpiece and raised it up. "Same here." He glanced at the cloth. "Best burn that before it gets lost."

Glancing at the refuelled fire, Vernon remembered the uncomfortable questions surrounding his friends and tossed the cloth into the flames.

Orfain tapped his back. "Got a drink waiting for you already."

Vernon sat beside Lysia, and she grinned at him. "So how are you finding Erium?"

He slouched onto the leather padded chair. "It exceeds all of my dreams." He took the untouched tankard and stared at the yellowish ale. He frowned. "What of you though? Do you know what you're going to do here?"

"Thought that'll be obvious." She took a gulp of ale. "I'm gonna reopen business here."

He remembered her hidden storehouse and stiffened. "I'm supposing you aren't referring to this tavern."

All joy left her expression. "Not exactly." She took the black crystal necklace from her pocket and placed it on the table. "All three of us are going to start making a business from this."

Orfain grinned. "Four when Grayfern returns."

Vernon was flabbergasted. "But I-I don't even know where to begin or what to do."

Orfain placed his palm on one of the black hexagonal blocks of the wall. "It's a shame this stuff shatters when you cut it after its heated. Plus it's a shame only a few noble families are allowed to forge with it." He turned back to Vernon. "Truth is, we need someone to enter Erium's records chamber and steal the specific dutiful tablet belonging to the Gallaper family. Unfortunately, they're the only one who doesn't live in Sidium."

Vernon's eyes widened.

Lysia added, "It should be easy to convince Reethial that you'll need to enter the chamber. After all, it contains every name created by the priests and past emperors as well as their specific duties to the country."

Vernon shook his head. "I can't do that. I'll easily be caught."

Orfain guffawed. "You think the guards will be searching through every satchel and bag of the many, many stewards who go there?"

Lysia leaned forward. "Once we have that bronze tablet, we won't need to ask anymore of you." She touched the braid hiding her spiral ears. "I needn't remind you of why we are forced to do this."

He was left speechless and turned his gaze into his tankard. With guilt overcoming him, he turned back to her. "Very well then. I'll ask Reethial in the morning if I can be allowed in the records chamber."

"Thank you." Lysia sipped some ale.

Orfain patted Vernon's back. "Good man. Now let's get some drinks in ya, and we'll talk places you need to visit in Sidium."

Vernon took a hearty gulp, trying to dissuade nervous thoughts from engulfing his mind as he half listened to Orfain.

Chapter eleven – Light in the Dark

Sixth eclipse, thirteenth day

In the waking hours of the day, Vernon held back a yawn as he stood beside Iyessa outside the embassy's living room. Despite the sun only just breaking the horizon, they could hear glasses of whiskey clinking together inside. Throughout the entire time in Sidium, Reethial had lacked any effort or care to do his representatory job, a fact that disgusted Vernon. So he felt no qualms about fooling the elite into entering the records room.

The door opened and out stepped a man in brown embroidered leather who barely hid his smirk as he marched out of the manor. Iyessa entered the room with Vernon following close behind, and they stood before a tipsy elite lazily slouched in his armchair.

"Did I call for either of you?" he asked.

Iyessa held out two filled parchments for him. "I have the full list of Erium commanders you asked for."

Reethial refilled his crystal glass tumbler. "And what is the name of *that* commander."

Iyessa glanced at Vernon with disdain. "I don't believe it is wise to talk about such matters in front of a commoner."

Vernon's arms seized with a sudden rage.

Reethial leaned back in his soft chair, glaring at Iyessa. "I will not have you lecture me on what is wise and what is foolish, Synthion." He pointed his finger at Vernon. "This is the son of an utter failure, and yet he has a far greater standing than you will ever reach."

The edges of parchments crumpled in Iyessa's hands. "I mistakenly had not realised the representative of Felliet would require lecturing."

Reethial brought his whiskey tumbler to his lips without another word.

She inhaled a long breath through her nose. "I will give you that commander's name in the afternoon."

As she turned to leave the room, Vernon saw her incensed eyes glare at him.

Once the door closed behind her, Reethial sighed. "This is why those with lesser names should always know their place." He took another sip of whiskey. "Would you agree, *Meyorter*?"

Vernon's hands tensed, but he managed to hold back his hatred. "I believe everyone, from the commoners to the greatest of names, have a duty they must uphold."

"Diplomatically put." The vulgar elite seemed almost disappointed as he leaned back into his cushioned seat. "So what reason did you have for coming before me?"

Taking a deep breath to calm himself, Vernon explained, "After much consideration, I believe Felliet would have an edge in the great chamber if you were to meet with the most recent names Emperor Anisious created."

Reethial frowned. "Do you think me incapable of representing Felliet?"

"The opposite." Vernon swallowed his pride. "I believe the Erium nobles incapable of representing Erium. If you were to meet with them, especially the newly appointed, some may let slip faults in Erium which you can exploit in the great chamber."

The elite leaned back in his seat, taking another sip of whiskey and grinning. "Then make this list of noblemen and their duties."

"The quickest method would be for me to enter the records room."

"Fine, fine," Reethial said. "I shall draft a letter for you and Cendion to enter this evening. Now unless there's anything more, leave me."

Vernon turned his back to the egotistical man and, without another word, stepped out of the room. He wondered how he would conceal his true intentions from Buckley as well as the crypt's guards.

With little thought of pushing his way through the small crowd gathered along Innill's road, Jornis watched from a restaurant balcony as a line of fresh swordsmen paraded through the city. They had been outfitted with Gildren's famed curved swords and gilded square shields; however, from the way they merrily waved back to the cheering crowd, it was abundantly clear none of them had seen combat.

Copias smiled. "Those Rauders don't stand a chance."

Jornis barely glanced at him. "In open battle perhaps, but the Rauders have so far eluded both Erium and Gildren fleets, exclusively raiding only weak, isolated villages."

The swordsmen passed beneath them.

"Then wouldn't more soldiers help defend those places?" Copias asked.

"It would take a far greater force to safeguard the vast coastline of Gildren," Jornis explained. "What you see before you is a simple appeasement for the common people."

A restaurant maid approached with their ordered cups of sage tea. Jornis sipped his, feeling the mellow herb soothe his tongue.

Once the maid left, Copias whispered, "I think the woman on the far table is watching us."

Jornis turned his gaze to a woman loosely holding a theatre booklet. "Most likely she is a spy of the Marble Wheels."

"What should we do?"

"We should *do* nothing," Jornis replied at the foolish question but noticed the boy's eyes glance back to the spy. "It is quite understandable the Marble Wheels head is suspicious of us. After all, our intentions are unclear to them."

The boy looked dumbfounded. "But we spoke the truth."

"Precisely." Jornis took another refreshing sip. "*We* spoke the truth."

The parade of swordsmen exited the city's gatehouse, taking the festive atmosphere with them. As the cheering crowd dispersed, the Marble Wheels head herself, in practical silken attire, entered the restaurant and offhandedly gestured to one of the maids. Not a single bodyguard or companion accompanied her.

A chair was quickly brought to their table along with a pot of minted tea, and she approached. The boy's eyes had grown wide and his body visibly stiffened as the leader of the siloin calmly sat before them.

Jornis said, "I had not expected the leader of the Marble Wheels to so causally traverse outside her residence."

"Is this not my city?" she asked as she poured the minted tea from pot to cup.

Jornis grinned at the unretortable answer.

She brought the tea to her nose and took a sip. "I heard rumours you doubt Gildren's ability to defend its coast."

"And I heard other rumours saying the Rauders can easily outmanoeuvre Gildren's and Erium's combined navy," he replied, glancing at the last of the swordsmen leaving the gatehouse. "But I doubt you are content with merely sending more soldiers."

"Your doubts would be correct." She took another sip. "The siloins of Gildren have commissioned our esteemed engineers for a particular project that will counter this threat." She set her teacup down. "To ease your worries, I would like to invite you to the coastal town of Delport."

"I humbly accept." Jornis wondered why Gildren's famed engineers would be needed.

She turned to the boy. "And you?"

"I am very curious to see what you're building," Copias answered and stupidly added, "But I'm most curious about your name."

She turned to Jornis. "I shall see you in Delport tomorrow."

"I look forward to it."

She stood and left their presence.

Jornis took a sip of his sage tea, explaining, "Unlike Felliet or Erium, it is customary in Gildren that no one asks a person for his or her name."

"So how do people know who's who?"

"The person will state their own name when they feel who they're addressing is worth it."

Copias sighed.

"Relax, I'm sure she has had plenty of experience dealing with foreigners." Jornis finished his tea. He wondered why he felt the need to reassure and comfort the boy, especially since he was the son of a Dictorate member. He abruptly said, "We should prepare our horses to depart for the Silk Shores."

Copias rose from his chair. "Then let us go."

With Erger back, the forge was able to keep pace with the unending requests for repairs and forges. Niyaa had even practiced engraving some of her drawings on many of the tools they made. At long last, Erger left her to make a mattock all on her own and engrave it with whatever symbol she wanted.

Taking the stone bowl of melted agron out of the furnace, Niyaa wondered if the mattock's pointy tip would be strong enough. As she neared the mould, Kivy stepped inside, followed by a cheerful-looking brown-haired woman with an enormous leafy basket strapped to her back.

Kivy stepped towards Erger. "Got any stem axes?"

Erger glanced at Niyaa. "Keep your attention on filling the mould and make sure none of it spills."

Niyaa spun her gaze back to the heavy bowl and nervously poured it.

He replied to Kivy, "Afraid we don't have any stem axes at the moment."

"Why not?" She crossed her arms.

"Cause we haven't had a request to make one."

"But I guess you've had a request to make drawings then," Kivy grumpily said.

Niyaa's hands shook, wobbling the thick goo pouring into the mould.

The basket-carrying stranger walked to the shelves. She asked Niyaa, "Did you do these?"

Keeping her gaze focused on the mould, Niyaa nodded.

"Well, I absolutely love them." The stranger watched the last drop of agron plop into the mould. "Could *you* make me my axe?"

Niyaa looked at the woman and eagerly turned to Erger who gave a single nod. She smiled. "I can."

"Wonderful," the basket carrier said.

Kivy rolled her eyes with a loud sigh.

Erger turned to the woman. "Should be ready tomorrow."

"Perfect," the stranger said. She kneeled before Niyaa. "Do you think you can add a little something to my axe?"

"Like what?" Niyaa asked.

The woman glanced at the other engravings. "Could you draw some waves?"

"What are waves?"

Brief surprise crossed the stranger's face, and she put her hand to the back of her head. "Suppose we are a fair way from the coast."

Erger chipped in. "I'll show her how."

"Thank you," the woman said, straightening up.

Kivy spoke up from the entrance. "That'll be twenty brass coins."

Erger stepped between them, folding his arms. "You don't get to decide how much I charge for my service." He glanced at the stranger. "Ten brass."

Kivy marched to Erger, standing before him with an infuriated scowl.

The basket carrier spoke up. "How bout fifteen, halfway between the both of you."

For a tense moment, Kivy kept glaring at Erger. She yielded. "The village will get all of that fifteen."

"Fine," Erger replied as Kivy stormed out. He turned to the woman. "Don't mind her. She makes for foul company but has her heart in the right place."

Niyaa was unable to tell if he was serious.

Erger proudly put his hand on Niyaa's shoulder. "I can at least guarantee the extra you're paying will not go to waste. Niyaa will make the best stem axe you can find in all of Felliet."

"I look forward to seeing it," the basket carrier replied. "In the meantime, I'll be gathering herbs and other plants in the nearby canopy."

Niyaa asked, "What's your name?"

"Cabi," she answered, looking to both of them. "And yours?"

"Niyaa."

"Erger," the smither grunted. "It'll be ready by tomorrow afternoon."

"I look forward to it," the basket carrier replied and stepped outside.

Treading along the polished granite path with the great chamber's glistening white wall to his side, Vernon gazed up in awe at the gargantuan Imerial palace. Its colossal black crystal walls soared far above the great chamber and the colossal hexagonal base it towered from. Countless chainmailed tribowmen and swordsmen patrolled the glistening ramparts of the immense base. This home to the Imerial family filled Vernon with pride and admiration. He arrived at the bronze-lined entrance to the underground records crypt to the side of the palace's immaculate gateway.

All marvel and astonishment gave way to nervousness as he and Buckley approached the half dozen swordsmen guarding the stairs. Vernon's heart pounded as the guards thoroughly searched the stewards' satchels both leaving and entering. Despite knowing his satchel had a hidden pocket, his nerves didn't ease as he and Buckley approached the guards.

The closest guard asked the pair, "What business do you have in the records crypt?"

Buckley stepped forward, presenting the signed parchment from Reethial. "By the esteemed representative of Felliet, the two of us have been given permission to enter."

The guard took the paper and read it. Vernon glanced at Buckley, his thoughts filling with gratitude and relief easing his nerves.

The guard returned the parchment. "I'll need to check your bags."

Vernon stiffened and wondered whether the guard would notice the hidden compartment. He remembered *The Foundations* was still inside, and his eyes widened. The guard rummaged his gloved hands around the book inside and returned the silver satchel. After checking Buckley's grey satchel, the guard stepped aside. "You may pass."

Assured his hidden satchel pocket wouldn't be noticed upon leaving, Vernon relaxed and walked past the guards. He gazed down the brass-lined granite stairs stretching far below the surface. Unlike the steward's staircase in Ellity's academy, at least a handful of wall lanterns guided the way down. Taking a deep breath, Vernon began the decent.

Keeping his eyes low to avoid misstepping in the dim light of the staircase, Vernon thought of Buckley's description of Reethial. He glanced at the boy and wondered how anyone could describe that elite as *esteemed.* He returned his gaze to the shimmer of flickering light at the distant end of the underground staircase.

Reaching the final step, Vernon's eyes widened. A dozen thick colossal stone walls stretched across the vast marble-floored underground chamber. The thick walls housed thousands of scrolls and books with sliding iron ladders to reach the most distant. The shadowed arched ceiling brought a presence of grandness in the stuffy air as Vernon realised these colossal shelvings were the supports holding up the Imerial palace.

Following Buckley's stride, Vernon gazed down each row of records. Each began with short descriptive words engraved in bronze on the marble floor. The engravings were difficult to read as only a single wall lantern opposite either end of the thirteen rows shone in the massive chamber. A chainmailed swordsmen stood beneath each flickering lantern, and Vernon's awe vanished as he remembered the real reason he was there.

Passing the first two rows, Buckley stopped and asked, "Shall we start with the lesser names?"

Brought out of his harrowing thoughts, Vernon turned to the words *lesser nobles* engraved in the marble floor in a row filled with brass tablets. If the Gallaper family were in any way lesser nobility, they wouldn't have permission to forge black crystal.

Vernon said, "I think it would make the job easier if we split up. That way we can cover twice the number of books."

"But surely the newly appointed names would be all *here*. We need not split up."

Vernon desperately tried to think of an excuse and blurted out, "We need to be discreet."

"Excuse me?" Buckley asked.

Thinking on the spot, Vernon leaned closer and whispered, "We are foreigners here. Who knows who could be watching us. One of us should create a list of newly appointed nobles while the other does something completely meaningless."

Buckley glanced at one of the guards and at one of the Erium stewards taking some notes on one of the wallside writing podiums. He quietly said, "Very well, I'll search for something random while you make the real list."

"No." Vernon replied before anxiously saying, "I mean we should alternate."

"Alternate?" Buckley asked.

"Yes." Vernon felt sweat across his forehead. "If we keep swapping places, we will throw off anyone watching."

"I see." Buckley took a moment to consider it. "That seems reasonable. Not to mention we can both be searching in different places along the brass tablets."

Vernon relaxed. "You make a start on the real list, and I'll come a little later to swap with you."

Buckley nodded and departed into the row of lesser names.

Finally separated from Buckley, Vernon wandered through the crypt determining which row would contain the dutiful tablet belonging to the higher nobility. At the furthest row, he found the engraving *honoured duties of the revered nobility* which housed thousands of bronze tablets in the colossal stone shelving. Standing beside the wall lanterns and writing podiums was a black chainmailed swordsman, sternly observing the empty row. Vernon took a deep breath and ventured into the row.

The bottom row of bronze tablets were engraved with a specific duty or authorisation as well as the noble family's insignia. The thousands of bronze tablets were grouped and organised into specific families in ascending order of their lineage. The sheer scale of the duties and responsibilities in these vast shelves overwhelmed Vernon with inspired pride and awe.

He trekked towards one of the iron ladders. After arduously combing through many shelves, he came to the Gallaper family. Among a couple dozen dutiful tablets he found the specific bronze tablet.

In the name of Cloresious Imerial, those who possess the name Gallaper shall be granted permission to enter the hill of night spears and make use of the crystalline forges. This decree shall hence forever remain till either the Emperor of Erium or Grand Bishop of the priesthood deem it otherwise.

Vernon cocked his head slightly at the mention of the priesthood having the power to revoke a decree installed by the emperor himself. He realised this tablet would have been made before the disastrous culling when almost all of the priesthood was rightfully stripped of its authority.

Before he climbed down the ladder, Vernon glanced at the guards watching him from the far ends and knew not to place the bronze tablet into his satchel's hidden compartment. He grabbed several other Gallaper tablets and descended the iron ladder.

Stiffly approaching one of the writing podiums beside the guard, stack of tablets in his arms, Vernon anxiously tried to avoid eye contact as he neared it.

"Quite the selection you have there," the guard said.

Vernon set the bronze stack down on the podium, jokingly saying, "The person I'm working for wants to know as much about a particular noble as possible before meeting him. I figured this would be the best method."

"Why don't you ask this noble's stewards?" the guard asked. "Word spreads quickly around them."

Vernon nonchalantly placed his stiff hand to the back of his head. "Guess I didn't think about that."

"Guess you're new to this." The guard smirked. "Just remember that for the future. Saves you having to comb through this place."

"I will, thanks." Vernon took out a couple of blank parchments and his ink feather and scattered the bronze tablets around the small writing podium, placing the important black crystal forging permission tablet beneath the parchment he wrote on. After listing all the irrelevant duties of the Gallaper family, he grabbed both the parchment and tablet, hiding the dutiful tablet from the guard's eyes as he carefully moved it towards his satchel. Seeing the guard's attention was elsewhere, Vernon slowly placed the tablet inside his satchel's hidden compartment. He stacked the other bronze tablets on the podium and stiffly walked away.

"Aren't you forgetting something?" the guard asked.

Wide eyed, Vernon turned back to the guard.

"It's not our job to clean this up for you."

Vernon was overcome with relief. "Oh, right. Excuse me."

"Just make sure you put it back in the right place," the guard added. "I'll be watching to make sure you do."

"Of course." Vernon grabbed the bronze stack and returned them to the correct position, shuffling the section to avoid a noticeable gap. Stiffly walking past the guards, he breathed in a long sigh of relief.

With neither of the moons rising in the starry sky, the Felliet and Erium armies halted, for ahead lay an empty, wide bridge over the border river, beyond which stood the dark silhouettes of Iorden's homes. Though only a pale glow of the fallen sun shone from the distant horizon, Iyna managed to see the town's streets. Not a single barricade or wall was built around the stem-roofed town, nor was there any sign of soldiers or a garrison at all. The unshaken Therra marched forth, their glowing eyes and weapons lighting the way along the bridge. Her breath deepened as she realised there would be no pause before the assault.

Alexan hastily whispered an order to his two spear units to form their shield walls, and the spearmen formed their two rows and locked their shields behind the two other armies.

The Erium commander in his black armour was difficult to make out in the dusk light, and being so close to the river, his hushed words were faint. However, with every soldier anxiously awaiting the battle, no other voices carried over the gentle breeze, so she managed to make out his confident speech. "Our objective is to occupy this place as fast as possible before any Fyoreten can escape or resist. We will thus rush in and surround every last building while they sleep. First unit, circle round the town's left; unit eight, circle right. Everyone else follow me into the heart of the town."

Iyna glimpsed part of the commander's saddle shimmer as he turned his horse toward Iorden. Four hundred sets of hooves steadily followed their black-armoured leader across the empty stone bridge.

Alexan rushed to Orbert's spear unit, whispering something before returning to his own place, between Iyna and Barcial. His voice was quiet but stern. "Keep the shields tight and your walk slow." A slight pause hung in the cramped shield wall until he gave the order, "Slow march forward."

Each spearman trudged forth, following the sound of trotting hooves with only a narrow view through the swaying gaps in the triangle shields to guide them. Iyna remembered the bolts battering her shield and tightened her grip on it. She glanced at Sareesa hunched in front of her and turned to Barcial and Darius on the other side of Alexan. Their faces were calm and their spears steady.

Feeling her sandals step onto the stone of the bridge, Iyna returned her gaze ahead and stared longingly at the silhouette of the town.

The river below was calm, making only the lightest of trickling sounds beneath the bridge, a sound that faded into the noise of the numerous Erium horses arranging themselves on the grass plain between the river and town.

The orange glow of the Therra's eyes reflected off the grey buildings as they, in a single uniform column, entered the wide street cutting through the town. The red glow of their weird spiral weapons grew brighter as they pointed their blackened pipes forward. Iyna's breath deepened as a shimmer reflected off the Erium commander's sword when he unsheathed it and held it high. The other horsemen readied their lances.

His voice blared out for all to hear. "All charge!"

Iyna's heart raced as she felt the ground shake in the wake of four hundred sets of galloping hooves pounding the ground toward the town.

"Don't follow!" Alexan demanded. "Keep your pace slow and the shields tight."

The Erium horses thundered into the town, their hooves echoing across the cobblestone streets. Marching ever closer to the town, a familiar unease grew within Iyna as she realised not a single lantern or candle shone from any of the buildings, leaving only the distant glow of the Therra nearing Iorden's centre to illuminate the way.

Iyna's breath quickened as the shield walls came halfway between the bridge and the dark town, bringing much of the closest buildings in view.

Alexan yelled, "Halt! Everyone halt!"

The spearmen stopped, their faces flooded with dread. Iyna darted her gaze from one corner of the narrow shield gap to the other, desperately trying to spot any danger, till she noticed a slight shimmer in one of the nearby upper windows.

"Crossbowmen in the windows!" Alexan announced.

As soon as his voice left his mouth, Fyoreten crossbowmen revealed themselves, unleashing bolts onto the spearmen from the glassless windows. The shield gaps closed to the pelting, and Iyna felt the unending shower batter her shield. She gritted her teeth at the ambush, and a familiar horn sounded from up ahead. Her eyes widened with shock as another horn blasted, then another, till the entire town was engulfed in a single blaring alarm.

Crossbows snapping and horse shrieks followed, filling the dark air with a nightmarish sound of slaughter and carnage. Erium horsemen were overcome with bolts from the surrounding windows and rooftops. A bright reddened glow shone from the town centre, casting long shadows at the spearmen's feet.

Iyna's mouth gaped open. Long jets of red flame rose into the air from the Therra, bathing the horrific slaughter of the Erium riders in crimson light.

Town doors sprang open to mobs of Fyoreten farmers and craftsmen in a chaotic attack against the Erium and Therra.

Alexan shouted, "Slow march back!"

With the bolts still pounding the shields, the two walls steadily backed away as the dismounted Erium soldiers became overwhelmed by the ferocious mobs. Behind them, the jets of red flame violently swung along the ground, sending roaring fires through the streets, filling the air with horrific screams and shrieks.

A Therran covered in bolts marched down the main street and punched the blackened tube of its flame weapon through a window. A torrent of fire flooded the hose. A Fyoreten man charged from behind, imbedding his axe halfway through the creature's neck. The Therran turned to look at the man, axe still in its neck. It pulled its spiral weapon from the window, still spewing fire. Just before it turned the jet of flame to the stupefied man, a bolt struck deep into its left glowing eye, and it fell silently to the ground.

A splatter of blood struck Iyna's cheek. Turning to her side, she saw Darius fall with a bolt lodged in the back of his head. Barcial surged away from the wall, dropping his spear and defending his friend's body from the barrage.

"Halt!" Alexan demanded. "Crossbowmen to our rear."

Iyna spun around. A dozen Fyoreten behind a small, spiked barricade dripped water that glistened in the fiery red light. Their hands held both pikes and crossbows. A bolt thudded against Iyna's shield from the town ahead.

Alexan yelled, "Those on the sides, defend our backs!"

The pair of spearmen on each side rushed behind the rear row. One fell to the forward barrage. With only a few shields guarding the rear, Iyna felt exposed and desperately glanced to Orbert's unit only to find a similar sight.

The Fyoreten mob massed near the edge of town, all seething in rage at the Felliet spearmen as the red and yellow flames grew tall and wide. Barcial still held his shield over Darius and himself with bolts scattered in the dirt around them.

The bolts from the town ceased.

Alexan ordered, "Fast march west!"

The two spear units fast marched in the direction of the river, but Barcial remained at Darius's side.

As her shield wall moved away from him, Iyna broke formation, sprinting to him with her shield raised. She grabbed the back of his chestplate and yanked him away from Darius. Finding him too heavy to pull to his feet with her spear arm, she kept tugging him, until a bolt sliced across her right shoulder. Barcial got to his feet and ran with her, their shields raised towards the bridge.

Still feeling bolts pelting her shield, Iyna sprinted with Barcial after their unit, catching up with them in their desperate, near scattered route.

Iyna looked back to see if any of the mob were giving chase only to see an inferno consuming every part of Iorden. The Fyoreten people rushed to the river, buckets in hand. A handful of horsemen silhouettes

218

galloped away in the opposite direction. She returned her wide-eyed gaze forward and kept running.

Chapter twelve – Persevere

Sixth eclipse, fourteenth day

Trudging through the long Fyoreten grass, Iyna heard only the flowing waters of the border river and the wearied panting of the other spearmen. The rising reddish-orange sun took away the cover of the moonless night while bringing a stark reminder of that horror, lowering everyone's gaze.

Iyna heard a nearby thud and turned to see Barcial on his knees clutching the dirt. Like the other soldiers, Iyna and Sareesa halted, all staring hopelessly at him without any energy to comfort him.

Alexan marched to him, telling the others he passed, "Keep moving. We're not to rest till we cross the river."

Sareesa obeyed, turning her weakened body forward and following the other soldiers, but Iyna stood there watching.

Alexan knelt to Barcial's eyelevel. "We are to keep moving."

He shook his head. "I can't."

Iyna glanced at the shield on Barcial's back and, without thinking, trudged towards them.

"We *will* recover Darius's body," Alexan explained. "But to do that, you need to stand and keep moving."

Barcial said nothing.

"If you stay here then—"

Iyna punched Barcial's back-strapped shield, and he turned his bewildered gaze to her. She said, "Darius told me where you hail from, but I don't care." She knelt down with a firm grip on her spear. "It's your job to lead the unit, so stop wasting time back here and get your arse to the front."

Barcial turned away, his eyes watering. "He was all I had left."

Iyna stomped the ground with her spear. "And what will you do to the people who took him?"

He remained silent.

She narrowed her eyes. "Will you let his death go unanswered?"

Barcial sat back, and his eyes drifted to his empty hands. "I don't know."

Alexan stepped in. "Decide at the camp how you will honour him. Right now you need to stand." The commander held out his hand to Barcial. "I want you to set the pace at the front."

Barcial stared at the commander's palm and grasped it. Gradually he was pulled to his feet, and he closely followed Alexan to the front of the slogging army.

After a long while, they all reached a spot where the waters were calm and shallow.

Excitement and nervousness flowed through Vernon's veins as he, Lysia and Orfain neared the white iron gate of the hill of night spears. Several swordsmen in bronze-lined robes pearl robes patrolled the thick ramparts of the bronze-lined wall surrounding the hill. Vernon knew they were soldiers of the priesthood and he glanced to the hefty coin bag in Orfain's hands. Vernon pondered whether the sale of black crystal was what had kept the priesthood alive since the culling. Why had the emperor, both current and past, not regained control of the night spear hill from the priesthood, especially as it was *the* place where Rochious Imerial founded the empire?

Lysia marched ahead. Vernon and Orfain approached the single priesthood guard standing before the white swinging gate and presented the Gallopers' bronze tablet along with a folded parchment. Vernon's body stiffened as he watched the armoured swordsman take both, reading the note and examining the bronze tablet.

The guard returned the tablet and parchment. "Sixty bronze worth?"

"That's correct," Lysia replied, glancing at the bag in Orfain's hands.

The guard turned his head up to the ramparts, shouting, "Lower the scale!"

Atop the wall, a ruby encrusted crane turned till the bronze bowl it held was overhanging the wall. It steadily winched down.

Once the bowl was a mere foot off the ground, the guard explained, "Place the coins and written request inside."

"With pleasure." Lysia refolded the parchment and gently placed it inside. She turned to Orfain.

Orfain took the coin bag to the bowl, and they watched it gradually ascend before disappearing from view as the crane turned back.

An uncomfortable quiet wait followed, worsening the concerns plaguing Vernon's head, but the extravagant crane turned again.

The guard took out a sealed letter from within, broke it and read aloud, "As the overseer and protector of the hill of night spears, I, Priestlord Thirrentus, shall grant Lysia Gallaper the right to enter and purchase a full unforged block." He handed the letter to Lysia and banged thrice upon the solid white gate.

A moment later its chains steadily pulled it up, swinging it forwards and casting a dark shadow over the floor. Vernon's eyes widened with awe as he gazed at the wonderous silver hill from which grew giant, grey crystals whose five sides glistened in the morning sun. In a single moment, all his worries vanished, and he followed Lysia and Orfain into the birthplace of the Empire of Erium.

The silver grass on the hill's gentle slope was softer than any fur carpet, and a rich earthy scent entered Vernon's nostrils. The three passed a half-cut crystal, and Vernon could see it steadily growing a new layer. Several pairs of white-robed stewards were delicately cutting the crystals into hexagonal blocks, and he wondered which part of the city they would be sent to. A discomforting thought entered his mind as he pictured Reethial wearing several pieces of this glorious symbol.

Trying not to linger on the disheartening thought, Vernon followed Lysia and Orfain to one of the cutters where she asked for a large unheated block.

A renewed gust of chilling wind flowed past Jornis as he passed over the deep moat and through Delport's yellow gatehouse. The coastal town had a more industrial atmosphere than Innill, even if its buildings were of the same sandstone. Not only were the port town's cobblestone streets winding, but the people walking along them were poorly groomed labourers. The silk dyeing workplaces gave off a flowery perfumed scent, masking much of the commoner stench. Jornis shouldn't have been surprised by this, for it made simple logical sense to locate the dye stations within the same place the silk trenches were cultivated.

After stabling their horses, Jornis and Copias trekked past many weavers and dye stations till their sandals reached Delport's brick pier. Moored far into the calm waters was a long copper-plated warship with an unusual second level built on the deck.

Copias pointed towards the large vessel. "Is that what Gildren is building to counter the threat?"

Jornis rolled his eyes. "What else would the siloins construct to battle the Rauders?"

"I was assuming they would be improving their walls and towers."

"Coastal towns and villages cannot wall off the sea." Jornis glanced to the small wall surrounding the town and the thick tower overlooking the pier entrance. "And I have yet to hear the Rauders attack from the land."

The boy gestured to the elongated beach and the lengthy kelp trenches uniformly stretched to the water's edge. "But should they not at least add stakes and walls to their beaches?"

Jornis glanced at the numerous raised poles alongside the trenches and the nests of silkworms they held. "The heart of Gildren's wealth lies in trading silk. Understandably, the idea of disrupting even a small portion of its production never came to them."

"So instead they allow the Rauders to disrupt it," Copias said.

224

"Afraid that's correct," Jornis admitted as he looked back at the warship. "But let us first see what the wise council of Gildren have planned."

The lengthened raised platform of the duel-masted warship and the bustling deck it spanned from were lined with as many tribow stands as humanly possible. Clearly the idea was to bombard a passing boat with a multitude of bolts, perhaps in a single volley. Glancing up at the square sails, Jornis pondered whether this warship could even intercept the Rauders in time.

Passing several labourers filling the copper-plated agron hull, the two of them walked up the gangway and stepped aboard the bustling deck. The Marble Wheels head was speaking to a man in yellow silk at the warship's bow, and Jornis approached them, ending their conversation.

"Ah, you must be Jornis Meyorter." The man in yellow silk grinned. "Tell us, how was your travel to my town?"

"Gildren has the smoothest highways in all the federation," Jornis replied. "Though I'm doubtful it will remain that way forever."

"I have heard a fair amount of your doubts," the man replied, placing his palm on the nearest tribow stand. "But I would love to hear them expressed in your own tongue."

Jornis obliged. "Gildren has prominent rivals to its north and south, its trade network has been threatened by the Fyoreten's demise and its coast is now being raided by unknown people. It would be foolish not to question your nation's future."

The Marble Wheels head folded her arms. "And what if I told you this ship can unleash a hundred tribow bolts from either side?

Furthermore, every siloin has commissioned a ship similar to this one. As for our *prominent* neighbours, you can rest assured we are building up our forces to match."

Jornis held in an exacerbated sigh. "Eight new warships added to your trading fleet and you believe this, combined with Erium's neglected navy, will protect your coast?" He gestured to the kelp trenches along the beach. "The very heart of Gildren is threatened at a time of increasing uncertainty."

"It is quite certain these creatures will meet their end at these warships." Delport's governor shrugged. "Perhaps you two would also feel this certainty once you witness the results of the *Russlet Warden* and the Rauder bodes it brings back."

"Do not mistake my arguments for simple malice or ignorance," Jornis said. "You must understand Gildren is at a dangerous crossroads right now."

He smirked. "I will allow you to stay in Delport so you may see your concerns laid to rest. Now, if you excuse me, I have other matters that require my attention." He marched away without a further word.

The Marble Wheels head stared at Jornis. "Gildren has always been on a dangerous crossroads ever since it established itself as independent of Artor and especially during the culling."

Copias argued, "But the Delflare region came under your nation's control. Surely the culling would have been a benefit to you."

She stared at the boy and returned her gaze to Jornis. "Do not think us weak or incompetent."

"I only ask that you not think yourselves invulnerable," Jornis replied. "For even the strong and capable will eventually fall."

She turned towards the sea. "You will find suitable lodging in the inn at the far side of the town."

Jornis left her staring longingly out at the calm waves.

Niyaa giddily undid the clamps of the axe head mould as she imagined what it would look like when pinned to the handle she'd prepared. Her mom and dad had even come to the forge to see the results of her hard work, so with them and Erger watching, she opened the mould.

Niyaa steadily prised the stone pieces apart. The long, curved axe blade hadn't warped or fractured.

Erger stepped forward. "Aren't you gonna *properly* examine it?"

"Right." Niyaa was flustered as she lifted the tool head from the cooled stone and brought it close to her face as she carefully stared at each bit of the long thin blade.

Darryam patted his daughter's shoulder. "It looks great."

"Yeah." Niyaa smiled widely and eagerly turned to the smither. "I don't see any chips at all."

Erger nodded. "So would you now like to test the sharpness?"

"Al...all right." Her hands shook a bit as she brought the blade close to her thumbnail.

Darryam turned to Erger in half panic. "What is this? What are you teaching her?"

Erger said, "You test the sharpness of a blade by lightly scraping it against a thumb or fingernail."

Niyaa gently placed the long axe blade straight against her nail and nudged it forward. To her delight, it left a slight scratch mark.

Erger glanced at it. "Seems you forged it correctly."

"Thanks." Niyaa shook with excitement.

Darryam touched the top handle ring of the axe head. "You did absolutely great."

"Now all you need to do is engrave it." Erger grinned. "Then you can add the handle."

Niyaa felt unsure of what to do, so she looked to her parents. "Cabi said she wanted waves engraved on it."

"Waves?" Darryam wondered. "Afraid I wouldn't know how to draw that."

Mysia giggled. "You can just do some curvy lines." She turned to Erger. "Do you have something I can use as an example?"

Erger nodded and handed her the etching tool with a scrap piece of agron.

She scratched out three short, wavy lines that narrowed at the left end.

"Are those waves?" Niyaa asked.

Mysia smiled. "The sea is never flat. It goes up and down, up and down all the way to the horizon. That wobble's called waves."

Niyaa tried to imagine it, only for her thoughts to picture a glass of water filling and emptying.

Darryam rubbed the back of his head. "I don't really understand it either."

Mysia shrugged. "Well, it's only cause I grew up near the coast."

Niyaa couldn't picture it at all. "Can we go there one day?"

Mysia smiled slightly. "Maybe."

Erger said, "I reckon that engraving will work." He turned to Niyaa. "Remember to engrave only the strongest areas. In this case it'll be just below the holding pin."

She nodded and gently brought her etching tool against the axe head. Slowly and steadily, she scratched out the three wavy lines, trying to keep the curves matching. Niyaa turned to her mom. "How's that?"

"It looks perfect."

Erger held out the agron handle. "Now to finish."

"All right." Niyaa slotted the handle through the axe head's holding ring. As she pinned it through the little hole, Niyaa held the stem axe at arm's length, proudly staring at it. She was certain that when Cabi returned from foraging in the canopy she would love it.

Body devoid of energy, Iyna trudged her way back into the blue hill camp with the other exhausted spearmen, and her body collapsed. Her iron shield came off her shoulder, clattering to the trampled blue lilies, with the other shields and spears dropping to the ground around her. Iyna's spear hand relaxed and she immediately regrasped it, before noticing eighty new faces.

She gave no smile to the Felliet reinforcements nor to their red-faced armoured leader marching towards Alexan.

"Who gave you permission to take command of this army?" the man demanded.

Alexan kept his wearied body composed. "As I mentioned in the letter I sent, no one else could have commanded this army, and had I waited for permission, everyone you see would have died at Iorden."

"What of Orbert?" the commander asked. "You should know his name is superior to yours."

All eyes turned to Orbert, who replied, "Alexan is superior on the battlefield."

Alexan said, "Now with the pleasantries out of the way, I need you to send word to Ellity that Erium's advance force and the Therran army have been wiped out. Fyoreten resistance remains as fierce as it was during the culling."

The elite gave no answer as his face went pale.

Alexan stepped closer. "After our defeat, Fyoreten will greatly desire retribution, likely targeting this very camp. Now you can either stay here and argue your experience in battle, or you can inform the Dictorate of the dire situation and have them send further troops."

The elite hesitated. "Fine. But be warned they will debate your actions when the conflict is over." The man stubbornly turned away, marching to his horse near the main tent with several bodyguards following suit.

A moment later, the elite galloped out of the camp and Iyna steadily got to her feet.

Alexan turned his attention to the reinforcements gathered before him. "Who are your unit leaders?"

A clean-shaven man grasping a spear stepped forward followed by a ponytailed woman firmly holding a tribow.

"If you two would step inside the command tent." Alexan turned to his army. "Orbert, Barcial and Iyna, follow me. Everyone else, get some rest."

The spearmen groaned as they moved towards the tent, leaving their weapons scattered across the ground. Iyna realised she too had been called. She glanced to Barcial trudging after Alexan inside the command tent and tentatively followed.

Inside the thick cloth tent hung a soft hammock on one side while the other held several water barrels and crates with only an empty map table filling the space between.

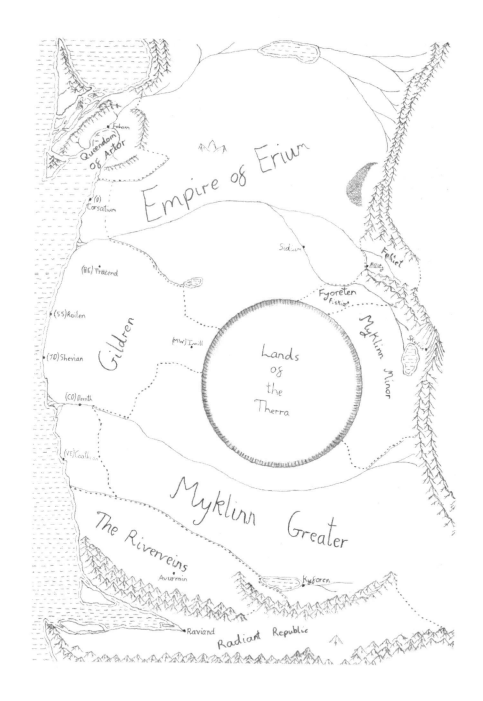

Alexan filled several tankards with water, placing each on the table, and turned to the two unfamiliar unit leaders. "Could you two introduce yourselves?"

The woman stepped forward, pointing her tribow to the floor. "My name is Tarrow, and I lead forty of the best tribowmen in Felliet."

"And I am Feeliath Coriate," the man proudly said. "My unit is comprised of the strongest men and women from Milnet. No matter what we face on the battlefield, I guarantee none of my unit will ever yield."

Alexan darted his eyes up and down the man. "What *is* your experience on the battlefield?"

Feeliath said, "I am the top of my unit and have won many wall clashes."

"And outside of training?" the commander asked.

The man's prideful look vanished. "Well, some of us helped the garrison capture a handful of Beast Riders trying to sneak into our town."

Iyna's eyes widened with shock that the Beast Riders would try to attack a town so far from the desert. She breathed in relief that the town was spared the savagery of those monsters.

"Anything else?"

Feeliath scowled. "No."

The commander marched around the table, approaching Iyna with his gaze locked on Feeliath. "During last night's battle, this one demonstrated incredible courage and leadership. Even risking her life for a fellow comrade."

Iyna glanced at Barcial, whose face still lacked any emotion, and she realised what her commander meant.

Feeliath stepped forward, bitterly asking, "Are you saying *she* will replace me?"

"I am," Alexan answered. "The battlefield is different to any training you might have had. Furthermore, I don't know you well enough to entrust the safety of my army in your hands."

"Then let me prove it to you. Let my unit take any of yours on in a shield wall clash." He grinned at Iyna. "Then we can see who—"

"My decision is final!" Alexan snapped. "If you want to prove yourself, start by demonstrating your ability to follow orders."

Feeliath fell silent and turned away, leaving the tent.

Alexan held out the water tankard to Iyna. "Though you have much to learn, I trust *you* to quickly make the right decisions and lead your soldiers so they may see another sunrise."

Hesitantly taking the tankard, she stared longingly into the water as she pictured herself leading a unit of her own. The memory of the body pile crept its way into her thoughts.

Alexan turned to the other unit leaders. "Does anyone object?"

Barcial picked up one of the other tankards. "I believe she is not only capable but the perfect choice to lead a unit into battle."

Surprised, Iyna stared at him as her weary body relaxed, easing her horrid thoughts.

Orbert without uttering a word picked up a tankard and nodded to her.

All eyes turned to Tarrow and she calmly spoke. "I too know not the experience of battle, but I strongly agree those who have, especially those who have shown true leadership, should be the ones to lead." She raised her own water tankard to Iyna. "I will do what I can to support you."

Seeing their approval, Iyna lifted her head to her commander. "I accept."

Alexan grabbed the last cup for himself, and all the tankards came together.

Stepping from the command tent, Iyna noticed many bitter glances from Feeliath and the people around him. The distrust and resentment on the faces of those she would be leading returned Iyna's exhaustion. She sighed and trudged to the sleeping tent.

Chapter thirteen – Storm Clouds

Sixth eclipse, thirty-second day

Day after day in the dreary camp, Iyna overheard mutterings and snickers by the very soldiers she was supposed to lead. No matter how many of their names and backstories she remembered, all forty of them still looked to Feeliath for leadership, giving her not a shred of recognition. Combined with the utter lack of information about the war throughout the many idle days spent guarding the hill of blue lilies, Iyna was left frustrated.

As the morning sky drizzled with a misty rain, Iyna trudged along the third trench line being dug around the camp and spotted Feeliath lazily sitting with a man and woman on the grass.

Exchanging bitter looks with them, Iyna turned her attention to the easterly landscape with a firm grip on her spear. She spotted a single, grey-robed rider emerging from the rain's mist and galloping towards them.

Feeliath boasted, "Maybe this messenger will rid us of this bitch."

Furious, Iyna turned to him. "Do you have something to say?"

"I do." He stood. "You aren't fit to be our leader."

Her teeth gritted together. "And why is that?"

"Because you're an outsider," he said. "Because you don't truly know any of us, how we all trained together or how we've protected Milnet."

"You mean how you helped the garrison that one time?"

He crossed his arms. "Well I bet *you* won't ever defeat any Beast Riders."

All of Iyna's muscles tensed in sheer rage, and she stiffly marched forward, but the rider halted before them.

"I carry an important message from the Elite Dictorate," the messenger said. "Where is Alexan Brige?"

Iyna turned to the grey-robed messenger and begrudgingly answered, "I'll lead you to him."

The rider dismounted and, leaving the horse untied, climbed over the damp trench.

Feeliath stepped aside, smirking to Iyna. "Better not keep him waiting."

She turned away from him and led the messenger up the blue hill, over the other two other trenches and into the command tent. Inside, Alexan and Orbert were discussing something over an old map but ended their conversation when the messenger entered.

The messenger held out a wax-sealed letter to the commander. "I bring word from the Elite Dictorate."

"Thank you." Alexan took the letter and broke its grey shield seal. After reading it, he let it fall onto the map table and turned to the messenger. "Ride swiftly back to Ellity. Tell the Dictorate Felliet's army is ready to march."

"With pleasure." The messenger rushed out.

The commander turned to the two unit leaders standing before him. "Orbert, Iyna. A serious matter needs to be discussed. Wake Tarrow and find Barcial. He should be in the supply tent."

They nodded and ran out into the rain. Iyna wondered why Barcial would be in the supply tent but realised she hadn't seen him much since the attack on Iorden. She rushed to the nearby supply tent and stepped inside its cramped space.

She walked along the narrow passage dividing the water barrels, weapon racks, crates of training spears and food sacks. Barcial was chopping mushrooms atop an agron barrel at the far end.

She said, "We're needed in the command tent."

He kept his blank gaze on the task. "Do you think tonight's dandelion and mushroom stew would go better with potatoes or pink lettuce?"

Iyna stared at him. "Right now, there are more important things to discuss."

He paused and turned to her. "More important things?" He leaned against the green barrel with a weird smile. "You know. I've always wanted to become a chef, make beautifully crafted dishes for all kinds of people. Then I'd watch them savour every bite." He set down his cutting knife, and his smile vanished. "Suppose I will never get the chance to cook for…"

She stood there without an idea of what to say, leaving only the sound of the drizzling rain pattering the tent's cloth to fill the air.

He sighed and walked towards Iyna. "Let's go, shall we."

Iyna dumbfoundedly nodded.

They returned to the command tent with the other unit leaders. Alexan looked grim as he explained, "The main armies have finished gathering and have already departed from Garhurn. Reportedly Erium's force numbers ten thousand with further thousands from Gildren, Artor and Myklinn Greater."

Orbert asked, "When will they arrive?"

"Early tomorrow."

Barcial added, "No doubt the emperor wanted to wait till the next great chamber meeting to announce it."

Alexan nodded. "That would be the only reason to explain their delay in this war they started."

Iyna's body tensed in fury.

Alexan stared down at the map. "Inform your units, have them ready and rested by sunrise. We are to march with them and once again assault Iorden."

An uncomfortable moment hung in the air. Tarrow said, "You can rest assured my tribows will be ready for battle."

Like the others in the tent, Iyna glanced at the inexperienced woman till Alexan sternly replied, "Glad to hear it."

Without another word, the unit leaders left the tent to inform their units. Iyna stood in the misty rain, her body still tense with anger at the sheer injustice of the war. Remembering Feeliath's arrogance, she returned to the supply tent to grab a pair of training spears and marched her way down the blue hill.

Yet again she saw him merrily chatting away with his friends in the unfinished trench, and her grip on the straw spears tightened.

He asked, "So have they come to their senses?"

Iyna marched directly to him, planted her spear into the wet dirt and tossed him the other training spear to his feet. "You said before that you were the best in your unit. I want you to prove it."

He grinned. "If you really want to." He took the iron shield from his back and stepped within duelling distance of her. "I can't wait to knock you onto your girly ass."

Taking her own triangle shield from her back, Iyna readied herself for the duel and took in a long deep breath to settle her anger before speaking. "Come on then."

He charged forward, bashing his shield against Iyna's, forcing her off balance, and thrust his straw spear at her head. She narrowly dodged the attack. His shield bashed her a second time, nearly pushing her over before she leapt back.

"Losing your step?" he asked.

The others in her unit gathered around them, with many cheering Feeliath, and she steadied her breathing. Watching him raise his shield once more, Iyna knew he planned to charge again, and a smirk crossed her face. "You really are unfit to lead a unit."

Feeliath barked back, "You'll see who's unfit!"

He charged again. Iyna sidestepped, thrusting her straw spear into his open side.

His face flooded with surprise and rage, and the cheering around them vanished. He jabbed at her shield.

Iyna stepped back as she struggled to defend against the unending attack. But she remembered the first duel with Barcial. She waited for an oncoming strike and swung her shield, bashing his training spear far to the side. In the same movement, Iyna thrust her spear forward. He raised his shield, blocking his head and his vision. Iyna rushed forward, swinging her straw spear at his undefended legs and thrashing his shin. He grunted and lifted his leg. Iyna bashed his shield, toppling him into the mud.

Standing over Feeliath, Iyna turned to her unit gathered around and said, "A large Erium army will arrive early tomorrow. We are to join them and march on Iorden." She pointed her training spear down at Feeliath. "Do you want to be led by a pitiful sore loser or someone who's seen real fighting?"

He leaned his body up. "We've all seen real fighting."

Iyna glared at the fool. "Have you ever felt crossbow bolts batter your shield, cutting down those around you? Have you ever stared down an oncoming horde of horsemen?" Her voice grew louder and angrier. "Have you ever watched your village burn down around you? Watch as the monsters butcher defenceless people? Kill the person closest to you and make off into the night?"

He darted his eyes away.

Breath seething, she turned back to her unit. "I don't care if you like me or not. I don't even care if you despise me, so long as you do as I say because then you might see many more sunrises." She tossed the other straw spear onto Feeliath. "Follow this one and you'll find yourselves become just another corpse flung onto a pyre."

The former stonemasons and quarrellers gave no response.

She stepped closer to them, staring at each of their stunned faces. "Erium has forced this war on us without care if we live or die. If we are to survive, we need to become a solid, unwavering unit that can withstand any barrage or charge." Again she heard no objections, snickering or otherwise. "I want every one of you right now to prepare our supplies for the journey."

They left for the supply tent with only Feeliath staying.

Iyna pulled her iron-tipped spear from the wet soil. "I said everyone."

He quickly got to his feet, face red with anger, and glanced at the rest of the unit walking up the hill. Biting his bottom lip, he followed.

In the midst of Erium's finest diplomats, merchants, nobles and scholars, Vernon held his head high as he ascended the glistening white stairs towards the immaculate doors of the observers stand. His smile twitched as he remembered the remarkable descriptions of the magnificent great chamber and imagined the emperor's decrees sounding off the glistening white walls. Vernon could not contain his excitement at being able to witness authority directed to the nations of the world from the very heart of Erium, to the point he cared not that Buckley and Iyessa were accompanying him.

Passing the pair of silver-armoured swordsmen, Vernon set foot onto the bronze-lined observers stand and was in total awe at the grand chamber before him. The glistening white walls stretching far and high bathed the entire chamber in ambient sunlight despite the clouded outside, and its pearl floor was beautifully polished. Gobsmacked, Vernon admired the simple design of the Federal Throne, depicting the emperor's bronze seat placed above all nations of the world. No doubt it was the ultimate symbol of the Empire of Erium's authority over the world.

Descending the stand, Vernon's eyes were drawn to the pearl floor below, where sheathed in the centre was the greatest aspect of the chamber. His grip on his satchel tightened as he reminded himself of how Rochious Imerial forged the white crystal sword and used it to bring down the last captain of the Royals. Vernon thought of the lasting peace and prosperity that followed as Erium's first emperor united nearly the whole world's people under a single, shared goal.

Glancing at the bronze representative seats on either side of the glorious sword, Vernon remembered the stubbornness and foolishness that pointlessly divided the world after Rochious's unfortunate passing. With the reminder lingering in his thoughts, he slumped near the front row between Buckley and Iyessa with much of his wonder fading.

It took a while for the observers stand to fill, and they had a further long wait before the grand doors below the stand opened. Vernon's awe returned as Emperor Anisious Imerial trekked along the pristine pearl floor in silk clothes of pure white. Vernon had always imagined the emperor to adorn himself in the grandest of colours, and he wondered whether the white was to appease the other nations.

Shortly after the emperor's loyal advisors took their seats beside their ruler, the first of the representatives entered. A man fully covered in yellow silk and bronze jewels flaunted the vast wealth of Gildren before everyone present. The next two arrived as a pair, a bearded man in grey fur alongside a woman in brown cloth who both glared at the Gildren representative as they took two of the opposing seats.

A strange scraping noise echoed along the polished floor below the stand, and stunned looks swept across the faces of the emperor, his advisors and the three representatives as they all watched the new arrival. Vernon's eyes widened as Reethial appeared in a humongous robe of black crystal pieces that dragged along the pearl floor. The elite had no shame as he marched his way to his seat, leaving the chamber aghast and silent as all eyes fixed on this appallingly arrogant display.

Iyessa stood, with a subtle pleased grin, and left the stand. Turning back to Reethial and his egotistical strut across the great chamber, Vernon hardly noticed the other representatives trickling in. Only when the grand doors closed did he finally notice everyone was seated.

"This session shall now begin." Emperor Anisious announced. He turned to the man in yellow silk. "I would first like an update on the ongoing pillaging happening along Gildren's coast."

"Since our last gathering, several villages have been attacked by these creatures of the sea." The man of Gildren seemed oddly smug. "However, I am glad to say the siloins of Gildren have ensured the safety of our glorious coast. I can now say with confidence that no more of these raids shall take place." He turned to the woman in brown cloth. "Artor may now have the protection of Erium's navy."

She scowled back without a reply.

The supreme commander swiftly turned to his emperor. "I believe it is wise to see their council's solution in action before we order the navy moved."

"Agreed," Anisious Imerial replied to his advisor.

The man in yellow grinned. "It would be an honour to demonstrate Gildren's ability to defend the federation before Erium's mighty warships."

"We will await the results." The emperor turned to the other representatives. "Next issue, the subjugation of Fyoreten. I would first like to thank Gildren, Myklinn Greater and the Therra for providing forces to aid this final offensive." He narrowed his eyes at Reethial and took a short, irritated breath. "Felliet especially played a crucial role in this conflict and was first to battle the Fyoreten."

A wide, unearned grin crossed the elite's face. "It would be an honour to inform the Elite Dictorate of your approval."

The emperor stared unimpressed at Reethial and turned his attention to the observers stand. "Trade will soon flow freely across the mountain route. Caravans and wagons will no longer be slowed by the decaying roads of Fyoreten, replaced by smooth highways funded by the Empire of Erium. Merchants and traders will freely travel to the region, bringing its towns and cities much-needed wealth."

Relaxed, Vernon smiled at the idea of prosperity coming to the people of Fyoreten.

"As for which family will take control of the region, the Pellsias name has proven itself more than capable in both governing and diplomacy." The emperor turned to the delegate of the citizens advisor. "I decree that those with their name shall have the honour of—"

A snapping sound came from the front corner of the observers stand, and a bolt struck Emperor Anisious in the chest.

Vernon rose from his seat, turning to the assassin reloading his miniature crossbow. A sudden rush of swordsmen charged from the entrance, obscuring his view. The observers stand filled with panic and terror as the guards drew their swords.

Vernon returned his gaze to the scene below where he watched the emperor collapse from his throne, coughing blood onto the pearl floor.

The supreme commander was the first to rush to the emperor's side, defiantly shielding Anisious from any further bolt, while the other advisors and representatives froze in place. A yell sounded from the assassin as a sword buried itself in his stomach and further blades struck him down.

"Meyorter." Buckley tugged at Vernon's sleeve. "We should leave."

Distraught, Vernon turned to Buckley but returned his gaze to Emperor Anisious as a pool of blood grew around him. He replied, "I'll meet you at the estate."

"Very well then." The boy hastily left.

The observers stand dispersed, leaving only a handful of onlookers to watch in silent horror as Emperor Anisious Imerial slowly became still.

Half a day had passed since the Marble Warden set sail. Jornis remembered the ecstatic look of the warship's captain when he received reports of a raid happening south of Delport. The man's haste to depart had left Jornis strangely uneasy, so he resided at the pier's end, awaiting their unsuccessful return. Staring out at the rough sea with dark clouds blanketing the sky, he pondered how long it would be before the vessel came into sight, especially as he found his thick coat greatly inadequate for the brisk salted gale.

Copias arrived with a small tray of buttered bread rolls and cups of sage tea.

Taking the hot drink, Jornis saw the bewildered expression on the boy's face. "You're wondering why I don't wait beside an indoor fireplace."

"The ship will take just as long to return no matter where you place yourself," he replied.

"I want to witness the sailors' expressions as soon as they dock. Specifically, I wonder whether they will be prideful or not." Jornis sipped the warm tea and relaxed at its fine taste.

"When they return, their captain will surely announce their success or failure to everyone," the boy said. "There's little need for you to spend the day here."

Jornis took another calming sip. "You can wait inside a tavern if you wish."

Copias held the tray in one hand and took one of the bread rolls. "If you believe I came all this way to relax, then you're deeply mistaken." He took a bite of the bread.

Long after finishing the tea and the bread, Jornis noticed something brown moving along the high, violent waves. He marched to the furthest edge of the pier and squinted at the unusual small dot before spotting three others following it.

"Are they back?" Copias asked.

Every hair raised across Jornis's body, bathing him in a dreaded chill. Approaching the town's submerged beach were four brown kite sails hurriedly skipping small boats along the rough waves.

Copias stared at them. "Who are they?"

A bell rang from one of the two towers overlooking the bay.

Wide eyed, Jornis said, "The Rauders are coming." He turned to the ramparts around the small town and saw a handful of tribowmen running along its ramparts. "Did they supplement the ship with the garrison?"

"I see them!" Copias pointed his finger to the lead boat.

Jornis looked again. Each skipping boat housed four hulking grey creatures; each hunched on two giant arms with a single bulbous leg and no head or neck to speak of. One stood itself on its thick leg, stretching its enormous body along the lead boat's mast. The creature loosened the kite sail with its three-fingered hand, letting it drift further into the sky, and the other boats copied. Jornis watched helplessly as their pace quickened towards the town.

Copias grabbed Jornis's arm, tugging him away from the pier edge, and they ran back along the brick pier.

A few tribow strings snapped. Rising panic gripped the town, and the labourers scrambled towards the only gatehouse. The boy glanced back as further desperate tribowmen released their bolts.

Jornis said, "Keep your gaze ahead. Tuning back will only slow your step."

Copias obeyed.

At the pier's end, the winding streets were in complete disarray. Jornis realised it would be foolish and dangerous to head for the gatehouse, especially if the intent of the Rauders was to attack the civilians. He turned to the thick wall tower closest to them and informed Copias, "We'll find safety in there."

Copias glanced at the fleeing crowds of silk harvesters and dyers. "I'll trust your judgement."

Glad the young man had listened, Jornis led him to the tower's iron door. It swung open, disgorging almost a dozen chainmailed swordsmen. The soldiers with their small, polished square shields rushed towards the water's edge as the Rauder boats skipped past the silkworm nests held high above the water.

Copias said, "Isn't that the garrison leader?"

Jornis glanced at the one ordering the terrified men to form a line along the shifting water line but was unable to answer.

"Does that mean those men are the only ones who aren't tribowmen?"

Glancing up at the few tribowmen rushing along the ramparts, Jornis again was unable to answer.

Closing in on the tower's iron door, Jornis heard the boats scrape along the sand and glanced back. He watched the Rauders leap off their boats into the shallow water, almost galloping on their three hefty limbs towards the shrunken beach. Jornis and Copias rushed inside the tower just as the hulking creatures smashed through the line of swordsmen, sending cries of pain and terror sounding in the air behind them.

Bolting the iron door shut, Jornis breathed out, his heart racing in his chest. He dropped to his knees as his thoughts dwelt on the soldiers' screams and the chaos sounding across the town's streets. He managed to calm his breathing. "They should not bother ... following us."

"What makes you say that?" Copias stared anxiously at the reinforced door.

Jornis rose to his feet. "The Rauders have thus far carried out small, fast raids against farmhouses and small villages. I doubt they will waste time breaking through a tower door when an entire town of riches lies before them." He glanced around the bare room, finding only a few stacks of shields beside the door and a pair of barrels alongside the sandstone stairs. "With any luck those barrels hold water and not—"

A ram-like object battered the door, echoing in the bare room and leaving Jornis turning to the entrance. Another strike pounded the iron.

"We need to leave." Copias tugged his arm. "Now!"

Jornis was brought out of his frozen state, and the two of them hurried up the stairs till they were standing on the ramparts overlooking the town. The Rauders were scattering into the town, breaking into random buildings without hesitation. Jornis turned his attention to the tower's entrance and spotted a single Rauder denting the iron door with nothing but his lumbering fist.

One of the tribowmen along the ramparts rushed to them and aimed his cranked weapon at the Rauder battering the tower's door. The tribow snapped its string, sending the bolt swiftly through the air. It pierced the creature's shoulder. The Rauder, however, continued his assault against the reinforced iron, seemingly unfazed by the bolt in his shoulder.

Fear shuddered throughout Jornis as he heard the door's hinges begin to give way as further sounds of screaming and looting grew throughout the town. His hands shook and his breath deepened.

Copias said, "We can jump down here."

Jornis turned and saw the young man staring over the other edge of the wall.

The guard hurried to the edge. "It should be deep enough."

Seeing the guard climb atop the defensive stone, Jornis approached the edge and stared at the moat below.

"I'll go first." Copias perched on the crenel. "Wait till you see me surface before following."

Jornis nodded. Wide eyed, he watched the young man drop feet first off the wall, loudly falling into the water below. He and the guard stared anxiously down for a lengthened moment till Copias finally resurfaced.

Jornis stood atop the wall edge, heart racing, as he stared down at the seemingly narrow water. He took a deep breath and stepped off the wall.

He hit the water, going below its surface as the air escaped his mouth. He flailed his arms till they struck the dirt bank, whereupon he grabbed hold and began climbing.

The guard plunged into the water near him with great force, and Jornis felt his grip loosen in the shifting water. He brought his body along the mud bank, desperately clawing up its surface till he broke the water's surface.

Coughing to regain his breath, he found Copias holding out a muddied hand.

Jornis accepted it and stood out of the moat with the weaponless guard following suit. He looked up and saw the assaulting Rauder moving along the rampart without a single glance at the three humans below as they turned to flee.

Redrawing the wavy lines onto a piece of scrap agron, Niyaa remembered Cabl's delighted smile when she received the axe. It was a shame she had to leave so soon afterwards as Niyaa would have loved to make more things for her.

Erger also seemed happier and was using his own etching tool in the corner of the forge, making some symbol on a spade head. Noticing a proud grin on his face, Niyaa tried to sneak a look at whatever he was drawing.

He set the etching tool down. "That's it," he whispered and took the spade head over to her, showing an impressively drawn hammer whose head was a rounded brick furnace.

"If I had the right dye paste then I would add colour to it." He shrugged. "Guess there's no point complaining about it."

"It looks amazing," Niyaa said. "Did you draw this on all your tools when you were in Ellity?"

"I did indeed." He looked wistful and leaned against the hammering table. "Honestly, I'm thinking about heading back there to restart my business."

"You should!" Niyaa blurted out. "What's stopping you?"

He shook his head. "Doubt I will make much of a living in the city if I have to start from nothing. I'm especially sure of that when I know there'll be a ton of smithers already working hard there."

Her voice softened. "You should still try."

"It's a nice thought but afraid I won't be able to."

Niyaa stared down at his symbol on the spade head, knowing he would be much happier away from there.

"Anyway," Erger said. "Prepare a handle mould while I light the furnace."

As she picked up one of the scrap agron pieces, she heard a familiar voice angrily shouting outside.

Erger stared at the entrance. "Keep working. I'll take a look." He rushed out into the misty rain, leaving Niyaa in the forge by herself.

Heaving the stone handle mould onto the hammering table, Niyaa recognised the furious voice and her eyes widened. She followed after Erger, her worried thoughts wondering what Governor Seveck would do about his things being taken.

Poking her head around the corner of the forge, she watched the governor scream at Kivy while Erger and several others gathered around them.

"...have no right! No right whatsoever to sell my belongings!" Governor Seveck shouted.

Kivy, in her usual bitter tone, replied, "And you ain't got a right to leave this place for the comforts of the city. You leave us 'ere with not a coin spare." She crossed her arms. "Wonder how much whiskey and buttered bread you scoffed with your elite buddies."

The man's eyes widened in anger. "How dare you accuse me of forsaking my duty, thief!" He glared at the others gathered around. "All of you did absolutely nothing as this woman robbed your governor. As far as I see, you're all just as guilty."

None of them responded, leaving only the gentle patter of the misty rain to break the silence.

"Some governor you are." Kivy scowled. "I reckon you left thinkin' the Beast Riders might come back."

Seveck gritted his teeth. "Return everything you stole, this instant"

She shook her head. "Not for a coward like you."

His hands clenched into tight fists. "Very well then." He walked away, heading towards Pelight's gate.

All eyes turned to Kivy as the governor marched from their sight.

Erger stepped towards her. "Seveck will not let this go unpunished."

She shrugged. "Doubt anyone will bother listening to a selfish coward like him." She turned to the others. "You lot should get back to work."

No words were spoken as the small group trickled back to their homes, workplaces and fields.

Erger's eye caught Niyaa's, and he sighed. "Let's finish that spade."

As she trudged back to the forge, a large, uneasy feeling took hold of Niyaa.

Not being allowed to leave the muster's square for most of the day, Vernon was overcome with sorrow as the sight of the emperor's death ceaselessly plagued his thoughts. Even as the silver-armoured guards searched his and Buckley's satchels, the sound of the mini crossbow lingered in his mind.

Vernon had followed Buckley away from the inner wall and returned to the Felliet embassy. Vernon looked at the grey shield emblem prominently displayed on the black crystal walls, and all of his dread turned to anger. Noticing an ornate brown carriage with leather-armoured soldiers guarding it, Vernon furiously realised yet another Erium noble wished to boast and laugh with Reethial. The arrogance of that elite knew no bounds.

Muscles tensed, Vernon followed Buckley inside and was guided by one of the grey-robed stewards to the elite's study. The door swung open to reveal Reethial sitting red faced behind his wide slate desk with the black crystal robe neatly folded before him. Surrounding him were brown-leathered bodyguards whose gloved hands firmly grasped their sword hilts. Surprised by the sight, Vernon turned to a tanned young man in dark brown armour standing by the crackling fireplace with Iyessa to his side.

The door shut behind the two students, and the unfamiliar man turned to them with a delighted grin. "Meyorter, Cendion, I understand you two came to work for Reethial Zenth at the same time the talented Iyessa Synthion did. Is that correct?"

Buckley replied, "We did."

Vernon, thinking they might be on trial, let out no words, answering only with a simple nod.

The man turned to Reethial with a disgusted look. "It is quite a tragedy this man's buffoonish audacity was one of the last things our glorious emperor saw."

His words stuck true for Vernon, who glared at the elite with a burning hatred.

The brown-armoured noble refused to move from the warmth of the fireplace as he turned to Iyessa. "My dear, could you tell us why this *elite* would be so bold as to cover himself in the symbol of our great nation? No less than in the great chamber before the emperor himself."

With a triumphant smirk, she turned at Reethial. "I remember he strongly expressed a foolish desire to be seen on the same level as the Imerial name."

"Quite a troubling notion." The noble turned to Vernon and Buckley. "Would you two be so kind as to share your thoughts about this lowlife who knows not his place."

Buckley's eyes narrowed at the man, and he stepped forward.

Vernon said, "This man is an ignorant fool and is an embarrassment for any nation." All of his hatred released itself as he turned to Reethial. "He lacks all humility and understands nothing of the wider world. Nor does he hold any passion for anyone or anything, instead choosing to spend his time and effort selfishly bragging about his possessions and titles." He returned his gaze to the brown-armoured man who wore a look of delighted surprise. "He did not deserve to take a step in the great chamber, let alone adorn himself with any piece of black crystal."

Reethial seethed at Vernon, and Buckley marched around the granite desk. Standing beside the elite, Buckley scowled at everyone in the room.

"Reethial is a proud member of the Zenth family, a family which flawlessly leads the Elite Dictorate. He has done many great things for Felliet and without question deserves … no, has the *right* to represent our great nation in the chamber." His voice and passion grew. "And I will say that anyone bearing the name Zenth *is* equal to the emperor's family and is superior to any other."

The red in Reethial's face faded as he looked at Buckley.

"I respect your loyalty." The man in brown armour stepped away from the fireplace. "However, you are greatly mistaken to place it in this man." He smirked at Reethial. "I spoke directly with your Dictorate, and they agree no one is on the same level as the emperor or his family."

Buckley and Reethial staggered back at this news.

The noble leaned on the desk. "When I heard Felliet's representative planned to wear black crystal in the great chamber, I felt it my duty to inform the leaders of your puny country." He placed his palm on the black crystal robe. "Such an elegant robe should *only* be worn by the most righteous person in all the—"

Reethial brought his fist down onto the desk. "You have no right to take it!"

A nearby bodyguard stepped closer, his hand firmly grasping his sword handle, and his leader gestured him back. "You are to return to Felliet with your title as representative forever removed."

The pathetic elite slumped back in his chair.

"This residence is permitted for Felliet's representative and accompanying stewards only." The noble turned to his bodyguards. "If you could escort Reethial Zenth and Buckley Cendion from the building."

The swordsmen marched closer to the two of them as the elite lifted himself from his seat. The two of them left the study, and Buckley gave a furious, betrayed glance towards Vernon, who smirked back.

Once the doors closed behind them, the man in brown armour returned to the warmth of the fireplace, turning his attention to Vernon. "I find it odd that you would speak so ill of him."

"I only spoke the truth," he replied.

The noble chuckled. "Then considering you were so honest about his shortcomings and the elites like him, I must ask where *your* loyalties lie?"

Only a single clear answer came to Vernon. "Since the fall of the Royals, only one of the four founding nations has truly sought to bring peace and prosperity to the world. It is undeniable that Felliet and its people would have greatly prospered had it stayed a part of Erium." He darted his eyes to the black crystal robe. "I choose to place my loyalty in the Imerial name."

Iyessa drifted her gaze to the dancing flames.

"Few outside of Erium would utter such words, fewer still born to foreign families." The man approached the desk, picking up the robe. "I believe such an insightful honest person would be wasted doing menial tasks for Felliet's elites. As such, I, Gallale Henite, the nobleman of the triplet pillars, shall offer you citizenship in our empire. You may spend your days here however you choose, and if anyone dare ask, you are a true man of Erium."

Vernon was overwhelmed with joy. "Thank ... thank you."

"It is always gratifying to hear someone speak so truthfully of the emperor's greatness and of those who wish him harm." Gallale moved towards the door. "You will be more than welcome to come to Trissiup if there is little else for you in Sidium."

He left the study with Iyessa closely following but avoiding Vernon's gaze. He was left utterly dazed in the midst of the study trying to comprehend the unbelievable great news. Joyous tears rolled down his cheeks.

Chapter fourteen – Sudden Journey

Seventh eclipse, first day

In dampened clothes, Jornis had marched along the flat coastal land, through the brisk night wind as he and Copias followed the tribowman. Yet no sense of anger coursed through his veins; instead, he felt an unusual relief during the arduous journey from Delport. As dawn broke on the vast flat landscape, the silent trio reached the Gildren camp.

Hundreds of gilded tents encircled a single narrow tower, yet foolishly no defensive perimeter of any kind surrounded the large camp, allowing them to march forward unhampered. Jornis observed with a growing sense of disgust that nearly all of the waking soldiers they passed were hungover. Each of them glanced bewilderedly at the three dampened strangers marching toward the centre of their camp.

Arriving before the oval command tent at the foot of the narrow tower, Jornis approached its two guards. "The town of Delport has been raided by the Rauders. We must speak with this army's commander."

The guards looked to one another, and one shook his head. "We can't just let anyone inside."

Jornis crossed his arms. "The council of Gildren have underestimated the Rauders, and their strategy has failed. The longer you deny us entry, the further attacks your towns will suffer."

The same guard glanced at Delport's tribowman and said, "Wait here."

Watching the guard disappear inside, Jornis turned his attention to the growing number of curious soldiers gathering around them.

Copias said, "Shame that we have to appear in these dirtied clothes."

"At least we're appearing at all," Jornis said with a contented smile he wiped away.

The guard returned from the tent. "You may enter."

Jornis stepped onto the reddened fabric that made the tent's floor. At an ornate oval table, a balding man in gilded chainmail sat opposite a pale man in orange silk. The latter leaned back in his copper seat. "You have something to report?"

"Rauders drew away the warship at Delport and raided the undefended town," Jornis explained as the two men glanced at one another. "Its citizens fled along the road. I cannot say where or in what condition."

The Delport tribowman stepped forward. "They may be seeking refuge in Towin."

"Most likely," the armoured man replied, rising from his chair. "Thank you for this information. You will find fresh clothes and food in the supply tent opposite."

Jornis kept his gaze focused on the chainmailed man. "If you wish to continue treating me and my partner like common messengers, then many opportunities will be squandered."

The man in orange silk leaned back in his seat, squinting at the two damp men. "Forgive me, but when you arrive before us in such attire, it is impossible to discern who you are from the regular rabble."

Ignoring the insult, Jornis sat at the end of the table. "I am Jornis Meyorter, former representative to Felliet and current diplomat of the Elite Dictorate."

The man in orange silk huffed. "You claim you are *that* Meyorter whose leaders so easily discarded?"

"They had already discarded much of their sense before that day," Jornis coldly replied.

Copias said, "But much has changed in our lands. The Dictorate is entirely different than in those days, and our industries are far stronger."

Jornis darted his eye to the gullible young man and returned his attention to the two seated men. "Much has changed in *all* our lands for the better and worse. Regarding that, I strongly believe yours will greatly worsen in the near future, if nothing is done."

The armoured man shrugged. "One raid does not spell disaster."

"Invasion would," Jornis said. "The Rauders were able to draw away the ship moored at Delport before launching an attack on the town. This implies they are not mindless beasts. Far from it, they are coordinated and understand your capabilities." He glanced at the tent entrance where he could hear the passing hungover soldiers. "I imagine you gathered this army here to organise which soldiers will go where. Unfortunately, this will only spread your forces thin, making for easy prey. Pulling troops from your aggressive northern and southern rivals will not end well."

The armoured man crossed his arms. "And what would you have us do?"

The silken man interjected, "Actually, we have important guests arriving in a couple of days. I believe it will be an ideal time to raise your suggestions then." He rose from his copper seat, gesturing to the tent entrance. "I suggest you take the time to find suitable clothing, *former* representative of Felliet."

Jornis held back his disdain for the man and stood. "It would certainly be interesting to see these guests of yours and *their* suggestions."

As Jornis turned towards the exit, the Delport tribowman stepped forward. "If I may ask, what will become of me? Am I to return to Delport?"

The man in gilded chainmail grinned. "I believe I have a task for you."

Jornis pulled back the entrance curtain and turned back to the young man standing still. "Are you coming, Copias?"

A surprised smile came upon the boy's face as he walked through the curtain Jornis held open.

Following him outside, Jornis pondered the young man's surprised expression and realised he had never spoken his name aloud before. Combining this with the events of last night, Jornis halted between the command and supply tent and slowly turned to the young man. "On the Delport battlements … I …" Jornis's gaze drifted away as a strange ache settled in his stomach. "Your actions were prompt and wise. Had you…" He hesitated.

"It is unnecessary to give further praise," Copias replied.

Jornis had no thought of what to say.

Copias turned to the supply tent. "Let us hope they have more than armour inside."

Unable to look at the young man, Jornis replied, "I expect Gildren's armies are supplied with plentiful spare outfits for their messengers." Following Copias inside, Jornis felt his stomachache worsen.

Standing in the midst of the vast crowd gathered in the muster's square, Vernon gazed up at the emperor's palace. Atop its soaring black tower burned a single pyre for all to see. It was truly a sorrowful day, yet Vernon heard only suspicious whispers from the nobles, priests and merchants around him, none of whom favoured the upcoming coronation. Instead, they muttered questions and rumours about how the emperor's brother was coincidently in the city yesterday or wondering whether he was even fit to rule. Vernon had a strong headache that only intensified as further influential people poured into the square.

Long into the proceeding, Vernon spotted Orfain in silk clothes pushing his way through the densely packed crowd.

Vernon walked up to him. "Didn't expect you to be here."

Orfain stopped and grinned. "But I expected you'd be 'ere." Orfain lowered his voice. "Lysia and I heard what happened to Reethial. Does that mean you're to leave Sidium?"

"I will never return to Felliet." Vernon smiled. "In fact, I am now a citizen of Erium."

Orfain grinned. "You work fast." He leaned closer. "In that case, would you be willing to help us expand the business opportunity you gave us?"

Vernon nodded. "It would be my pleasure." The crowd quietened as the first of the emperor's black chainmailed guards marched into sight. "Are we to meet in the same place after this?"

Orfain nodded, and the two of them turned their attention ahead.

The four advisors walked behind the guards, placing themselves before the black stairs, their stern expressions staring down at the crowd.

Orfain brought his mouth close to Vernon's ear. "Think one of 'em did it?"

Vernon's eyes widened at the ridiculous question, and he whispered back, "Why would you say that?"

"Just wondering." He shrugged. "So, who'd you think did it then?"

Vernon pondered the question for a while. "Anyone who fears a strong, decisive leader. The assassin would've been someone foreign, though I don't know which—" His words left him at the sight of the black crystal robe he had helped make being worn by Merchasious Imerial, the emperor to be.

"Would you look at that?" Orfain smirked.

With the black crystal glistening in the day's ambient sunlight, Merchasious marched to the pinnacle of the black staircase, standing between his four advisors.

Taken aback by the incredible sight, Vernon turned to the advisors and wondered which of them would announce the coronation. A prolonged silence came upon the vast crowd as everyone awaited the answer to the emperor's symbolic priority in his reign.

The supreme commander stepped forward. "Before you stands Emperor Merchasious Imerial, ruler of the people of Erium, final voice in the great chamber and leader of the strongest force in the world. Any who revel in his glory shall enjoy the prosperity his reign will bring. Those who wish misfortune upon his life and empire shall see a swift, merciless end."

He turned to the new emperor. "May the all-seeing mother guide his path to greatness."

An uncomfortable moment of hesitation hung in the air before the crowd erupted into an orchestral cheer. Vernon felt his heart proudly race at the rejoicing people surrounding him and gladly contributed his own voice.

Long after the emperor and advisors returned to the glorious palace, the crowd dispersed from the muster's square. The hushed rumours and whispers that had filled the air gave way to a mutual accepted silence.

Mind at ease, Vernon followed Orfain away from the inner wall, returning to the long, quiet tavern. Inside, Grayfern was sitting next to Lysia at the far table. Vernon sprinted to them. "It's great to see you."

The brawny man glared back. "Had it not been for you, the Welcomerry Band would still be intact."

Guilt and awkwardness overcame Vernon, leaving him unable to speak.

Lysia intervened. "Afraid none of us can change the past." She waved to Orfain. "Bring the Red Excen, would ya?"

"Will do," he replied.

Vernon tried to lift the mood. "I presume you're not going to hire a barman."

Grayfern leaned back. "Won't need one."

"I suppose now you're here, this tavern will function just fine." Vernon took the seat opposing them. "And the quietness of the area will make it ideal."

Lysia shrugged. "We would've preferred an obvious place along the main road, but when one is lacking choice one can't be fussy."

Vernon stared back. "Would a secluded place not be better?"

Orfain returned, placing a familiarly heavy cask heavily on the table. "Having a business packed with regular folk and the occasional guard makes for easy cover."

Lysia placed her hand on the cask tap. "Well, I'm sure we can make this place bustling in no time." Springing the top open revealed the container half filled with black crystal pieces. "There was a fair amount of unused pieces from that block we cut."

All the awkwardness faded as Vernon longingly stared at the glistening treasure.

Orfain put his arm around Vernon's shoulders and turned to Lysia. "Since this one's stayin' in Sidium, he ought to be part of this little business of ours."

She reached inside the cask and plucked a black crystal ring, setting it on the table. "We won't force you to help us. But if we are to forge jewellery for Erium's nobility, we feel your talents would—"

"I accept," Vernon interrupted. "I greatly want to see you three prosper in this city and especially if it's by sharing the symbol of Erium's greatness to the nobility governing its people. I honestly doubt I could think of a more perfect role."

Grayfern folded his arms. "And the payout has nothin' to do with it."

Vernon shook his head. "If I wanted coin, I would've thrown myself at becoming one of those despicable elites, and I certainly wouldn't have gone against Reethial." He turned back to Lysia. "Though I doubt I will be much help forging jewellery or finding buyers."

She grinned. "Which is why you will be personally selling to the people I scout. Also…" Lysia reached inside her pocket, took out a small purse and slid it across the table. "Almost forgot to give you your cut."

Vernon picked up the purse and felt a small stack of coins. "Thank you." He placed the purse inside his satchel. "Anyway what do you mean, people you scout?"

"The rich in this city love to visit plays, restaurants and luxurious stores," she explained. "I'll simply find and court the ones who would love wearing the symbol of Erium. At a fair price of course." She glanced at Orfain. "Plus if they want something specially crafted then we will arrange it."

Vernon pondered the scheme. "So how do you avoid getting caught selling to a lot of people?"

"A lot of *rich* people," Lysia corrected. "Few would question their fashion choices and fewer would question their sources."

Orfain added, "Plus I reckon I can make a few forgeries of black crystal that I can sell for basically nothing."

Vernon grinned. "Flood the underground market with fakes to hide the real thing."

"Exactly," Orfain said. "Though I'll have to give 'em to someone else to sell. Wouldn't want those rich folk thinking we're selling knock-offs."

"But have you found somewhere to store them?" Vernon asked.

Grayfern said, "This place is under my name now and can hide many goods … but the tracker might be a problem." The atmosphere at the table became tense as he explained to Vernon, "A couple days after what you did, a masked man in bronze armour turned up. He questioned everyone high 'n' low in the city, and somehow, he managed to find many of our buyers in Ellity."

Lysia added, "We heard he interrogated each of them with torches and whips before letting them go."

Vernon's body weakened as his guilt worsened.

Grayfern clenched his hands. "He even checked the safehouse along the wall. Though he thankfully didn't find the storeroom, he had a guard posted along the street there."

Orfain leaned his chair back. "Then there's hope he won't look for us here."

Lysia brushed the braid along her temple. "The priesthood never gives up in their hunt for…" She shook her head. "We can't change the past, so let's do what we can in the now."

Vernon stiffly picked up the ring. "Have you found someone to sell this to?"

She nodded.

Rattling chainmail, trotting hooves and marching boots sounded across the hilly landscape, encasing the Felliet soldiers in a stunned dread. Steadily marching towards their camp was the gargantuan invasion force with its vast array of differing armies followed by a multitude of supply wagons in colours of black, gold, brown and iron grey.

Iyna was fixated on the ten thousand men in black chainmail leading the force; paraded above each of their many tribow and sword units was a bronze-tipped black crystal perched atop an iron pole. A chill engulfed her as she compared Erium's army to Felliet's as even their cavalry trotting along the force's right flank numbered more than two thousand riders. The sheer number of men in black chainmail dwarfed the thousand gilded horsemen along the other flank as well as the two thousand brown-clothed macemen behind Erium's tribowmen. Only the five thousand grey fur-covered bowmen marching near the wagons seemed to stand out in the vast sea of black-armoured soldiers. The sight of it all filled Iyna with a depressing sense of the powerlessness.

The humongous force halted before the blue hill's base where Felliet's hundred-and-forty-strong army stood in formation. The commanders from the four armies galloped to them, and each halted their horses before Alexan.

"I am Nelthan Huljis, commander of Erium's principal army," the rider in black chainmail said. "But I must say that I am truly grateful to finally meet you, Alexan Brige. Had it not been for you and your men, Fyoreten would have attacked many more in this region."

The female commander in thick brown cloth added, "They wouldn't have attacked at all had Erium thought not to conquer them."

The Erium commander turned to her. "Does Artor object to this conflict?"

"Not at all." She shrugged. "It's as good excuse as any for my men to see a real fight."

The man in grey furs scoffed. "A real fight is waiting to pounce on an enemy at their weakest. This is merely a mindless one-sided assault."

Alexan turned to Myklinn's greater commander. "At least it will bring this war to a swift end." He addressed the other three. "I suggest Felliet be placed at the rear of the armies, to cover the archers and tribowmen."

"I was to propose the same thing," the Erium commander replied, turning to the other commanders. "Are we in agreement?"

The woman in brown grinned. "It would be good knowing someone held the rear, especially since I hear the Fyoreten are fond of surprise attacks."

"Agreed," the Myklinn commander said.

All eyes turned to the gilded rider who stared judgingly at Alexan till he finally spoke. "I hope you prove Felliet worthy."

Alexan smirked. "And I hope Gildren proves itself more than a bunch of wealth-obsessed merchants."

Without another word, the Gildren commander steered his horse away and galloped back to his horsemen.

The Artor woman respectfully nodded to Alexan. "Good luck in the upcoming fight." She left for her army, followed by the man in grey furs.

Once they were out of earshot, the Erium commander turned to Alexan. "A friend of mine lives near here, and after I was told my superiors would not replenish his small garrison, I worried the Fyoreten would attack his town." Nelthan steered his horse towards his gargantuan black army. "I truly meant what I said about being grateful to you and your army."

Watching him ride away, Iyna wondered whether the rulers of Erium even cared about their own people.

Alexan turned around, facing each of his unit leaders. "We are to guard the rear of the invasion force. Tarrow, have your tribows march ahead. Orbert, Barcial and Iyna, have your spears following closely behind with a keen eye on our rear." He turned ahead and raised his voice. "March forth."

Iyna glanced at her unit whose faces were filled with anxious dread and repeated the order. "March forth."

Staring out of the mill's window, Niyaa watched the blue and green stars twinkling away in the night sky as the gentle breeze brushed against her face. The sound of only a few voices at the gate left the village nice and quiet.

Her mom said, "Dinner's nearly ready."

A scrumptious pot of dandelion stew was bubbling away. Niyaa picked up her clay bowl and sat beside the turning mill column.

Darryam sniffed the stew. "Smells nice. Did you add chickweed?"

"You'll have to find out." Mysia smirked.

The sound of glass breaking outside drew their attention.

Darryam shrugged. "Probably just some drunkard."

Niyaa turned away from the window and handed her mom her bowl. "Today I thought about making some kind of symbol on my work."

"A symbol, huh?" Mysia asked, filling the bowl.

"Yeah, Erger says all the best smithers do them," Niyaa explained, taking the bowl and bringing it close to her nose to breathe in the vibrant vegetal stew.

Darryam smiled. "So what kind of symbol do you want to make?"

"I don't know," Niyaa said, blowing on her spoonful of stew. "Maybe flowers coming out of a furnace?"

Mysia joked, "And why not coming out of one of our tankards?"

Darryam chuckled. "Yeah, exactly. You could spread the word about our brewery business."

Niyaa grinned. "Think it has to be related to smithery."

Mysia filled her husband's bowl. "In that case, why not make it a symbol about forging a cask of ale or—"

A shout outside quietened the three of them.

Darryam rushed to the window. "Some brawl perhaps?"

Mysia set aside the dinner and stepped closer to her husband. The mill's door burst open below. Niyaa ran to the ladder and saw two unfamiliar soldiers barging inside. They grabbed the agron brewing pot.

Darryam rushed to her side, yelling at them, "What do you think you're doin'?"

The soldiers hardly glanced back as they took the brewing pot outside.

"Niyaa, you wait here," Darryam told her before climbing down.

Mysia followed, leaving her daughter anxiously standing in the mill as she heard other doors breaking. She rushed to the window and watched as other soldiers broke into homes and workplaces throughout Pelight, hauling out all kinds of pots, pans, tools, cutlery and other agron items. Each of them carried the stuff towards the gate, where Niyaa spotted a large cart with a growing pile of green metal. One of the soldiers used his spear handle to shove aside an elderly man clinging to an agron lantern in his doorway. Without thinking, Niyaa ran to the ladder and followed after her parents.

Running along the dirt street passing homes being looted with frightful shrieks filling her ears, she reached the cart. She hid herself around a shadowy corner of a building and spotted her parents yelling at the handful of soldiers surrounding the cart. Staring at the pile of agron in the cart, she saw her family's brewing pot. A soldier tossed a spade onto it, denting its side.

Niyaa gritted her teeth at the sight and spotted the governor with a bunch of soldiers, escorting Kivy in shackles.

"Put her inside," the governor ordered and turned to Darryam and Mysia.

Darryam loudly asked, "What is the meaning of this?"

"I thought that would be clear." Seveck crossed his arms. "You all did nothing while this vile woman stole my belongings. As such, I seek immediate repayment."

Mysia pointed to the brewing pot. "Then how much for that? We will gladly work it off."

The governor looked at her with disdain. "You think it would be so easy to get away with thievery?"

Darryam furiously stepped towards him, and the bodyguards came between them. Niyaa's dad glanced at each of the spears in their hands and took a deep breath. "What happened was the result of a few and not the whole village. If you want to maintain your image, then you must—"

"I will not let thieves go unpunished!" Seveck shouted back. "And as far as I have seen, the *entire* village allowed my possessions to be taken away! You all will be punished accordingly."

Niyaa nervously watched as Governor Seveck's face reddened with rage at her dad.

Darryam shook his head. "Don't punish the people like this. Just let them work for the items taken instead of—"

"I damn well intend to!" Seveck interrupted. "After I sell this junk for the pitiful amount it's worth, I intend to make every one of you work till your legs give way."

"But why?" Mysia asked. "We haven't done anything to you."

The governor glared at her. "This is to send a message to everyone in this rotten place that *I* am in control. That whatever orders I give, you will follow." He paused for a moment and turned back to Darryam. "Perhaps it's best you help me spread that message." Seveck glanced at his soldiers. "Have him sold to the Atimah as well!"

Stunned, Darryam turned to the soldiers advancing on him. "What? No, I—"

One of the soldiers hit his stomach with the back end of his spear, bringing Darryam wheezing to the ground. Niyaa sprinted towards them.

Mysia grabbed Seveck's arm. "You'll anger everyone by doing this!"

"Good." He yanked his arm free. "Perhaps then you will learn who is really in charge."

The soldiers pulled Darryam to his feet before Niyaa reached him. She grabbed his hand tight and shouted at the governor, "Don't take him away!"

Seveck scoffed. "Do you wish to join him?"

Niyaa stared at him, utterly defeated. Her dad's hand brushed through her hair. "It's … it's gonna be fine." She slowly turned to him and saw a forced smile beneath his watery eyes. He turned to his wife. "I … I'm gonna miss you both so much."

Niyaa gripped his hand tighter. "Please don't go."

Tears came down his cheeks.

Mysia embraced him too, her voice choking up. "I love you, so … so much."

One of the soldiers grabbed Darryam's arm, yanking him away from his family, and he tearfully said, "I love you both so much."

Shackles enclosed around his wrists, and he was shoved into the cart alongside Kivy.

"Take them from my sight," Seveck demanded.

Grief overwhelming her, Niyaa watched the cart wheels turn.

Few clouds had gathered in the night sky above, yet throughout the march, the air had been filled with the sound of so much rattling chainmail and metal that anyone could've easily mistaken it as rain. Worsening Iyna's feeling of powerlessness was that the sheer mass of men, armour and carts travelling ahead of Felliet's army meant she couldn't even see what lay ahead. It was only when she glimpsed the dark silhouette of Iorden's rooftops that she finally knew where she was.

The vast force slowed as they neared the border river, no doubt to allow them all to cross the stone bridge in a calm manner. Waiting at the back of the enormous invasion force, Iyna's thoughts returned to the sight of the inferno engulfing the town. She caught a faint scent of ash and rotten meat hanging in the air.

Stepping onto the stone bridge, she overheard the Erium tribowmen ahead saying the scouts had reported the town abandoned. An insufferable guilt swelled in Iyna's stomach, and she heard breaths of relief and cheer from her unit. She turned back, scornfully silencing their joy. "We are still marching into enemy territory. Keep your wits about you." She watched as their relief faded. She caught a glimpse of Barcial clutching his stomach as he led his unit alongside hers.

Stepping off the stone bridge, Iyna watched the armies ahead scatter into the darkened town, clearing the way for her to see ahead. Her eyes widened as she spotted rotting bodies littering every space along the scorched streets, filling the gentle breeze with a nightmarish decaying stench.

The Erium and Artor soldiers rushed ahead, breaking into the blackened buildings and leaving the bowmen, horsemen and wagons behind.

Alexan turned to his army. "Tarrow, prepare a pyre. The rest of you, defend the bridge."

Iyna spotted a small line of familiar bodies lying near the edge of the town, and she turned away. Seeing the faces of her unit staring at the horrific streets before them, she quietly ordered, "Keep your faces on the rear."

They turned their aghast faces to her.

"During our assault on this town, the Fyoreten ambushed us from that bridge." Every pair of eyes glanced back to the empty stone bridge. "We are here now to ensure the same thing does not happen again." Iyna glanced at the single Felliet supply cart pulled by a couple of Tarrow's tribowmen. "We'll form a barricade with our barrels and sacks. Tyria and Mayfern, scout underneath the bridge. Everyone else start unloading the cart.

Of her unit, only Feeliath seemed reluctant to head for the supply cart.

Iyna glanced at her spear and turned back to the line of Felliet bodies lying near the main street. Barcial was approaching Darius's body. She went to help him build a pyre.

Chapter fifteen – Power Dynamic

Seventh eclipse, third day

For two miserable nights, the soldiers slept and ate in the ruins of Iorden with the unending stench of decay and rot lingering long after the many pyres died down. When the march on Fiskior began, it came as almost a relief to the armies.

However, as midday neared, the green spiked ramparts of Fiskior appeared on the horizon ending any feelings of relief. Erium scouts had informed the entire invasion force that Fyoreten had amassed nearly the entirety of their troops in the capital, meaning there would be no negotiation or compromise.

Nearing the city, Iyna took her shield from her back and turned to her unit. "Prepare yourselves."

Each had the same nervous and fearful look as they slung their shields from their backs. Only Feeliath was slow readying his shield and spear as he glanced bitterly at Iyna.

Not long after, Erium's gargantuan army spread wide, swordsmen raising their triangular black iron shields ahead of their tribowmen who began cranking. The many supply wagons of the four massive armies split up, placing themselves on the flanks between the archers and horses, leaving covered wagons at the back. One of those wagons unfurled its covering, revealing a strange iron square platform lined with solid railings on which stood two unarmoured men. Iyna's heart raced as she watched scaling ladders being unpacked from two other wagons. The central wagon unfurled its covering, revealing a large ballista ram.

Erium's swordsmen and Artor's macemen were standing with shields raised outside the wall's crossbow range with ladders in hand, and the ballista ram had been pushed to the front line, its hefty cord drawn back. All that was left was the single messenger futilely sent to issue demands before the city's iron-plated gate.

Staring through the numerous soldiers, Iyna managed to glimpse the messenger return from the gate, and her breath deepened at the impending assault.

The Erium commander trotted to the strange iron platform behind the Myklinn archers and Erium tribowmen and said something to the men inside before returning to the centre of his army. The two platform men undid clamps at the platform's four corners, and Iyna watched as the iron square rose into the air with a thin silvery thread connected to the wagon below. She stared up at it in disbelief as the platform rose as high as a wall tower before the thread became taught, halting the square without a single wobble from the wagon below.

Alexan raised his voice. "Form a shield wall away from the assault! Our role is to protect the rear from any surprise attacks!"

Iyna turned her back to the city and ordered her speechless unit. "Form a shield wall." She watched her unit rush into the practiced rows and walked around it, ensuring the locked shields were tight. Entering the lead position, Iyna stared through the tiny gap in the shields at the hilly, canopy-ridden landscape as a familiar unease settled in.

She heard Tarrow order her tribowmen to take aim at the city ramparts, and Iyna glanced over her shoulder just as the Erium commander raised his sword for all to see. Nelthan pointed the blade at the city. "Slow march forth!"

With a rattle of chainmail and shields, the swordsmen advanced with the tribowmen close behind till Iyna heard the sound of crossbow bolts pelting shields across the entire frontline.

Nelthan shouted a second order. "Volley!"

A thunderous applause of thousands of tribow strings snapping at once rang loudly in Iyna's ears, followed by the cavalcade of their bolts sharply striking every foot of the stone wall. A long while later, the volley faded to the sound of cranking.

The Myklinn commander raised his fur-covered arm for his bowmen to see. "Quick draw!"

Thousands of arrows flew through the air at the ramparts, arching over the advancing swordsmen and rapidly plinking at the ramparts. The ballista ram neared Fiskior's gate, and the macemen charged forth with their own ladders, passing the black-armoured swordsmen in a mad dash through the sporadic hail of crossbow bolts.

"That's not our fight!" Alexan yelled, turning Iyna's attention to him. "Keep your gaze facing away."

She pried her gaze away from the assault to the nothingness she could barely see through the shields. The sounds of battle cries and pain-filled screams overwhelmed the clamour of exchanging bolts and arrows. Helplessly listening to the sounds, Iyna gritted her teeth.

The ballista ram snapped its limbs, crashing the ram head into the gate with a thunderous ringing sound. One of the floating platform observers cried out, "Fyoreten riders on the right flank!"

Iyna turned but saw nothing through the wagons and dark horses on the right side of the archers. Nelthan galloped to his cavalry, ordering them to give chase. The ground shook as the Erium horsemen rode fast, and another tribow volley followed, drowning out the sound of hooves beating the ground.

An unbelievable long moment later, the cranking restarted, and Iyna glanced around at the empty landscape before her, desperately trying to spot any Fyoreten ambushers. She spun her gaze towards the right flank, as in the wake of the pursuing Erium riders, she realised only the wagons were defending the right side of the tribowmen. She turned ahead, staring through the small gap in the shields at the many canopies dotted across the hilly landscape. Her heart pounded, and she looked up at the two observers in the floating platform. One kept his gaze on the distant Erium cavalry while the other focused only on the assault.

Without thinking, Iyna sprinted away from her shield wall towards the floating platform's wagon, stopping just short of the surrounding guards and shouting up to them, "Look to the rear!" The two observers didn't seem to bother looking down.

Alexan's shield hand furiously grabbed her shoulder. "What are you doing?"

"I think they were a distraction," Iyna said. "Remember how in the first and second battle they had a group lying in ambush?"

"Would those riders not have been them this time?" he asked.

Iyna shook her head. "They would've known this invasion force was coming the moment it was formed." She pointed her spear towards the deserted wagons. "I think they planned to have a small group show themselves to lure away the Erium horses, leaving everyone exposed on the right side." She glanced ahead and saw the swordsmen and macemen climbing ladders wedged in the moat, battling with the defenders along the entire rampart as friendly arrows and bolts arched into the city itself. The ballista ram smashed into the gate again, breaking off the last of its iron plates. Iyna said, "They knew they would be greatly outnumbered, so they must've come up with *some* plan to save themselves."

Alexan glanced to the tribowmen and archers and to the undefended wagons. "So you believe they have a second force waiting to strike at our vulnerable right flank?"

"I do," Iyna confidently replied.

"Very well." Alexan turned to the observers above. "I am the commander of Felliet's first army. We believe a second group of horsemen lies to the north or northwest."

Iyna breathed in relief as she noticed the observers finally paying attention.

"Keep a keen eye on any movement in those directions," Alexan added and marched back to his army. "Tarrow! Have your tribows lined up at the wagons along the right flank. Use the barrels and crates inside them to form barricades!"

She hesitated at the sudden command but swiftly obeyed.

He turned to Barcial and Orbert. "Have your spears follow the line of wagons diagonally to cover the rear corner of the armies! I'll go to Myklinn's commander and have his bowmen protect the rear in our stead." He turned to Iyna. "Well done realising their trap. Now go set up your shield wall alongside Barcial and Orbert."

She sprinted back to her unit, saying, "A Fyoreten attack is coming! Follow me to the right flank." They turned to one another in the cramped rows, so she furiously added, "Do as I say, and we may yet live!"

Slowly at first, they broke apart the shield wall and followed Iyna to the right flank with the other two spear units close behind. As they reached the wagons, a faint horn blast carried across the wind, and their pace quickened.

Upon reaching the edge of the wagon line, she yelled to her unit, "Shield wall, now!"

The ballista ram smashed apart Fiskior's gate with a loud crash. A river of black-armoured swordsmen charged forth, slamming into the defenders through the broken gate. It became a dense clash in the opened gateway as Erium and Fyoreten soldiers viciously threw themselves at each other, both sides trying to control the breach. The ramparts seemed overwhelmed with Erium and Artor soldiers, routing the crossbowmen entirely.

Glancing at the Erium tribowmen still cranking, Iyna spotted Alexan speaking with Myklinn's commander. Returning her gaze ahead, she realised the spears in her shield wall were quivering with fear.

"Reaffirm your grasp" she told them as her own heart pounded in her chest. "So long as we stand together, we can take on any charge." Iyna noticed all their eyes desperately looking at her, so she smiled. "You lot were the guardsmen of Milnet, the ones who fearlessly stopped a bunch of Beast Riders from slaughtering your people. Prove to me now your strength and courage."

Their spear points steadied as they brought their eyes forward.

One of the observers from the floating platform cried out, "Riders approaching from the rear right."

Glimpsing the oncoming Fyoreten horsemen through the tiny hole in the shields, Iyna tightened her grip on her spear and deepened her breath. "Keep the shields tight and you *will* see the next sunrise."

She felt the faint tremor of oncoming hooves and sighted a horde of perhaps three hundred axe-wielding riders charging towards a force less than half their size. She glanced to her sides once again and, seeing the fear return across their faces, told them, "These men will cut down anyone who tries to flee. To survive, you *must* stand your ground."

Her words seemed pointless as the sunlight shimmered off the riders' raised axes, causing the spearpoints to tremble once more. Iyna's muscles stiffened and her breathing quickened as she saw the oncoming horde bear down.

A deafening sound of thousands of bowstrings snapped behind her, and the landscape ahead rained with arrows onto the oncoming horsemen. As horse and rider screams echoed across the landscape, Iyna glanced back and saw the Myklinn bowmen releasing another volley, with Alexan standing beside their fur-covered commander. Tarrow's tribowmen released their bolts from the line of wagons, and many of the horsemen fell, greatly slowing their charge.

"We aren't alone!" she yelled. "We have nothing to fear of them!"

The trembling of the spearpoints vanished as the sound of further volleys arched overhead, felling many more riders and tripping others. The Fyoreten charge spread their horses wide as they bore closer to the shields. Iyna realised they weren't retreating or turning.

She tightened her grip and tensed her body. "Brace yourselves!"

Iyna's breath frantically panted till the frontal horses slammed into the shield wall and wagon line, filling the air with horse squeals and battered shields. Iyna was thrown on her back as she stabbed a horse trying to leap over the shield wall. The dead creature collapsed on its front legs far beyond the line of spearmen as several other horses crashed through the walls, leaving the rest pushing against the shields.

Regaining her senses, Iyna felt a sharp pain pulsate in her shield arm. Upon sitting up, she saw many of the Fyoreten riders thrown from their saddles across the line of shields as many other horses behind them tried to push through. Almost all the spearmen had retracted their spears as they tried to push against the Fyoreten. The wagons were a mess of panic-stricken horses crippled over makeshift barricades that Tarrow's unit madly released bolts upon, trying to keep them at bay.

Realising her spear was still stuck in the horse's chest, Iyna rushed to her feet. The rider, who had also been thrown far back, had gotten to his feet. The man staggered towards the back of her unit, shortaxe firmly in hand, and she charged at him with pain throbbing through her shield arm as she raised the heavy metal to her chest.

The man raised his shortaxe and charged at her. She leaned back, letting his axe swing miss, and brought her shield smack against his head, toppling him onto the ground. A sharp pain rang through her battered arm. The man tried to swing his axe at her legs. Jumping back, she stared down at the man, tightening her grip on the shield.

Without thinking, she stomped forward, dodging another desperate swing and stepped on his axe arm. Iyna brought her shield down on his head, bloodying his face, and slammed it down again, then again, then again, until no feeling of resistance remained in his body.

She got to her feet and rushed to pull her spear from the dead horse. Her shield wall was bulging from the sheer weight of the pushing horsemen, and she sprinted towards them.

She thrust her spear through the gap where her shield had been, stabbing at a dismounted rider, and locked her shield in place, pushing back.

The sound of hooves beating the ground behind her made her glance back. She relaxed as she spotted the Gildren cavalry circling around the shield walls towards the Fyoreten. No longer hearing the foot soldiers assaulting the city, Iyna realised those riders had only just heard what was happening.

One by one the Fyoreten axemen scattered, till each was running in a desperate retreat. Feeling no further push against her wall, Iyna let her shield arm wearily drop to her side and watched the Gildren horses pass them by, pursuing the fleeing Fyoreten.

A relieved breath came from every Felliet soldier as they relaxed their exhausted bodies. The bloodied ramparts and gatehouse were empty as the swordsmen and macemen moved uncontested inside. She glanced at the rider she had pummelled into the dirt and turned back to the Felliet spearmen. Incredibly all of them were still standing.

Feeliath wearily raised his spear to the sky. "We have victory."

A sickening feeling engulfed Iyna's stomach.

Silence hovered over the oval table, for none of the seven siloin commanders gathered in the Gildren tent dared to speak in the presence of a foreigner without their host present. Many suspicious glances were directed at Jornis, clothed in purple silk. Rather than responding to such foolish distrust, the elite instead kept his attention to the map laid across the oval table.

Staring at the numerous towns and cities spread across the vast coastline, Jornis couldn't help but notice the pitiful development inland. Why hadn't the counsel of Gildren invested into a suitably large navy? Remembering the discussion he'd had with Copias, he realised constructing more ports to house extra warships would have disrupted the silk industry. He sighed at the shortsightedness of it.

The balding commander for the Silk Shores entered, stepping into the flickering light in full gilded chainmail. He had a grim expression as he passed his peers and took his seat at the far end of the oval table.

Avoiding eye contact with Jornis, the grim-faced commander said, "It is good you all came on such short notice. As some of you are aware, the town of Delport was recently attacked and looted, leaving little of its industry intact. I have thus sent three hundred of my men to bolster its defences and replenish its moth nests, but it is now undeniable that this threat must be dealt with as soon as possible."

The man sitting to his immediate right stroked his trimmed beard. "The Velvet Enclave has just finished constructing its warden, completing the final unstoppable vessel. We should expect to be rid of these seafaring pests before long. I see no reason why we must concern ourselves about this issue any further." He glanced at Jornis. "Nor do I see how a Felliet diplomat could be of use to us."

All eight gilded commanders turned to Jornis as he explained to the bearded fool, "Unlike you, I was there to witness the Rauder attack. I saw how they drew away the *unstoppable* vessel and watched them skip across the water like a disc stone, taking the town of Delport by surprise." He turned to the balding Silk Shores commander. "To counter these attacks, you need to divert the Rauders away from your coast while easing tensions with Artor and Myklinn Greater."

The bearded commander scoffed. "And how do you propose we divert them away when we cannot even communicate with these creatures, let alone meet with them?"

The Marble Wheels commander seated beside Jornis joked, "You mean the Rauders or Myklinn Greater?"

His pointless babble faded in an awkward silence, and the Silk Shores commander turned to the elite. "What is your proposal?"

"We need not meet with the Rauders to lead them away." Jornis leaned across the table, bringing his attention to the map. "I advise the construction of unmanned beacons along your coastline, each displaying a detailed map of the federation's coast. We should depict Gildren as having an impressive army inland while depicting the Radiant Republic as both undefended and prosperous."

Half the armoured men seemed to seriously consider the plan while the others seemed dismissive.

The bearded man asked, "Wouldn't that give these monsters precise locations of our towns and cities?"

The Marble Wheels commander replied, "If they can lure away our ships, they already know where our cities and towns are located. Furthermore, we need not depict the inland cities nor mention Gildren is a collection of separate siloins." He turned to Jornis. "But why the Radiant Republic and not Artor?"

"While I did consider it," Jornis lied, "I realised it would only lead Artor to bolster their navy in much the same way you have. Not to mention their cliffs and narrow island passes would prove difficult targets to raid."

The Silk Shores commander added, "Furthermore, if they were to learn of this ploy, it would undoubtedly cause *problems*."

The bearded man folded his arms. "I admit there is little to lose with this idea."

The tent fell silent as the commanders stared at the map in consideration. The Marble Wheels commander said, "These beacons would need lanterns or a firepit which will need to be kept lit throughout the night."

The Silk Shores commander leaned back in his chair. "My esteemed engineer will provide the design and requirements."

In the midst of the deliberation, an exhausted messenger rushed inside, drawing everyone's attention, and marched to the far end of the table to whisper in the host's ear.

Shock showed on the commander's face. "You've done well bringing this news. You may go and rest."

The exhausted messenger graciously nodded and left.

The Silk Shores commander leaned forward, stroking his clean-shaven chin. "Emperor Anisious Imerial has been assassinated in the great chamber, and his brother now holds power."

The tent fell silent as the commanders turned to one another, unsure of what to say.

Jornis rose from his seat. "I believe you all will have much to discuss regarding this urgent matter, so I will take my leave." Without a further word, Jornis turned and left the tent.

Copias was waiting outside, and Jornis told him, "Walk with me."

Leaving the presence of the tent bodyguards, Copias asked, "Did they agree to your plan?"

"Yes, however they now need to address an even larger matter." Jornis waited till no soldiers were passing them before quietly explaining, "Emperor Anisious was assassinated."

"What?" Copias blurted out and lowered his voice. "Who did it?"

"The messenger didn't say, so clearly no one knows yet." Jornis pondered the likely suspects but pushed such tangential thoughts from his mind. "What matters is how this new emperor acts on the Federal Throne."

Anxiety crept across Copias's face, an expression Jornis couldn't fault.

Opening her eyes to the mill's dull ceiling, Niyaa lay on the straw heap blackly staring up at nothing. A bowl of warm soup was placed next to her, and slowly she turned her gaze.

"Your dad wouldn't want to see you like this," Mysia said, crouching beside her.

Niyaa rolled on her side, facing the blank wall.

Mysia gently brushed her daughter's hair. "I miss him too."

Niyaa's eyes watered. "Why did he have to be taken away?"

No answer came.

Niyaa turned to her mom. "I don't know what to do."

Mysia grasped her daughter's hand. "The only thing we *can* do is to keep moving forward." She looked down. "If we stop now, we wouldn't be able to carry on."

"But without Dad…" Niyaa felt her voice croak and noticed her mom's saddened eyes.

"I know it'll be hard without him," Mysia said. "But we must keep going for our sake and his. If he were to return and see you giving up, what would he think?"

"But he's not coming back," Niyaa replied.

"I'm sure he will," Mysia said, faking an optimistic smile. "You just have to keep hoping."

Niyaa sighed. "That won't do any good."

"Nor will staying cramped up in here," Mysia said, nudging the bowl of soup closer to her daughter. "We both need to keep our strength."

Niyaa forced herself to sit up and drank the soup.

Her mom scooped her own bowl from the last pot they had. "Make sure you fill your stomach. There's plent…" She stopped herself. "I made some extra today."

Niyaa glanced at the empty third bowl sitting motionless beside the bubbling pot, and a wave of weakness overcame her body, making the rest of the soup even harder to swallow.

Shortly afterwards, Niyaa reluctantly stepped outside, her eyes bombarded by the bright midday sun as she walked towards the forge, leaving her mom to go to the fields. Trudging along the dirt streets, Niyaa passed several weary farmers, who all, like her, held their heads low. Governor Seveck had truly rid all hope and joy from this place

Entering the forge, she widened her eyes, for nearly all the tools and agron pieces were gone, even the little quartz engraver. Erger stood red faced before the simmering furnace, staring longingly at the melting green cutlery.

"What happened?"

"What'd you think?" he furiously muttered. "That *leader* of ours took pretty much everythin'."

Niyaa walked to the empty shelves and realised most of the moulds were also missing. "Is there anything left?"

He picked up a hammer lying beside him and pointed it to a handle mould by the hammering bench. "Our thoughtful governor decided to let us keep one mould, a pair of the tongs and a single hammer."

Niyaa leaned against the empty shelves in defeat, unable to think of something to say.

Erger sighed. "Afraid I won't be staying here for much longer."

Niyaa wasn't surprised.

He avoided looking at her. "All honesty, I didn't want to leave you alone to tend this forge again, but I just can't stand it here any longer." His hands became tight fists. "I should never have left Ellity."

Niyaa felt her body collapse against the shelves as she remembered the awful time she'd had working by herself.

"You can hate me if you want," he mumbled. "I know I would in your place."

"I don't hate you," she replied. Anger gripped her body. "What I hate is this place. So *so* very much."

"Well…" He turned to her. "When you're older and can travel places, I would be glad to see you in the city." He smiled. "Just look for my mark."

"I will." She forced a smile. "Perhaps one day you could look for my mark."

He nodded. "I'd like that."

Following the waitress past the numerous midday patrons to the prebooked table along the glass-roofed balcony, Vernon pondered the words he would say to the noblewoman. After ordering a sage tea, he glanced to the chefs filleting alkrays and sautéing wild vegetables for all to see. The patrons filling the other tables were of all classes. Vernon smiled at the unifying sight and thought of how he would present the ring to the scouted noblewoman.

Taking a sip of the herbal tea, he spotted the noblewoman enter following the same waitress. She took the chair opposite him. "Pleasure to meet you Vernon Meyorter."

"The pleasure is mine, Tillia Sellice," he replied and turned to the waitress. "Could I have the Alkray?"

"Certainly," the waitress said, turning to the noblewoman.

"Just mint tea for me," Tillia politely said.

Waiting for the waitress to leave, Vernon glanced at the black, glistening street. "Such a wonderous city this is."

She took a sip of her tea. "Afraid neither of us came for simple chatter."

"Very well," Vernon said, taking the ring from his pocket and placing it gently on the table.

She smiled and longingly stared at its glistening black surface. "It has quite a remarkable shine, does it not?"

"It perfectly reflects the glorious name of Imerial," he said.

She dated her eyes at him. "And what would you know of the Imerial name?"

Vernon grinned. "I know much of Erium's proud history and the prosperity the line of emperors has ensured for all its citizens." Vernon glanced again at the city landscape with a slight smile. "Without the Imerial name to guide the nobles and people, Erium would not be the glorious empire it is today."

Sellice stared back. "You would say the emperor guides the nobility?"

"There must always be a single voice, a single leader to make decisions for a nation," Vernon argued. "If every noble acted in their own way and freely governed the way they saw fit, the vast Empire of Erium would immediately shatter into a hundred squabbling states. In short, without the emperor to guide everyone from above, there would be anarchy."

She grimaced and took a sip of tea, relaxing a little. "As a noble myself, I have to believe my duties are vital to the empire and my actions, though small, contribute to the empire's wealth and glory. However, I greatly admire your loyalty to the emperor." She smiled and took out a small coin purse. "Your partner told me the ring would cost six bronze, but if you allow me, I would be glad to pay eight."

"That won't be necessary," Vernon replied. "I simply wish to see the symbol of greatness worn by as many of the truly righteous people as possible."

Her smile grew. "I must say, you are far from what I expected of a Felliet elite."

"Actually," Vernon corrected, "on the final day of the sixth eclipse I was nominated a citizen of Erium."

Surprise filled her expression. "I see."

The grilled Alkray dish arrived, brightening Vernon's mood as the delicious scent of the river fish wafted to his nose.

Sellice turned to the waitress. "I've changed my mind. May I have a salad with a side of sweetened oatcake?"

"Certainly," the waitress replied, taking her leave.

The noblewoman turned back to Vernon with a delighted smile. "Well you may rest assured, the ring shall be worn often."

Chapter sixteen – Consequences

Seventh eclipse, fifth day

As the sun rose over the flat landscape, the entire Gildren camp was a hustle of dismantling tents and loading wagons. Surrounded by the organised fervour, Jornis and Copias followed the Silk Shores commander far past the single tower. It was quite remarkable to see the swiftness in which the siloin commanders agreed on the number and placement of these future garrisoning soldiers, especially as each siloin was different in both population and land.

Before long, the gilded chainmailed commander glanced over his shoulder. "The engineer is not too far away now."

Copias asked, "Afraid I don't understand why you would show us to him as I thought Gildren's engineers were highly renowned and sought after."

"They most certainly are," the armoured man replied. "However, the idea of the beacons came from you both. It would be a wasted opportunity not to have you meet him while you are here."

Jornis pondered whether this was instead a plan to improve relations between Felliet and Gildren, or perhaps ideally, himself and Gildren. Either way, he grinned with pride as he knew the plan was progressing.

"We're here," the Silk Shores commander said, arriving at a large tent surrounded by guards.

Inside, numerous sketches, models, and weapon parts cluttered across every chest, drawer and worktable that filled the large interior. Standing in the midst of this cramped disorder was an unkempt man drawing three rings of increasing size.

The commander stepped towards him. "Roudal. Do you have the beacon diagram?"

"Yes, yes," the engineer dismissively said, keeping his gaze on the drawing before him.

"Well?"

Roudal walked further into the tent and searched through a pile of diagrams left haphazardly on the floor.

Copias glanced at the rings he drew. "Are these supposed to be some kind of cart wheel?"

The engineer excitedly turned to him. "No, no, definitely not, my dear boy." He plucked out a large drawing of a scaffolding-like tower and rushed back to the three-ringed sketch. "This will hopefully be my recreation of an ice eye."

Copias stared wide eyed at him. "Will it work?"

"Of course it will." Roudal stretched his hand past miniature models of crossbows and tribows. He pulled out a set of three rusted rings attached them upright to a mould-spotted leather bracer.

Jornis stared at the devastating weapon as a sickening feeling gripped his stomach.

Copias grew excited at the captured weapon. "Will this shoot frost water then?"

"Well…" Roudal hesitated. "I still haven't figured out how the Radiant Republic made the frost water or how they make these ice eyes send them hurtling out. But I assure you I will find out soon enough."

The Silk Shores commander said, "Can you make that work *after* you show us the beacon design?"

"All right, all right," the engineer replied, laying the drawing flat. "I figured your design of a large fire bowl at the top would need the occasional relighting, so I made it easy to climb."

Jornis forcibly pried his gaze from the abhorrent ice eye to the beacon sketch.

The commander pointed to several dangling strings in front of the map at the beacon's underside. "And what are these?"

"Pieces of jewellery, bronze and silk of course," Roudal explained.

The commander stared at him. "You wish to reward them?"

"Of course." Roudal grinned. "If you want these things to seek these beacons out, then there's no better way than to tempt them with precious valuables." His eager attitude grew serious as he asked, "Will you build any for the Riverveins?"

Copias interjected, "Their coast is almost entirely formed of steep cliff faces. Since it would be impossible for the Rauders to climb them, I can comfortably assure you it would be entirely pointless to construct any beacons there."

"Are you at least gonna tell them about this plan?" the engineer asked, darting his eyes between the men standing before him.

"Word will be sent within a few days," the commander answered, turning his attention to Jornis. "I will see to it this design is copied for our siloin neighbours."

"The quicker the better," Jornis replied, anxiously turning to the ice eye. "There must be as little warning as possible for the Radiant Republic."

The commander nodded. "Agreed."

Copias asked, "Will you be returning to Roilen?"

"No, I am to stay here as a reserve force and arrange certain meetings." The commander promptly turned to the engineer. "Thank you for your hard work, I will see construction begin immediately." He glanced at Jornis who remained focused on the worn rusted rings and left without another word.

The engineer eagerly returned to his drawing. "Just you wait. I'll replicate the Radiant Republic's prize weapon and make it superior in every way."

Jornis's stomach withered with disgust as he pictured this devastating weapon in the hands of all armies in the federation. He rushed outside in the cold breeze of the dawn.

Copias followed, asking, "What's the matter?"

Unable to block the thoughts, Jornis became engulfed with the memory of watching his wife leave for the Southern Campaign, and he muttered, "It's nothing."

Copias paused.

Jornis remembered what the Dictorate had said on that day, and his hands clenched into tight fists.

Stepping onto Fiskior's weed-covered street, Iyna glanced back at the home she and her unit had occupied and thought of the displaced families across the whole city. A bunch of Erium soldiers staggered from other

Fiskior homes, still hungover from their constant celebration in the city. She scowled and watched them uncaringly trek through the looted city. She stiffly marched down the quiet main street.

Nearing the ransacked city centre, Iyna passed an open air tavern filled with smug Erium swordsmen, joking and laughing together as a Fyoreten barwoman bitterly served them further ales. The barwoman scornfully glanced at Iyna in her thin green chestplate and dome helmet and turned away. Iyna lowered her head and continued marching further along the street.

Iyna reached the looted governing house in the heart of the city. The three other unit leaders waiting outside its large, broken doors in grim silence.

Glimpsing the litter strewn about the green-veined marble hallway, Iyna asked, "Is Alexan still inside?"

"He is." Barcial let out a long, depressed sigh. "There was word late last night that the rest of Fyoreten had given in."

Iyna's body felt weak.

Barcial looked up at the stem rooftop of the governing house. "The Fyoreten people are strong and fearless. I guarantee there will be much resistance to Erium occupation."

Tarrow grimly said, "At least our role in this is over."

An awkward silence fell over the four of them. Alexan emerged from the ransacked governing house and marched to his unit leaders. "We are to remain in this city until we have final confirmation that every Fyoreten town and village has yielded."

Barcial's hands tightened into fists. "Have they said what will happen to the populous?"

Alexan shook his head. "Nelthan only said the tributes Fyoreten has failed to pay will be forgiven."

Barcial grunted. "So no mention of how they will be treated."

Tarrow asked, "How long do we have to stay here then?"

"It shouldn't be long," Alexan answered. "I suspect Erium wants the other armies away from Fyoreten land as soon as possible."

Iyna glanced at a tall black crystal tipped with bronze being escorted into the square, heading towards the governing house. Her hands became tight fists at the sight of Erium's emblem and she muttered, "So they can rule as they see fit?"

"There's nothing more we can do," Alexan replied. "Or could have done."

Barcial shook his head. "We could have stayed away from this war entirely."

The commander stepped closer to him, whispering, "Felliet is in no position to provoke the Empire of Erium. The Elite Dictorate understands that, and you should too."

"Felliet should not be helping them." Barcial's bitter voice quietened. "It's only a matter of time before the emperor decides a random town has grown too large on *your* border."

A tense moment lingered in the air until Orbert folded his arms. "Then we best prepare for that day."

"Agreed," Alexan said, looking at each of the unit leaders. "See to it you and your soldiers are well rested in these next few days. Now if you excuse me, I am going to properly thank the other commanders for their role in the battle." He marched away.

Iyna's arms tensed as she thought about what Erium would do now Fyoreten had fallen.

Stepping into the tavern, Vernon spotted a small group of customers at the far table and noticed Orfain chatting to Grayfern at the bar. He marched to them, quietly asking, "So who am I meeting next?"

Grayfern picked up an empty tankard. "Hazel ain't back yet."

Hearing her old name, Vernon glanced at Orfain who shook his head, clearly indicating that he shouldn't say anything.

"Did you want a pint then?" Grayfern asked.

Vernon hesitated. "Yes?"

Grayfern filled a tankard while glancing at Vernon over his shoulder.

Orfain turned to Vernon. "I've got something to show you." He placed two identical black crystal bracelets on the bar. "Bet you a drink you can't tell which is real."

Vernon glanced at the strangers talking at the far table and whispered, "You finished the fakes?"

Orfain nodded. "Took a while to get the right shine, but in the end, I think I coloured the glass just right."

Picking up the smooth bracelets, Vernon examined them close to his face and turned around to view them with the fireplace behind. One let a slight hint of light through its edge, and he placed that one before Orfain. "This one's the fake."

"Lucky guess." Orfain shrugged. "But you see how this can work."

"So how many have you made?"

"Just a few chests," Orfain answered. "But we'll save most of it for when we can't get black crystal anymore."

Vernon looked at him in confusion. Grayfern placed the filled tankard down.

"You didn't think our little ruse would hold up forever, did you?" Orfain sarcastically asked.

"I guess not." Vernon sipped the ale. "Just thought it would be a shame if we were to only sell fakes."

Grayfern rolled his eyes. "What difference does it make if they're near identical?"

"One's a genuine symbol of greatness while the other is just blackened glass," Vernon argued.

"Only in *your* eyes," Orfain replied. "To anyone else, it's genuine black crystal."

"I suppose." Vernon relaxed. "I suppose even fakes can still spread the symbol of Erium's greatness."

"Exactly," Orfain said. He excitedly muttered, "And we may be selling it across Erium soon."

Vernon's eyes widened as he pictured black crystal travelling along the many routes Orfain had spoken of. He wondered just how far they were going to take this business. He then remembered their storehouse in Ellity's wall and smiled. "With all of your expertise, we can't fail."

Orfain patted Vernon's back. "With all of our expertise."

Vernon chuckled. "Afraid I can't offer much."

"Says the only one of us who's a real citizen of Erium," Orfain argued. "Not to mention, you are the only one who can reliably approach those nobles."

Grayfern turned away.

Vernon shrugged. "I guess you have a point." He raised his tankard. "I'll do what I can."

"Good man," Orfain replied and took a hearty gulp of ale.

Biting into the hardened bread after another lonely day in the forge, Niyaa wearily turned to her mom who tried to hide her exhaustion and sadness, leaving them both without words. The small room was left with only the squeaking of the mill's turning column and the brisk evening breeze against the closed shutter.

They heard a familiar woman's voice call to them from the bottom of the mill's ladder. The two of them rushed to the ladder and looked down. Cabi was standing there with her large basket still strapped to her back.

"Can I come up?" she asked.

Mysia stared suspiciously at her. "What do you want?"

After a short pause, Cabi answered, "I heard what happened and I … I want to offer you both a new home. A place where you'd truly feel welcome."

Niyaa's eyes widened. "A new home?"

"Yes." Cabi lowered her voice. "Could I climb up and talk to you about it?"

Hopeful excitement overcame Niyaa, and she turned to her mom who relented. "All right, come on up."

Without taking off the giant leaf basket from her back or loosening its thick round straps, Cabi climbed the ladder rungs and clambered onto the upper mill's floor.

Mysia folded her arms. "So what did you mean, *a new home?*"

Cabi smiled. "I come from a place that is home to a close community of people who would joyously welcome newcomers."

Niyaa eagerly asked, "They'd welcome us?"

"Without question," Cabi cheerfully replied. "We especially would love new forgers and brewers to come."

"Really?" Niyaa blurted out. She noticed the suspicious look on her mom's face, so she asked, "Where's the axe I made you?"

"Oh, I didn't want to worry your guards so left it with my friends back at our camp," Cabi explained. "I have to say though, it works perfectly."

Mysia narrowed her eyes. "How come you and your friends are camped outside the village?"

Cabi's smile faded into a nervous frown. "Well … I…" She took a long, deep breath and said, "What I said was honest. The place I come from is filled with all kinds of friendly people who *will* gladly welcome the both of you … but…" She paused, darting her gaze away, quietening her voice. "I know you both came from Edenor ... I am so, so sorry you lost your home. I and my parents know the feeling well."

Mysia stepped back, unfolding her arms. "Who are you?"

Cabi nervously looked away, and her hands grasped her elbows. "Those who attacked Edenor, they were ... misguided. That third purge drove them to foolishly lash out in anger. They were only supposed to go after the soldiers and priests. They should never have torched it."

A sudden terror gripped Mysia's face, freezing her on the spot.

Niyaa asked, "Are you ... are you with *them*?"

Cabi turned to look at them in their eyes. "I think it best I show you, but please, *please* don't be afraid." She bit her bottom lip and took a deeper, longer breath. The basket's thick round straps wiggled, steadily pushing the leaf basket away from Cabi's back till it fell to the ground with a light crunch. Cabi stretched the six crab-like limbs emerging from her back, flexing them wide.

Niyaa and her mom stared in utter shock.

Cabi explained, "I want to make up for what happened in Edenor and take you away from Pelight, from these elites, away to a place you *will* be welcomed."

Stunned silence engulfed the mill's air as both Niyaa and her mom were left speechless.

Cabi slowly bent her limbs inwards towards her back as she pleaded, "I know it might be difficult to trust someone like me, especially after what happened, but I tell you the truth about where I come from. It was created by exiles across the world, both Beast Rider and normal folk. We now live as a giant family with plentiful food and shelter. We will welcome—"

"No," Mysia interrupted and looked away.

Her answer stunned Niyaa.

Mysia returned her gaze to Cabi, chin held high. "I can trust neither your words nor you. Now, you should go before someone sees you."

Cabi opened her mouth as if she wanted to speak but no words left her lips. Instead, she picked up her basket and wriggled it onto her back limbs.

Mysia leaned against the wall near the shuttered window, looking down at the heap of straw on the mill's bare floor.

Cabi set her foot onto the first ladder rung. "My group are camped where the stream enters the nearby canopy. We'll be there for a couple nights, so if you change your mind…" She stopped herself as Mysia shook her head.

Watching her disappear down the ladder, Niyaa rushed to her mom. "Shouldn't we go with her?"

Mysia once more shook her head.

"It's gotta be better than here," Niyaa argued.

"Best we get some sleep." Mysia stiffly walked away from the wall. "We both have a lot of work to do tomorrow."

The two of them lay atop their straw heaps in complete darkness, yet Niyaa couldn't sleep at all, for Cabi's words kept spinning around her head. The chance to leave Pelight and go somewhere wonderful kept her heart racing.

She sat up and turned to her mom sleeping peacefully on her huge mound of straw. Niyaa wondered what her mom would do if she left, whether she would be better off or even happier without someone to care for. Niyaa glanced at the ladder and crept towards it without daring to look at her mom.

With sandals on, she stepped onto the first rung and glanced to her to her mom still fast asleep. Perhaps one day she would return for a visit, or better yet, after spending time in the new place, she could convince her mom to head there herself. She wondered when she would see her mom again. Determined, Niyaa nodded to herself and placed her other foot on the next rung and snuck outside.

Instead of heading to the gate, she rushed atop a nearby empty stretch of wall and stared down at the little moat below. Niyaa knelt down at the edge and lowered herself. She let go, loudly splashing into the shallow water.

Utterly soaked, she ran through the nightly brown fields, following the stream towards the canopy as she felt a sudden freedom from the rush of wind against her face. Her body was full of energy and joy as she left Pelight behind.

As the parasoller stems were within reach, she heard her mom's voice call to her, "Niyaa! Niyaa!"

Turning back, Niyaa saw her mom sprinting towards her at an incredible pace. Niyaa's excitement vanished, and she pushed her body harder, making her little legs go as fast as they could. Entering the moonslit shadow of the canopy, Niyaa felt a wet hand tightly grab her arm, stopping her.

Mysia furiously shouted, "What do you think you're doin'?"

"Let go!" Niyaa tried to yank her arm away. "I can't stay there. I won't!"

"Listen to me." Mysia crouched to her daughter's level. "I know it's hard, but we have to."

"Why?" Niyaa gave up trying to break free as her voice grew louder. "We're utterly miserable there! None of them like us!"

"I know," her mom replied. "But your dad and I would want you to grow up safe."

Niyaa shook her head. "I don't want to be safe. I want ... I want friends."

Mysia hugged her tightly. "I know."

"But why can't we go somewhere else?" Niyaa desperately asked. "Why do we have to stay here?"

Her mom broke the hug, shaking her head. "We can't trust her."

"But she's different from those other Beast Riders. She's kind and nice," Niyaa pleaded. "We *can* trust her."

"We can't, Niyaa." Mysia tightened her grip around her daughter's arm. "They're dangerous."

"The governor's the dangerous one," Niyaa argued back. "He took Dad away and might take us away too."

"That won't happen."

"You don't know that."

Mysia relaxed her grip. "I will make sure Seveck never does anything like that again."

"But you can't," Niyaa replied. "He has complete control over the village and everyone in it."

Mysia bit her bottom lip, unable to argue back.

A moment later, the sound of something climbing down a nearby stem drew their attention. Cabi, happy and relieved, descended the sticky stem with her back limbs.

Mysia shot to her feet, looking around in fear.

Nearing the ground, Cabi spoke. "It's just me here. Our camp is actually a fair distance away."

Mysia placed herself in front of her daughter, keeping her anxious eyes focused on the Beast Rider.

Touching her feet on the ground, Cabi's back limbs released their grip on the stem, and she stepped forward. "Afraid, I couldn't fully trust you guys either."

Mysia didn't say a word.

Cabi sighed and sat on the ground, her back limbs comfortably propping her upright. "I don't blame you. What happened at Edenor was a stupid act of revenge after that third purge." She rubbed the back of her neck. "If it makes you feel better, had they really hated you lot, they would've never allowed anyone to leave Edenor."

Mysia asked, "You think by lettin' us live, we'd be grateful?"

"No." She shook her head. "What I meant to say is that they didn't mean any harm to come to the people."

"Had it not been for you Beast Riders, my husband and I would still be together, brewing in our home," Mysia argued. "It's thanks to your raid that our family was forced to move to Pelight in the first place."

Cabi got to her feet. "Well, had it not been for the culling, my parents would never have been driven to the desert." She let out a long breath. "I suppose had there not been any elites, governors, priests or nobles, neither of us would've lost our home and family."

Mysia paused, relaxing her tense muscles. "I'm sorry for what befell your people, but we can't join you."

"We aren't a different people to you," Cabi replied. "Every soul in this world is of the same blood. It matters not where they hail from nor what they look like. We are *all* the same people."

Niyaa jerked her arm away from her mom and rushed to Cabi.

"Niyaa!" Mysia yelled.

She turned to her mom begging, "Please. We can find some happiness with them."

Mysia stared at the two of them for a long, worried while, and her face fell in defeat. She sighed. "All right then. We'll go with them."

Relief and happiness overwhelmed Niyaa as she noticed a slight smile on her mom's face.

"You won't regret it," Cabi said and lead them beyond the canopy.

They were escorted to a fireless camp where a large, brown-cloaked man with huge round biceps sat alongside a skinny man patching a shirt.

"Hey guys," Cabi said. "This is Mysia, and this is Niyaa. They'll be joining us back to Reeffewd."

Niyaa noticed a huge six-wheeled cart filled with all kinds of foraged plants and flowers with a few agron and iron tools. She spotted a purplish scaly horse tied alongside a fluffy yellow mule.

The cloaked man stood up with a wide grin. "Cabi told us about you two back when you made that axe for her, but I'd never thought people round here would see us for who we really are." He knelt down before them. "I promise you you'll be safe and welcome with us."

"He's Borren by the way," Cabi said and pointed to the other. "And the one sewing is Semy."

"Glad to make your acquaintance," he said.

Niyaa stared at the skinny man. "You're not a Beast Rider?"

"I took after my mother's side." Semy patted the side of his ribs. "But I'm a Beast Rider through and through." He grinned. "I sure when I have kids they'll be gifted with their own unique appendages."

Cabi joked, "You'll have to find someone to date first."

Semy chuckled. "I'll find someone, don't you worry."

Cabi cheerfully turned to Niyaa and Mysia. "We've gathered much more than what we've needed, so we can set off early tomorrow if you want."

Mysia hesitantly nodded. "The earlier the better."

Hearing that answer, Niyaa turned towards the eastern horizon and wondered what lay beyond the desert.

Chapter seventeen – Unforeseen

Seventh eclipse, fourteenth day

Iyna's gaze was kept low as she led her unit through Ellity's westerly gatehouse with the rest of the Felliet army. It was uncomfortably early in the bright morning, yet even so, crowds of people flocked along the clear street awaiting their return. As the soldiers marched past them, the people offered no cheers or applause; instead, only curiosity and confusion filled the surrounding faces. Glancing at the joyless people around her, Iyna felt a strange sense of pride overwhelm her as she realised just how many of them also hated the war they were in. She raised her sorrowful head up and kept marching along Felliet's main street.

The small army arranged themselves on the magnificent shield plaza, and Iyna was once again staring up at the gargantuan Gallery with the pleasant scent of lavender filling her nostrils. The grand doors opened wide and out stepped a grey-robed man who approached the commander. "Alexan Brige. The Dictorate would like to personally congratulate its commander and unit leaders."

Alexan glanced to his army. "And the fighting men and women?"

The steward grinned. "They will be handsomely rewarded by our new military overseer."

"Military overseer?" Alexan asked.

"Correct," the steward explained. "The Dictorate believed it wise to appoint someone with the sole task of supporting Felliet's army. He will oversee the supplies, funding, messages and other necessities for our brave soldiers. However, I must stress that he shall not lead any troops into battle nor issue orders to you or your men."

"Very good," Alexan replied and turned to his unit leaders. "Tarrow, Orbert, Barcial and Iyna, shall we head inside?"

Stepping through the pristine brass doors into the bright light beaming through the Gallery's glass roof, Iyna gazed around the long Gallery in complete awe. The long walls either side of her were filled with an assortment of ornaments, flowers, tapestries and stained glass around each shield-engraved elite name. At the far end stood a glistening granite stand above which hung eleven bronze shields, the largest of which had the name Zenth engraved in ashen grey. Iyna turned her attention to the eleven finely dressed people sitting behind the shiny stand and filling her with confidence that they knew how to steer Felliet towards a bright future.

Standing in line with the other three unit leaders, Iyna glanced proudly at Alexan as he stood ahead of them, staring up at the Elite Dictorate.

The central elite spoke. "You have done well, Commander Brige. Your efforts have ensured Felliet retains its prominent place within the federation."

Iyna's shoulders slumped at hearing the confirmation their reason for joining the war was simply not to provoke the Empire of Erium.

"I appreciate the praise, Eythiam Zenth," Alexan replied. "However, it would be wrong of me to take the glory away from the brave and loyal soldiers who fought fiercely to defend this nation."

The elite woman sitting to Eythiam's left said, "Yet were it not for your decisive actions in the opening battle, my husband would never have been avenged."

Alexan hesitated. "He was a brave commander."

Iyna darted her eyes to Alexan in confusion as she remembered the first commander galloping away during the battle of the blue hill. Glancing at the Elite Dictorate, she realised it must have taken a great deal of courage to volunteer to lead the first ever army.

"That he was," she replied. "As are you. In recognition of this, you will remain as Felliet's commander."

Eythiam added, "We will, however, require far more soldiers; therefore, you will return to the Plythiat tower and train a fresh force."

"It will be my pleasure," Alexan said.

"We have, however, heard disturbing reports that some Fyoreten riders escaped into the mountains, so the Moain fort will need to be garrisoned." He darted his eyes to the unit leaders. "Three of your units should be adequate."

The large elite far to the left leaned back in his chair. "We need not send Orbert Cendion. The other three units should be enough."

"Only two will be necessary," Alexan argued. "Felliet's army should be as strong as it can be with the finest leaders it can have." He gestured to Barcial. "This one has proven himself exceptional in combat and in leadership. He and Orbert are essential to ensuring the safety of our border. With their proven experience, we can better train any new recruits."

Iyna glanced at Barcial, who seemed just as surprised by Alexan's suggestion.

Eythiam shook his head. "Only one unit is needed to help train soldiers. Our priority as of this moment is to snuff out any and all

Fyoreten resistance, lest they attack our lands from the south." He grinned. "If your man is as skilled as you say, then there will be no issue."

Alexan seemed to be struggling to think up an argument, but he reluctantly agreed. "Very well, we shall obey the Dictorate's wise decisions."

"Good." Eythiam rose from his chair followed by the other elites. "We eagerly await your results."

"You shall not be disappointed." Alexan turned away.

Following the commander out of the Gallery, Iyna saw several stewards handing out hefty coin bags to each of the soldiers, bringing joyous surprise to their faces. She turned to the brass cart the bags came from and spotted a man covered in a huge robe made of hundreds of tiny grey glass pieces.

Alexan calmly approached him. "Are you the new military overseer?"

The man hesitated. "I am."

"Could you give me your name?" Alexan asked.

The man took a deep breath. "Reethial Zenth."

Iyna was shocked as she realised Eythiam Zenth's own brother was supporting the army. She smiled, knowing the Dictorate was looking out for them.

"I apologise," Alexan said. "I had not expected such a senior elite to oversee our army."

"That's quite all right," Reethial replied. He drew his attention to an approaching boy in a similar robe of grey glass.

"The stewards have finished handing out the reward," he said.

"Good work, Buckley," Reethial said. "See the remainder returned to the academy."

"With pleasure." The boy nodded and guided the stewards to cart the few remaining coin bags away.

Alexan returned his gaze to the elite. "How much was in each bag?"

"One hundred brass."

The commander shook his head. "That will not be enough to cover food and other supplies."

Reethial glared back as if insulted. "You think me so incompetent to have the army supply themselves?" His bitterness eased as he turned to the cheerful spearmen and tribowmen. "Since I am to maintain this pitiful force, I will ensure they each are given all the equipment and food they require."

Iyna glanced at her own thin agron chestplate and turned to the chainmailed guards outside the Gallery doors. "Could we all have new armour?"

"I can't exactly allow my army to charge at an enemy force unprotected," Reethial replied. "But first I will see to it the Plythiat tower receives a sufficient number of men before the comet arrives."

Alexan gave a single nod. "You have my thanks."

The elite averted his gaze. "You each have your orders. See to it they are carried out." Reethial walked away without another word.

Alexan turned to his unit leaders. "Tarrow, Barcial and Iyna, who among you is going to lead your force at the Moain fort?"

Barcial shook his head. "If we are to face Fyoreten resistance fighters then I … I can't be the one."

"Very well," Alexan said.

Seeing Barcial's grief, Iyna answered, "I'll do it."

Alexan turned to Tarrow, awaiting her opinion.

She spoke in sincerity. "If it weren't for Iyna's quick thinking in the battle of Fiskior, we would have been slain by those Fyoreten riders." Tarrow turned to Iyna. "I'll feel comfortable knowing you are leading us."

"Thank you," Iyna replied and turned back to Alexan. "I'll do what I can to safeguard the people of Felliet."

He grinned. "A good answer."

Niyaa had always imagined the desert to be as hot as a furnace, but throughout the whole journey, the gentle breeze was just as cool as it was in Felliet. It was weird to see not a single cloud appear in the clear blue above or find any strand of green anywhere on the vast sandy landscape. Still, the company she and her mom had for the many days and nights travelling east was wonderful. Borren, with his huge furry arms, easily pulled the big cart not only laden with all the supplies but with Niyaa and her mom as well. Semy had somehow knitted a pair of woollen gloves while in the red scaly saddle of his fluffy yellow horse. Cabi chatted nearly endlessly about the city of Reeffewd with its many, many kinds of people, as well as a small town named Lorish, with the cool, flowery oasis it was built around. All of Mysia's worries and suspicions seemed to have disappeared along the long journey as she talked of how she could restart the brewing business. In the early morning, the jagged pink walls of

Lorish came into sight, and Niyaa stood in the cart, excitedly staring at the nearing oasis town.

The pace of the cart and beast horses quickened as Niyaa made out a narrow pink tower overlooking the town's scaly red curtain gate. Semy put away his knitting and gripped his horse's red scaly reins. "Can almost smell the pluff flowers now."

"Same here," Borren said and glanced over his shoulder at Niyaa and her mom. "Welcome to Lorish."

Nearing the oasis town, Niyaa spotted someone with enormous antlers waving to them from the top of the tower, and the scaly gate rolled upwards. As it furled above the gap in the rough wall, a bunch of welcoming people flocked to the entrance, with an array of pink craggily homes to their backs.

Borren pulled the cart faster, shouting to them, "We're back!"

Before they even reached the small crowd at the gate, two guards came rushing out to greet them, one with toad-like skin across her body and the other weighty with a long orange snout.

Borren set down the cart and clasped hands with the snouted man. "Good to see ya, Goreth."

"Yeah, you too," the weighty guard replied.

The toad woman looked at Niyaa and Mysia and cheerfully asked, "Who're they?"

Cabi trotted her purplish horse near them. "They've come to join us."

The toad woman smiled at the two newcomers. "Glad to see new faces round 'ere."

322

"Definitely," Borren agreed, releasing his grip from his friend.

Niyaa leapt out of the cart followed calmly by her mom, and the snouted man grabbed the cart's handles. The guard pulled it towards the growing crowd beneath the rolled-up gate with Borren walking beside.

The toad guard turned to Cabi. "Should I get Fewttyre?"

"He's here?" she asked. "Never thought he'd go so far from his lab."

"He's been here for a while now," the toad woman explained.

Semy shrugged. "Maybe he figured by coming here he could escape his duties."

Cabi smirked at him. "I'm sure it's not that." She climbed off her saddle and turned to the toad woman. "Yeah, if you could find him, Leeli."

"I won't be long." Leeli practically sprang on each smooth leg as she ran back.

Watching the toad guard rush back into the town, Mysia whispered to Cabi, "Won't her skin dry out quickly?"

"Of course, but the oasis inside has never run dry," Cabi said, steering her horse toward the furled up gate. She casually added, "Also, you don't have to worry about the people here struggling to get used to their beastly limbs. It comes naturally to everyone from birth even if their limbs differ from their parents." She smirked. "Funnily enough a lot of people find it weird that I don't mind sleeping on my back arms."

Entering the small crowd of beast people, the group was overcome with joyous greetings and praises from all sides. Niyaa looked around, and though she saw all kinds of strange beastly limbs, she felt a kind warmth from their friendly welcome.

Leeli returned with a worn slate tray, carrying a bunch of misshapen cups of milk. Behind her came a normal-looking man with tired eyes and scruffy bed hair.

Semy took the closest cup, turning to the man. "So how come you're not with the rest of the pioneers?"

"Ah, well." The man shrugged. "Someone has to inspect the outposts. Besides, Fericka's keeping the others in check."

Semy sighed. "Sure."

The man looked at Niyaa and Mysia. "It's a pleasure to invite newcomers to our community."

Mysia asked, "Are you the governor of this place then?"

"Governor?" He chuckled. "Oh, we don't have those around here. But more importantly, I honestly never thought I'd see the day when I'm not recognised."

Niyaa asked, "Are you famous here then?"

The beast people surrounding them giggled.

The man cheerfully explained, "My name is Fewttyre Alorcha."

"Alorcha?" Mysia shouted in amazement. "You don't mean you're related to Uthering Alorcha, do you?"

"He was my grandfather," he proudly answered. "I'm guessing the rest of the world believed they wiped out all of the surgeons."

Semy took a sip of milk, gloating. "Not that you've ever performed one on a person yet."

"The future can yield many wonderous surprises," Fewttyre replied and turned back to the newcomers. "So what shall I call you two?"

"I'm Niyaa, and my mom's named Mysia."

"You both have lovely first names, but what about your family name?" he asked.

Niyaa looked at him in confusion. "Family name?"

Mysia shook her head. "Afraid we aren't elites."

"Nor are the people here." Fewttyre smiled. "Here you can choose whatever name you want for your family."

Cabi proudly patted her chest. "Mine's Graspen."

Borren copied, heartedly pounding his chest. "Lugger's mine." He patted Goreth's shoulder. "And this one's Sniffer."

Niyaa's head filled with all kinds of ideas about what she and her mom should name themselves. She glanced at Semy who smirked. "Weaver."

Fewttyre raised his voice. "You see, out here there's no authority telling you who you ought to be. Either of you can be whoever you want."

Niyaa saw the proud faces of the surrounding crowd and felt her heart race with even more excitement.

Fewttyre turned to Cabi, asking, "Shall we give them a tour of Lorish?"

"Afraid I've kept my man wating too long." She cheerfully looked up and waved at the antler man watching everybody from the narrow tower. "Besides, one of the great pioneers would do a much better job than I can."

"I suppose," Fewttyre said, darting his eyes away and turning to Niyaa and Mysia. "Then if you would follow me, I'll first show you the beauty of the oasis."

Mysia nodded. "That'll be wonderful."

Following Fewttyre further inside the pink town, Niyaa noticed most of the beast people scatter back to their workplaces and homes with the rest following. They came to a large round sparkly blue pond with hundreds of little red and orange flower balls growing around.

Fewttyre picked one of the flower balls. "Have either of you ever tried pluff balls?"

Mysia was stunned. "Haven't seen one since I was a girl." She turned wide eyed to him. "I thought they only grew along the rivers in Artor."

"Not anymore." He popped it whole in his mouth.

Niyaa knelt down, picked a light orange one and sniffed it. To her surprise it didn't smell of anything, but upon popping it in her mouth, a delicious bittersweet taste filled her mouth.

Approaching the extinguished beacon with the Silk Shore's commander and his personal guard, Jornis and Copias observed many of the items had been taken, including the large agron fire bowl from atop the beacon. Furthermore, the site had a multitude of three-legged tracks imprinted around the area, a fact that bothered all of their horses as they neared the site. However the silk clothes, pearls and glassware were still dangling from the ropes beneath the beacon.

The commander turned to the two Felliet riders. "Why do you suppose they left *these* items?"

One of the bodyguards suggested, "Perhaps they were in a hurry."

Jornis shook his head. "Unlikely." He pointed to the top of the beacon. "Especially if they had the time to climb up and prise off the fire bowl."

The Silk Shore's commander narrowed his eyes. "So what do you suggest?"

Returning his gaze to the few items remaining, Jornis struggled to rationalise the Rauder's actions.

Copias gave an unexpected answer. "Perhaps they are not interested in wealth." All eyes turned to him, awaiting further explanation. "We see silk, jewels and well-crafted glass as valuable. Perhaps these Rauders do not."

They collectively paused to ponder the strange idea. Jornis said, "Nevertheless, we can at least assume they will soon begin raiding the Radiant Republic."

The commander glanced at the empty space where the map had hung. "While I will not allow my guard to be lowered, I can certainly be hopeful your plan works." He steered his horse away from the beacon. "In that regard, shall we now depart for Bilhyn?"

"We?" Jornis asked.

"Of course," the commander replied. "If Gildren and Felliet are to build a stronger relationship then they should be seen as taking a stand together."

"Understandable," Jornis replied, still surprised by the decision. "So when are we to depart?"

"Immediately." The commander steered his horse back to Jornis, staring suspiciously at him. "Show us Felliet can be of use to *all* of Gildren."

"I swear on all of my experience as representative of Felliet that the lands and resources of my country will become of great use to all eight siloins of Gildren," Jornis said. He added, "For once in so very long, the whole federation will be brought closer to true balance and peace."

Walking along the winding granite path through Sidium's public gardens, satchel to his side, Vernon breathed in the flourishing scents of perfume and ink lilies filling the air. Even more refreshing was witnessing such a wide diversity of people enjoying this spacious delightful place, from loving couples to ivory-robed moon worshippers to quiet book readers to playful kids. Vernon could not think of a more pleasant place to trade the black crystal bracelet than this place.

Approaching the finely dressed noble reading on one of the garden's gold-veined granite benches, Vernon cheerfully greeted him. "It's a pleasure to meet you, Dowsian."

"The pleasure is mine, Meyorter." The noble set aside his book. "Especially on such a fine day as this."

Taking his seat next to the noble, Vernon glanced at the cheerful family strolling past and said, "There truly is no better place than this city.

Never have I seen people of all kinds thriving in such prosperity and harmony."

"Agreed," Dowsian replied. "Does this mean you hail from a different part of Erium?"

"Felliet actually," Vernon explained. "All my life I've lived in that pathetic country whose leaders either act uncaringly or moronically." He smiled with pride. "Now I can say I am a man of Erium."

Dowsian turned back to the people walking by. "If I may ask, what made you decide Erium was your true home?"

Vernon took *The Foundations* from his satchel. "I grew up with this book and learned much of Emperor Rochious, the glorious empire he founded and his victory over the corrupted Royals." He caressed the worn cover. "From as young as I can remember, I had dreamt of travelling to the black city. However, never could I imagine I would step inside the great chamber, let alone be named a man of Erium."

The noble hesitated. "You're loyal to the Imerial name?"

"Without question," Vernon answered. "Only *they* can unite the world."

Dowsian paused, putting his hand to his chin. "So why sell black crystal?"

Vernon looked at him in confusion. "Afraid I don't understand."

"Forgive me, but I assumed you and your friends sold black crystal simply to make plentiful coin." He darted his eyes to the satchel and back to Vernon's face. "Was I mistaken?"

Vernon didn't hesitate. "If I wanted coin, I would have sold my dignity and pride to the elites long ago." He glanced at the clear sky above. "I do this to spread the symbol of the emperor's name and glory to as many people as possible."

The noble opened his mouth ready to speak but stopped just as the moon worshippers passed them.

"I've rambled enough," Vernon said, taking the black crystal bracelet from his satchel and placing it on the granite bench. "I heard you're also loyal to the Imerial name."

"Indeed I am." Dowsian let out a long weary sigh. "Six bronze, correct?"

Vernon nodded and returned his book to his satchel.

The noble coughed once and wordlessly rose from the bench.

Vernon stared at him. The pair of moon worshippers marched to them with scornful looks in their eyes.

Dowsian said, "I advise you not to make a scene."

Terror stiffened Vernon's body as he darted his eyes from the three serious-faced men standing over him to his calm surroundings. Other men in ivory robes were scattered throughout the garden, defeating any chance of escape and leaving him no other choice but to slowly rise from the bench.

The noble pocketed the bracelet and walked along the dark garden path.

One of the robed men whispered to Vernon, "Walk in front and keep your head forward."

Vernon turned his head towards the noble and nervously followed with the moon worshippers to his back. His breath deepened as his thoughts were plagued with horrific outcomes, and he wondered what might befall his friends. He realised they wouldn't be harmed at all, for it was only him in possession of black crystal and only him selling it to the nobility. Vernon lowered his head as he tried not to think on whether he had intentionally been put in danger.

Leaving the garden, it became obvious he was being led to the inner wall area, and seeing the chainmailed garrison patrolling its mighty black ramparts, Vernon felt his body anxiously slow.

When Vernon passed through the gatehouse, a renewed sense of dread hit him as he was being led not towards the mustering square or the emperor's palace but along the wall itself. They came to one of the wall's soaring towers whose iron door was guarded by a pair of black chainmailed swordsmen. Without a word spoken, the pair opened the thick reinforced door, allowing the noble and him to enter and leaving the ivory-robed men behind.

The iron door shut, sealing the outside light from the black walled inside. Vernon wondered why there was no longer an armed escort but realised he had no possible way of escape, even if he tried.

"I advise you not to keep her waiting," Dowsian said.

Vernon turned to him. "Who?"

The noble gestured to the tower's ascending stairs, and Vernon obeyed, marching up with Dowsian following. They reached the ramparts at the top of the wall, and Vernon was escorted to an unguarded door alongside the stairs. His heart pounded in his chest as Dowsian's knuckles tapped its surface.

A stern female voice emerged from within. "Enter."

The noble opened the door, revealing a dimly lit, square room with a single stone desk at its centre. Sitting behind the desk was an irritated woman in full black chainmail with a curved dagger held upright in a special stand weighting down a letter she was writing.

She darted her narrow eyes from her paperwork to the noble and captive.

Dowsian placed the bracelet on her desk. "I have brought the seller."

"Good." She turned her gaze. "Your name is Vernon Meyorter, correct?"

Vernon felt his heart sink as he nodded.

The noble stepped back. "I shall take my leave, however…" He glanced at Vernon. "I must admit I finally understand your reasoning about this one."

She leaned back in her stone chair as Dowsian left and only when the door closed did she ask, "Do you know who I am?"

Vernon looked around the small room, finding the black glistening walls entirely bare. "I would say you were a high-ranking member of the garrison."

"You are not entirely wrong." She glanced to the dagger. "I am the leader of Sidium's garrison, Elleasious Imerial."

Shock engulfed Vernon, and he stumbled his words. "You're … you're the emperor's sister." He averted his gaze to the ground. "I had no idea … I—"

"You have been profiting from my family's name," she said.

"I wouldn't dare!" Vernon shouted but calmed his next words. "I would never use the emperor's name for my personal gain."

"I dislike liars," she said, slowly picking up the bracelet. "How much did you charge for this?"

Vernon kept his gaze fixed on her. "Six bronze."

"And you say you deny using this money for your personal gain?"

"I do." Vernon stepped forward. "To devote your life to amassing fortune is a wasteful and pitiful thing. What matters is ensuring you do right by the people around you and for the nation as a whole."

"The nation? Are you referring to your home of Felliet?"

Vernon shook his head. "To consider Felliet a proper nation is deeply misguided. In truth it is a pitifully tiny nation with few resources that should never have left the greatness of Erium." He realised she and Dowsian had known of his past long before the arranged meeting. He took a deep breath. "When I was in the muster's square on the day the new emperor was announced, I heard many people whisper damning rumours and suspicions. I couldn't bear listening to their foul tongues, knowing it was the Emperor Anisious and his predecessors who had made the empire"—he shook his head—"no, the world safe and prosperous."

"So you did this to improve my brother's image in the eyes of the nobility and high merchants?"

Vernon gave a small nod.

"Then why not simply offer the black crystal pieces without charge? If you truly wish to spread the word of my brother's greatness as you just declared."

Vernon hadn't considered the idea and drifted his gaze to the bracelet glistening on the desk. A moment later he realised the reason. "Giving them away without cost is akin to saying they hold no value."

She paused for a long while, leaving dreaded silence gripping the room. "You and your friends misled the priesthood into entering the hill of night spears and had a block of the crystal reserved for new building blocks cut. Then, without the approval of the emperor nor any of the authorised names, you had it forged into various items before selling them to the nobility under the pretence of spreading loyalty to my brother. Furthermore, you openly claim many of the nobility whom my family have entrusted are openly spreading rumours and lies."

Vernon's body fearfully shook.

She grinned. "Your actions have been greatly useful."

Bewilderment struck him, leaving him unable to move or speak.

"I would like to reward you with an official position under my direct supervision." She crossed her arms. "The small town of Rerrunter lies to the far north and owes ninety-three bronze and three brass." Elleasious's grin widened. "I order you to collect them."

Vernon was in a state of confused disbelief. "But why me and not Erium's coin collectors?"

"I feel you would be more suited for this role." Her tone harshened. "But if you speak of this to anyone, you will find yourself on my *worse* side." She picked up the bracelet and stretched her arm out. "Wear it."

Vernon hesitated at the command but accepted the bracelet, placing the black crystal on his right wrist.

"There is a barge that you can take to Converrium this evening. From there, you will travel on foot to the town." Elleasious turned her attention back to drafting her letter and offhandedly said, "And I expect you and Lysia to provide suitable contributions from your business."

Stunned at the mention of her name, Vernon stood there for a long moment before leaving the room as quietly as he could. Setting foot outside the tower, his body nearly collapsed from relief. He glanced at the black crystal around his wrist and realised he would need to depart immediately.

Halfway up the mountain slope late into the clouded evening, the fort finally came into sight, greeting the marching soldiers with sheer disappointment. Not only were the fort's two towers tiny, but the three short walls not overlooking the steep craggy cliff were crumbling ruins. Worse still, the rigid ground along the narrow passes up the mountain showed no sign of forage or wildlife, and the chilling wind lingered in the air. At least Reethial had added a bunch of blankets to their food and water cart before they left Ellity.

Marching across the small rocky clearing before the fort, Iyna led her army across the dry moat and through the unhinged, barred gates and stepped into the tiny courtyard within. Inside, nearly all the fort's stonework was broken and cracked. The mossy well in the centre had a rusted bucket.

She sighed and turned to her weary army gathering in the small courtyard. "Feeliath, Barcial, have your units clean out the sleeping quarters and repair the well. Tarrow, take your unit along the ramparts and take first watch. Feeliath, have your unit take the second."

Feeliath asked, "Do we have to keep watch tonight?" All the exhausted soldiers turned to him. "I mean we've travelled all this way; we should all rest, at least for tonight."

Iyna wondered whether it was wise to allow him to become the unit leader in her stead but reminded herself only Feeliath had volunteered. She shook her head at the reckless idea. "We are to protect this area from a Fyoreten force in the mountains. If they find us resting, no matter which night, they will waste no time taking revenge." She glanced at Barcial who was looking away, "But with any luck, we need not fight them."

"What do you mean?" Feeliath asked. "The sooner we fight them, the sooner we can leave this mountain behind."

Tarrow glared at him. "You wanna kill people that badly?"

Feeliath crossed his arms. "If they threaten our lands and want to kill our people, then yes, without question."

"You think they *wanted* war?" Iyna asked, marching towards him. "You think Felliet wanted to fight them or that we wanted to help the Empire of Erium conquer their lands?" Her voice grew louder. "Don't be so foolish to think anyone but Erium won that war."

He wordlessly looked away, gritting his teeth.

Barcial repeated, "With any luck, we need not fight them."

She nodded and turned to the decaying walls. "Maybe if they see an intact, manned fort, they'll look elsewhere."

Feeliath rested his spear on his shoulder. "And how do you expect us to fix this place?"

"We'll start by repairing the well and clearing the ramparts. If we need anything more, I'll write a letter to Reethial." She smiled and remembered all the times she had argued the pointlessness of reading and writing.

Chapter eighteen – Encounter

Seventh eclipse, eighteenth day

Stepping over many of the rocks scattered across the crumbling rampart, Iyna spotted an unarmoured man pulling a small cloth-covered cart towards the propped-up gate. She leaned her head through the cracked stone gaps above the gate and shouted down to him, "Morning. You the stonemason I asked for?"

He shook his head and shouted up to her, "I'm the smither Reethial requested!"

"Do you at least know anything about stonework?" Iyna asked.

"A little," he replied. "But from the looks of it, you're gonna need a true expect to mend this place."

Iyna sighed.

The man shrugged. "Agron can bond to stone fairly well. Could use some of that to mend parts of the wall."

"All right then," she said, feeling hopeful. "What's your name anyway?"

"Erger," he answered. "One of the best smithers in Felliet." He hauled his cart closer to the gate. "Reckon I'll take a look at mending this thing first."

"That'll be a big help." Iyna watched him examining the gate. "But get some food and rest after your journey."

"Thanks, but I'm gonna start straight away if you don't mind," Erger replied as the gate opened for him.

After constant days of her soldiers not wanting to repair and clean the fort, Iyna was taken aback by his eagerness. "Yes, that'll be brilliant."

Iyna climbed down from the wall, and the smither uncovered his cart next to the well, revealing a mini furnace alongside a bunch of agron and iron bars. Erger picked up the glass jar tied to the well's rope and held it up with an eyebrow raised.

Iyna shrugged. "We found the bucket completely rusted so we made do with that."

Erger shook his head. "Could you not just patch it up."

"Patch it up?"

"Yes, with leather." He frowned. "Did you at least keep it?"

Iyna looked away. "It *was* broken."

He sighed.

One of the scouts she had sent out came running through the gate into the small courtyard to wearily stand before them.

"What is it?" Iyna asked.

"I spotted a Fyoreten camp." She huffed. "Two leagues from 'ere."

"That close?" Iyna's eyes widened. "How many were there? What were they doing?"

"I think there's maybe forty of them," the scout answered. "Some I saw digging trenches while others seemed to be doing target practice."

Iyna glanced at the soldiers atop the walls and in the courtyard around her; each of them were looking at the scout with ears wide open. She returned her attention to the scout. "Have Barcial, Feeliath and Tarrow meet me in my room and then get some breakfast down ya."

"Thanks," she said and rushed into one of the two towers.

Erger grabbed a scrubbing brush from his cart. "I'll start with the gate then."

Iyna nodded. "That'll be smart." She marched inside the right tower and trekked down into the underground storage area. Returning to her cramped, cold room after the half-filled storage room, Iyna lit the half-melted candle resting on the dented agron barrel beside her dusty hammock.

Barcial and Tarrow entered, begrudgingly followed by Feeliath.

"One of the scouts came back," Iyna quickly explained. "A Fyoreten camp is only two leagues from here."

Feeliath was the first to reply "Then we should attack before they know we're here."

Iyna hesitated to argue as she thought about the pitiful state of the fort.

"No," Barcial replied. "We need not attack."

Feeliath turned to him. "They clearly intend to fight us and then push into Felliet."

Barcial stared back at him. "I'm just thinking we can resolve this through dialogue rather than battle."

Tarrow shook her head. "I doubt they would even listen to us."

Barcial glanced at Iyna before taking a deep breath. He turned to the other unit leaders. "They might if it's a fellow Fyoreten."

"What do you…" Feeliath's eyes widened. "Are you saying you're one of them?"

Barcial hesitated. "My full name is Barcial Synthion. My parents used to govern the Fyoreten region before the culling." He glanced away. "But once they were ordered to purge the Beast Riders, like the rest of the world, a full rebellion ensued. Fyoreten's resistance to the emperor's decree was one of the most vicious in the federation." His hands tensed. "It wasn't long before most of my family was struck down by the mobs. In fact, only my sister and I were able to flee to Erium. However, not long after the culling, the nobles decided we were no longer of use and the last two Synthions were forced to leave Erium."

Iyna muttered to herself, "If it weren't for the Beast Riders."

Feeliath crossed his arms. "You shouldn't be here then. No one would be able to properly fight their own people."

Iyna said, "He has never once shown cowardice or hesitation towards the Fyoreten soldiers, no matter how horrific the battles got."

Her words left the small, dim room silent.

Tarrow turned to Barcial and asked, "Why would they listen to you? Surely you are the one they hate the most."

"I have as much reason to despise the empire as they do. I will simply remind them who the true enemy is. Besides, I cannot allow any more of my countrymen to be killed by my hand."

"Your countrymen?" Feeliath said. "You've been tasked with defending *Felliet*. You should pay no heed to protecting the enemy."

Iyna brought her fist down upon the agron barrel where the candle flickered. "They have as much right to live free of Erium as us!" She stomped towards Feeliath. "Our enemies are to the east and west *not* the south."

Feeliath shook his head. "Our enemies are who the Dictorate say they are, and I have yet to hear them speak ill of Erium."

"Like Fyoreten's leaders?" She crossed her arms. "Erium and its emperor don't see us as equal let alone as an ally." She glanced to the others. "We all know it won't be long till they turn their massive army towards us."

Feeliath turned to Barcial. "What would you even say to them then? That you regret fighting *your people*?"

"I will say what we all know to be true." He scowled. "The true enemy lies to the west."

Feeliath shook his head. "I'm sorry you've been thrown into this mess, but we can't do anything other than defend Felliet against your countrymen."

"I have to try," Barcial said.

Feeliath's voice grew louder. "They will kill you before you can say you're sorry."

"I won't apologise," Barcial replied. "I am not responsible for the culling forced upon the people of the federation nor am I responsible for Erium's conquest of my nation." He hesitated. "As for my role in the war, I will speak the truth. I did it to survive, so that one day Darius and I could return home."

Silence once again filled the small, cold room.

Tarrow gently placed her hand on Barcial's shoulder. "Are you sure you want to do this?"

"As I said, I want no more of my people's blood needlessly shed," he answered. "If I don't return, Sareesa can lead my unit and…" He paused. "And I would like my body burned on the outskirts of Iorden."

A wave of dread and grief engulfed Iyna as she said, "It's decided then. Barcial will follow the scout to the Fyoreten camp and meet with them alone." She turned to Feeliath and Tarrow. "The rest of us will prepare the defences, but let's hope they're not needed."

Giddily crossing the little pink bridge over the sparkly moat, Niyaa was amazed as Reeffewd's scaly gate rolled upwards between the city's craggy pink walls. Inside, a very long sandy street was packed with all kinds of unique beast people of all sizes and strange appearances, all going about their business. One of the guards standing beneath the gate tower merrily waved his taloned hand to the returning scouting group while his friend with a wide toothy smile patted his chest.

Setting foot inside, Niyaa's excitement drew her to the front of the group as she looked around the pink craggily buildings whose glass windows sparked in the bright sunlight.

Mysia called to her daughter, "Don't wander too far."

Realising she was a fair distance ahead of the group, Niyaa turned back, but an enormous glass tunnel soaring above the southern pink homes caught her eye. She stared at the curved glass wall that stretched from one side of the city to the other, overshadowing the rocky wall alongside it. The glass wall flourished with vines of greens, yellows and reds within.

Fewttyre caught up with her. "That's the Florision."

Mysia stared wide eyed at the shining surface and asked, "How did you build such an enormous thing?"

"I guarantee it wasn't easy or quick," Fewttyre explained. "It took the efforts of every man, woman and child in the city to just gather and smelt the sand. But when it was finished, our food crisis was finally over."

Cabi turned to Mysia and Niyaa. "You should have seen the celebrations we held when we harvested the first vine berries."

The antlered man stepped closer to Cabi. "That was the day I asked this one out."

She smiled at him. "You mean when I asked *you* out."

The couple giggled together, and Fewttyre gestured further down the street. "Shall we show them the forge?"

Semy shook his head. "Afraid my family's probably dying to see me, so I'll catch you lot at the gathering."

"All right," Cabi replied. "Just don't be late."

As the small group wandered down the street, Niyaa turned to Fewttyre. "Gathering?"

"Oh." He pointed ahead. "You see that thin pole overlooking the saltless sea? That's where the pioneers and people gather to set rules and sort out any disagreements. It's a place where everyone's invited and can speak their mind about the state of the city."

Niyaa relaxed at the idea of living free from any elites or governors.

Mysia looked to him. "Saltless sea?"

"I suppose you can't see it from city's gateway." He grinned. "I can't wait to see the look on your faces when you see it."

Cabi patted Mysia's shoulder. "I guarantee you haven't seen anything like it."

The group arrived at a roofless, three-walled open forge located halfway down the sandy street. Along the left wall stood a huge semicircular furnace while the right wall was covered with red leaflike scales that seemed to grow downwards. Between them was a cracked hammering bench with a little stool on which stood an incredibly short, grey-skinned woman with four backwards-jutting horns below her ears. She was hammering pinning holes into a scaly chestplate. Niyaa couldn't help but look at the many tools and scrap pieces scattered around the sandy floor and picture Erger's shocked face had he seen his forge looking this messy.

The smither glanced up and crossed her arms. "So you're back then. Suppose you need stuff fixing?"

"Yeah, but it can wait." Cabi stretched her back limbs. "I actually passed by cause we have someone joining us who's good at smithery."

Niyaa confidently stepped forward.

The beast person gave one glance at her before returning her gaze to Cabi. "Little young, don't ya think?"

Mysia replied, "She can make reliable tools and casks."

"Metalwork then." The smither pointed her thumb to the wall of red scales. "I'm guessing she's never worked with this stuff then."

"I can learn." Niyaa approached the stone hammering bench. "I promise I won't get in the way."

The smither jumped off the stool from behind the bench, stepped closer to Niyaa and stared up at her. "You know, I've never had someone come to me asking for work, let alone an outsider."

Fewttyre replied, "They aren't outsiders anymore."

Looking down at the grey-skinned smither, Niyaa wondered whether she would even be allowed to help her.

Cabi said, "You know, we brought some agron back. Maybe Niyaa can show you how to use it."

The smither spun her widened gaze to Cabi. "You mean work with actual metal?"

"But only if Niyaa's allowed to become your assistant." Cabi smirked.

The smither sighed. "All right, you have a deal." She held her hand out for Niyaa to clasp. "I teach you and you teach me."

Niyaa accepted, placing her hand in the smither's tiny, slightly furry grip. "I can't wait to make things with you."

"And me you." She smiled. "Mithen by the way."

"What about your last name?" Niyaa asked.

"Never needed one." Mithen shrugged, releasing her grip. "Anyway if you're headin' to Florision, could you bring back a couple of ribbon roots?"

Cabi nodded. "Was gonna head there now actually."

Leaving the open forge, Niyaa and Mysia were led through the colourful city, passing yet more unique beast people till they reached the edge of the city. The two newcomers stood mesmerised at the sight of an unmoving sea, endlessly sparkling beyond the horizon. Beside them and across the entire water's motionless edge flourished vast swathes of pink lilies, yellow stalks and red pluff flowers filling the air with ambient flowery scents.

Niyaa couldn't turn away from the sparkly, endless water. "It's so beautiful."

"It really is," Mysia placed a hand on her daughter's shoulder.

Fewttyre pointed to a circular craggily pink seating area a long bridge away from the left side of the shore. "That's where we'll be holding the gathering later today."

Turning to the pink stadium-like platform, bridged far from the shore, Niyaa knew there couldn't be a more beautiful spot to hold the gatherings. Without a doubt, she and her mom had found a truly wonderous place to call home.

As the first of many drawbridges lowered before the Gildren and Felliet riders, Jornis pondered his words for the Lord of Bilhyn. They marched their horses inside, and the only welcome they received were suspicious and bitter looks from the numerous bowmen lining the castle's many walls and towers. Even as the group passed by a collection of hide-roofed homes and inns enclosed between the many layers of defences, they were greeted with further discontent especially towards the gilded chainmailed commander. Observing such spite towards Gildren, Jornis pondered whether it was devious manipulation by their king or whether it was actually warranted.

Escorted further inside, the small group was led through the final gatehouse and into Bilhyn's impregnable keep. Looking up at the purple and grey fur of the gargantuan wind flap soaring above the enormous keep, Jornis pondered the sheer amount of coin it would have cost to build and supply this fortress.

Dismounting before dozens of scornful bowmen, Jornis looked around and saw not a single servant or steward come to take their horses. Realising none of them would be staying a night within these walls, he sighed.

Copias stepped closer to Jornis. "A little excessive, isn't it?"

"The nation of Myklinn once stretched far along the coast," he explained. "It is understandable that their monarchy fears losing further lands and resources to Gildren."

The Silk Shore's commander said, "What should be understandable to everyone is that Gildren desires not to push inwards."

"Not for the country that used to have a coastline," Jornis said, turning his attention to the opening iron gates of the keep. "For a country to lose a piece of their territory to a young, expanding nation is both terrifying and shameful."

"No one alive can even remember when Myklinn held the Velvet Enclave," the gilded commander replied.

Jornis avoided criticising Gildren's council of their ignorant diplomacy and instead said, "It is a mistake to view past lifetimes as separate from your own. Many of Myklinn Greater could point to this territorial loss as the start of their decline, and considering the Myklinn civil war that broke their country in two, you can almost understand their paranoia."

As the gates opened wide, the Silk Shore's commander said, "Lingering on past grudges and claims will only cloud a ruler's judgement in the present."

Jornis looked at the armoured man, forcing himself not to respond to such a misguided, foolish notion.

Traipsing with Copias and the gilded commander, Jornis was unsurprised to find the short arched chamber filled with suspicious bowmen and astute guests. Nary a single piece of artwork hung on any of the plain stone walls, not even any engravings on the iron casted throne Lord Orther Hulld sat on. While pleased not to fine pointless decorations in the hall, Jornis remained despondent, for he observed Lord Orther's grimace in his thick iron woven fur at the approaching three foreigners.

The gilded armoured man bowed his head. "As the commander for the Silk Shores, I humbly bid you a fond greeting."

The lord gritted his teeth. "Save your breath for only what needs to be said."

"Then allow me to explain." The commander lifted his head. "The days grow uncertain and dark. Fyoreten has been conquered and Emperor Anisious Imerial killed. I strongly advise that we improve relations between our nations, that we work together to form a lasting peace where trade and culture can flourish across our respected border."

The lord crossed his arms. "You think me so foolish as to trust the manipulative venom-like tongue of you lowly merchants?"

Jornis said, "It would be foolish to so readily dismiss this idea of coexisting peace."

"And you would be?"

"I am Jornis Meyorter, former representative of Felliet and current diplomatic voice of the Elite Dictorate."

The lord paused and stared at the elite. "Tell me, *former* representative. What purpose does Felliet have for involving itself in matters not relating to itself?"

"To believe any part of the federation is isolated from the dispute between Myklinn Greater and Gildren is troublingly misguided," Jornis explained. "However, the belief that a continued build-up of forces along this border is benefiting your nation is far more reckless."

"And what if you were named Lord of Bilhyn and entrusted with the security of the west?" Orther asked. "Would your course of action be to send all of Myklinn's armies away and hope the council of Gildren keep their word?"

"Obviously, I would not to send a single soldier away," Jornis answered. "However, I would allow trade to freely cross the border without the reliance on individual merchants and citizens. This would not only provide Gildren with the iron and agron it needs, but it would provide your vast nation access to the markets north of the Therra. From purely an economical position, it would greatly benefit Myklinn Greater."

The Silk Shore's commander glanced at Jornis as if doubting the answer.

"A purely economic stance perhaps." Lord Orther shook his head. "But it appears you clearly do not understand the long history between Myklinn and its enemies."

"History is history," the siloin commander replied. "Do not let it dictate your actions to inevitable misfortune."

"Our iron and agron will go where we see fit and will *not* go through Gildren lands." He rose from his throne. "Now, unless there is anything more, you will take your leave."

The bowmen lining the walls stepped forward, escorting Jornis, Copias and the commander from the keep.

Before long, the small procession was led out of Bilhyn entirely, and once they were far from earshot of the first drawbridge, the commander halted. He turned to Jornis. "Why did you offer their traders passage through Gildren?"

"Two reasons," Jornis explained. "The first is simply to appear willing to compromise and be fair. The second is to confirm my suspicions that their monarchy already possesses a route to Artor and Erium." The elite grinned. "The fact Lord Orther refused so quickly despite the great need for trade for their primary production is clear proof of this."

"That is quite a strong accusation," the commander said. "Especially when it comes from a single lord's refusal."

"Did he not say *iron and agron will continue to go where they see fit*?" Jornis asked.

The commander said, "You are suggesting they are already transporting metals."

"Precisely," Jornis said. "And there is only one possible route Myklinn Greater's traders and officials can take: through the ports of the Riverveins."

Copias asked, "But surely it would have taken a lot of effort to convince the Riverveins to even meet in secret, let alone ally themselves with Myklinn Greater."

"I highly doubt it is a proper alliance," Jornis responded.

The gilded commander crossed his arms. "If the Riverveins are so bold as to help transport metals to Artor, then it all but guarantees an alliance."

"Only from Gildren's perceptive," Jornis argued. "To everyone else it can be seen as a simple trade arrangement."

"Either way, it is no good to simply speculate." The commander steered his horse forward. "Rest assured, I will have this fully investigated."

Moving his steed to follow, Jornis pondered what Myklinn's monarchy offered to have the Riverveins change its neutral stance.

Trudging along the muddied road, Vernon saw nothing through the towering reeds enclosed around the winding road, leaving him wondering how long it would be till he reached Rerrunter. Orfain had once spoken of the awful smell residing throughout the flat northern marshes, but to personally breathe in its putrid stench of egg and manure made Vernon wince with every step. When he finally caught sight of the town's gate at the far end of the corridor road through the enormous reeds, he sighed in relief and quickened his feet.

Beyond the open clay gate, the buildings were made from tar-thatched straw atop a base of blackened stakes. Before he could enter, something large rustled the reeds to his left, stopping him in the midst of the muddied road.

Vernon stood unmoving as several large legs stomped louder and faster than any horse closing in on him, and he felt the ground quake in its wake. A fully grown reed cutter emerged onto the road, its six spindle-thin, brown-haired legs soaring over the carriage high reeds while somehow supporting its enormous cylindrical body.

Vernon stared at the huge creature's sharpened, pike-length fangs under its six slit-like red eyes and noticed a beige-armoured rider sitting bareback atop the creature with a thick hooked spear held high. The armour was comprised entirely of animal rib cages pinned and strapped to a full leather, padded suit. The helmet was a tight configuration of curved tusks, leaving only a narrow visor for the rider's eyes.

The rider tapped the enormous reed cutter with the hooked spear, and the creature lowered its enormous body. A female voice emerged from the helmet. "You're too well dressed for someone wanting marsh work, so what brings you to my place?"

Stunned, Vernon stared up at her for a long awkward moment. "I was sent by Elleasious Imerial to collect taxes owed by this town."

"That so?" She paused. "What's your name?"

"Vernon Meyorter."

Her voice changed to delight. "Did you realise a coin collector has to investigate the surrounding area before determining the amount of tax owed?" She leaned forward on the creature, tapping the tip of her spear against the side of its body. The reed cutter lowered its body further, setting it on the muddied road. "And since it would be foolish and dangerous to go through the marshes on foot, I suggest you climb up."

Bewildered, Vernon stared at the rider and approached the side of the creature where he found an ascending handful of muddied stirrups bolted onto the creature's tough skin. He placed his foot into the first and grasped one further up, feeling the soft mud squelch through his fingers. He climbed up the stirrups until he was kneeling on the huge creature.

"I suggest you hold onto me," she advised. "You certainly would not want to fall off."

Vernon edged his way along the hardened back of the creature till he sat behind the rider and grasped the rib cages covering her back. Tightening his grip, Vernon asked, "What's you name?"

"Awelin Grittion." She glanced back with smug eyes. "Now you better hold on tight." She tapped the creature again, bringing its body into the air. Pulling himself closer to the rider, Vernon gazed across a flat landscape filled to the horizon with brown reeds where only Rerrunter and a few distant reed cutters jutted above the unending brown.

The rider pointed her hooked spear forward and the reed cutter charged ahead, bringing Vernon's head rearing back as he desperately tightened his grip. The creature surged through the reeds, moving its spindle legs faster than any horse as its cylindrical body skimmed the tips of the reeds. Vernon peered over her bone-armoured shoulder and saw they were charging towards a pair of similarly dressed riders harvesting reeds in a small clearing.

Reaching the clearing, the female rider tapped the back of the reed cutter, bringing the creature to an abrupt halt. Catching his breath, Vernon turned to the woman, hiding his discomfort.

She asked, "How'd you find the ride so far?"

Vernon forced a smile. "Certainly a lot faster than walking."

In the clearing, one reed cutter effortlessly cut the reeds while the second used its incredibly sharp fangs to delicately pick up the felled reeds and place them into the other's huge storage saddle. This dual rotating system was astonishingly efficient in harvesting reeds leaving no doubt reed production in the town remained high.

Awelin waved her free hand to the other two riders. They stopped harvesting the reeds and used their hooked spears to charge to her.

"Got a tax collector here who needs to look around." She pointed her thumb at Vernon. "Why don't you tell him a bit about your work."

The rider with reeds stacked on his saddle shrugged. "Not much to say really, other than it's a dirty, miserable job."

The other rider crossed his arms at Vernon. "All to make some paper for those nobles in the cities."

"The books made from the reeds are used to record history, famous events and current issues," Vernon said. "Additionally, these reeds are used to make rope, which is used by every kind of person."

"Books don't put food on my plate," the man replied. "And the rope goes mostly to the sailors and tribowmen."

Vernon shook his head. "Those tribowmen and sailors protect Erium and its people. But on your first point about history not being relevant, I'd argue it allows everyone to look back at past events, mistakes and successes that we *all* can learn from."

The female rider shrugged. "Only for those who can actually afford books."

"Has demand for books and rope fallen?" Vernon asked. "Because if not, then your town would be quite wealthy."

"There are plenty of other marsh towns that we contend with," she said. "Plus you can make paper from parchment as well."

"The demand for books and rope is considerable throughout Erium without even factoring in the other nations," Vernon said. "Furthermore, parchment is far too costly and thick to be used for anything other than messenger letters."

The rider with the reeds stored to his back snorted. "And what would you know about our work?"

Vernon stared back with dispassionate eyes. "I know reed cutting is a lucrative industry and that Rerrunter should have more than enough coin to pay its taxes."

Awelin replied, "Then perhaps I should show you our records." She glanced to the two other riders. "Perhaps then you can see just how bad the situation is here."

She raised her hooked spear back to the town, and Vernon tightened his grip on her bone armour. The reed cutter surged across the reeds once more. At an enormous clearing to the rear of the town, seven reed cutters crouched in a large circle with a hooked spear planted in the dirt before their faces.

Awelin caressed her hooked spear in her creature's neck, guiding it to an empty spot near the rear gate of the village and had it crouch down. "You can let go now."

"Thank you." Vernon released his grip and nudged himself backwards to the stirrups, watching the female rider stand up straight on the creature's back. Climbing down, Vernon landed on the muddied ground, and the rotten stench reaffirmed itself in his nostrils. His clothes were encrusted in dirt and muck.

Awelin climbed down her reed cutter in her full rib cage armour and marched to the head of the creature. She planted her hooked spear in the ground before its sharp fangs, leaving each of its six slit red eyes staring motionless at the curved blade.

Following her through the rear gate, Vernon walked along a muddied path through a disordered clutter of raised homes. Not a single sound emanated through its blackened straw walls, leaving the town eerily quiet. Further along the mud-covered street, the stench lingering from the vast marshes hadn't faded. He remained undeterred by the appearance, for he knew the coin made from this industry was, without question, vast.

Vernon was led to a long building at the centre of the quiet town where he found a short closed-off entranceway after a set of clay steps. A smaller set of bone armour hung on the entranceway's side wall. Awelin removed a pin from the chin of her helmet and took it off, revealing a scarred face beneath short brown hair. She placed the helmet on an empty hook opposite the other armour set and shouted towards a closed door.

"Wealt! We have a guest!" Awelin removed pins from the rib cage spines covering her body, carefully arranging each of the rib cage bones on the wall.

Staring at the scars covering her face, Vernon asked, "Why isn't your armour made from iron or agron?"

"Cause rib cages snap," she explained. "It can break your fall from a height, whereas metal would just make the landing heavier." She grinned, revealing several missing teeth. "Would you like some food after your journey? My sister and I are having something special for dinner today."

"Yes, that would be nice."

"Perfect." She removed the final rib cage and led Vernon to a cramped dining room. "Shall we?"

No decorations adorned the tar-thatched walls or sealed window, with no sound of a crackling fireplace anywhere inside.

A younger girl in similarly worn leather clothing entered, balancing three plates of dark orange meat chunks and odd brown leaves. As she set them down on the table, Wealt smiled at Vernon. "It's rare to find someone so compassionate willing to visit our humble town."

Vernon said nothing as the three of them took their seats around the plain dining table.

Wealt cut into the meat chunk, oozing a yellowish liquid onto the clay plate. "So what brings you here?"

"He wants to collect taxes," Awelin answered.

The younger girl appeared shocked. "But we don't have the money."

"I know," Awelin replied. "But you shouldn't fret. I'm sure he means to be fair in his judgement and never take *too* much from us."

Vernon felt insulted at this dishonest performance. "You can rest assured I will only ask for what is owed."

"That's a shame," Awelin replied, cutting into her meat chunk. "I would've liked to have some fresh food brought here."

Vernon lifted his knife to carve into the foul meat and reminded himself of the wealth and popularity of the book industry. Raising a small piece of the orange chunk to his mouth, he winced at the abhorrent stench flooding his nostrils.

"Do you not like oig thigh?" Wealt asked, nearly hiding her smirk as she took another bite.

Hearing those words, Vernon plunged the meat into his mouth to the torment of his tongue. Chewing the meat, Vernon forced himself not to gag and quickly swallowed to the displeasure of his stomach. "It certainly has a distinct taste." He stared down at the rest of the meat and begrudgingly cut another piece. "I certainly will need to get accustomed to it when I am to return in the next cycle."

Awelin stopped eating. "When you return?"

He stopped cutting and turned to look her in the eyes. "Would it not make sense to have the same coin collector for the same region?"

She folded her arms with the knife still in her hand. "If there were coin to collect."

A tense silence filled the small room as the two of them stared at each other. Vernon finally got straight to the point. "I understand reed harvesting is grimy work, but I know it to be a profitable trade. I will not be fooled into believing your town or its people are impoverished, so I shall not leave until you have paid your debt in full."

Awelin's stern expression didn't change as she glanced to the knife in her hand. "And what if you were to have lost your way in the marshes and accidentally fallen into one of the many mud pits around here. Would you still be demanding I pay my debt if that were to happen?"

Stunned into silence, Vernon froze.

"Well?" she asked, twiddling the knife in her hand.

"Well, I…" Vernon pictured his body lying amongst the reeds gripping him in fear, and he considered the consequences it would bring the perpetrators. "Even if I'm gone, you will still have debt looming over you and your town. I highly doubt it would end with me."

Wealt cheerfully cut off another piece. "It can at least buy us some more time."

Vernon turned in disbelief at her merriment as she ate another piece. "The Imerial family does not consist of fools. They will not sit idle if I do not return."

"Is that so?" Awelin asked. "You believe the emperor's personal family, the most powerful people in the world, are concerned about *your* wellbeing?"

"They are concerned about the wellbeing of the country," Vernon replied, remembering details from *The Foundations*. "Throughout all of the empire's history, each emperor has sought a bright, prosperous future for all of his citizens. I assure you, he or his family will not overlook the murder of one who intends to collect what you hoard."

Silence flooded the small room once more as Awelin kept her gaze focused on Vernon. She rose from her chair, scraping it against the floor.

Vernon bit the inside of his cheek, hiding his fear.

A long, dreaded pause ensued before she stuck her knife in the meat chunk and sat with an amused smirk. "I think I can see why Elly offered you the test."

Bewildered, Vernon stared wide eyed at her, unable to say a word.

"You really think she would just give you an official position after you dared do something so egregious?" She took out a folded letter from her chest pocket. "I've known Elly since we were kids and *I assure you*, I know far more about the Imerial family and its history."

"She wrote you a letter beforehand?" Vernon asked, taking a moment to understand. "Which was how you noticed me before I even reached the town gate."

She leaned back in her seat. "If you had, you would have noticed the transport hub."

"Transport hub?"

"It's where the workers' earnings go," Awelin explained. "From there, an escorted carriage takes it to their families across Erium."

Wealt chuckled. "All cause they're too delicate to settle here."

Vernon relaxed as the explanation sunk in. "So is that where the tax money is held?"

Awelin shook her head. "Like all the other marsh towns, Rerrunter has never once been sent a coin collector. In fact, every now and then, Sidium sends us coin to keep the reed harvesting running smoothly."

Thinking of the exhausting journey travelling here, Vernon sighed. "So there's nothing for me to collect?"

"I didn't say that." Awelin glanced at her sister who rose from her seat and left the room. "Long ago I made a bet with Elly. I said no one would bother risking their life over collecting something as insignificant as a pair of coin bags just out of the sake of loyalty." Her grin widened. "Guess I lost."

A sudden wave of pride washed over Vernon and he asked, "But how did you know I was loyal to the Imerial name and not just lying?"

She held up the folded letter. "Because Elly said so."

"I see." He nodded in and asked, "Elly?"

"It's what her brothers and I called her when we were young." She leaned back in her seat. "But if I were you, I wouldn't call her that."

An amused smile crossed Vernon's face, and he pondered how this woman used to play with the current emperor and his siblings. He wondered how she ended up in charge of Rerrunter.

Wealt returned, carrying two hefty coin bags in her hands, and placed them in front of Vernon. "I honestly never thought we'd lose the bet."

"And I thought I'd be tested on the job itself," he replied.

Awelin rose from her chair, turning to her sister. "Shall we prepare a proper meal now in our proper dining room?"

"Gladly," Wealt replied.

Vernon breathed in relief and cheerfully stood.

The beautiful smells of the vast greenery inside the Florision stayed with Niyaa the whole time she and her mom explored the pink city. The two of them were sitting on the front row of the circular gathering stands watching all the other colourful beast people gather around them. Niyaa even saw a bunch of beast people with fins and webbed feet bobbing in the sparkly water beside the bridge leading to the coral stands. She wondered if any of them could actually breath underwater and turned to the six pioneers in the centre of the empty sandy clearing.

Cabi pressed her back limbs against the stone seating and leaned closer to Niyaa. "How do you like Reeffewd so far?"

"I love it," Niyaa said. "There's no better place in the world."

Mysia added, "I admit it's hard to imagine a more inviting place."

"You'll have to thank Elixsis and Grenis for that." Cabi pointed to a couple of the pioneers. "You see the green-scaled guy with the long face and that woman standing next to him in the long white dress?"

Niyaa stared at the bold green man and the golden-haired lady standing close together. "Yeah?"

"They're the ones who really made this city grow and flourish," Cabi explained. "Without them, Reeffewd would be just another camp along the saltless sea."

Mysia turned to her. "Are there other places for your people?"

"We all have the freedom to do as we please out here." Cabi turned to her antlered boyfriend sitting beside her. "We were even thinking of heading to one of the quiet settlements one day."

Anthile leaned closer to her. "It won't be quiet with kids in the picture."

She snuggled into him. "Absolutely."

Mysia suggested, "If you're waiting for coin, then I don't mind giving you some I earn from brewing. After all, I owe you for bringing us here."

Cabi shook her head. "No one uses money here. We all work for the benefit of those around us, and we usually know when someone's done a good or bad deed."

Anthile explained, "We're actually waiting till everyone's sure we'll be safe from any more purges."

"Purges?" Niyaa asked.

"What you call *expeditions*," Cabi replied. "After the last one reached Lorish, the pioneers all agreed we could no longer sit idle while waiting for the next one to come our way."

Mysia said, "That's why you all decided to gather information and supplies in Felliet."

"I only wish all the pioneers agreed on it," Cabi said. "See that one with the cane?"

Niyaa turned again to the pioneers and stared at an elderly man with a strange iron brace on his left leg leaning his taloned hand on a cane.

"That's Tovern," Cabi said. "He's the one who wanted an all-out attack on Felliet."

Niyaa turned to her. "He wanted to attack us?"

"Thankfully, no one supported his idea," she replied. "Even Romult, the founder of Lorish and Reeffewd, rejected it."

Relieved, Niyaa glanced to the greying red-furred pioneer sitting in a copper wheelchair. "That's good to hear."

Anthile shrugged. "It was just as stupid as Fericka's proposal."

Cabi said, "She wanted to experiment adding a second animal limb to someone."

Niyaa looked at the normal brown-haired woman whispering to Fewttyre. "Is that bad?"

"It's dangerous, that's what it is. The body would struggle handling a second beast limb."

Mysia asked, "So why did she propose it?"

"She believes everyone's abilities can eventually be perfected, so by adding a second limb that complements the first, we will be closer to that perfection." Cabi shook her head. "So glad only Fewttyre knows how to perform the surgery."

"It's a wonder how she managed to become a pioneer then," Mysia said.

"Well…" Cabi said. "She's the one who helps the children adapt to their beast limbs. She even makes person-specific items to help their beast-specific needs. In fact, Fericka was the one who wove that basket for me to hide my back limbs."

A moment later, the green scaly man raised his voice. "Thanks for coming everyone." He gestured his green palm to Cabi. "As most of you know, we called the gathering because Cabi's team has returned with news from Felliet." Cabi, Semy and Borren all stood. "Were you able to gather any info on Felliet?"

Cabi fixed her gaze on the pioneers as she raised her voice. "We discovered Felliet has created an army and sent it to attack Fyoreten."

Confused mutterings and worried talk sprang up around the stands, and Niyaa realised Iyna could be in danger. Unable to do anything, Niyaa slumped in her hard seat, wondering whether Iyna was in this army or a garrison somewhere.

Tovern hobbled his cane a step forward. "How large is this force?"

Cabi shook her head. "I wasn't able to find out."

He turned to the other pioneers. "We should strike now while their army is distracted."

Fewttyre replied, "It is foolish to attack a force not knowing their size or purpose."

"But we know their purpose!" Tovern argued. "They've created this army to threaten us."

Fewttyre crossed his arms. "So explain why they used it to attack Fyoreten?"

"It doesn't matter," Tovern said. "Sooner or later they will use that army on us."

The green scaly man asked Cabi, "Did you learn their reasoning?"

All gazes turned to her once more. "We believe it was done at Erium's request as a kind of joint invasion."

Fewttyre stroked his chin. "That would imply Erium wishes to take back the lands they lost in the culling."

The scaly man crossed his arms. "Then why would Felliet help Erium?"

"I can't say," Fewttyre said. "But we can at least say that Felliet's focus is now on their western border."

"And what happens if Erium conquers Felliet?" Tovern asked. "Would *their* focus be to the west?"

Fewttyre struggled to answer.

The pioneer in the wheelchair raised his voice. "If another purge happens, we will respond without mercy. However, I will not condone a preemptive attack." Nods came from all but Tovern as the greying red-furred man turned his chair towards Cabi. "Now, was there any news of - Parred's group?"

She darted her eyes away. "I regret to say they were caught in Milnet."

Shock and fear filled the stands as the beast people all looked to one another in horror.

"We heard they were sent to the Atimah," Cabi said. "Though we cannot say how many of them made it there."

The pioneers glanced at each other. The furry man in the wheelchair nudged himself closer. "What else did you learn from your time in Felliet, my dear?"

"We discovered the residents of Edenor had moved to the neighbouring village of Pelight. Not long after, their governor betrayed them, taking a great amount from them in their time of need." She turned to Mysia and Niyaa. "Which was why two of them have joined us."

Niyaa watched as every pair of eyes turned to them, and Mysia rose from her seat. Niyaa copied, stiffly standing beside her mom.

"My name is Mysia. I have travelled here with my daughter so we may find a peaceful, happy life. I can brew good ales, and my daughter Niyaa can forge tools. I just hope we prove ourselves valuable to your community."

Niyaa lowered her head as she wished her mom could've introduced her dad.

The green scaly man said, "I deeply regret what happened after we forced those spearmen from our lands. The raid on Edenor should never have happened."

The golden-haired woman spoke up. "I know it won't be much to repay what befell you both, but I can at least say you will be welcome here. I even have a small cottage overlooking the water that you may have."

Noticing the scaly man nod to his wife, Niyaa felt strangely relieved.

"Thank you," Mysia replied, sitting back down with her daughter

Following Tarrow down one of the fort's towers, Iyna was overcome with relief that Barcial was returning to the fort. Nearing the darkened courtyard, she tried to imagine what kinds of things he had said to the Fyoreten and what he must be feeling.

From the small shadowy courtyard, she watched him stagger over the moat bridge. All sense of relief faded as he passed through the gate, head low and hands tucked in his armpits.

Iyna and Tarrow sprinted to Barcial. Blood dripped from his hands.

"What happened?" Iyna asked.

His head stayed low as he removed his hands from his armpits, revealing both his thumbs had been sliced off.

Iyna tore a long strip from the bottom of her grey undershirt and covered one of the wounds.

Tarrow turned towards the clouded mountains through the bars in the gate. "Damn them!"

"I deserved this," Barcial muttered.

"You're wrong," Iyna told him as she knotted the shirt piece across his hand. "You weren't the one who started the culling, and you weren't the one who declared war."

He shook his head. "I helped Erium conquer my homeland."

Iyna grabbed his shoulder. "Look at me."

Reluctantly, he lifted his wearied head to look her in the eyes.

"Fyoreten would've been conquered with or without you," she said. "You are *not* to blame."

He silently turned away.

Tarrow asked him, "What did they say?"

"They said I wasn't even worth killing and I should instead watch as my puppeteers fall before their bolts. They took my thumbs so I can never grasp a spear, ink feather or … or anything else ever again."

Iyna tore off another strip from her shirt. "What's important is that you're alive."

He didn't reply.

Wanting to break the silence, Iyna asked, "How many did you see there?"

He hesitated. "A little greater than forty and without any horses."

Tarrow turned to Iyna. "The scouts were right then. We outnumber them three to one."

Wrapping the second shirt strip across Barcial's other hand, Iyna felt the chilling night wind blow under her thin chestplate. "How do you think they will attack us then?"

"Maybe they'll wait for us to leave the fort," Tarrow suggested. "Strike us out in the open."

Barcial remained silent.

Knotting the shirt strip, Iyna's mind was filled with ideas of how the Fyoreten group could force her army out till she realised they wouldn't. Her army would not be allowed to leave the mountain at all as the sheer number difference would put Fyoreten at a great disadvantage. If they wanted revenge against Felliet, they would avoid her army retreating even if it was a desperate scattered route down the mountainside. The Fyoreten group would avoid a pitched battle and instead focus on wearing down her soldiers.

"When will they attack then?" Iyna asked herself. Glancing at Barcial, she turned to the dark clouds blanketing much of the sky and looked to Tarrow. "You need to ready your tribowmen for an attack right now."

Tarrow nodded and rushed to the tower's stairs.

Iyna shouted to the soldiers watching them from the surrounding ramparts. "Prepare yourselves! They're attacking tonight!"

They turned to the blackened mountainous landscape and rushed to their defence positions along the wall.

Barcial drew his bandaged hands close to his chest. "I should command my unit."

"Sareesa will do it. You need those wounds tended to." Iyna turned to the furnace placed alongside the well. "Go see that smither. His furnace could seal those wounds."

Barcial looked at her with wide eyes and gave a slight nod. He trudged towards the tower where Erger slept with the other soldiers. Iyna turned to the barred gate and the pair of soldiers guarding it.

"You two, step away from there right now." Her command seemed to surprise them. "That is unless you want to be struck by a crossbow bolt."

They obeyed, stepping to either side of the gate with a tightened grip on their spears. Iyna turned to the tribowmen rushing along the ramparts and set off to join them.

Much of the ramparts were still covered in rubble with some of the edges overlooking the courtyard badly crumbling. She spotted Tarrow above the gate ordering her unit to crank their tribows and get in position.

Iyna turned her gaze outward, trying to glimpse anything in the dark mountainside to no avail. Before long, the cranking stopped, leaving only the chilling wind harassing the stone walls to fill the silence. Staring at the vast black landscape waiting for the assured attack was agony.

A long while later, Iyna heard a crossbow string snap, and a bolt struck the stone below her. Further strikes followed, plinking at the wall just short of the ramparts.

Tarrow loudly bellowed, "Enemy attack!"

Iyna squinted at the dark landscape, trying desperately to spot any kind of shimmer. A bolt struck the stone next to her, forcing her to duck below the opening. Turning her gaze down the rampart, Iyna saw to her dismay all the tribows were silent as the soldiers also struggled to spot anyone. Each of their faces were filled with terror, and many of them released their tribow bolts randomly into the darkness.

Remembering the reload speed of both their tribows and the Fyoreten crossbows, Iyna shouted, "Don't reply to them!" A handful of tribowmen turned to her in confusion, and she ordered, "We'll wait it out tonight. So stay out of their sight and don't respond to them."

The handful in front of her reluctantly obeyed, ducking their heads and bodies. The rest hadn't listened, forcing Iyna to march along the debris-ridden rampart with her head kept uncomfortably low.

Passing each of the tribowmen, Iyna repeated, "Don't respond. Keep your head low."

She found most of them obeying while the rest she had to yank away from the gaps, each time nearly throwing herself off balance on the crumbling wall. She reached Tarrow. "We'll wait it out tonight. Make sure your unit doesn't release their bolts unless they charge the gate."

"Are you serious?" Tarrow asked. "We can't just wait here."

"It takes ages to crank the tribows," Iyna said. "We can't needlessly waste our shots against people we can't see."

Tarrow stared at her commander and asked, "So we wait till sunrise?"

Iyna nodded.

"All right then." Tarrow moved further along the wall, telling her unit the plan.

Crouching next to the stone gap above the gate, Iyna bit her bottom lip as the sound of the bolts striking the stone continued to ring throughout the night.

Chapter nineteen – Application

Seventh eclipse, nineteenth day

As the sun peered over the mountainous horizon, the Fyoreten crossbowmen finally fled, filling the exhausted Felliet soldiers with relief. Not for a single moment throughout the cold night could any of them catch any sleep, leaving them all wearily watching the empty landscape, still unable to spot the attackers.

Turning away from the brightening mountainside, Iyna saw the relieved and dismal expressions on the soldiers along the ramparts. She walked up to Tarrow. "Have your unit rest, and join me in my room."

Tarrow nodded and directed her unit off the walls.

Iyna looked down at Barcial and the smither wearily sitting beside the smouldering furnace and went to check on them.

In the courtyard, Iyna approached them and stared at Barcial's scorched hands. "How do you feel?"

He held up his shaking hands, avoiding her eyes. "Better than last night."

Erger patted Barcial's shoulder. "Sorry about the poor job I did. Never tended to someone's wounds before, you see."

"I'm just glad I passed out before you did my other hand," Barcial replied.

"Again, sorry 'bout that," the smither said.

"So…" Barcial held up his pale thumbless hands. "I won't be able to use a spear now."

"Only if you don't want to," Erger replied. "I can strap your spear to your forearm and then add a handle for your fingers to grip."

Barcial stared wide eyed at the smither. "Are you sure?"

"Who do you think I am? Some backwater apprentice?" Erger asked. "When I say I can make something, I mean it."

Iyna nodded to the smither. "See to it right away."

He sighed. "Was hoping I would get a proper rest after carting this thing up." He tapped his warm furnace and rose to his feet. "Right, I'll see this one swinging a spear before nightfall."

Barcial said, "Thought my life ended yesterday."

Iyna held her hand out for him. "Even if you weren't able to grasp a spear anymore, I would still want you in my army."

He stared at her palm. "Why?"

She smiled. "Cause you're one of the smartest, most skilled fighters I've ever seen."

Barcial looked at her in disbelief and burst out laughing.

"What?" Iyna asked.

"I'm sorry." He took her hand. "It's just I would have heard that from my sister when I was a small kid."

Iyna lifted him to his feet. "That's not something you should say about your commander."

"Nor should a commander say such childish things." He gave a wide smile. "Anyway, let's join Tarrow and Feeliath. I imagine there's much to discuss."

Trekking across the courtyard and into the tower, Iyna was glad to see the relieved smile staying on Barcial's face despite his hands still quivering from the ordeal. Feeliath and Tarrow were waiting with the lone candle lit in her room. She closed the door behind the four of them. "Thankfully we didn't lose anyone last night."

Tarrow rubbed her eyes. "But it's likely they'll return every night now."

"In that case"—Feeliath turned to Iyna—"we should attack them while we still can!"

Iyna leaned her back against the door and remembered the vengeful looks the Fiskior people had given her. Barcial's smile had vanished.

"Well?" Feeliath asked, turning to the other three. "We can't just wait within these walls till the food runs out."

Barcial replied, "Nor can they expect food to appear on the mountainside."

"Actually it will," Feeliath said. "The supplies that have been sent for us. All the Fyoreten have to do is seize them as they travel up the narrow mountain passages. Then we'll starve." He crossed his arms. "Our only option is to attack their camp, destroy all their food and water, and then force them off these mountains."

"They intend on us leaving the safety of the fort to attack them in the open," Barcial said. "When we leave here in our groups towards their camp, they'll ambush us from all sides. Essentially we would become easy prey for their crossbows."

Tarrow said, "Then we better defend against them." She turned to Iyna. "If we light fires along the opposite slopes, we can see where they are and take them out before anything happens."

Iyna imagined bonfires scattered across the entire clearing and the slopes opposite.

Feeliath shook his head. "Even if we had that much straw and stem pieces, the light wouldn't last long enough. Besides, it will make it harder to see any figures moving where the fires don't shine."

Tarrow grew angry. "Well, we have to come up with some kind of plan to defend this place. Otherwise, night after night, they'll wear us down till we're nothing."

"Then what about attacking them at night?" Feeliath asked. "We know they'll be there at nightfall. Why not charge out the spearmen to attack after their first volley?"

Barcial looked him in disbelief. "You want to charge your unit into pitch darkness towards a hidden enemy with the light of the fort behind you?"

Iyna pictured the scenario from the Fyoreten perspective. Barcial was right; the spearmen would be easy to spot and surround. In that image, a realisation came to her. "I think I know a way to defeat them and perhaps a way that can take them prisoner." All three of them turned to her, awaiting the explanation. Iyna stared at the single candle flickering in the small underground room and held her thumb up to it. She turned to Barcial. "You remember what happened at Iorden?"

After a cosy sleep on a cushiony feather bed, Niyaa walked with her mom through the pink coral streets till they arrived at the open forge. Mithen hadn't arrived yet. Niyaa wondered what she could possibly be doing and noticed the red scales covering the wall had grown lower since yesterday.

Mysia crouched to her daughter's eye level. "If anything happens, I'll be in the Florision looking at possible ingredients, all right?"

"I'll be fine, Mom."

"All right then." She stood up. "I'll bring back a wide bunch of ingredients for us to test."

"For *us* to test?" Niyaa grinned.

"Of course. Unless you'd rather watch."

Niyaa shook her head. "Not a chance."

"Good. I'll see you back at the cottage this evening then."

Niyaa turned to the tools, broken scales and sand scattered across the ground. Spotting an old scruffy brush lying beneath the wall of red scales, she began cleaning.

Niyaa placed the tools atop the cracked hammering bench and got on her knees to brush the dust and discarded scales off the floor.

Halfway through, she heard Mithen's voice. "You're up early."

Niyaa looked up from the ground and saw the smither standing at her eye level. "Erger would always start this early."

"Erger?"

"He's the smither I used to work for." Niyaa got to her feet, looking down at Mithen. "He always wanted me to get to the forge nice and early."

"Well, you don't need to do that here." Mithen picked up her stool and set it at the base of the wall of growing scales. "Look closely." She stepped atop the stool, twisted a scale from the midst of the wall and handed it to Niyaa. "You see how there are no veins, lines or anything? That means this one is fully matured and is now as stiff as a horn, unlike"—she hopped off the stool and tore a scale from the very bottom row—"these new ones."

Niyaa bent her knees, bringing her eyes closer to the scale and noticing tiny vein-like lines all over the red scale. "Does that mean these aren't stiff?"

"It does." Mithen placed the scale between her thumb and finger, bending it slightly. "And that is why the newer ones are perfect for armour and saddles."

Niyaa remembered how agron had to be bent with many hammer strokes. "So these bendy ones can be easily shaped."

"Exactly." Mithen plucked other bendy scales. "The mature ones are useful for things like shields and doors."

As the smither plucked more scales, Niyaa noticed a thin tangled network of pale red veins drooping behind the scales. "Is that what the scales grow from?"

"Yep. A new layer will be ready tomorrow, so long as we give it the milk it needs, that is."

"Milk?"

"Oh right. So when Wellore…I mean Fewttyre's dad created these plants, he said milk's the best thing for them to grow." Mithen shrugged. "Guess it must need a certain nutrient or something."

After plucking the last scale off the bottom row, Mithen took them all to a metal grill overlooking the furnace. "Right, we're gonna heat them a little so we can punch holes in 'em."

"So what are we gonna make with them?" Niyaa asked.

"A chestplate. Exactly what our fighters need."

"A chestplate?" Niyaa's excitement faded.

"Should stop any kind of slash."

Niyaa remembered the night Edenor was attacked and the red armour they had all worn. "I ... I don't think I can do that."

"Why not?" Mithen looked confused. "Don't you want the people venturing out to be safe?"

Niyaa couldn't bring herself to answer.

Mithen raised her arm and patted Niyaa's shoulder. "Don't worry. I don't make weapons in this forge, only things that'll help protect the ones protecting us."

Niyaa's worries eased. "So you don't forge anything that causes harm to others?"

Mithen shook her head. "Don't have the iron or agron for it anyway."

Niyaa felt a wave of relief wash over her.

"Now let's quit dawdling and light the fire."

Jornis rode his horse behind the commander of the Silk Shores and his bodyguards. The marble walls of Innill came into sight. Unsurprisingly, the vast number of traders and merchants along the roads entering the city hadn't changed despite the raid on Delport. The polished orange-veined walls of the city were still covered with gilded ivy, and the flow of traffic entering the city still remained unslowed.

Copias moved his horse closer to Jornis and asked, "Is it me or are the Marble Wheels being complacent?"

"It would appear so," Jornis said. "However, you must consider their lands are far from the threats along the coast."

"The Marble Wheels cannot grow silk and would be in a dire situation if the other siloins fall," he said. "Your plan with the beacons may have directed the Rauders elsewhere for now, but it doesn't address the threat from Artor or Myklinn Greater."

Jornis turned to him. "How would you suggest the counsel of Gildren handle the current situation?"

Copias lowered his voice further to avoid the ears of the gilded commander and his bodyguards. "Each of the siloins need to demonstrate its ability to fight on the battlefield and on the sea. That way it can demonstrate to its neighbours its ability to stop any invasion."

"I don't like that answer," Jornis said. "Once Gildren's armies display their might, their neighbours may see it as a threat. Personally, I would prefer a resolution without violence."

"Without violence?" Copias asked. "Were you not the one warning the siloin commanders of the threat from Artor and Myklinn?"

"It would be foolish for a nation to act self-assured in its safety," Jornis said. "However, there can be no denying that Myklinn Greater and Artor are both fundamental parts of the federation. Without them, the close trading networks that bind the world and its people together would cease to function."

"I don't understand," Copias said. "Are you suggesting those hostile nations are necessary?"

Jornis quietened his voice. "Their lands are vast and complex with resources used daily by all citizens across the federation. Their people are culturally different from any other and hold a unique history vastly unlike the one we share. In short, it would be foolish to assume they play no role on the world stage or that an outside nation can tame them." Noticing Copias's frown, Jornis added, "I didn't say their leaders' attitudes to their neighbours or the rest of the federation should or will be tolerated."

Copias looked back. "Afraid you can't do that without the threat of violence."

Jornis smiled and shook his head. "What would you say the goals of a nation are?"

Copias looked off in the distance for a moment. "It would have to depend on the leaders ruling them."

"Not at all," Jornis said. "Each one of those leaders has to ensure their country's safety, wellbeing, and longevity. The only difference between them are the methods they use."

Copias paused. "I suppose that makes sense, but it still doesn't explain how a nation or its leaders can be convinced to withdraw its forces."

"There are countless more ways to resolve disputes than through violence or the threat of such. If the nation in question is concerned with its safety then a mutual agreement can be arranged, and if its people's wellbeing is in question, then resources can be exchanged or gifted.

Peaceful, ever-present dialogue between a few large nations can ensure the world continues to flourish."

"You mean how the federation currently acts?"

Jornis shook his head, his smile vanishing. "The emperor of Erium dictates the discussion between members, focusing most of the attention on matters north of the Therra. Furthermore, having smaller nations…" Jornis stopped his tongue and returned to the original discussion. "At least you understand why I dislike the idea of Gildren or any other nation displaying a show of force."

Entering the city gatehouse, the small group was greeted by a messenger. "The head of the Marble Wheels urgently wishes to meet with you."

With any notion of respite lost, Jornis steered his horse alongside the Silk Shores commander as the armoured man demanded, "What happened?"

The messenger took the reins of the commander's horse. "I would not delay."

Jornis and Copias followed the gilded commander inside the orange-marbled residence. A half dozen yellow chainmailed guards welcomed them, with the Marble Wheels head standing at the forefront.

She glared at Jornis. "It appears your ruse has failed."

"Have they raided another town?" Jornis asked.

"Worse," she replied. "The Rauders have built a small fort at one of your beacons along the Silk Shores coastline."

The gilded commander clenched his fists. "They dare settle in *my* lands?"

"All because this man suggested showcasing Gildren wealth," she said.

Jornis shook his head. "If they constructed a small fort, then it would indicate they have been planning this from the start."

Copias added, "Not to mention they only took the metals displayed at the beacon."

"Either way, your plan has failed," she said. "So what other *suggestion* might you provide before I have you sent back to your Dictorate in disgrace?"

Jornis glanced at Copias and pondered their earlier discussion. "I believe we could use this to establish communications."

The Silk Shore's commander turned to him. "You would have us greet them when they have raided our coast and invaded my lands?"

Jornis's confidence faded as an upsetting realisation came to him. "It would be unreasonable to ask you to speak with a hostile force currently inside your territory." Remembering the raid on Delport, Jornis hesitated. "Further, it would be wiser to have a speaker of an uninvolved nation begin the talks. To rebuild the trust between the siloins of Gildren and myself, I will personally volunteer to open communications with the Rauders."

Shock crossed every face in the room.

The Silk Shores commander crossed his arms. "There isn't a need for you to throw your life away. I'll gather my armies and crush them before they can utter a single word."

"It will take time for your armies to gather," Jornis replied. "In that time I can meet with this base of Rauders and perhaps resolve this matter."

The Marble Wheels head said, "Very well. I will detach a handful of my men to escort you to the fort. In the meantime, I suggest you prepare what you will bring and discuss."

"You have my thanks," Jornis said, hiding his nerves.

She turned her attention to the Silk Shores commander. "I would like to know what you discussed with the Lord of Bilhyn."

"Of course," he eyed Jornis and Copias, indicating they should leave.

Stepping onto the smoothened streets, Copias turned to Jornis. "What were you thinking? You can't possibly meet with them."

"I told you there are countless more ways to resolve disputes than through violence." Jornis darted his eyes away from the young elite. "Now, shall we discuss what the Rauders want with iron and agron?"

Approaching the copper walls of Minitium, Vernon couldn't help but marvel at the elaborate defences surrounding the city while dreading the plumes of white smoke consuming the sky from within. Nearing the first of several gatehouses, he wondered how the hundreds of guards patrolling the vast copper ramparts could live in such unpleasant air.

As Vernon crossed the blackened waters of the city's moat, he looked to Minitium's copper gates and saw an engraved symbol of a ruby atop an iron podium. He had never imagined such a symbol being left in all of Erium, yet before him, engraved onto Minitium's gate, was the symbol of the Royals.

Inside, Vernon explained his purpose to a pair of red-robed guards, showing them he had nothing but the coin bags and his singular book within his satchel. He was permitted to venture through the proceeding two other gatehouses alongside the wall, and finally the last gate opened before him.

Stepping onto the blackened cobblestones, Vernon felt the heat emanating from the numerous crucibles lining the entirety of the lengthy narrow street. Each had several labourers pouring liquid bronze into various moulds, clouding the air with white smoke Vernon could taste. Further along the street, several red-bricked homes abutted the forges, and Vernon wondered how anyone could possibly stand to live there, even if this city was the centre of bronze production for the entire federation.

Several swordsmen in black chainmail stood outside a long, fort-like warehouse at the far end of the street. Knowing they had to belong to Elleasious's procession, Vernon approached the swordsman with a black ring pinned to his chest. "Excuse me, could you tell Elleasious Imerial that Vernon Meyorter has completed her request?"

The man darted his eyes to the red-robed guards staring from atop the flat roof of the warehouse and whispered, "Wait till she's finished."

Vernon realised the tension grasping the clouded air and noticed the red-robed guards watching each of the newcomers with suspicious, alert eyes. He stepped back from the wide reinforced warehouse door and waited with the soldiers in black chainmail.

The door slid open, revealing an enormous room brimming with tin and copper bars. Elleasious wore full black armour and stood alongside a crimson-robed man covered in ruby jewels. Both had similar frustrated scowls and neither said a word of farewell to the other as they left the fortified warehouse, departing in opposite directions. Elleasious marched with her personal guard away from the main street.

Vernon rushed within her line of vision. "I've completed your task."

Her pace and frustration didn't ease as she glanced at him. "Keep your tongue still and follow me."

Vernon obeyed as he wondered why this city would be so antagonistic towards the emperor's sister.

Following her away from the heat of the crucibles, he arrived at a modest black crystal building placed between two wall towers. Again, the red-robed guards patrolled the copper ramparts, staring suspiciously at them and the Sidium soldiers.

Few decorations or comforts were found in the building; instead, the few furniture pieces within the short hallway were small and plain. The handful of stewards standing ready lacked any of the standard black robes; instead, each wore a simple black crystal pin on their plain clothes.

Elleasious turned her attention to the head bodyguard. "Have the horses saddled and ready to leave." She raised her voice to the stewards. "Our business here is concluded, leaving us with no further reason to stay. Load the wagons and ensure no items from Sidium are left."

Immediately, the entire residence descended into a flood of action as every soldier and steward readied their procession to depart.

Still in the hallway, Elleasious turned to address Vernon. "May I see what you have brought?"

"It would be my pleasure." Vernon showed her the two coins bags. "I'm glad I passed your test."

"Test?" She crossed her arms.

Vernon looked at her in confusion, thinking about his wording and wondering whether the stewards around them were trustworthy. "I mean to say I succeeded in following your orders."

She paused for a moment and glanced at the stairs. "I want you to see something."

He was led up to a bare room with an enormous circular window overlooking much of the city. Elleasious gestured for him to look outwards. "Where does this city's loyalty lie?"

"After seeing the Royal symbol on the gate, I cannot say," Vernon answered. "How is such a thing even possible?"

She stepped closer to the window, staring at the white smoke engulfing the city. "I remember hearing you own an old copy of *The Foundations*. While it is a remarkable book that details much of Erium's rise, you will not find any reference to Minitium or the forging of brass and bronze."

Vernon thought back to the text and realised she was correct. "Why was it left out?"

Elleasious turned to him. "In the time of the Royals, coins were of scarlet gold, a rare metal found only in a few deposits where Myklinn Minor stands today. Before the Royal dynasty collapsed, they forged vast amounts of coins made of similar more common metals. The entire world became filled with them and its worth plummeted." She returned her gaze to Minitium. "When Rochious Imerial came to power, he had this city become the sole overseer of coin production so no emperor may be tempted to forge more than is required."

"Are you saying the emperor has no authority over this city and the amount of coins it makes?" Vernon asked.

She kept her gaze silently on the smoke rising from the crucibles.

Vernon's mind raced with the ramifications of this system. "But wouldn't that create a divide between the emperor and the owner of this city?"

Elleasious turned away from the window and changed the subject. "You may keep the coins you collected as a reward, but I expect you to be in the observers stand of the next great hall meeting." She walked towards the door and halted. "I advise you travel in one of my wagons for Sidium instead of lingering in this city."

"Thank you," Vernon said, relieved he wouldn't have to walk.

Just as she left the room, he glanced out the window at Minitium and wondered why Rochious Imerial would create another system limiting his power. Perhaps it was intended to show solidarity to the masses or forge trust with the other founding nations. In any case, Vernon knew, had Rochious known what it would have led to, he wouldn't have done it.

With her stomach lying in a freshly dug pit on the firm slope, Iyna peeked through the cover of the cloth as the last glow of sunlight faded from the mountainous horizon. Constantly plaguing her thoughts was the question of whether the spearmen's grey hammocks and the small pits they dug were enough to hide them on the opposing slope. Fortunately, dark clouds blocked much of the light from the crescent moons rising into the sky, leaving only the fort's exterior lanterns shining out. Even so, the fear of being spotted before the Fyoreten released bolts at the ramparts lingered, for it would take only a single spearman making a noise for her plan to fail.

Slowly moving her head, Iyna glanced to the nearby pits and the hammocks covering them. She could only glimpse a few nervous faces but saw none of them looked to flee. Reassured, she returned her gaze towards the brightened fort and awaited the attack.

Figures moved along the base of the slope, their silhouettes easy to spot with the fort's lanterns further ahead. Their crossbow strings rang out, filling the night air with bolts distantly striking stone, and she steadied her spear's grip.

Exactly as planned, Tarrow's tribow unit yelled and shouted, drowning out all other sounds and allowing the spearmen to rise to their feet. Erger had insisted on padding the shield's edges with cloth, so when they all came together in a single row of shields, they made hardly a sound.

Glancing to her sides, Iyna squinted at the spearmen far to the ends of the long line, knowing they were held by Feeliath and Barcial. Heart racing, she took a deep breath, steadied her spear and whispered either side of her, "Pass this on, keep the shields raised and watch your step." The whisper carried from person to person till it disappeared from earshot.

The spearmen at the sides steadily advanced, followed one after another by the rest of the spearmen in the line till her entire force was marching down. The slope was rocky, steep and covered with shadows, slowing their quiet advance, but the tribowmen's shouts kept the scattered Fyoreten's attention.

Closing in on the crossbowmen, Iyna whispered down the line once more, "Get ready to charge."

Waiting for the message to carry, Iyna squinted at the Fyoreten silhouettes till she saw one of them glance back. She let out a thunderous cry. "All charge!"

The spearmen broke into a run, charging at the crossbowmen in a single line of shields. Disorder and panic set into the scattered Fyoreten as they fled from the line of spearmen, towards the fort, with only a couple releasing bolts against the shields. Feeling one stick into the cloth padding her shield, Iyna knew the plan was working, and she smiled.

Reaching the flat clearing after the mountain slope, Iyna glimpsed Barcial and Feeliath leading their sides further ahead, bending the line around the panic-stricken Fyoreten. They clumped together in their chaotic retreat from the spearmen. A moment later the forty or so Fyoreten were surrounded by the line of shields with the fort's wall to their backs. Tarrow's unit revealed themselves on the rampart above, aiming their tribows at the defeated crossbowmen.

Tarrow yelled loud and clear. "Drop your weapons!"

The distraught crossbowmen turned to a single man wrapped in a green cloak over his agron chainmail, who stepped closer to the fort and shouted up to Tarrow, "What will be done to us?"

Tarrow turned her gaze to the middle of the curved shield line, and Iyna lowered her shield and raised her voice. "*I* am the commander of this army!" She watched the man turn and march towards her. "I ask you to drop your weapons and leave these mountains at once."

"Leave these mountains?" The man stopped short of her spear length. "Are you saying you *won't* parade us in your capital or send us to the Atimah?"

"We have a common enemy," Iyna replied. "It will not be long before the Erium Empire turns against *us*."

The man's grip on his crossbow tightened. "So why did you help them?"

Iyna hesitated. "I have seen Erium's gargantuan army, and I speak honestly when I say that even if Fyoreten and Felliet united, it wouldn't nearly be enough to defeat them."

"So you acted through fear," he said. "Like little frightened mice."

"After thinking long and hard about it, I finally understand the Dictorate's decision," Iyna said. "They joined the war to buy time so we may all have a chance to defeat them."

The man stared suspiciously at her. "What's your name?"

"Iyna."

"No last name?" He glanced to his force. "So, Iyna, what would you have us do after we leave the mountains back to Fyoreten? Charge hopelessly against the *gargantuan* forces of Erium?"

"Whatever they want out of your homeland, I ask that you deny it," she urged. "If it's the mines, destroy them; if it's trade, cut it off; if it's simply pride, make them utter fools in the eyes of the world."

He paused. "I never thought I'd see the day Fyoreten resistance would rise anew." He turned once more to his men and to the surrounding

Felliet before returning his attention to Iyna. His crossbow fell to the ground, and he brought his hand to his chest. "Then it shall be known that I, Reegar, one of the last unit leaders of the Fyoreten army, shall agree to your terms." He raised his voice to his men. "Do as she says! We will return to our lands and make Erium pay for taking our homes!"

The other crossbows fell to the ground, and Iyna stepped aside, raising her voice. "Make an opening!"

The Fyoreten group marched past them, heading southwest before fading into the darkness of the mountain landscape.

Chapter twenty – Judgement

Seventh eclipse, thirty-second day

Standing at the head of a mere handful of anxious bodyguards, Jornis stared at the iron thorns surrounding the beacon and the monstrous creatures within. Though the wall of iron thorns was thick, he could still observe perhaps fifty Rauders with a dozen skipping boats along their fort's beach. The beacon had been transformed into a spiked scaffolding lookout with one Rauder stretching high on its large single leg, far above the fort, bringing all the Rauder's attention towards the approaching small hesitant group.

Nearing the wall of thorns, Jornis turned to the handcart of metal goods one of the bodyguards pushed and said, "Leave that with me. I will go alone."

The bodyguards immediately set the handcart down and stepped back.

Copias glanced at Jornis. "The siloin armies are gathering nearby. There's still time to leave."

"Even if we were able to outrun the Rauders to our horses, I would prefer an attempt at spoken dialogue. Without such an act, it will be extremely difficult forging trust between the siloins of Gildren and myself." Jornis held a sealed letter to Copias. "But if I am to fall here, there needs to be someone who can relay this message to the Dictorate. You must wait with the guards."

Copias took the letter and watched the Rauders use their enormous fists to pull a gap between the wall of thorns. "You're a brave man."

Jornis couldn't bring himself to look at the boy. "Ensure that letter reaches every elite in Felliet."

"Only if you fall," Copias replied and left.

Keeping his anxious gaze ahead, Jornis stood his ground armed only with the handcart of supplies and a single altered map emphasising the Radiant Republic along with a clear depiction of the Rauder fort.

A single Rauder stomped out, its enormous three legs lumbering towards the unmoving elite. Its thin horizontal eyes were focused only on Jornis; the elite forced himself not to turn away to the horses far behind him.

The Rauder halted before Jornis, its enormous imposing body overshadowing him as it stared unblinkingly at the man.

Jornis forced his hand to gesture towards the handcart. "I have brought some gifts for you."

The creature didn't turn its headless body; it kept its slit eyes focused on Jornis.

"I believe you and your kind are after the Radiant Repub"—Jornis hesitated as one of the Rauder's fists lifted from the ground—"Republic. We also desire their downfall and are willing to"—it slowly brought its fist closer to Jornis's head—"assist you in that effort…" The creature's thick fingers bent back, and numerous crimson tendrils emerged from within the creature's large palm. Jornis tried to remain composed as the tendrils stretched closer, touching his neck.

They wriggled further across his neck and extended further from the creature's palm. His mind raced with fear.

He remembered the map in the handcart. "We brought a gift…"

"Gi…ft." A voice emerged from beneath the creature's chin.

"Yes." Jornis pulled himself away from the light touch of the tendrils and reached into the handcart. He showed the creature the map along with an ice eye replica. "This gift"—he held out both for the Rauder—"is for you."

The tendrils surged at it, wrapping around the ice eye and yanking it back into the creature's grasp as the tendrils retreated back into its palm. The Rauder slowly brought it closer to its slit eyes, examining the markings around the three iron rings. The creature stomped it into the ground under the power of its fist.

Jornis pointed to the damaged ice eye. "Rade-ie-unt Re-pub-lic." Watching the creature return its slit eyes to him, Jornis tapped the bottom of the map. "Rade-ie-unt Re-pub-lic."

The other fist rose from the ground, and its tendrils emerged. Jornis held out the map for it to grasp. The Rauder's tendrils crumpled the edges of the parchment and brought it closer to its eyes. It turned to the spiked beacon and looked at the map once.

An unbearably long moment later, the creature stomped towards the handcart, dropping the map inside and dragging the entire load back to its fort.

Jornis stood there entirely dazed at the whole interaction. The thorns hauled back into place and one of the boats set sail.

He stood there unmoving until Copias came to him. "Did they take the message."

Jornis glanced to the bent ice eye half buried in the ground. "I'm unsure." He turned to the bodyguards already atop their horses. "We can at least be sure they can learn to speak."

Standing before the Gallery doors, Iyna took a deep breath, for despite knowing her actions to be right, she had little idea of what the Elite Dictorate would say. She knew they would either be grateful to her for ending the threat or merciless for letting them go; there would be no middle ground. Alexan stopped beside her.

An uncomfortable silence hung in the air between them. Iyna eventually asked, "How are the new recruits faring?"

"They're doing well." Alexan kept his eyes facing the doors and whispered, "The elites sent me a letter saying you let the enemy go free. Is that true?"

"It is," Iyna muttered back. "I don't regret what I did."

He turned wide eyed at her and returned his focus to the closed doors, further quietening his voice. "Now I understand why the Dictorate passed this off as a review of our performance."

Hearing him condemn her actions, Iyna wondered what the punishment could be, leaving a daunting silence hanging between the two of them for a longer while before the doors opened.

Inside, none of the beautiful displays filling the walls eased her worries, not even the bright sunlight beaming through the curved glass roof, for she noticed the irritated faces of all eleven finely dressed Dictorate members behind the black stand.

The Zenth man in the centre said, "Commander Iyna. You have been brought before the Elite Dictorate to explain why you allowed a Fyoreten army to go free after they attacked the fort."

Iyna replied, "Because they are not our enemy."

"Why do you say that?"

"Erium brought us into a war with them because they wanted to show off their strength in front of all the other nations." Iyna's arms tensed. "It won't be long before they do the same to us."

The female elite under the Lawver-engraved shield said, "We have our own strategy to ensure that does not happen."

"What do you mean?" Iyna asked.

The elite woman glanced to a large elite and to another in priesthood clothes. "We believe securing a powerful ally will stave off any notion of Erium conquest."

"Then why can't we ally ourselves with this Fyoreten army?" Iyna asked. "They absolutely detest the Erium Empire, do they not?"

"They are too weak," the Lawver elite argued. "And even if that were not the case, they simply cannot be trusted."

The large elite leaned back, creaking his chair. "Besides if the Empire of Erium were to discover us aiding any Fyoreten resistance, it would signal a declaration of war."

"But we can't sit idly by while they fight our enemy." Iyna raised her voice. "We should be looking for as many allies as we can to counter the Empire of Erium."

Her words bounced off the decorated walls without a response.

The Zenth elite said, "As Pryias Lawver has mentioned, we already have a plan in motion that will dissuade the Empire of Erium from conquering Felliet. However, we believe there is a task you can aid in that matter." He held up a letter with a broken black seal. "The emperor is to announce a fourth expedition that, in his own words, will finally rid the world of the Beast Riders."

The news gobsmacked Iyna into silence.

"This force will be composed of armies from every nation without exception," he explained. "We strongly believe this is an attempt to demonstrate the strength of Erium's army under this new emperor." He leaned forward, staring closely at Iyna. "We need a commander to lead our force, demonstrate Felliet's strength to the world and demonstrate our nation's commitment to its allies."

She stared at them in disbelief. "Are you saying I am to lead Felliet's army into battle with the Beast Riders?"

"Considering your apt resolve and cunning in battle, it is a clear to us you are best suited for the task." He turned to Alexan. "Brige, you will continue to remain here and train further soldiers."

"I will see they are thoroughly trained," he replied.

Delight and unease clashed in Iyna's mind as she stewed on their decision.

The elite in religious clothes grinned at her. "It should be quite the honour for you. You will be among those finally ridding the world of those foul creatures."

His words overwhelmed Iyna's thoughts, and she raised her head. "I accept your kind offer and assure you I will defend Felliet and crush all threats to its safety."

Ascending the black stairs towards the great chamber, Vernon glanced at the black crystal bracelet around his right wrist and wondered why Elleasious had allowed Lysia and him to continue the trade. Certainly, she was to receive a contribution from Lysia for every transaction, but it wasn't as though the emperor or his sister needed the coin. He put aside his questions and returned his attention to the great chamber.

Stepping into the observers stand, Vernon was once again in wonderous awe at the magnificent glistening white walls of the great chamber. Staring down at the Federal Throne, he was reminded of the assassination and his amazement vanished.

Elleasious sat on the left front corner overlooking the edge with a hefty, scarred man sitting directly behind her. Clearly, he was one of her personal guards and likely concealing a weapon of some sort. Moving past the merchants, messengers and nobles taking their seats, Vernon noticed several other serious-faced men scattered throughout the observers stand. Seeing them watchful and alert, Vernon breathed a sigh of relief, assured the assassination would not repeat itself before he took his seat beside Elleasious.

Her gaze was fixed on the Federal Throne as she spoke. "You were here when my brother was killed, were you not?"

A sudden unease gripped Vernon's stomach. "I was."

"There may come a time when I lie dying at the hands of an assailant." Elleasious turned to him. "Every man and woman who bears the name Imerial must demonstrate absolute courage, wisdom, leadership and authority."

"I understand."

She shook her head. "How can you?"

Vernon turned to the Federal Throne. "I have read and reread *The Foundations* countless times. No matter how often I read the words, I can always feel the duties and responsibilities Rochious Imerial and his sons had to endure."

"Not to a personal level it seems," she said. "But at least you have a vague idea."

After a lengthy moment of tense silence Emperor Merchasious entered, gliding his black crystal robe across the pearl floor. Seeing the glistening of that metallic robe on the emperor overwhelmed Vernon with pride.

Marching behind was the supreme commander, minister of scales and delegate of the citizens, each with a look of confidence to them. Far behind hobbled the elderly grand bishop who seemed frustrated and somehow slower than before.

As the frail man approached his bronze seat, Elleasious whispered, "The priesthood chose him to lead because of his disloyalty towards the emperor and his nobles."

Shocked, Vernon darted his gaze to her. "Is the divide between the faith and empire that wide?"

"Wider," she explained. "The priesthood still refuse to acknowledge their fault for starting the culling."

"How can that be?" Vernon whispered. "The priests and the families they named were the ones who started purging the Beast Riders. Had it not been for them, the emperor could have simply let the surgeries continue."

"Perhaps they believe refusing acknowledgement of the truth will somehow return them to their former glory," Elleasious suggested. "As if that would happen."

The representatives entered, in much the same order as before, with the exception of Felliet's new representative who wore plain grey silk and only a silver pendant. Furthermore, he closely followed Gildren's representative rather than boasting his appearance by himself.

Once all the representatives took their seats, Emperor Merchasious rose from the Federal Throne. He raised his voice in a booming tone similar to his late brother. "To all leaders and followers, men and women, named and unnamed, it is time for the culling to finally end." His words echoed across the chamber, bringing every observer to a wide-eyed silence. The emperor turned his attention to the representatives. "I announce one final expedition composed of an overwhelming force, with armies from every nation led by ten thousand of Erium's finest soldiers. This combined force shall depart across the desert and eradicate every last Beast Rider from the world." He looked specifically at Myklinn's representative. "How many does the kingdom of Myklinn Greater offer?

The man in grey furs stood. "Four thousand of the finest bowmen."

"And for Myklinn Minor?" the emperor asked, turning his head.

The man in silver embroidered wool hesitated, perhaps at the insulting name, before he stood. "Five thousand crossbows."

The emperor turned to the Therran. "And how many flames?"

The creature echoed its voice from its mouthless face, "Nine hundred and sixty."

As the other representatives stated their contributing numbers, Elleasious whispered, "This expedition is unlike any other before it and even overshadows the Southern Campaign." She lowered her voice. "As a result, considerable coin is required, hence why the emperor and I agreed to dispatch a tribute procession to Myklinn Minor."

Vernon thought about it for a moment and realised this was the reason Elleasious had met with the leader of Minitium and why Lysia was allowed to continue trading. He whispered back, "I understand why you may need tributary coin before the first cycle's eclipse, but why Myklinn Minor?"

"Fyoreten's lands are restrictive, its population small and its wealth lacking, yet it managed to accrue several hundred horsemen and crossbowmen." She darted her pupils to him. "Speak none of this anyone, you understand."

Vernon realised the danger in her words and gave a single nod.

"And lastly Felliet," the emperor said to the man in grey.

"Two hundred fearless souls," the new Felliet representative said to the understandable eye roll of all present.

Vernon wondered whether Iyna would be forced to participate in this expedition and realised Felliet's army would never be placed at the front lines anyway. He wondered whether she was patrolling the streets of Ellity or of the Felliet towns, for he knew even the Dictorate would never send fresh recruits to the war with Fyoreten. He relaxed at the thought of her safe and sound, perhaps even finding other friends she could spar with.

The emperor raised his voice to the observers stand. "That brings the total number to thirty thousand. Aside from Felliet's army, all the forces will gather before the walls of Sidium and march when ready."

"The tributary procession leaves at sunrise tomorrow," Elleasious whispered. "You will accompany Jofinian Tritas and be present when he addresses the king of Myklinn Minor."

Vernon wondered how he would explain to Lysia and Orfain about disappearing for a long journey once more, though at least this time he could give them forewarning. He turned to Elleasious. "I will do my best."

All around, colours of all kinds flourished as Niyaa breathed in the refreshing flowery, herbal aromas floating in the Florision air. She could never tire of seeing the bountiful vines of green, gold, grey and red climb their way up the humongous curving glass walls. Nor could she bore of trekking along the cute gravel paths, marvelling at each of the bountiful garden beds, each flourishing all kinds of vibrant herbs and flowers. The enormous glass tunnel even had many baskets dangling overhead, filled with all kinds of pink and violet stalks. But the sound of the growing, rustling plants and the little water wheels streaming nourishment from the saltless sea was simply delightful. Niyaa could think of no better place for her and her mom to gather ingredients for a delicious ale.

The two of them came to a wavy flower bed packed with thick grainy stalks with thin dropping red leaves.

Mysia scraped off a handful of the reddened grain, holding it close to her daughter to smell. "When I fermented these, it became quite a heavy drink with an interesting taste."

Niyaa brought her nose closer to the grains; it smelled like a dark, heavy barley. "That's really strong."

"Which is why I need something to mellow it out," Mysia said.

"You mean something sweet?"

Mysia nodded. "Everything in here is edible, so you can choose whatever you like."

Niyaa beamed with excitement and pranced through the Florision sniffing as many of the colourful flowers as she could. She stumbled upon Fewttyre uprooting a tiny, pyramid-like bulb. "Good day, Fewttyre."

"Good to see you too, Niyaa." He uprooted a second bulb. "So what brings you here today? You having a day off from the forge?"

"Yep. I'm helping my mom find ingredients for her ale. It needs to be sweet to balance the dark grains."

"I'll be interested to hear what she ends up using," he said, closely examining the two bulbs.

"You'll be one of the first ones to try some when it's ready."

"Afraid I don't drink." Fewttyre put his hand to his chin. "But Cabi does."

Niyaa felt a little disappointed. "But you're gonna miss out."

"So long as everyone else is happy, I won't miss out." He uprooted a third bulb. "You know, I do have some rare plants in my lab, a couple of which might be what you're looking for."

"Really?" Niyaa asked. "That won't be a problem, will it?"

"Not at all." He stood up. "We can go there now if you like."

She agreed, and they trekked through the rest of the enormous Florision till they emerged out the other end. Niyaa followed Fewttyre to a circular building that poked up higher than the other homes around it.

He walked up an outside staircase following its curving wall. "I guarantee you will love seeing my lab."

"What's a lab anyway?" Niyaa asked as they passed the second floor.

"You'll see." Fewttyre grinned and took out a long skinny key from his pocket to unlock the topmost door.

Stepping inside, Niyaa looked up in delight at the flat glass ceiling that filled the spotless circular room with clear sunlight. The sapphire floor was as smooth as marble, and the curved walls were plastered chalk white with strange wall plant pots hanging along it. The countertops following the round wall were filled with organised bottles, jars and spotless weird tools; even the cushiony single bed in the centre of the polished floor was cleaned thoroughly.

Niyaa followed the wall, looking closely at each of the plant pots; one was filled with thin yellow arches that curved back into the soil, and she instinctively prodded at one of the yellow arches. The bouncy arch changed to an orange colour under her finger and a greenish blue near the soil. She turned to the other plant pots. One had a single spiky black spindle poking straight downwards while another had a spiralling cup of tiny cyan scales pulsating above the soil.

Fewttyre walked across the spotless room, passing the single bed and arriving at a set of glass shelves filled with clay pots and clear jars of various powders. He placed the pyramid bulbs in a clay pot and grasped a spoon. "What kind of grain is Mysia using?"

Niyaa thought back to the plant. "The one with the thin red leaves."

"Fountain stalks then," he said, examining the many glass jars and taking one half filled with a purplish powder. "This one is made by peeling back the stems of the crimson vines, drying them out and crushing them into a fine powder."

"Can I try it?" Niyaa asked.

He opened the jar and filled a spoon with a small bit. "Of course."

Taking the spoon, she dipped it into her mouth. Her face lit up with joy at the sweetness. "It's delicious."

"Thought you might like it." He smiled. "So, do you think it will it work with the fountain stalks?"

Niyaa licked the spoon. "It will."

He resealed the jar and handed it to her. "Well, you can take this to your mother. I'm sure she'll be happy to use it."

"Thank you," Niyaa replied, leaving the strange lab.

Chapter twenty-one – Altered Fate

Eighth eclipse, second day

With sunlight pouring through the carriage's glass roof, Vernon reached his hand in the compartment beneath the silk padded seats and grasped a random book from the small selection. Placing it on his black-trousered lap, his eyes widened with delight, for the cover depicted the white crystal sword in all its glory above the words *Erium's Founding*.

The noble in white leather grinned from his opposing seat. "I can attest *that* book makes for a good road."

"Well"—Vernon eagerly reached for his satchel hanging between the carriage's windows and took out *The Foundations*—"if it is anything like this book, then I will thoroughly enjoy every word."

Jofinian leaned forward, staring at the worn cover. "I believe I've read that version. Though I admit I've seen the comet pass many times since." He held out his unjewelled hand. "May I?"

Placing his favourite book in the noble's palm, Vernon said, "I don't believe there are any tales better than how Rochious defeated the Royals and built the foundation of Erium."

"What of him founding the heart of the empire and bringing the then town of Sidium's impoverished residents into true prosperity?" the noble asked, turning the first page. "If so, then you may find *Erium's Founding* a fine read."

Vernon lowered his gaze to the pristine cover and opened the book.

The procession crossed a stone bridge, and their attention was drawn to an approaching sound of hammers, stonework, scrubbers and laden carts. Vernon edged closer to one of the windows and gazed beyond the tributary bodyguards at the approaching town of Iorden.

Along the main street, labourers were tiling roofs, stonemasons repairing doors and cleaners scrubbing the blackness off the walls. Families on the street had baskets or carts brimming with food, clothes and furniture. Many glanced curiously at the tributary processions, especially at the elaborate bronze chestwagon with its four columns representing the founding nations.

Vernon smiled. "Was this all funded by Erium?"

Jofinian looked out the window. "Before his unfortunate passing, Emperor Anisious wished the people of Fyoreten to live with all the comforts and necessities of the rest of the empire." He pointed up. "We are already replacing their cheap stem rooftops with reliable tiles from Trissiup."

Vernon stared at the families walking along the street. "It won't be long before they feel the prosperity of Erium."

"Precisely what Emperor Anisious wanted," Jofinian replied.

The procession entered the town's centre square, and the noble pointed to a small group of soldiers in black chainmail drinking outside an open tavern. "See those guards over there? They're the same Fyoreten soldiers that fought us at Fiskior."

Vernon turned to him wide eyed. "You mean we have enemy soldiers guarding this city?"

"They are not the enemy, at least not anymore." Jofinian leaned back in his seat. "When you consider their bravery to fight against such overwhelming forces, it would be a tragedy to send them to the Atimah.

Not to mention it would certainly leave a sour taste for both the people of Fyoreten *and* Erium."

A smile crossed Vernon's face as he considered the emperor's kindness and generosity.

The procession stopped before a green building with a bell tower protruding above the heart of the city. Jofinian said, "Now that peace has finally arrived to the region, the Fyoreten people can prosper."

Following the noble outside the white carriage, Vernon stared up at the green bell tower and noticed many streaks of blackened soot across its surfaces. "Are you not going to remove these scorch marks?"

"We're going to remove the tower completely," Jofinian said. "In its place shall be an even greater bell tower whose walls could never blacken."

"So Fyoreten will fully return to the empire." Vernon relaxed at the thought. "The memory of its reckless independence will really fade."

"In time." The noble turned his gaze to the bronze tributary chestwagon with its sandstone, iron, sapphire and black crystal columns cornering the code-sealed chest. He glanced at other town residents. "The Fyoreten people will also not incur any reparations for the tributes its leaders failed to pay. I also imagine they will all see their taxes greatly lowered for the foreseeable future."

Vernon glanced at the civilians watching from new, spotless windows and felt proud their lives would improve.

Jofinian glanced at the thirty bodyguards surrounding the procession on horseback. "Perhaps we should not have taken this many soldiers."

Vernon shrugged. "It's always better to be safe than not.'"

"I just hope it won't appear too aggressive."

"The bodyguards will stay with the procession along the entire journey, not just through Fyoreten," Vernon said.

"True."

The head bodyguard steered his horse alongside the noble. "Jofinian Tritas, we have found a guesthouse that will provide suitable lodgings for you and your guest."

"Well done," Jofinian replied. "See to it all your men share similar accommodation and that each room is paid double their worth."

"Thank you, but only twenty beds will be required," the armoured rider said. "As a third of my men will be on night watch."

The noble sighed. "Very well, but remind them these are now Erium citizens and should be trusted just as much as those from Sidium."

The head bodyguard nodded and ordered his men to dismount.

Vernon chuckled. "The elites of Felliet would never have treated their stewards or bodyguards with respect, let alone any commoners."

The noble smirked. "Then perhaps the elites of Felliet have no sense of duty and responsibility."

"That they do not," Vernon agreed.

The Dictorate's decision engulfed Iyna's mind in a mix of eagerness and unease throughout the chilling trek up the mountains until the fort came into sight. A daunting realisation struck her; she would have to explain why her army would be marching to the desert and battling the Beast Riders. She stopped in her stride as the thought of leading them to such a dangerous place settled in. But the fires at Edenor engulfed her mind, and all hesitation vanished.

Marching over the dry moat, Iyna stepped into the small courtyard filled with soldiers staring at her. Erger was strapping the modified spear to Barcial's forearm. This time the straps were made of better leather, and the U-shaped agron handle was a better fit for Barcial's fingers to grip. A freshly engraved symbol below the iron spearpoint depicted a hammer with a brick furnace as its head.

Barcial practiced thrusting his modified spear.

Erger looked up at her. "So you've returned in one piece. Did they reward you then?"

Iyna couldn't answer the question and instead turned to Barcial. "How does it feel to wield?"

He smiled at her and raised the spear to the sky. "It's surprisingly easy to use and direct, although admittedly it feels as though I am simply punching with it."

Erger slapped his back. "So long as it works."

"Cannot argue with that," Barcial said and turned to Iyna. "It's good to see you back."

"It may not be so good." She sighed. "Afraid we have new orders."

Barcial looked at her with worry in his eyes. "I'll get Feeliath and Tarrow."

Erger shook his head. "You're gonna wander around with that spear still strapped to your arm? I'll get them."

412

Barcial glanced at the strap. "Very well."

As Erger rushed into one of the towers, Barcial battled with the forearm strap with his thumbless left hand. "I gather they were less than pleased with your action."

Iyna helped him remove the spear strap. "They certainly weren't happy with me letting the Fyoreten go."

"I can imagine," he frowned. "So do these new orders mean we are to pursue them into the mountains?"

Iyna undid the last strap, letting the spear swing downwards in his finger grip. "No, we're not."

"Then we're to relocate to somewhere else?" Barcial set down his modified spear.

"I'll tell you with the other unit leaders but…" Iyna hesitated as she glimpsed the surrounding groups of spearmen watching them. "I can't say whether it's good news or bad."

Erger returned with Feeliath and Tarrow.

Feeliath yawned. "So how come you aren't in shackles?"

Barcial said, "Because she defeated an entire unit of crossbowmen without losing a single man or woman."

Feeliath shrugged. "I simply figured the Dictorate was wise enough to punish a commander for letting an unscathed enemy army go free after *they* attacked *us*."

Iyna crossed her arms. "If you aren't going to be helpful then I'll be happy to send you back to Milnet."

He hesitated. "Just suggesting you shouldn't do something so reckless again."

"I'll decide what's reckless and what isn't."

Tarrow asked, "So what *did* they say?"

All eyes around the courtyard turned to Iyna as she sighed. "The emperor of Erium has announced an enormous expedition that will wipe out the Beast Riders. We are to march with all the other armies of the federation."

Stunned surprise engulfed every expression.

Jaw dropped, Tarrow asked, "Are you saying we are to march into the desert?"

Iyna nodded. "Alongside all the other armies of the federation, yes."

Tarrow shook her head in disbelief. "But we don't have the supplies to do so."

Feeliath said, "Not to mention the third expedition ended in disaster."

Barcial looked at Iyna with concern.

Iyna knew she had to convince them. "Those things fight like a bunch of savage animals preying on the weak." She grinned. "Believe me when I say they won't stand a chance against the might of the entire federation."

Feeliath and Tarrow looked at her, unable to say a word.

"It appears none of us have a choice." Barcial placed his thumbless right hand on Iyna's shoulder. "I'll be with you all the way."

She smiled at him and raised her voice for all the onlooking soldiers to hear. "We'll march out as soon as we get permission and set up a strong base just before the desert." Her voice grew with excitement. "The time has finally come to rid the world of this scourge."

A cheery smile lay across Niyaa's face as she threaded the scales together, knowing it would make a pretty sleeveplate. Mithen seemed bored as she punched the holes into a batch of heated scales. No doubt because she had to forge the agron Cabi had brought into dull cutlery rather than anything exciting, whereas Niyaa was more than happy to show off her forging skills. Just a shame the metal didn't last long.

A guard rushed into the forge to tell Mithen, "They're back."

Mithen dropped her puncher and hammer. "Finally."

The guard left to rush along the street, loudly repeating the news to everyone he passed. A bunch of people rushed towards the gate.

"Who is it?" Niyaa asked.

"My brother in law," Mithen answered, hopping off her stool. "Come on, I'll introduce you."

Niyaa followed her through the pink sandy street as many faster beast people overtook them in an excited scramble towards the gate. Seeing the ecstatic faces on the crowd of people charging towards the gate, Niyaa wondered what he might look like, thinking he would look just like Mithen.

Reaching the cheering crowd around the rolled-up gate, Mithen pushed her way through with Niyaa close behind. Just before Niyaa stepped from the cluster, her excitement turned to stunned dread, for entering the city was a dark violet horse-like creature with long lilac features and bright sapphire eyes. In its red scaly saddle rode an enormous bear-like man with a gargantuan pole axe strapped to his back.

Her knees felt like giving way as the once-forgotten sound of that priest's scream engulfed her thoughts. The other riders following the bear-like man were the same Beast Riders that had looted and brought terror to Edenor, yet this crowd welcomed them. She was frozen on the spot, staring wide eyed at them all.

A hand grasped her shoulder, and she jumped, only to find her mom and Fewttyre looking at her.

Mysia grabbed her daughter's hand. "Come with me."

Niyaa's weakened body gave no fight as her mom led her out of the crowd.

Fewttyre led them towards the circular building, mumbling, "I didn't think they'd be back so soon." He turned to Niyaa with an overly forced smile. "I've got a little treat for you in my lab."

Niyaa lowered her eyes to the sandy ground as the painful memories swirled in her thoughts.

Walking inside his lab, Fewttyre approached his jars, picking up a glass jar with tiny greenish balls.

Mysia said, "You can take today off from the forge if you like."

Niyaa said nothing.

Fewttyre brought the jar of sweets over to her. "They taste strongly of herbs when they first hit your tongue but soon become particularly sweet."

Niyaa turned to them and asked, "Why did he attack us? And why is everyone happy to see them?"

Mysia and Fewttyre glanced at each other, and he gestured to the bed. "It's best you take a seat for this."

Turning to the soft bed in the centre of the spotless blue floor, Niyaa trudged over to sit on it, her legs dangling off the edge.

Fewttyre knelt to her eye level, asking, "So what do you know of the culling?"

She shook her head. "I don't know anything."

He glanced to Mysia who hesitated. "I'm sorry … I guess I hoped I wouldn't have to explain it to her."

He paused. "I understand. It is certainly a painful subject that's difficult to explain." Fewttyre returned his full attention to Niyaa. "It all started long ago when my grandfather discovered how to merge the beauty and strengths of nature with the human body." He smiled with pride. "His wife eagerly volunteered to be the first to undergo the surgery, and after it was performed, she had a beautiful feathery tail that glistened in all the colours of the rainbow. News of her transformation spread far across the whole of Artor and soon the entire federation knew of it. Numerous people from all levels of society flocked from across the world to have the surgery, and soon after, my grandfather began training new surgeons. Before long, many people were skilled in the art."

Niyaa asked, "Why did they all want to become beast people?"

"Everyone was excited with the idea of having stronger arms, faster legs, lighter bodies, clearer eyes, better ears and much more. Honestly, the wonders and variety the surgery brought were endless."

Mysia added, "Most of them were poor, weren't they?"

Fewttyre nodded. "My grandfather was too kind to rob anyone of their hard-earned coin so charged only a paltry sum in addition to the ingredients." His face grew grim. "Sometimes I wonder how things would've changed had he charged a fortune for his service. Or if he had exclusively offered it to Artor's highborn."

Seeing his face grow sad, Niyaa asked, "What happened?"

"It expanded and grew rapidly. No longer was the surgery limited to people from Artor, far from it. Tens of thousands of *commoners* across Artor, Erium, Glldren, and Myklim Minor had undergone the surgery." He paused. "Then in a one great chamber meeting, the grand bishop declared a ban to all surgeries across the federation, with harsh punishments for those who refused."

"That's when the riots began," Mysia added.

"Almost immediately afterwards," he replied. "And flaring up in most cities across the entire world. It swiftly escalated."

"Attacks against the wealthy, priests and highborn worsened." Mysia sat beside her daughter. "That's when my parents and I decided to flee Artor."

Niyaa turned to her mom in disbelief.

She smiled. "Though if we hadn't, I wouldn't have met your father's family in Edenor."

"The priesthood were the ones causing the riots and chaos," Fewttyre said. "They did everything in their power to scorn and humiliate the Beast Riders, even driving them away from their homes. The riots and clashes grew deadlier till eventually the emperor announced the beginning of what we now call the culling." He looked down, his voice softening.

"Across the entire federation, the soldiers descended into the cities and countryside, slaughtering all Beast Riders they found. My grandparents tried to resist but were no match for professional armed soldiers and became among those desperately fleeing into the Therran land. A large Erium army gathered and pursued."

"The first expedition," Mysia said. "Only a handful of the soldiers returned."

Fewttyre raised his head. "But no Beast Riders."

Niyaa gently placed her hand on his shoulder. "I'm sorry to hear that."

His voice croaked. "All of us here have lost homes, friends and family at the command of the emperor and the priests while the majority of non-turned people pretended all was fine, refusing to acknowledge the truth." He looked at Niyaa. "Do you understand now why some of us may want to lash out?"

She withdrew her hand and gave a single nod. "I know how hard it is to lose a home and someone you love."

Mysia placed her arm on her daughter's back.

"In that case." Fewttyre rose to his feet. "I promise you both that one day, however distant it may be, we *will* reclaim our homes."

Niyaa got up off the bed. "Then I promise to help you with that as much as I can."

Unable to communicate with the Rauders, each of Gildren's armies began their march along the nightly flat ground ready to make battle. Riding alongside the eight commanders, Jornis observed the two thousand shields and swords shimmering in the moonslight above. This force, along with the ceaseless rattling of the two thousand bolt quivers behind the swordsmen, ensured the Rauders would notice the eight siloin armies long before the assault on their fort. At least each of the commanders was wise enough to order their men to remain quiet.

However, as the combined force neared the coast, it was clear no fires or torches shone from within the silhouetted wall of iron thorns. Not even a single shimmer moved in the silent beacon fort, leaving a strange unease hovering over the entire force.

Copias whispered to Jornis, "Is it possible they can see at night?"

"Perhaps they already knew the armies were gathering to attack." Jornis glanced at the third quarter moons. "At least in the moonslight they wouldn't be able to ambush us from the flanks."

"With their enormous size and loud legs, I doubt they could surprise us in complete darkness," Copias replied.

Jornis pondered whether the Rauders would await a vast army to march on their fort without a plan in mind. "Perhaps they intend to flee to their boats once battle starts."

Copias shook his head. "They should know several wardens and Erium vessels are anchored nearby. Besides if they wanted, they could have fled long before tonight."

His answer worsened Jornis's uncomfortable dread as he stared at the distant thorn wall silhouetted along the tide-swallowed beach. One after another, the siloin commanders halted their troops and galloped their horses to the rear of their respective armies.

Directly ahead of Jornis and Copias, the Silk Shores commander ordered his tribowmen, "Inflame your bolts!"

The other commanders followed suit, and two thousand flickering lights appeared along the span of the army's rear, brightening the entire force and filling the air with the smell of oil.

"Release!" the commanders successively ordered.

Jornis's ears rang with the sound of a multitude of snapping tribows as the air over the swordsmen filled with scores of arching lights before landing across the entire fort. In an instant, the wall of iron thorns was lit up for all to see the Rauders within, but and not a single one appeared to be fazed by the onslaught of fiery bolts.

Staring wide eyed at the fort, Jornis realised only eight grey bulbous figures were within while the number of kite sails illuminated in the sporadic light remained the same. He kicked his horse into a sprint and caught up to the Silk Shore's commander. "I observed fifty of the creatures yesterday."

"Are you sure?" he asked.

"I am," Jornis answered. "There are far fewer than before."

The commander turned to his men. "Stand firm! We will wait for them to come to us!"

Copias and the other commanders joined them. The yellow chainmailed man from Innill demanded, "Why have you ordered your men to stand firm?"

The Silk Shores commander said, "It appears there are too few Rauders inside the fort."

"Have they already fled?" the Marble Wheels commander asked.

Jornis shook his head. "The same number of boats remains unchanged from yesterday. Therefore, we should assume there remain fifty Rauders, not eight."

The yellow-armoured commander relented. "It figures these monsters of the sea would attempt something underhanded." He turned to his peers. "I suggest we keep giving them volleys till they come at us."

The other commanders agreed and returned to their places, ordering their men to begin cranking.

Jornis breathed in relief. "Thankfully, the siloin commanders understand time is on *their* side."

Copias steered his horse closer. "I almost expected they would recklessly charge their soldiers against the fort."

Jornis shrugged. "Fortunately, Gildren's leaders have a far wiser understanding of war than Felliet."

"Excuse me?" Copias scowled.

Realising his foolish words, Jornis said, "In terms of experience, Gildren has a long history of contending with Artor at sea and Myklinn on the land, not to mention its role in occupying Delflare during the culling. Whereas Felliet has only now formed an army of its own."

"Experience doesn't necessarily reflect skill," Copias said. "Besides each of those clashes between Gildren and its neighbours took place over the course of a couple centuries. Aside from the culling, this divided nation has yet to see any real conflict for an entire lifetime. *Whereas* Felliet's soldiers were the first to confront the Fyoreten forces this very cycle."

"You make a reasonable argument," Jornis lied. "Perhaps it's best to see how Felliet's army progresses in relation to the other nations before judgement."

"Indeed," Copias replied as if victorious in his absurd argument.

The cranking ceased, and in quick succession the siloin commanders ordered a volley. Once more, Jornis's ears were filled with the cracking of tribow strings, yet in the darkness of night, he saw none of the unlit bolts, only hearing them piercing the air over the swordsmen. To his delight, he watched one of the hulking silhouettes collapse in the dwindling fires scattered throughout the fort.

Hearing the tribows crank once more, Jornis's relief faded as he glimpsed one of the Rauders climb the scaffolding beacon. The creature stood tall on the short tower, seeming to observe the four thousand men in gilded chainmail. Stranger still, the other six Rauders left alive in the fort made no attempt to attack or flee; instead, each of them stood where they were as the cranking continued.

Long after, a third volley sounded. This time the two thousand strong barrage was directed almost entirely against the single observing

Rauder, pelting the hulking creature with hundreds of bolts. The creature was thrown off the tower, slamming against the beach. The six remaining Rauders erratically stomped their fists onto metal disks lying on the ground, drowning out the cranking.

Copias asked, "What are they doing?"

"Sending some kind of signal," Jornis replied, glancing around at the flat, empty landscape.

The Silk Shore's commander yelled, "Prepare for a frontal assault."

Seeing no sign the wall of iron thorns was about to be pulled open, Jornis once again looked around at the dark coastal surroundings. He bit his bottom lip. "Where are the others hiding?"

"Perhaps they fled inland," Copias suggested.

"There would have been numerous tracks leading from the fort, and as you said earlier, their large bodies stomping the ground wouldn't be able to surprise…" Jornis realised the creatures wouldn't attempt an attack on land, and he turned his attention to the sea. Upon seeing many rocks near the water's thrashing edge, Jornis bolted his horse, shouting to the siloin commanders, "Look to the sea! The Rauders are submerged! Look to the sea!"

They took heed of the warming and directed their swordsmen units to face the waters either side of the fort. A flurry of water sounded across the right side of the fort as over forty bulbous Rauders came surging out, galloping on their three legs towards the swordsmen.

The Marble Wheels commander shouted, "Stand firm!"

Without a moment to relax, the hulking creatures smashed through the front row of shields and swords, bringing them deep in the midst of the force. The Rauders used their giant fists to sweep aside the startled swordsmen surrounding them.

The Silk Shore's commander demanded, "Overwhelm those animals!"

His words brought about a frenzy throughout the eight armies as the swordsmen pushed their way towards the surrounding bulbous creatures. Dozens upon dozens of swords hacked them down.

When the cranking sound faded, the Marble Wheels commander yelled for a final volley. Vast numbers of tribow bolts flew over the swordsmen's helmets, striking the final ten Rauders as their hulking bodies stood above the swordsmen bringing them down.

The night air was filled with victorious cheer.

Copias smirked. "I cannot believe they thought they could route such an enormous force with so few of them."

Jornis noticed the six Rauders in the fort depart in two of their boats and head in differing directions. Deducing one was a decoy for the awaiting warships to allow the other to escape, Jornis replied, "I don't think tonight it was *them* underestimating *us*."

Chapter twenty-two – Ideals

Eighth eclipse, third day

As dawn's light filled the sky, the extent of the carnage was revealed. All forty Rauders who had charged were left scattered about the battlefield with wide trails of blood where they had carved through the swordsmen. Grimly, far more soldiers were dragged to the pyres than the hulking creatures, leaving the combined siloin armies eerily quiet. Only their commanders searching the thorn-walled fort and the skipping boats seemed positive, albeit prideful and relieved.

Walking his horse along the bloodied ground, Jornis carefully looked at the Rauder bodies, each one still imbedded with many swords and bolts, while the sight of the two boats leaving lingered in his thoughts. He asked, "Are there other Rauders the fleeing boats went to?"

Copias said, "Perhaps they simply fled."

Jornis shook his head. "They could have left the moment they saw the large armies. It seems almost as though they waited to the last possible moment to leave."

"You think they were testing Gildren's might?" Copias asked.

Glancing at the ten skipping boats beyond the iron thorns, Jornis replied, "It's too soon to say."

"In any case"—Copias walked his horse closer to the gap between the iron thorns—"with this victory, Gildren shouldn't see any more raids."

Turning to the stripped beacon, Jornis wondered whether the cart of agon and iron had been taken. He moved his horse forward as he pondered what weapons and ships the Rauders could forge, for their palm tendrils could indeed grasp objects. A daunting realisation struck him: the Rauders were planning and preparing for an invasion from their islands far to the west. He reaffirmed his grip on his horse's reins and quickened its trot to the commanders.

Reaching the eight men, Jornis said, "I believe the Rauders will soon strike your coasts in a single great force."

The armoured men turned to him, and the Silk Shore's commander said, "We are well aware of that."

"So what is your council's plan to counter them?"

The Silk Shore's commander glanced at the growing pyres. "We learned their speed and strength is unlike any force the world has seen before. We have therefore decided to develop a fast-moving army for every coastal siloin, equipped with long pikes and mobile ballistas."

The Marble Wheels commander grinned. "And if they attack the Radiant Republic, we can learn far more of their tactics and strength."

Jornis considered the plan and nodded. "Much of the Rauders remains a mystery, especially their true numbers. Creating a force made to counter and learn from them is a wise decision." He paused. "I do not believe there is much more I can advise."

The Silk Shores commander said, "You may inform your Elite Dictorate that your advice throughout these recent eclipses has been much appreciated." He paused, glancing at the other commanders. "Furthermore, you may inform them all eight siloins of Gildren have agreed to your offer of direct trade for information. However, it will not be limited to the Marble Wheels."

Hiding a foolish, relieved smile, Jornis replied, "I will be glad to inform the Dictorate of your wise decision."

The Marble Wheels commander turned to his peer. "Surely you can simply tell them yourself when you arrive at Ellity."

"While I will visit them when I lead my army through Ellity, I feel it would be politer to notify them beforehand." The Silk Shores commander returned his attention to Jornis. "I will be the one leading this force, as well as our cavalry sent to Fyoreten, into the desert."

Jornis widened his gaze.

Copias asked, "Are you saying there will be another expedition?"

"Unlike any other before," the Silk Shores commander answered. "Every member of the federation will send their armies. against this common foe. Without a doubt, I truly believe this will bring an end to the Beast Riders, for good, or for ill."

Jornis shook his head. "If all nations of the federation unite and defeat a shared enemy, it will teach every leader the importance of cooperation."

"Only so long as that shared enemy exists," he said. "Either way this will be the last time I see you for a while, so I shall bid you a peaceful journey home," he replied. "Also, my full name is Koren Illion Mander."

Jornis smiled. "I wish you happy hunting Koren Mander."

Focusing her thoughts only on her work, Niyaa was proud to see the scaly sleeve taking shape as she threaded the final scales where the knuckles would be. She glanced at Mithen who was plucking more scales off the red wall. "Nearly done."

"Make sure you use only three straps," Mithen reminded her. "We only have so much string."

"One for the shoulder, the elbow and wrist, right?" Niyaa asked, reaching for the box of string.

"*Above* the elbow," Mithen corrected and turned to the entrance. "So how long were you gonna wait there for?"

Niyaa looked up and saw the bear-like man walk inside with that horrid pole axe thing still strapped to his back and with a scaly saddle in his arms. She turned back to her work, hoping he wouldn't notice her.

"I need you to mend this," he said, dropping the heavy saddle on the hammering bench.

"I *only* mended that thing before you left," Mithen replied. She jumped atop her stool to examine the worn red saddle. "Half the scale threads have come off. How far did you go with this thing?"

"It was well used."

"Just not cared for." She sighed. "All right, leave it with us, and we'll see it shine again."

Hearing those words, Niyaa lifted her gaze from the scaly sleeve and stared into his grim black eyes. He gave her a single disinterested glance and returned his attention to the smither. "You have my thanks."

He turned his back to the forge, forcing Niyaa to see the gargantuan pole axe up close. She was unable to move a single muscle in her body as the huge man marched away.

"He sure knows how to wear my work down." Mithen shook her horned head and turned to Niyaa. "Why the angry look?"

"It's nothing." Niyaa took three lengths of string.

Mithen folded her little arms. "Now I don't know what's got you so worked up or why you vanished yesterday, but I know that when people are annoyed, they make mistakes."

Niyaa's arms tensed. "I'll be fine."

"No, you won't. Get some air for now. You can finish that sleeve when you've calmed down."

Niyaa let the sleeve fall from her hands. "All right."

Stepping out onto the sandy street, Niyaa took in a long breath of fresh dry air as the painful memories returned. Head lowered, she wandered along the sandy street towards the saltless sea. Perhaps the beauty of the sparkly water would take her mind off everything.

Passing other beast people, she glimpsed the horrific spiked axe head and saw the black-furred man heading in the same direction. Niyaa stopped in the middle of the street, her muscles tensed. She got a sudden urge to follow.

Tailing him all the way to the water's edge, she watched the bear-like man march to a house along the shoreline where his feathery violet steed lay untied just outside the door. For a moment she wondered why he was allowed to keep it away from the special pens and questioned why such an evil man would care to keep it so close to his home. She shook her head and rushed over.

As she approached the door, the horse-like creature woke, keeping its bright sapphire eyes focused on her. Feeling nerves overcome her, Niyaa stared motionless back at it for a long moment before she tiptoed to a little window beside the door.

Peering inside, Niyaa saw the huge man had leaned his pole axe against an empty dining table and grasped a gutting knife from the side of his plain kitchen. The horse-like steed huffed at her, and she darted her body low, leaving only her eyes poking above the windowsill. She watched him take the curved knife to a fresh coral fish and gut it. The bizarre sight of him casually preparing his super bewildered her. His purple steed whined.

Panicked, Niyaa ducked low, pleading with the steed to hush before the door burst open.

The man's black eyes glared down at Niyaa. "Why are you disturbing her?"

Noticing the curved, serrated knife firmly in his grip, she couldn't reply.

"Well?"

The screams of Edenor's priest thrust back into Niyaa's ears, and she sprang to her feet, demanding, "Why did you have to attack us?"

His face didn't change. "You aren't one of us, are you?"

Niyaa stared into his black eyes waiting for her answer.

"Did you come here from that village?"

She felt her hands tighten into fists. "Why did you have to kill the priest and guards?"

"I think you know why." He tossed the knife at her feet. "If you want revenge, then go ahead."

All of Niyaa's anger vanished as she turned to the knife.

He folded his bulky, furry arms and repeated, "If you want revenge, then go ahead."

Turning back to his dark eyes, she shook her head. "I don't want revenge."

"So what *do* you want then?" he asked. "An apology?"

"I just want everyone to get along," Niyaa blurted out as her eyes grew watery and her voice croaked. "I don't ever want someone to die."

He stared at her and unfolded his arms. He bent his legs, lowering his huge body to her eye level. "Even those who'd wish harm on others?"

"I…" Niyaa looked down at the knife. "I still wouldn't want them killed."

"Nor would I," he replied. "But these things must happen."

"But why?" she pleaded. "Can we not talk with each other?"

"You're far too naïve." He narrowed his dark eyes and straightened up. "Those kinds of people would never listen."

Niyaa's body relaxed as she realised who this man really was. "*You're* one of those people." She smiled with relief at the pitiful man. "You're just a bully, desperate for revenge."

His hands tightened into fists. "You believe those spearmen who marched on our home here would listen to anything other than a blade? Or those priests, who gladly sing songs of our destruction, do you think they will listen if we ask politely not to send our families to the chopping block?" His face grew more furious. "You're just a child who knows nothing of the world. Now get out of my sight."

Staring at his menacing look, Niyaa didn't feel fear; instead, she felt a strange mix of sadness and pity for him, leaving her standing there unmoved.

"Did you hear me?" His voice grew. "Leave me be."

Niyaa glanced at the knife lying at her feet and picked it up. "I can't forgive you for what you did, but I don't think I can blame you anymore." She held the knife's handle for him to grasp. "Please don't believe your problems will vanish when you've killed your enemies."

Without a single word, his black-furred hand took the knife, and she turned away, trekking back to the forge, her head high.

Stepping into the pouring rain onto the small courtyard, Iyna looked up at her soldiers repairing the last of the ramparts, noticing the bitter glances they gave her. It was understandable, as they had all been told to wait in the grim weather of the mountainside in case the Fyoreten returned. Most of them had grown bored of eating the same stew day after day while the rest were tired of redigging the moat and repairing the fort, leaving everyone utterly miserable.

As Iyna passed Erger's covered furnace, one of the spearmen above the gate shouted down to her, "Someone's approaching from the north."

A rush of curious, hopeful soldiers along the ramparts stared out.

Marching to the gate, Iyna asked the lookout, "Who is it?"

"Appears to be a black carriage and a grey wagon with a bunch of bodyguards in chainmail."

Watching them near the fort, Iyna didn't see any replacement unit, leaving her wondering just who this was.

The entire courtyard and the surrounding ramparts were packed with curious and excited soldiers as the gate opened to the arriving procession. The black carriage halted before the repaired well, with the wagon stopping just after the gate, and the unit leaders caught up with Iyna as confusion and disappointment spread across every face.

The carriage door opened, and Reethial and Buckley stepped out into the pouring rain.

Iyna stepped towards them. "It's good to see you again."

"And you." Reethial grinned. "I heard of your cunning victory against those Fyoreten fools and felt it was prudent to reward you and your army." He clicked his fingers, and the bodyguards proceeded to unfurl the cover on the grey wagon, revealing it was brimming with casks of ale and iron chainmail.

Iyna stared in disbelief at the clean, new armour as the surrounding soldiers cheered at the sight of the ale. "Is this really for us?"

Buckley replied, "Your army has done much for this country and its people. It would be remiss of any elite not to reward you."

"Indeed," Reethial said. "I will ensure every one of your needs are met until the expedition sets out across the desert."

Iyna turned to him. "Thank you."

"No, thank you," Reethial replied. "Your swift, decisive action against the Fyoreten has done much to protect the interests of this nation. The news of you and your reputation has already spread throughout Felliet."

"My reputation?" Iyna asked.

"Of course. Word of a female commoner leading Felliet's army in victorious battle has become quite the sensation among the masses." He grinned. "So when you return triumphantly from the desert, you are sure to be met with vast celebratory crowds. I even suspect the Elite Dictorate likely to gift your deeds with a family name of your choosing."

Stunned, Iyna hesitated.

Barcial stepped forward. "I would also imagine anyone supporting her would also revel in that celebration."

"Of course," Reethial replied. "The unit leaders would indeed be considered heroes of Felliet."

Iyna noticed a stern look in Barcial's eyes and realised this elite might be doing this more for his own benefit than hers. Even knowing that, she felt sincerely grateful. "So long as Felliet remains safe, I don't care if I acquire a name or reputation."

Reethial grinned. "A true leader if ever I have seen one."

Feeliath gestured to the wagon. "There appears to be more armour than we have people."

"Correct," Buckley answered. "In an eclipse or two, you will be joined by two other units."

Reethial added, "That will bring your army to a total of just under two hundred."

Iyna smiled as she thought back to her training. "If they're trained by Alexan Brige, then I eagerly await them." She turned to the surrounding soldiers staring at the casks of ale and raised her voice. "There won't be many chances to celebrate when the expedition starts, so tonight, make the most of it."

Thunderous cheers rose throughout the fort.

An unending drizzle had followed the procession since leaving the Fyoreten region, and though Vernon and Jofinian were kept dry in their white, glass-roofed carriage, they both felt sympathetic for the thirty bodyguards riding alongside. As the sun neared the horizon, they took solace at the sight of the approaching mountain city of Skylvin.

Glimpsing the wonderous vertical city through the carriage windows, Vernon leaned his head out into the damp air. Incredible clusters of white vines hovered on islands and towers along the entire mountainside wall of triangular-roofed homes, all interconnected by glistening silver bridges. Yet despite the gusts thrashing the heavy rain against the mountainside, not one of the many floating structures swayed, not even a little.

An enormous pyramid-roofed platform ascended along the mountainside city, stopping at small clearings on separate levels. Figures stepped onto it, with several other platforms ascending and descending across the vertical city. Vernon even glimpsed one as it rose through the darkening blanket of distant clouds.

As the procession neared the unroofed, ivory gate, the light from the westerly horizon faded, and with it, the city grew ever more wonderous. Across the mountainside, candlelight emerged, transforming the vertical city into a star-like array of reddish-orange lights with shimmering threads of silver that glistened along every bridge and beneath every lift.

"I had that same look when I first arrived here," Jofinian said.

Vernon brought his head back inside and smoothed his soaked hair. "Never thought it would look so incredible in person."

"One can never truly capture the beauty of a place from a book or secondhand telling. It's why I am so thankful for my appointment."

"Not to mention the tributes collected benefit the whole world."

The noble's prideful smile faded. "If only the other nations could see it."

"What do you mean?" Vernon asked. "Surely they can see Erium invests that money into projects across the federation, aiding their own prosperity."

"Unfortunately, they can only see the coin in their hands at the present moment and not what such an investment would later bring." Jofinian shrugged. "You'll see soon enough."

The procession passed over the rapid waters of the city's moat, through the open ivory gate and into the shadow of an overhead guard tower. Vernon peered out once more and saw numerous hooded axemen and crossbowmen lining the ground-level ramparts and realised their eyes were filled with suspicion.

Turning to the smoothened street ahead, Vernon saw a constant stream of water pouring from the overhanging pyramid roofs, flooding the gutters abutting the steep sloping street. Even so, families and labourers gathered along the wet street to watch the tributary procession pass. Noticing their disgruntled looks, Vernon retreated into the privacy of the white carriage and gazed through its glass ceiling. Many onlookers stared down from the overhead hovering towers and glistening silver bridges.

Jofinian leaned back and turned his gaze upwards. "It's quite a sight, is it not?"

Staring up at the numerous floating towers and islands filling the overhead darkening sky with a growing multitude of flickering candlelight and glistening bridges, Vernon relaxed.

Before long, night had fully descended and the procession reached one of the enormous lifts, readying to ascend the vertical city. After a dozen of the bodyguards escorted the horses off the iron platform, the Myklinn Minor guards raised the netted rails along each of the lift's sides.

Jofinian opened the carriage door and stepped outside, turning back to Vernon. "Let what you are about to witness reside in your mind for as long as you can."

Vernon stood beside the platform's netted railing, facing away from the mountainside city. The spiralling skyline wheel beneath the lift released.

Vernon felt a strange sensation of his body pulling downwards as the platform rose, and he gazed across the wet pyramid rooftops of the grounded houses. The orange glow scattered across the mountainside reflected perfectly on the flowing water gushing down the steep rooftops and across the slim waterfalls falling from the hovering towers.

As the platform rose further, Vernon gazed beyond Skylvin's grounded wall and spotted distant lights across the hilly landscape. The platform rose alongside a floating towerblock. He exchanged looks with passing families and couples of all ages as they watched from their aloft windows, and he saw people walking along the towerblock's shimmering silvery bridge. Passing beyond the tower, Vernon became transfixed ahead as the landscape widened before him, bringing farmhouse lights across the entire region into view.

For the long ascent, Vernon was mesmerised by the incredible vast sight. After an unknowable time later, he felt a weird sensation of his body moving upwards as the platform halted. Staring down at the hovering towers above the brightened grounded rooftops, Vernon realised he was a mere story away from the misty blanket of dark clouds covering the sky. The wind was both stronger and crisper than on the ground. The lift had halted before the pair of giant silver doors of Skylvin's mountain-carved palace. Glancing to the dark cloud layer hovering above, Vernon wondered just how many ballistas stood cranked and loaded out of sight as he and Jornis stepped away from the edge.

The hooded palace guards lowered the closest railing and opened the grand doors to the tributary chestwagon. Vernon noticed the serious look upon Jofinian as the two of them marched inside the unwelcoming palace.

As the grand doors shut behind them, Vernon was standing on the bottom step of a wide ascending chamber leading to King Asceld Silvex, staring down at them from his mirror throne. Vernon's eyes widened as he noticed the ballista bolt that had slain the king of Myklinn Greater in their bygone civil war still hung above the throne. Evidently the rulers of Myklinn Minor were stubborn fools, holding onto irrelevant past grudges.

Glancing upwards in the dim light of the stepped chamber, Vernon noticed many shadowy balconies filled with cloaked crossbowmen. He followed Jofinian up the steps.

Halfway up, the king raised a hand, halting the pair, and his voice echoed across the tall mountain-carved walls. "Why has Erium sent for our tribute two eclipses before the traditional date?"

"Now is a time of great need," Jofinian explained. "Much coin is needed for this final expedition as well as the urgent need to repair many of the roads along the mountain trade routes."

The dim stepped chamber grew silent for a long while before King Asceld's voice echoed once more. "Why has Erium sent for *our* tribute two eclipses before the traditional date?"

Jofinian stood his ground. "The aim of the federation is to establish a lasting peace where all eight nations cooperate for the benefit of all." He glanced to the balconies above. "The short-lived nation of Fyoreten threatened that desire by refusing its tributes and offering no aid to the federation's endeavours. It was therefore—"

"Endeavours such as the Southern Campaign?" King Asceld asked. "One of the few regrets I have for my reign was sending many of my finest warriors to that disaster."

Vernon said, "But at the time, you, like the rest of the world's leaders, would have seen the benefits ending the Radiant Republic would have brought the world. Fyoreten was the only nation to have refused, simply because their leaders thought only of their hatred towards Erium."

The king scowled. "Do not attempt to claim to know my decisions."

"Regardless," Jofinian said. "Every nation of the federation must contribute to the overall good of all. That in mind, it was decided with all the other nations that since you did not take part in the Fyoreten war we have agreed your tribute should be paid early."

Silence gripped the stepped chamber as King Asceld leaned back in his mirror throne.

Jofinian added, "It would demonstrate your nation *is* committed to the unity and protection of the federation."

Without uttering a word, the king glanced to one of the nearest balconies and gave a single nod. A pair of silver-furred servants carried a small chest through a side door at the top of the chamber. Vernon knew the size of the singular chest was far smaller than what had been demanded.

As it was placed on the step above the pair, King Asceld said, "This is a sign of *my* commitment to the federation and its goals of *unity.*"

"How much is in this?" Jofinian asked.

"Two hundred."

Vernon raised his voice in disbelief. "That is less than a third of what is owed."

"True Myklinn owes no one, least of all the Empire of Erium." King Asceld rose from his mirror throne and marched towards the side door.

Jofinian asked, "And what of the promised skyline?"

Neither glancing back nor slowing his step, the king left without an answer.

The tributary bodyguards brought the pitifully small sum to the chestwagon, and Jofinian entered its combination, springing open its pristine white-velveted inside. Two hundred bronze coins were poured inside, barely covering its velveted floor.

Standing once more at the edge of the platform with the vast landscape before them, Vernon whispered to Jofinian, "Does he not see the benefits the tribute system returns or why he has to pay it early?"

"He is no fool." The noble bitterly lowered his voice. "Perhaps it is his pride or ego preventing him from seeing reason."

"A leader shouldn't make rulings based on such things."

"Unfortunately, leaders are still people." Jofinian leaned over the netted railing, gazing at the wall of lights and silver bridges below. "If a man has never bothered questioning his country's place in the world, he will be blind to the inevitable mortality of nations."

"So he believes Myklinn Minor to be the strongest country in the world?" Vernon asked.

"Wholeheartedly."

Vernon turned his eyes down to the floating towers hovering over the network of candlelit streets glowing in the night. "A man like that threatens to end such a wondrous place."

"Agreed," Jofinian muttered.

The platform began its decent.

Chapter twenty-three – Familiar Road

Eighth eclipse, sixteenth day

Taking her seat with the beast people around the gathering stands, Niyaa and her mom restlessly watched an exhausted horse-legged man whisper something to the pioneers. Unease gripped everyone around the central clearing as the pioneers' faces filled with worsening shock and dread the more they listened. As soon as the horse-legged man finished his muttered report, Fewttyre handed him a water bag which he heartedly drank.

The golden-haired lady turned and addressed everyone still taking their seats. "We are going to wait a moment for the others to arrive."

Mysia whispered to Cabi and her antlered boyfriend, "Who is he?"

Cabi's back limbs folded inwards against the back of the hard seat. "I think he's from one of the scouting groups sent to Felliet, but why is he alone?"

Anthile lowered his head, muttering, "Something must've happened to them."

The four of them went silent. The bear-like man entered the gathering stands, taking one of the closest seats alongside Mithen.

Semy sat down next to Anthile. "So what's this about then?"

"One of the scouting groups has returned," he explained.

Cabi shook her head. "But it looks like the others haven't."

It took an uncomfortable while for the last of the beast people to gather along the large stands. The greying red-furred pioneer spoke. "Everyone! This man has come from Felliet! He has something important to announce!"

The crowd went eerily quiet as the turned to the people gathered around, his breath still heavy. "I was part of a small team finding information in Felliet when we heard an announcement. It didn't take us long to confirm it and…" He took a long breath. "The entire federation is sending one enormous force against us, far larger than anything before." Stunned mutterings and gasps flared across the semicircular ring as the scout kept talking. "I was the fastest of my team, so we decided I would split off from them to send word to Reeffewd as fast as possible."

The crowd's worried talking nearly drowned out the scout's words.

"Silence!" the taloned pioneer yelled, tightening his grip on his cane. "Listen to what else he heard about this new purge."

Noises around the crowd faded, and the horse-legged man continued, "They say it could be as much as twenty thousand, but we know for certain that armies from across the world are involved."

Fewttyre asked, "Even the Therra?"

"We believe so," the scout answered.

Dread came over everyone's faces, bringing an unnerving silence over every head.

Grenis crossed his scaly green arms. "Do we know who leads these armies?"

"I know only two names," the scout explained. "We discovered the emperor's own sister Elleasious Imerial will lead Erium's army. She's the leader of Sidium's garrison, and word is, she's a ruthless commander. There's no doubt she will be the figurehead of this purging."

"And the second?" the green scaly man asked.

"She commands a small Felliet army and apparently played a large part in the Fyoreten war. She apparently even defeated a small Fyoreten group without losing a single man." He took another sip of water. "Strangely enough, she doesn't have a last name and only goes by Iyna."

"Iyna?" Niyaa shouted, bringing the attention of everyone in the gathering stands.

The pioneer in a wheelchair moved closer to her. "Young lady. Have you heard of this person before?"

Watching all the stunned gazes across the stands, Niyaa answered, "She's my friend."

"Your friend?" he asked.

Mysia said, "They were friends long before we crossed the desert, but as you can see, we haven't seen her since."

Niyaa overheard hushed whispers spreading throughout the semicircular stands and felt even more nervous.

The beast pioneer leaned forward in his wheelchair. "Could the two of you stand and make your voice absolutely clear for everyone present?"

Mysia rose, and Niyaa took a deep breath and followed suit.

The golden-haired lady asked them, "How are you finding the city, Mysia and Niyaa?"

"It's truly a paradise," Mysia answered. "The Florision especially is incredible. From it I have found all the ingredients to start brewing batches of ale, and my daughter is doing well helping Mithen in the forge."

"It's good to hear you've both settled in." Elixsis smiled.

The other elderly pioneer, leaning both hands on his cane, asked, "So what can you tell us of this Iyna person?"

"She's really kind," Niyaa said. "And really strong."

Mysia said, "She's a fair bit older than my girl. Her mom died in the Southern Campaign. However, she would've only just become a soldier after what happened at Edenor, so I couldn't say how she came to command an army."

"Gentle and inexperienced." A cruel grin crossed Tovern's face as he turned to the other pioneers. "Sounds like her army will easily fall before our walls."

"You can't!" Niyaa shouted. "We can talk to her! I know she'll listen."

Tovern guffawed. "You really think an enemy commander will listen to any of us?"

Niyaa glanced to the iron brace around the elderly man's leg. "*I'll* talk to her then. She'll listen to me. I just know it."

Mysia whispered in her daughter's ear, "Don't say any more."

Elixsis turned to the other pioneers. "Perhaps it wouldn't hurt to let her try."

The bear-like man rose from his seat and raised his voice. "Why should we trust an outsider to speak with the enemy?"

Fewttyre turned to him. "She is not an outsider. Niyaa and her mother belong here now."

Tovern asked, "And how do you know she won't simply side with her friend? After all, they both came from the same place and were close."

"I trust her," Fewttyre replied.

Tovern raised his cane to his chest. "I will put my trust in anyone born among us but never someone born under the rule of those nobles and their priests."

The mutterings along the stands flared up once more as Niyaa worried about their mistrust and misplaced hatred. Her thoughts were on her friend who, if nothing was done, would be ordered to attack Lorish and Reeffewd.

Fewttyre's hands tensed as he marched towards Tovern. "I know those two to be compassionate and kind. They will never betray us."

"Fewttyre," Tovern raised his voice. "We cannot have someone unchanged speak for us."

"Then change me into a beast person!" Niyaa shouted, quietening everyone as the pioneers turned their stunned faces to her.

Mysia stepped in front of her daughter. "She didn't mean that!" She desperately turned to her daughter. "Tell them you didn't mean that."

Seeing the shock and fear in her mom's face, Niyaa tried to reassure her. "I know Iyna better than anyone. If I become a beast person, I just know she will change her mind about this purge. Hopefully everyone will."

Mysia grasped her daughter's hand, pleading, "I don't want to see your body change in any way."

"But I'm the only one who can help these people." Niyaa felt her eyes water. "And I'll be happy to do it."

Fewttyre walked closer to them and asked Niyaa, "Are you certain you want this?"

She wiped away the few tears falling down her cheek. "I am."

On those words Mysia grabbed her daughter's shoulders sternly, staring at her. "Please think on this. You won't be you ever again."

Niyaa smiled. "I will *always* be me."

"But"—Mysia's grip weakened—"it means the governors and elites will send soldiers and priest trackers after you for the rest of your days."

"I don't mind." Niyaa glanced around at the many kinds of beast people around the stands and placed her hand on her mom's wrist. "If I have a chance to stop all the people here getting hurt, then I will gladly have the surgery."

Mysia stared wide eyed at her daughter, unable to say a word.

"It's all right," Niyaa said. "I want this."

Her mom's grip became a tight hug. "It still amazes me how your dad and I managed to raise the kindest person in the whole world."

Niyaa hugged her mom back and turned to the pioneers. "I want to do this."

Fewttyre knelt down, staring at her. "You cannot change back, nor will your body ever be the same again."

Niyaa broke away from her mom and glanced at her hands then to her body. "I understand."

"Very well." Fewttyre gave a single nod and turned to Tovern. "If she were to have the surgery, would that earn your trust?"

He grunted. "It would."

Fewttyre turned to the other pioneers, and with no objections, he raised his voice for all to hear. "I'll have the preparations ready for tonight. If this task succeeds, we will have an ally to help us survive this purge."

The chainmail weighed heavily on Iyna's shoulders and head, and its chain links constantly rattled as she moved. She had expected it to be a tight fit, especially with the agron chestplate and helmet worn over it; instead, she found it easy to move in. Erger assured her it meant all the soldiers didn't have to fret about cuts and slashes, leaving a confident grin on most faces as they neared the brown walls of Vellide.

The gatehouse's guards, in better-fitted chainmail, cheered at Iyna and her small army as they entered the town square. The scents of fresh fish, meats and perfume caught her nose as she stared ahead at the bustling market square packed with merchant stalls selling all kinds of food and crafts. Families peered out of windows and around corners, all proudly watching the passing spearmen and tribowmen.

An eager crowd gathered along the bridge to the market stalls. Iyna smiled and turned to her army. "We'll stay in Vellide's inns for tonight and set off at midday tomorrow. Tarrow, Barcial and Feeliath, come with me. The rest of you can do what you like."

Cheering, they dispersed towards the taverns, crowds and stalls, their full coin purses dangling from their belts.

As her unit leaders caught up with her, Iyna turned to the black iron door with Felliet's symbol bolted onto it. A ginger-bearded man, with a tiny iron pin of a stone bridge over a river of snakes pinned to his grey tunic, ambled out of the open door. Iyna recognised Vellide's governor, so she marched to him with her unit leaders closely following.

"You must be Iyna," he said. "I've heard quite a lot about you."

"And you must be Governor Sepp," she replied.

He raised his eyebrows. "I didn't expect you to know my name."

"I passed through here with Jornis Meyorter before the Fyoreten war," she explained.

"I see." He stroked his beard as his smile grew. "There's little point to just standing here in the street, and I imagine you are quite thirsty after the long march to my humble town."

Feeliath asked, "Do you perhaps have something stronger than water?"

"Only the finest whiskies you will find in Felliet," Governor Sepp answered. "As well as a wide assortment of complementing cheeses."

Iyna kept her gaze focused on the elite. "Only one drink for each of us, for we'll need a clear head when we leave tomorrow."

The four soldiers walked inside the governor's brightly lit home, passing a pink-haired girl in a red and white dress who took their weapons and shields. Iyna handed her spear to the woman without hesitation or concern and paused to reflect. Perhaps in an elite's home in the centre of Felliet, she could truly feel safe.

Parick Sepp led them to a bright lounge at the end of the hall filled with lavish paintings and glass furniture around a pair of long fur sofas. A subtle hint of mint came from the warm, crackling fireplace. Iyna took her seat in the midst of Tarrow, Feeliath and Barcial and watched another stewardess enter with a brass tray of cheeses and buttered fish cakes alongside five whiskey-filled tumblers. She set the tray down on the glass table standing between the sofas and placed herself at the back wall.

Governor Sepp picked up one of the crystal cut tumblers. "I must say it is truly a delight to have such courageous soldiers of Felliet in my abode."

Barcial frowned. "What makes you say we're courageous?"

"Your actions at the Moain fort, of course." The elite leaned back in his cushioned seat. "Not only does it take the strongest of wills to carry out such a bold attack"—he grinned—"but to stand against the orders of the Dictorate to do what is right, now that is what I call courage."

"My apologies," Barcial replied. "I misunderstood your words."

"No apology needed," Governor Sepp remarked. "It is quite reasonable to assume every elite does not understand the true horrors of war." He gestured to the other tumblers. "Please help yourselves."

Feeliath was the first to grab a drink. "You have my thanks, Governor Sepp."

He shook his head. "You four are leading an army to defend Felliet. There will be no such need to refer to me other than Parick."

"Afraid I cannot abide by that." Feeliath took a sip of whiskey. "The elites of Felliet run all aspects of the nation, and their names need to be held to a higher standard than the commoners."

Iyna glanced at him, wondering if that was the reason he disliked her.

"I respect your viewpoint, Feeliath Coriate," the elite said. "But personally I believe there are times when such titles should be relaxed. One such instance should be when discussing military matters and the state of the nation." Parick turned to Iyna. "On that note, is there anything you require that I can provide?"

"Reethial Zenth is the elite who's giving us the supplies and equipment we need." She picked up a tumbler, holding it in her lap. "But no one knows for sure how far the desert stretches, so I'm worried about supply carts not reaching us."

Tarrow explained, "A cart of bolts and spare agron would be welcomed."

The elite grinned. "I actually have a horse-drawn cart full of agron scrap I've been hoping to be rid of. I will be happy to have our forges make the required bolts and deliver them long before you depart with the rest of the expedition."

Barcial glanced at the tray of cheeses. "We will also need plentiful sacks of food and barrels of water."

The elite took another sip. "Afraid that will have to wait till after the comet, but I might be able to arrange a wagon filled with water, bread and ale."

"No ale," Iyna said. "We must have our full senses if we are to face the Beast Riders in their territory."

"Then I shall have the casks set aside for your glorious return." He grinned. "Now, I heard you are travelling to Edenor."

Iyna darted her eyes away. "It's the closest place to the desert."

"Well, I certainly will be glad to see its walls occupied once more, even if it means converting it to a fort." He raised his tumbler to the soldiers. "You can rest assured I will see Felliet's brave soldiers receive all the support they need."

"I'm truly glad to have the support of another elite," Iyna replied, raising her tumbler to him. Barcial, Feeliath and Tarrow followed suit, whereby all five heartedly clinked together.

Prolonging their stay in Skylvin had yielded nothing extra from their stubborn king, resulting in the procession leaving the vertical city with only the measly two hundred bronze. The insult left Vernon's mind wrestling with the reason behind it, to the point of distracting him from reading *Erium's Founding*. Jofinian had tried to lift the mood by explaining much of his travels across the federation, yet all his stories did was raise the prospect of other nations failing to pay their tribute.

"Such a beautiful day, is it not?" Jofinian said, gazing out the window at the hilly Fyoreten landscape.

Vernon said, "I don't know how you can be in such a good mood when we're a day or two from reporting that we failed."

"But we weren't the ones who failed." Jofinian leaned back in the carriage seat. "Truth be told, I was expecting a reduced amount."

"You were?"

"Of course. Name given or commoner, everyone searches for ways to avoid paying what they owe. I just never expected it to be insultingly small."

"Which is why they shouldn't have the choice," Vernon said, glancing to the thirty bodyguards riding alongside.

The noble shrugged. "Afraid none of us live in such a world where rulers of other nations can be bound to their agreements."

His words forced a frustrated sigh from Vernon's lips. "Is there enough coin to fully fund this expedition?"

Jofinian's shoulders dropped. "This tribute was supposed to fund the majority of the venture, offsetting Minitium's refusal to release new coins."

"Does that mean we will travel to other nations for tribute?" Vernon asked.

Jofinian shook his head. "If we were to ask the other nations of the federation to fund the expedition in place of Myklinn Minor, we would only achieve embarrassment for Erium."

"Then it leaves only tax revenue." Vernon sat back in disappointment.

"That would likely be the case; however, Emperor Merchasious is understandably reluctant to raise taxes at the beginning of his reign."

"But surely the citizens of Erium understand that it will go towards unifying the federation under a single banner," Vernon argued. "Surely they will be more than willing to pay?"

Jofinian smirked. "Name given or commoner, everyone searches for ways to—"

Something small slammed into the carriage wall followed swiftly by the sound of a horse screaming in agony. Vernon sat up straight, and a bolt smashed through the carriage window, skimming the air between the two passengers and striking the opposing door. They ducked low as the barrage slew their driver and horse.

They heard the surrounding bodyguards drawing their swords and the head bodyguard shouting for ten of his men to stay with the chestwagon. Vernon raised his head, poking it above the carriage windowsill just as twenty of the bodyguards galloped towards a distant line of westerly crossbowman.

With stunned eyes, Vernon watched them charge away. Jofinian yanked him away from the open window.

"I'd advise against keeping your head where a bolt just flew by," the noble said, keeping his head low. "The guards will protect us, so there's no need to fret."

Vernon obeyed, bringing his head to face the glass shards scattered about the carriage floor. Several horse squeals came from the pursuing bodyguards. Vernon bit his bottom lip as he fought off the instinct to look, and a strange horn bellowed across the uneven landscape.

"The guards will protect us," Jofinian repeated.

The noble's face was filled with fear, and Vernon's hands were trembling.

One of the outside bodyguards staying with the chestwagon shouted that attackers were coming from the other side. Vernon hurled himself to the easterly window and glanced out. To his horror, he saw a couple dozen men in green chainmail sprinting towards the procession with crossbows and axes.

"What do you see?" Jofinian asked.

"There's a large group of them coming this way. I think they're Fyoreten rebels." Vernon glanced to the ten remaining bodyguards and saw them in disarray; three charged the oncoming attack, a couple dismounted and the rest remained unmoved in their saddles. He ducked his head below the window once more, looked about the carriage and grasped one of the glass shards.

Jofinian whispered, "You don't intend to use that, do you?"

Staring at its jagged point, Vernon's heart pounded in his chest. "Better to have it than not."

"But can you use it?" the noble asked, just as the Fyoreten rebels came upon the remaining guards, filling the air with battle cries and iron clashes. "Can you actually take someone's life?"

Vernon turned to the carriage door closest to the carnage, unable to reply, and Jofinian opened the opposing door.

"What are you doing?" Vernon whispered.

"We're no longer safe in here," the noble answered as he stepped outside. "If you want to stay in the confines of the carriage, then be my guest."

Still gripping the shard of glass, Vernon followed Jofinian outside and to the front of the carriage, listening to the attackers overwhelm the bodyguards. Vernon lowered his head below the carriage wheels and witnessed many bloodied bodies in green and black fall around the tributary chestwagon as the chaotic fighting endured. Seeing the chestwagon's horse still alive, albeit huffing, he realised these attackers were after the bronze inside. His grip around the glass shard tightened.

Jofinian whispered in his ear, "We should head west and meet the rest of the guards."

Turning his gaze westward, Vernon could barely see the distant clash of riders and crossbowmen. He heard one of the Fyoreten men shout, "Let's get this treasure open."

An eager cheer rose from the rebels as Vernon returned his head under the carriage and saw the final bodyguard fall against one of the chestwagon's ornate columns. A Fyoreten man wrapped in a green cloak pushed aside the body and examined the chest.

Jofinian grabbed Vernon's shoulder. "They couldn't possibly guess the combination. We should hurry before they notice us."

Keeping his gaze fixed on the tributary wagon, Vernon thought frantically about how he could stop these rebels stealing the vital bronze.

The Fyoreten leader demanded, "What's taking so long?"

"It needs some sort of code, Reegar."

The Fyoreten leader turned to the distant fighting and ordered his men, "All right, everyone, turn this thing. We're gonna ride it away from the road."

He proceeded to sit in the driver's seat, tugging the bloodied reins of the horse, while his men went to turn the heavy chestwagon. Vernon's hand gripped the glass shard even tighter, and it cut into his palm. Glancing at the small cut in his hand, Vernon turned back to the chestwagon and realised there *was* a way to stop them and survive. He looked around for a better weapon and spotted a sheathed shortsword on the carriage driver's dead body.

"What are you thinking?" Jofinian quietly demanded. "You can't possibly fight them."

Pulling the sword from the sheath, Vernon whispered, "I'm not going to, but I won't let them take the bronze tribute either." Lifting the shortsword, he found it far heavier than he imagined, forcing him to grip its pommel with his other hand.

"They are experienced fighters," Jofinian said. "They just killed some of the best swordsmen in Erium, and you plan on using that thing against them."

"I told you, I'm not going to fight them." Vernon peered around the corner of the white carriage, observing the tributary chestwagon turning with their leader shouting at his men. He glanced back to Jofinian. "Catch up with the other bodyguards. I will stop these men from leaving and then afterwards I'll follow."

Before the noble could respond, Vernon crept along the edge of the white carriage towards the tributary chestwagon's horse. The man wrapped in the green cloak kept shouting at his dozen men, trying to hurry them as they heaved the corner of the heavy chestwagon, directing it to the side of the white carriage.

One of the other Fyoreten men pointed at Jofinian running westward. "Hey Reegar, there's a man running away!"

Vernon ducked to the edge of the white carriage, his breathing quickening.

"Leave him," Reegar demanded. "Just get this thing moved before those guards come back."

Watching the Fyoreten men return to straining themselves against the weight of the chestwagon, Vernon glanced at their leader and saw him yanking the reins to one side. Vernon crept forward. Nearing the horse, he raised the shortsword over his shoulder and saw the Fyoreten leader turn ahead.

Vernon dashed forward and brought the heavy blade down upon one of the horse's front legs. The sword crunched into the shin bone as the horse squealed in pain, raising its front legs and taking the implanted sword with it.

Vernon turned westward and ran just as the horse bolted forward in a panic, crashing the chestwagon into the side of the white carriage. Glancing back, he saw the Fyoreten group bewildered and stunned at the unexpected surge before they chased after him. He returned his gaze ahead to the fading sound of swords against crossbows and pushed his body faster across the uneven terrain.

Passing a couple of the bodyguard's riderless horses lying bloodied on the ground, Vernon forced his body to charge even faster, desperately trying not to look back. As his body began aching and his breathing grew heavier, he faintly heard scattered pursuing footsteps closing in.

Forcing his body to quicken, he heard hooves beating the ground beyond a hill, and fourteen of the bodyguards appeared, galloping towards him. He glanced back and saw the scattered pursuing Fyoreten flee in terror.

Vernon's body collapsed on the ground as the bodyguards in black chainmail charged past him to slay the rebels. Vernon spotted Jofinian trudging towards him from behind the horsemen, and a relieved smile came to them both.

Late into the evening, Jornis and Copias found themselves once again walking through the same pitiful narrow streets of Rubium with the same rotten stench residing in the air. However, the mood of the bystanders and labourers throughout the maze-like city seemed improved. Instead of the indifferent and envious glances they had previously been given, they saw a blend of ecstatic and joyous expressions. The putrid streets were filled with people despite the sun beginning to set below the ancient red wall.

Halfway through the strangely lively city, they found the narrow streets further congesting with excited commoners wandering towards the ancient wall with several ivory-robed figures mixed within. Unfamiliar with this festival Jornis approached the closest ivory-robed person. "Excuse me, young lady, could you inform me why so many are out so late?"

"Haven't you realised?" She smiled. "A single full moon will emerge tonight."

Copias asked, "Are you a moon worshipper?"

"Do you have a problem with that?"

Jornis went to his rescue. "My colleague merely wondered whether it would be safe practicing your beliefs with the priesthood's objection to it."

"Oh, that won't be a problem now." She giggled. "They left here several 'clipses ago."

Jornis and Copias glanced at each other with the same concerned look.

She turned her gaze to the darkening sky above the red wall. "Now we're finally able to praise both of them for keeping us safe in these hard times."

Copias said, "How many of you are here?"

"Why don't you see for yourself?" She gestured to the ancient red ramparts. "Everyone's gathering along the best place to see it."

Jornis said, "It would certainly be a wasted opportunity to miss such a sight when staying the night in this city."

"Great, I'll show you to a good spot," she said. "Name's Lienett by the way."

Following her eager strut, Copias whispered to Jornis, "If the priesthood are gone, can we trust that she will not lead us to some kind of trap?"

"If order were absent from Rubium, then we would have been robbed the moment we had our horses penned in the stables. Not to mention, we approached her, not the other way around," Jornis muttered. "But it is wise of you to keep an eye on those acting overly religious or charitable."

Lienett led them to an open stairwell in the thick brickwork of the ancient wall and ascended the candlelit curving steps. Above and below echoed the sound of many other people ascending the tower, leaving Jornis to ponder what had fuelled this rapid conversion.

Copias said, "Incredible how much moon worship has grown in so short a time."

Lienett smiled over her shoulder. "It's been around since the culling riots burned through our city, but now it's really taken root."

Copias lowered his voice. "Because the priesthood left Rubium."

"Now they're gone, no one's being judged or punished for their belief," she explained.

Jornis asked, "So why *did* they leave?"

"Don't know." She shrugged. "They didn't give any of us an answer and simply left in a single afternoon."

Clearly, major developments were happening in the priesthood that would affect Erium and consequently the federation.

Copias rubbed his hand along the red brickwork. "Quite remarkable how well kept these stairs are."

At first Jornis paid no heed to the comment, but he remembered the poor condition the ancient structure was in when they had first passed through the city. He darted his eyes to the dusted red steps and to the fresh candles interspaced along the walls and realised they had indeed been well maintained.

Lienett smirked. "The garrison's done a good job, haven't they?"

Jornis nodded. "I'm glad to learn the governor is finally maintaining this wall."

"That oaf does nothin' but take taxes we break our backs for." She scoffed. "It's the garrison and city folk who now keep our red wall lookin' nice."

Stunned by her comment, Jornis asked, "Then who is leading Rubium if not the governor or priesthood?"

Lienett stopped on the stairs and grinned to both the newcomers. "No one. The folk of Rubium have always fended for themselves, and we plan on keeping it that way."

Utterly bewildered by such a comment, Jornis asked, "Are you saying the people of this city are independent of Erium?"

She thought about it for a brief moment and nodded. "I suppose we are." She continued marching up the stairs. "You'll see for yourself."

Reaching the end of the stairwell, Jornis and Copias followed Lienett onto the wide ramparts where the city's sporadic rooftops and disjointed extensions lay clear for all to see. They stared wide eyed at the sheer size of the crowds filling every space across the vast red wall.

"So what do you think?" Lienett asked.

Jornis approached the edge of the ramparts and tracked his gaze along the giant wall surrounding the city. "I had no idea there could be so many practicing moon worship."

"Practicing?" she asked. "Every person you see knows the hope the two brothers provide and are *true* believers."

Copias also gazed across the city's rooftops. "Aren't there too few plumes of smoke?"

"Only those with newborns and sick family members really need the heat," Lienett explained. "This way there won't be anything blocking the view of the elder brother's glorious display tonight."

Jornis pondered how such a vast number of people could possibly be so organised and wondered who might be secretly leading them. He turned to Lienett. "So will the sermon begin when the single full moon rises?"

"I told you"—she smiled—"there aren't any priests here anymore."

Niyaa gazed through the lab's glass roof at the wonderous stars as the bright glow of the single moon passed overhead. Tomorrow she would be watching its little brother poking from behind his older sibling with a forever-changed body. Thinking long and hard about what she would look like, Niyaa asked aloud, "Fewttyre, what did you mean when you said my legs will change colour?"

He said, "Whenever you stretch your new legs, they will change from a yellow colour to a mixture of reds and blues."

She lifted her head up from the lab bed and saw him mashing some ingredients together in a little stone bowl. "Whenever I stretch my legs?"

"That will happen when you use your new legs to run, jump and crouch," he explained.

Niyaa rested her head back down and struggled to imagine the description once more. "I still can't believe I will be as fast as a horse and be able to jump atop rooftops." She lifted her head again. "Will it really work?"

"There's no need to be nervous," Fewttyre said. "I've perfected my skills with horses and pets as well as being taught personally by my parents. I assure you, the surgery's free of all risks."

Mysia marched to her daughter's side. "She's fine to be a little nervous since her body will be forever changed and, well … during the surgery."

"Where she'll be fast asleep and not feel a thing," Fewttyre said. "Afterwards I will give her something to numb the pain."

"So there *will* be pain then?" Mysia bitterly asked.

"I cannot simply pour the mixture over her shins and feet; it must infuse the separate organism with the entirety of her legs," Fewttyre explained, turning to his weird set of tools. "The *slight* pain she will feel will only last until her body adapts to her new limbs, which I assure you has never been longer than a day."

Niyaa placed her hand in her mom's. "I'll be all right."

"I know," Mysia said. "It's just … hard for me to see this."

Niyaa laid her head back down. "It won't change who I am."

Fewttyre picked up a tray carrying several spotless little clamps, a glass of pale white liquid and a stone mixing bowl filled with a thick greyish yellow sludge. He brought it to the lab bed, setting it on a small glass table and turned to Mysia. "You can still leave if you wish."

She shook her head. "I will watch every moment."

Fewttyre sighed. "This will be the last time you can object, for when it begins, that door must never be allowed to open."

"I will stay," Mysia replied.

He turned to Niyaa. "Keep staring up, all right?"

She turned her gaze upwards and heard him walking across the room to light a strong scented candle. He returned to the bed and picked up the glass of pale white. "Mysia, this will be unpleasant for you to watch."

Mysia grasped her daughter's hand tighter. "I will stay."

"Very well then." Fewttyre brought the glass close to Niyaa's mouth. "With your permission, I will adapt your body so its bound is greater than any creature. Are you happy to proceed knowing there is no going back?"

Remembering the joyous time with her friend, Niyaa took a long, deep breath and answered, "I am."

"Then I ask you to swallow this and fall asleep." He brought the glass to her lips. "When you wake, you will possess wonderous new limbs."

Drinking the thin sour liquid, Niyaa scrunched her face in disgust and relaxed her head on the soft pillow.

Fewttyre rested his hand on her forehead. "Just keep staring up at the sky."

"All right." Niyaa returned her gaze to the stars. She became really tired and, staring at the bright light in the twinkling sky, said, "The moon is ... beautiful tonight ... is ... isn't ... it?" Her eyelids drifted closed.

Chapter twenty-four – Different

Eighth eclipse, seventeenth day

Niyaa lifted her eyelids to the bright sunlight shining through the glass roof. A strange tingling feeling ran throughout her body, and she wearily turned her head. Her mom was leaning against one of the side counters on the far side of the blue floor, distantly staring into a mug of herbal tea. Niyaa weakly pulled her arms in, ready to sit up.

Fewttyre spoke from the other side of the room. "Don't get up straight away."

Niyaa relaxed and watched him rush to her side. "How'd it go?"

"Your body took to it perfectly," he answered, resting the back of his hand on her forehead. "I see your body temperature is returning to normal."

Niyaa wondered what he meant but noticed her mom standing beside her. "I did it, Mom."

Mysia's lips turned up in a slight smile, and she grasped her daughter's hand. "You were *so* brave."

Niyaa smiled, readied her arms to sit up and felt Fewttyre's hand on her back.

"Nice and slowly," he said. "It is not uncommon for a changed person to pass out after sitting up so quickly."

Mysia also placed her hand on her daughter's back and helped her sit up. "The hard part is over now."

Feeling exhausted, Niyaa was grateful to have both of them helping her sit up. Her eyes looked down upon her new lower legs, and she stared at them in stunned disbelief. Below her knees were upward arches made up of hundreds of yellowish strands, stretching all the way to the end of the curve where her toes had been. She found it strange that she had no feet anymore, yet for some reason she couldn't remember how someone would even wiggle their toes. It left her in a speechless mix of wonder and confusion.

She sat up and, without thinking, lifted her knees, straightening the arches against the bed. She watched in amazement as their curvy underside turned a pale green while their topside turned orange, creating a beautiful spectrum of colour around the strandy curves. Strangely, she could feel the very end of the soft bed through her feetless legs almost like feeling something beneath a fingernail.

Fewttyre proudly patted her back. "Now try bringing your lower legs closer to your torso."

Niyaa turned to him, confused.

"You control how much your lower legs can curve. You can straighten them to raise your height, as you would if you tiptoed or you can bend them even further, allowing you to crouch lower than you would have possibly done before."

Niyaa turned back to her curves. "So I just bend them?"

He walked to the end of the bed and placed both his hands on the end strands of her legs. "While keeping your knees still, think about moving your legs away from my touch."

Feeling his cold hands on the end of her strandy colourful legs, Niyaa pulled away. Her lower curvy legs bent upwards as the yellow colour returned across them both. Tightening the curves further, she watched as the topside strands turned deep blue while the underside went orangey red, swapping the colourful spectrum, and she felt the undersides of the curves come together.

She stretched her hand and prodded the deep blue spot on the top of her right curve; it turned a dark purple under her fingertip. "I did it," she said in disbelief, and eagerly turned to her mom. "Did you see? I actually bent them."

"You did really well," Mysia's eyes watered and she hugged her daughter tightly.

"Mom?"

"I just love you so much."

"I love you too." Niyaa hugged her back while her lower legs unbent back to the relaxed yellow curve.

Passing beneath Sidium's gate, Vernon gazed through the carriage's broken window at the shocked expressions on the onlooking faces. The bolt marks across the white carriage and the blood stains across the tributary chestwagon couldn't be hidden, nor could the fewer number of guards riding alongside. At least the city's garrison had cleared a path down the main street through the city, keeping all the traders and onlookers to one side. This only brought many more curious bystanders to watch the procession as it travelled past, causing Vernon to retreat from the windows, ashamed of the pitiful tribute and subsequent ambush.

Jofinian brought himself closer to the windows. "I doubt any of them could remember the days when the tributary procession was routinely attacked."

Vernon turned at him. "There were previous attempts?"

"Oh yes," he answered. "During the culling, desperate and vengeful people went after the tributes, sometimes attacking it before it even left Erium."

"How have I not heard of such acts before?" Vernon asked, glancing to *The Foundations* residing in his satchel.

"Do you think any emperor would put in writing that such thievery is happening in their land?" He muttered to himself, "Especially with ambitious nobles listening."

Hearing that comment reminded Vernon of the abhorrent elites, and he glanced out the broken window once more, observing the crowds had grown along the black streets. He whispered, "I understand Emperor Merchasious is reluctant, but do you think these people will face higher taxes?"

Jofinian's expression turned grim. "Afraid that's not for us to contemplate."

With the garrison clearing a path through the trading carts, messenger horses and bystanders, it took little time for the procession to enter the inside walls. The white carriage headed towards the wall tower housing Elleasious, and the tributary chestwagon left for the palace, no doubt to disappoint the emperor in person.

Jofinian knocked thrice upon the reinforced door, and they heard Elleasious's voice tell them to enter. Upon opening the door, they exchanged curious glances with a goliath of a man in full bronze platemail whose face was shielded by a grated bronze visor.

Elleasious stood behind her desk in her black chainmail and kept her irritated face focused on the armoured man. She grunted. "We will discuss this later."

Without a word, the bronze-armoured stranger marched out. Vernon saw the man's eyes through the visor staring suspiciously at him as he left the room.

Once Jofinian closed the door, he asked, "What is a beast tracker doing in Sidium?"

Vernon's eyes widened with fear.

"He is *my* concern." She sat down on her firm seat. "My men informed me of the damage done to the procession."

Jofinian said, "As we were returning through Fyoreten land, rebels wearing green armour ambushed the procession and nearly stole the tribute."

She crossed her arms. "Nearly stole the tribute?"

"A majority of the guards were drawn away in the initial attack, and a second group came upon us." Jofinian turned to Vernon. "Had it not been for the quick thinking and bravery of this young man, the assailants would have driven the chestwagon far from sight."

Elleasious turned to Vernon. "Is this true?"

"I merely maimed the chestwagon's horse before they could steer it off the road," he said. "I did none of the actual fighting."

"Nor would I expect you to." She grinned. "It appears your wit saved the tribute."

Vernon beamed with pride. "Thank you."

Elleasious turned to Jofinian, crossing her arms. "Now tell me what lies in the chest?"

The noble kept his eyes focused on her. "Only two hundred bronze."

She slowly uncrossed her arms as her expression turned bitter.

"King Asceld told us that was his sign of how committed he is to the federation, and that Myklinn Minor owes no one."

Silence gripped the small room for a long while, until Elleasious sighed. "I will inform my brother of this matter as soon as I am able. As for now, I thank you both for carrying out this task and for protecting the tribute, even as insultingly small it was." She turned her full attention to Vernon. "You can tell your friend that I would like to expand our previous arrangement to the betterment of both parties."

He nodded, realising this could be a viable avenue for obtaining the much-needed coin for the expedition. However, the thought of how he would explain to Lysia that a beast tracker was in the city removed any sense of accomplishment.

It was painfully slow riding through Sidium's main street, for the traffic of trading carts, messenger horses and bystanders was greater than usual. Jornis and Copias navigated their way through the slow gossiping crowds and arrived before the Felliet embassy. Dismounting from his saddle,

Jornis watched as a grey-robed steward marched from the black iron doors towards them.

"What business do you have here?" he asked.

Copias said, "This is Jornis Meyorter, former representative of Felliet and appointed diplomat by the Elite Dictorate." He raised his chin. "*I* am Copias Lawver, adopted son of Pryias Lawver, one of the eleven members of the Elite Dictorate, and I advise you not to keep us waiting."

Jornis glanced to the young elite with pride and returned his gaze to the stunned steward.

"I'm afraid I was not made aware of your visit."

"Nor should you have been," Copias said. "Now, there are matters that need discussing with our current Felliet representative, so I demand you let us pass."

"Of course." The steward escorted them inside.

The two of them entered the representative's study where they found a man and woman in grey silk talking beside a bright sunlit window. Jornis glanced at the unopened letters piled across the wide slate desk and turned his full attention to the couple. "I am Jornis Meyorter and this is Copias Lawver. We have much to discuss regarding Erium, Gildren and the federation."

The man grinned. "I heard much of the mission you had been tasked with and am glad to find you here, for there is much I wish to discuss with you." He walked towards the padded chair behind his unworked desk. "I am Bartun Coriate, and this is my dearest wife Vieceen Coriate."

She smiled. "It is quite a pleasure to meet the famous Meyorter, especially now that my husband has taken your old position." She took a side chair and placed it in front of Jornis, doing the same for Copias and stood beside her husband. "It would dishearten me to see you both stand after so long a journey. Especially, when traversing through the city on a day such as this."

Taking his seat alongside Copias, Jornis asked, "And what day would that be?"

"The tribute has returned from Myklinn Minor," she said. "However, it has returned with much damage done to its carriage and chestwagon."

Copias asked, "The first eclipse of the cycle should be when the tributes are sent out. Why was it sent so early?"

Jornis pondered why the target was Myklinn Minor and theorised it might have been their secretive support for Fyoreten. His arms tensed at the obvious vengeful attitude in which it was sent.

Bartun glanced at the sealed letters. "This fourth expedition will be the largest assembly of armies the federation has ever seen. Every soldier involved will need to be paid, fed and supplied throughout the journey across the vast desert, making it the most expensive venture the federation has undertaken."

Jornis remembered the colossal funding secured for the Southern Campaign. "Why hasn't the emperor taken a loan from Minitium with the security of the tributes?"

Bartun hushed his voice. "There are rumours that the emperor's sister attempted to but ultimately failed. Although we suspect they may have convinced Minitium's leaders to stop funding the priesthood."

Copias said, "Hence why they left Rubium."

The couple stared wide eyed at the news, and Vieceen asked, "Is that true? Did the priesthood truly abandon Rubium?"

"They did," Jornis answered. "The city of Rubium with its lack of nobility was an obvious expense for them. However, since the day they left, it has become a haven for moon worship."

The two of them glanced at each other and Bartun said, "Curious why we weren't made aware."

Copias shrugged. "Hardly any news travels from that city in the first place, and now that the priests have left, it truly belongs to the commoners."

Vieceen said, "An unruled city is a disaster waiting to happen."

Jornis agreed. "Without action, such an idea will spread across Erium, and before long we may see another uprising not dissimilar to the culling riots."

Bartun leaned back in his padded chair and sighed. "I will arrange a private meeting with the emperor so you two and I can swiftly deal with this matter."

"That would be wise," Jornis replied, considering the early tribute and the imminent invasion of the Rauders. "Such a meeting would also allow us to discuss other threats to the peace and unity of the federation."

Pushing the tavern door open, Vernon's gaze was drawn to a pair of guards drinking at the far end of the narrow room. Standing in the doorway, Vernon considered whether they were being watched and ventured to the bar where Orfain stood.

"Good to see you're back." Orfain raised his tankard. "Fancy a drink?"

"Sure." Vernon noticed the water in his friend's tankard and turned to Grayfern. "I'll have the same."

"That'll be two brass," Grayfern said.

Vernon played along, placing the coins on the bar and whispering to Orfain, "There are things I need to tell you."

"We can talk of your trip later. Right now we need to enjoy ourselves," he said, taking a large mouthful of his drink. "Now, I want to talk to you about this great place I found on the far side of the city…"

The two of them put on the act of a pair of friends enjoying themselves until one of the guards rose from the end table, stretching his back. "Right, think I'll call it there."

Orfain glanced at him, asking, "You got the morning shift?"

"Afraid so," the guard answered as his friend finished his drink. "Worst time of the day."

Vernon said, "Would have thought the night shift would be the worst."

The guard shook his head. "People can be a bit grouchy when they first wake, plus the morning's when all the traders start pushing to get in early." The two of them approached the exit as the first guard mumbled, "Such a pain when the market turns to a brawl."

After the door closed behind them, Grayfern explained, "Lysia is working, so if you want to discuss business, you'll have to wait till later."

"I don't care about the business right now." Vernon glanced nervously to the door and whispered, "There's a beast tracker in the city."

An unsettling tension gripped the air as the two of them stared at Vernon.

Orfain brought his fist upon the bar. "How did he find us?"

Grayfern leaned his back against the casks along the back wall. "It may not be the same tracker." He turned to Vernon, asking, "Did he see your face?"

"He only saw me as Elleasious's assistant," Vernon answered.

"So that's a yes then." Grayfern groaned. "Suppose there's nothing we can do about it right now."

Orfain frowned.

Vernon rested his elbow on the bar, staring at the water in his tankard. "He'll be looking for the commoner woman Hazel, not the noble courting Lysia."

An eerily quiet moment passed, and Orfain pushed his tankard away. "Think we'll need something stronger."

Grayfern obliged and took the tankards. "Heard the tribute was attacked."

"It was," Vernon said. "Fyoreten rebels ambushed us between Fiskior and Iorden."

Orfain said, "So they attacked you along the main road through Fyoreten. Might make traders nervous along the mountain route."

"I hadn't even considered that," Vernon said. "Perhaps they weren't even aware of the tribute passing through."

"Well, *we* weren't till it left the city gates," Orfain replied. "So, did they manage to get any of it?"

"None of the pitifully small amount was taken," Vernon let out a frustrated sigh. "King Asceld Silvex believes he doesn't need to pay more than a mere third of what he owes."

"Which is?" Orfain curiously asked.

Grayfern placed two tankards of ale down on the bar.

Taking a good gulp of the drink, Vernon answered, "Two hundred bronze."

Orfain smiled. "So the emperor is short about four hundred bronze?"

Grayfern grinned. "Think there may be an opportunity here."

Vernon nodded, "Elleasious has already asked me to expand the arrangement made with Lysia."

Orfain gave Grayfern a knowing look. "With this, all our worries could wash away."

Grayfern poured himself an ale and smiled at Vernon. "It looks like I was wrong about you."

"It's fine," Vernon replied as he remembered the glare he was given in the last chaotic moments of the Welcomerry Band.

Orfain raised his tankard. "To new opportunities."

Grayfern followed suit. "To safer lives."

Vernon stared at his ale and heartedly struck the other tankards. "To a brighter future."

All three took a hearty mouthful.

Iyna took a long, anxious breath as she stepped through Edenor's broken gate. The scorched walls along the abandoned street had changed little, yet it all felt so unfamiliar now. The atmosphere in the abandoned dirt street was eerily quiet without a hint of warmth emerging from the ash heaps filling the roofless homes.

Glancing back at her army, Iyna expected them to be disinterested, only to see they wore the same looks of disgust and horror as when they entered the ruins of Iorden. Returning her gaze ahead, Iyna felt a chill overcome her as she led her soldiers towards the cobblestone centre.

Setting foot onto the loose cobbles, Iyna's mind brought up the agonising scream amid the burning offering, and without thinking, she wandered towards where it happened. She had expected the heap of ash to still be there along with the crimson puddle, only to find a large grey smudge and a small patch of dark red staining the ground. Standing over the desolate area, her grip on her spear tightened, and she realised Barcial was standing beside her.

"Who did you lose?" he asked softly.

"Her name was Cairsie." Iyna's eyes darted to the scratches covering her spear tip. "She was the one who took care of me when my mom died."

"Sounds like she was a good person."

"She really was." Remembering the tales Cairsie would tell at the eating table, a little smile came to Iyna. "I wouldn't have ever known how to use a spear had it not been for her."

"She was a guard?" he asked.

"More than that," Iyna said. "Like my mom, she was a proper soldier, and together they joined the Southern Campaign." She turned to him with a wider smile. "And in one of the first sieges, I was born."

Barcial looked at her wide eyed. "You mean your mother was pregnant when she marched to battle?"

"No, her belly only began to grow in the first cycle of the campaign." Her smile faded. "Wish I could remember what she looked like."

"The campaign lasted six whole cycles," Barcial said. "So if your mother bedded a man in the first then you must have been around six at the most."

"I was actually five when she…" Iyna shook her head. "I know what you're trying to say, but there's no need."

"I'm trying to say that you shouldn't blame yourself for things you cannot control."

She glanced at the large grey smudge on the cobbles and turned back to him. "Guess we all just have to keep moving forward."

"Precisely," Barcial replied. "So what are your orders?"

Iyna took a deep breath and turned to her army gathered in the clearing. "Look around! This is Edenor, my home!" She stepped towards them with a firm grasp on her spear. "On the night of the harvest festival, the Beast Riders came and, without mercy, killed all who resisted! They torched every home and looted all they could carry!" She spotted Sareesa guiltily looking away and raised her voice further. "We are here to ensure this happens to no one else! We will rid the world of these monsters and defend Felliet with every breath we take!" She slammed her spear down against the ground. "So will you defend your homes with all the strength you can muster?"

Her army roared in a single voice.

Iyna shouted as loudly as she could. "Will you stand together in an unyielding wall against the monsters who would slaughter your friends and families?"

Every one of the soldiers yelled as loud and as long as they could.

Iyna pointed her spear towards the eastern horizon. "Right here we stand as the only line of defence against those desert animals. So grab your shovels and stone hammers, for we will turn Edenor into the mightiest fortress Felliet has ever seen!"

A loud thunderous cheer rose in her small army, and they all scattered to work.

Niyaa glanced up at the stars emerging in the darkening sky and readied herself to step off the bed and onto her new curvy, colourful legs for the very first time. Taking her mom's hand, she stretched her legs towards the smooth blue floor as the yellow strands straightened to orange on top and green underneath. She took a deep breath and hopped off the bed.

Landing on the floor, she wobbled as the curvy legs bent down, and she grasped her mom's hand for balance before she found the curves unbend back to the relaxed yellow position. Niyaa felt completely balanced on these forwards-jutting lower legs, and she looked to her mom, realising she was a little taller than before.

Mysia gave a proud smile. "You're doing wonderful."

Fewttyre offered to hold Niyaa's free hand. "Shall we try walking to the door?"

Niyaa nodded and raised her right leg; the other leg straightened, raising her up, and she took her first step.

It was wobbly walking up and down, but feeling the weird bounce that followed her, Niyaa felt giddily confident. She tried bending and straightening her curvy legs with every step, making the bounce even larger until she realised she was barely holding onto either hand.

Reaching the door, Fewttyre asked, "Can you touch the ceiling?"

Niyaa looked up at the flat glass roof. "But it's so high."

"I assure you, you can jump much higher than that," he said.

Mysia patted her daughter's back. "I believe in you."

"All right." Niyaa stared at the glass ceiling, and as she bent her lower legs, her heart drummed in her chest till she leapt up, easily slapping the glass with her palm. Dropping down, she took in an alarmed breath but landed harmlessly on her curves, bending them low to the blue floor.

Niyaa stared at her legs as they gradually relaxed to the yellow colour, raising her up. Fewttyre put his hand on her shoulder. "Those legs will also allow you to land from heights far greater than you think."

Staring at the beautiful legs, the disbelieving realisation of her new abilities settled in her mind. "They're incredible.'"

Mysia hugged her daughter. "You're the one who's incredible." She turned to Fewttyre. "I'm glad you were the one who did this."

"I should be the one who's thankful." He unlocked the door. "It is a privilege to provide such a unique gift for someone. To transform their bodies into something far superior." He opened the door, glancing at the empty wall plant pot, and turned to the new Beast Rider. "Now it is time to live your new life."

As the door opened, Niyaa felt the loving, gentle breeze against her body and proudly stepped her new legs outside.

Chapter twenty-five – Confrontation

Eighth eclipse, twenty-fifth day

Waking up to the sight of the distant cloth stretched over the high walls of Vernon's old house, Iyna felt overcome with dread. Not only did the ruined building feel hollow but the scorched marks filling the walls ensured she would never forget that night. The only comfort came from the cramped windowless room halfway along the short hallway as it offered an enclosed secure place to hang her hammock.

Stepping out of the old governor study, Iyna walked across the open hallway to the blackened lounge and climbed the ladder placed next to the empty fireplace.

Iyna reached the top rung and perched next to the glassless window overlooking Edenor's wall. The rubble mound surrounding the gentle moat had grown nearly half the height of the grey wall. She was glad Parick Sepp had called for volunteers from the neighbouring villages to help fortify the place. Less pleasant were the letters from the Dictorate explaining she would need to travel to Sidium to attend the great chamber meeting with the other expedition commanders. The thought of arriving at Erium's capital to display Felliet's commitment to the emperor's proposal left a foul taste in her mouth.

Someone knocked at the repaired front door, and she yelled down, "Come in." Descending the ladder, she glanced over her shoulder and saw Tarrow walking inside. "What is it?"

"One of the governors has arrived with some labourers."

"Ah, nice and early." Iyna grinned and stepped off the ladder. "How many did he or she bring?"

"He brought around twenty people," Tarrow explained and darted her gaze away. "He said most of them had lived in Edenor before."

Iyna froze. "Are you sure?"

"That's what he told me."

Remembering Niyaa's family departing off the main road with the rest of the villagers, Iyna wondered how her friend had found Pelight. She smiled with relief and mumbled to herself, "They wouldn't let her pick up a spade and dig trenches."

"What?" Tarrow asked.

"It's nothing," Iyna said and walked to her armour, shield and spear left beside the front door. "Have one of the water barrels brought to the gate. I'll welcome them inside."

After strapping on her chainmail and chestplate, Iyna marched empty-handed through the debris-cleared street, determined not to act friendly to any of the villagers. Passing the cobblestone clearing, she glimpsed the group through the stack of agron and stem spikes planted before and after the open gate. She watched them drink from the water barrel Tarrow had provided. None of Niyaa's family was there, and Iyna marched undeterred onwards.

"I am commander Iyna. Who is in charge of this group?" Iyna recognised Pern and Rioree holding a large cart filled with picks and spades, reminding her of them taking Cairsie's body away.

A slender man in a polished tunic stepped from the crowd. "I am Seveck Heef, governor of Pelight, and I must say it is an honour to be working to restore Edenor."

Iyna turned to the crowd behind the governor and raised her voice. "Edenor will not be restored!" She watched as dread and disappointment came upon her former neighbours. "With your help, we will turn this village into a fortress and stop the Beast Riders from raiding anyone else."

Pern stepped forward. "But this is our home. It shouldn't be turned into a fort."

She folded her arms. "This is no longer your home, nor mine. It now belongs to the army of Felliet."

Rioree followed suit. "You're Cairsie's girl, right? Surely you must want to see this place flourishing with life again."

"I'd rather Felliet be safe than watch this tiny village live." Iyna turned to the governor. "Seveck. Have your people start digging a trench around the rubble mound."

"With pleasure," he replied.

Iyna turned away and marched back into the gate as the governor ordered his people to start work. Once out of their sight, she sighed.

Standing before the glistening bronze doors to the emperor's mighty palace, Vernon stared up at its towering black walls in complete awe. His heart raced with the thought of setting foot inside this glorious structure and personally meeting the emperor himself.

Jofinian, adorned in his white tunic, seemed just as eager. "This will be my second time in these walls."

Vernon turned to him. "But the first time seated at the emperor's dining table, correct?"

"Indeed."

The grand doors opened, revealing an enormous black-floored chamber separated across the centre by a large railing, a protected area separating any entrants from the emperor's gargantuan black crystal throne. Above the separated area burned a bright fire in a bronze-tinted bowl, filling the room with ambient warm light that glistened off the black crystal walls. Even the black side doors on either side of the clearing were lined with bronze.

Vernon stepped towards the bronze railing, and peering over, he saw a black crystal map of the world with clear white lines depicting the mountains, rivers and coast. Lingering on the beautifully crafted sight, Vernon gradually noticed faint fracture lines riddling throughout the ornate map. No doubt the sheer age of this black crystal map had brought such marks to the surface.

The grand doors closed, sealing the outside light before Vernon realised four of the palace swordsmen had been standing along the back wall. A black-robed steward opened the left door. "Vernon Meyorter, Jofinian Tritas, if you would follow me."

Following the steward, the two of them entered the adjoining long dining room whose walls were filled with two dozen noble crests depicting the lands they oversaw. Under several glistening white chandeliers stood an elongated, granite table with two dozen bronze-lined, firm seats with a grand black chair at its head. Sitting beside the emperor's place, Elleasious wasn't wearing her armour; instead, she was adorned in a long black and violet dress.

She raised her bronze goblet towards Vernon and tapped the back of the neighbouring seat.

Walking around the table with the noble, Vernon couldn't help but stare at the dress till the steward asked, "Would either of you care for a goblet of whiskey?"

Jofinian spoke first. "That would be most kind of you."

"I would as well." Vernon took the unpadded seat next to the emperor's sister. "Thank you for this."

Elleasious shook her head. "You are here at the emperor's table as a reward of your efforts. There is no need to thank anyone for being here."

The steward returned, carrying a tray of two brass goblets, and placed them before the guests.

Taking the seat on Vernon's other side, Jofinian glanced at the many empty seats on the other side of the table. "I would never have assumed we would be seated at the emperor's table let alone have it to ourselves."

"Usually the dining table is filled with the various nobles of our lands or used by the occasional cousin and their personal acquaintances." She smirked and raised her goblet to her lips. "But today it shall only be us and Felliet's representative."

Completely taken aback, Vernon grasped his goblet of whiskey and tried not to think which egotistical fool had replaced Reethial.

Allowing Bartun Coriate to take the lead towards the emperor's palace, Jornis pondered whether Merchasious Imerial would display resentment or disinterest towards Felliet's newest representative. What would the man say of the rise of moon worship in his lands and of the possible Rauder invasion? These questions clearly weighed on Copias's mind also, for his breathing was heavy and his walking stiff as the three of them approached the oversized bronze doors.

Standing before the elaborate entrance, Bartun turned to Jornis. "Why do you suppose the emperor decided to seat us at his dining table rather than meet us in the great chamber?"

Copias said, "Perhaps because Felliet will be crucial in supplying the expedition, so Emperor Merchasious desires to ease tensions between our nations."

Jornis pondered such an optimistic thought and remembered hearing Merchasious choosing his military advisor to announce his coronation. "Unfortunately, I believe he is the kind of man to take a hard line against foreign nations. Even if there are reasons to cooperate."

Bartun said, "Then why would he agree to meet with us?"

Jornis had no clear idea.

Copias said, "It would be wiser to see for ourselves than speculate outside."

Jornis and Bartun nodded in agreement, and they patiently waited for the palace doors to open.

Walking inside, Jornis saw a map of the federation brazenly displayed before a throne of solid black crystal as though the emperor of Erium ruled the world. As his gaze lingered on the map, he noticed a multitude of fractures throughout its surface and thought it was rather fitting that such an arrogant display be riddled with tainted marks.

The guards behind them pushed the doors shut, sealing the outside light, and a steward wearing a black robe appeared before an open side door. "If you three would follow me."

Approaching the door to the dining hall, Jornis glimpsed the many crests hanging along the black walls and knew them to be as wasteful as the displays adorning the Elite Gallery.

Stepping foot in the room, Jornis's gaze moved across the many bronze-lined seats along the granite table. His eyes came to the far end, and shock froze him in place. Staring wide eyed, he saw his own son sitting between two Erium nobles. Vernon's shocked gaze met his father.

The two of them stared motionless at one another for a long, stunned moment.

Copias tapped Jornis's side, muttering, "We shouldn't delay."

Jornis prised his gaze away from his son and followed the steward to the seats opposing the three seated, with the emperor's black chair to their side. Taking the seat opposite his son, Jornis darted his eyes to the woman in the black and violet dress and to the man wearing the white tunic, wondering how his son came to know them.

The steward broke his moment of thought. "Would you care for a goblet of whiskey?"

Jornis replied without a glance, "No, thank you,"

Copias answered, "Just water for me."

"And for me also," Bartun added. He addressed the woman in the dress. "It is quite an honour to meet Elleasious Imerial."

Jornis turned to her with greater surprise.

"On the contrary, it is a rare thing to meet both current and former representative of a federation nation." She raised her goblet to her lips. "I would certainly love to hear of what you two think of each other."

Jornis realised this woman had orchestrated his son to be before him, no doubt a tactic to put him at a significant disadvantage. At this insult, he hid his anger and let Bartun speak first.

"Jornis Meyorter faced many obstacles during his duty as representative but without a doubt made the correct decisions for the good of the federation."

The man in the white tunic asked, "Did he not object to the Southern Campaign?"

Copias responded, "Considering the prolonged suffering each of the armies faced through the unending snow or in the bloody siege of Trioforn, I would say it was undeniably right to object to such a foreseeable disaster."

Vernon raised his voice. "Had the invading force been commanded by a single leader, the Southern Campaign would have been swift and decisive. Instead, we were left with eight separate armies with more interest in letting others sacrifice themselves than commit to the overall goal."

Embittered at his naïve words, Jornis corrected his son. "Had the invading force been led by a single individual, many more would have been needlessly sacrificed. No one can perfectly lead a vast array and will inevitably make mistakes in any task they undertake, which is why you need several leaders cooperating together, utilising their skills and past experience."

"But they didn't cooperate," Vernon argued. "They split up, taking different approaches and dragging the entire war out before losing miserably."

"Had they charged every soldier against the walls of Trioforn, the outcome would have caused far greater misery."

"Tell Mom that."

Jornis clenched his teeth in sheer rage. "How dare you."

A tense silence consumed the hall as they stared enraged at one another. The door behind the black chair swung open. Jornis and Vernon kept their furious eyes locked on one another as several stewards set covered dishes before the six people with a larger, seventh dish reserved for the emperor's place.

Bartun turned to Elleasious and broke the silence. "So what is on the menu?"

She smirked. "Honey roasted fanbird with a range of sautéed vegetables."

Jornis darted his eyes at her and lifted the cover off the plate, revealing it truly was the bird that flourished in the mountains around Felliet. Unamused with Elleasious, he cut into the meat.

The noble in the white tunic asked, "Are you not going to wait for the emperor?"

Taking a forkful close to his lips, Jornis glanced at the man. "I don't believe we have been introduced."

"I am Jofinian Tritas, the"—he hesitated as Jornis bit into the roasted meat—"the federation's tributary noble."

Jornis waited till he swallowed the bite. "So what does the tributary noble say about serving both former and current representative an animal found in their homeland?"

"I believe it was a simple effort to offer a food you were familiar with."

Avoiding the bait of stating the fact Felliet shares much of the same food groups with Erium, Jornis instead replied, "It was indeed a simple thought."

Elleasious leaned back in her seat. "Our esteemed chefs were simply wanting to learn how to properly cook fanbirds." She raised her goblet. "Especially since they will soon be cooking it much more often."

Bartun looked at her wide eyed. "Meaning?"

"Don't get the wrong idea," she said. "It's simply because our vast army may bring such animals with them when they return successfully from the expedition."

Copias said, "I doubt they would be spending enough time in our lands to catch any of them."

"I wouldn't be so sure." She took another sip of whiskey. "Our tribowmen are very accurate."

Jornis took another bite of the dish. "While your tribowmen may indeed be accurate, there are many factors that will prevent them from catching the fanbirds, let alone enjoying the spoils."

Elleasious grinned. "We shall see."

The tension returned as both sides of the table stared at one another until Emperor Merchasious entered wearing a shameless robe filled with black crystal. As the egotistical man took his extravagant seat, his haughty eyes turned to Jornis. "I would say you may start eating but it appears *you* already have."

Jornis carved another piece off the fanbird. "And it appears *you* have a false notion of superiority."

The emperor uncovered his fanbird dish. "Do explain."

"Seating us in the same chairs as your nobility, entering with that ridiculous robe and seating yourself at the head of the table rather than on an equal place. It is clear you see us as nothing more than your subjects."

"Except my subjects know their place in the world," the emperor replied, cutting into the fanbird as if the intended message was not clear enough.

Bartun's expression was filled with disbelief. "Felliet is on the same level as any other nation, including Erium."

"You are mistaken," Merchasious replied. "My lands are vast, my people enjoy every known luxury, and my armies are unmatched by any other. *Felliet* is nothing of the sort and is a mockery on the world stage."

Bartun pushed his plate away. "It appears I have lost my appetite."

"As have I." Copias rose from his seat.

The emperor continued eating. "Next time you wish to discuss matters relating to my empire in a position of equals or parade black crystal in the great chamber, I may finally decide to turn my armies towards your land and crush your *Elite* Dictorate."

Jornis rose from his chair and stared into Emperor Merchasious's eyes. "One who believes himself omnipotent is completely delusional." He turned to his son. "But those who follow such a man are gullible fools."

Vernon stood. "The ones who are foolish are those who believe a divided world will lead to peace and prosperity."

"True division comes from any lack of cooperation," Jornis replied "Which is exactly what you will find under one who removes any semblance of entrusting others."

"Only for those who are untrustworthy," Vernon bitterly argued.

The two of them stared at each other for a long, tense while.

Jofinian raised his goblet to the three guests. "Till the next time."

Jornis wordlessly turned away and followed Copias and Bartun out of the dining hall.

Marching outside the palace, Jornis heard the doors slam shut. His son's wrongful words engulfed his thoughts, bringing his body exhaustively still. He remembered the joyous day Vernon had been brought into the world and the following grand celebrations he'd had with his precious wife. His hands quaked as he lingered on those wonderful days.

Copias stepped closer to him. "That was your son, wasn't it?"

Jornis felt his eyes water and turned his gaze away. "I was not …
prepared."

"I doubt anyone could have been," Copias said. "Not even the great
Jornis Meyorter."

"I'm not great." Shame overwhelmed Jornis. "I couldn't even
correctly raise my son." He wiped his eyes and turned to the two of them.
"Afraid there is nothing to be done about that now."

Bartun replied, "Inform the Dictorate of this. I will do what I can in
the next chamber meeting."

Jornis gazed ahead at the great chamber's white glistening wall and
remembered the true reason he'd left Felliet. He took in a deep breath and
marched forwards with determination.

Long after he heard the grand entrance shut, Vernon sat back down on the
firm seat, and with stiff irritated muscles, he uncovered his dish. Gazing at
the thick glaze coating the fanbird, he took a deep, calming breath.

Elleasious tapped Vernon's goblet with her own. "You did well,
standing up to your father."

He grasped his whiskey and sighed. "I couldn't say why he so
stubbornly believes in the federation."

Jofinian uncovered his dish. "Perhaps he has only witnessed poor
leadership in his prime and so doesn't trust a single leader to lead."

The emperor stopped and darted his eyes to the noble. "Such as my
father?"

Jofinian stuttered. "I meant from Felliet's Elite Dictorate. It is well known they promote their peers based on wealth and stature rather than any ability."

"There's no need to deny it," Emperor Merchasious replied, setting down his cutlery. "My father made for a poor emperor whose short reign only accomplished wasting Erium's recovering armies in the Southern Campaign."

Elleasious added, "As well as allowing Gildren to keep Delflare."

"Quite right." Merchasious leaned back into his grand seat as his gaze drifted down the granite table. "I can still remember Jornis Meyorter speaking back to my father when he announced the Southern Campaign. He was a much younger man then but no less talented with his words. Just a shame he was Felliet born." He brought his attention to Vernon. "I trust my sister's word very dearly but to have someone born as a foreigner personally working for me … well, you can see why I needed to test your loyalty with my own eyes."

Vernon stared back. "This was a test?"

"Which you passed." The emperor raised his goblet to Vernon.

Pride overwhelmed Vernon. "I swear I will commit to you and your empire to the utmost of my ability."

"Then I shall hold you to your word." He glanced at his sister. "I imagine in the cycle to come we will need loyal, wise nobles to uphold the values of the empire."

She smiled. "I couldn't agree more."

"Nobles?" Vernon stared wide eyed at them.

The emperor took a sip of his whiskey and said, "I advise you design your own insignia before I change my mind."

Vernon spun his gaze to Elleasious who gave a single nod. The idea of becoming a noble, of the emperor himself gifting him with his own bronze or brass plate in the records crypt filled him with overpowering excitement. Vernon cut into the fanbird with giddy hands.

Bouncing to the top of a green hill alongside Semy and Cabi riding their snakeskin horses, Niyaa spotted distant lights on the hilly landscape between the darkening mountains. The gentle breeze brushed the sand off her hair, and she realised Edenor was alive again.

She turned to her friends. "It's my village. It's back."

Semy stared at the shadowy wall of rubble around the moat. "Seems to have been taken over by Felliet's new army."

Cabi's back limbs crunched her leafy basket. "We shouldn't have been surprised. This place makes an ideal spot for a fort."

"A fort?" Niyaa looked at her. "But they wouldn't turn Edenor into a place of fighting, would they?"

"Think about it," Cabi said, dismounting from her beast horse. "It's the closest place to the desert. Not to mention your friend knows the area well."

Disappointed, Niyaa turned back to the distant lights. "Do you think she'll be there?"

Semy jumped off his horse. "Felliet's army is supposedly pretty small, so I doubt there's a reason why she wouldn't be with them."

Ignoring the defences built around her old home, Niyaa focused her thoughts on seeing her friend again, bringing her excitement back, and without thinking, she stretched her curvy lower legs tall. She bent her curves back to their relaxed yellow colour. "I need to wear those boots, don't I?"

"Yes, you do." Cabi wiggled her basket off her back limbs and took out a pair of tall, purplish boots along with a very long brown skirt. She and Semy led the horses to the hidden side of the hill.

Pulling the long skirt over her clothes, Niyaa found it draping on the grass until she straightened her curvy lower legs, nestling them into the hidden straps inside the boots.

Standing nearly as tall her friends, Niyaa found it hard to balance. "How do you walk in these things?"

"Just take it nice and slow," Cabi explained. "Fericka made those entirely for *your* legs, so you should be able to walk comfortably."

Semy knelt beside Niyaa and tightened the boots' internal straps. "Just relax those legs of yours."

Feeling the straps tighten around the bottom bit of the straightened curve, Niyaa steadied herself. "Could you give my thanks to your family for making the straps?"

He shrugged. "You can thank them in person when we return."

"I will." Niyaa took a step forward. Unable to bend her lower leg curves was a weird feeling and with no bounce to her step, she wondered how she had ever walked before the surgery, let alone in sandals.

Cabi wiggled her back limbs around her leaf basket. "I'll stay here and tend to the horses, but I'll be keeping an eye out, just in case."

Semy nodded. "We'll come back safe."

She sighed. "Be sure you both do."

The sun was far below the horizon, allowing darkness to hide Niyaa and Semy as they crept far around Edenor's wall and rubble mound till they were standing on the dirt road with the open barred gate ahead. It was disturbing to see a bunch of spearmen chatting amongst sharp green spikes around the gate. She pushed aside her unease and marched forward.

Nearing them, Semy muttered to Niyaa, "Let me do the talking."

As the two of them passed into the light of the gate's lantern, they were met with but a few disinterestedly glances. Only when the two of them were about to pass through the open gate did someone speak up. "Where are your shovels?"

Semy stopped and forced a laugh. "Well … we actually came all the way from Vellide."

The clean-shaven spearman sighed. "Certainly did not expect any further volunteers arriving."

"Afraid we only heard about the volunteering today, so…" Semy shrugged. "Anyway, I must say, you're quite well spoken."

The man grew scornful. "I am Feeliath Coriate, second son to the head of my family." He glanced to the other soldiers and turned back to the two travellers. "You know, the other volunteers worked tirelessly the entire day and started as soon as they arrived."

"And you can be sure we'll work just as hard in the morning," Semy replied.

Feeliath shook his head. "I want to see you working now."

Semy looked bewildered. "Can we at least get some food?"

The man crossed his arms.

"Can my sister at least get some rest?" Semy asked, and Niyaa stepped forward. "The journey's been terribly long, and it would pain me to see her fingers worked numb before a proper rest."

"Fine." Feeliath pointed his spear down the familiar street. "Your sister can find some spare hammocks in the chapel. If not, there may be some in the houses near the commander's house."

Niyaa excitedly blurted out, "The commander's house?"

"It's the tall one at the far end," he explained, muttering, "Should be me in there."

She realised Iyna was staying in Vernon's house and smiled as she imagined her sleeping in his soft bed.

Semy patted her shoulder. "I'll meet you at the chapel, sis."

Niyaa smiled at him and replied, "All right, brother."

Stepping into the familiar dirt street, Niyaa looked around at her neighbour's walls and saw the burn marks had faded to grey while the ash that once covered the ground had been blown away. Despite the plain cloth stretched over the roofless walls, she felt comforted that her home had changed little since the fire. Knowing it wouldn't be long till people started living here again, she held her head up and wandered towards the cobblestones.

Spotting Pern and Rioree drinking water next to a portable furnace in the centre, Niyaa sprang into a gap between some homes. She had to hide from their sight, so she crept through the familiar shadowy gaps between the homes till she was walking alongside the grey wall. Thankfully, the spearmen atop them were all staring at the pitch-dark landscape and not the village behind them. She breathed in relief and tried not to break into an excited sprint as she followed the wall around Edenor.

She made it to Vernon's house, and just like the other homes, its walls were grey with stretched cloth covering its roof. Though it was disappointing to see the upper floor windows no longer there, at least the cracked thick windows of the ground floor lounge were still in place. Through those completely clouded windows, she noticed the faint flicker of a candle within, and Niyaa walked forward only to notice a woman soldier waiting outside the black door holding a spear in her shaking hand.

After a long moment wondering when this soldier woman would enter, Niyaa finally got the courage to confront her.

The female soldier noticed her. "Can I help you?"

Niyaa darted her eyes to the repaired black door. "I need to speak with Iyna."

"What about?" The woman stared suspiciously at the girl.

"I'm … I'm a friend of hers." Speaking those words, Niyaa relaxed.

"Oh." The woman looked away. "I heard some of the labourers were people who used to live here." She spun her gaze back, quietening her voice. "What was she like? Before the raid I mean."

Taken aback, Niyaa hesitated and remembered playing with Iyna and Vernon. "She was always so adventurous and strong." She smiled. "She'd always want to duel or race or something. She said she hated whenever Vernon tried to get her to read, but really, I think she liked hanging out with him and me."

"I can see that." The woman smiled and took a long deep breath. She whispered, "I think I'm ready."

Watching the woman place her free hand on the door's latch, Niyaa asked, "Could you tell her I'm here."

"Sure, what's your name?"

"Niyaa. And yours?"

"Sareesa." The woman pushed the mended black door and stepped inside.

Hearing the door close behind someone, Iyna turned away from the top window and climbed down from the ladder. "One moment."

Stepping off the last rung, she saw Sareesa resting her spear on the wall opposite her own and stiffly marched down the hallway.

"Hey," Iyna said. "What brings you here?"

"I…" Sareesa took a deep breath and stepped into the lounge. "I came here to apologise."

"What for?" Iyna asked, noticing Sareesa was avoiding her eyes.

"Ever since that first battle, I…" She stopped herself. "I've been avoiding you."

Iyna shrugged with a reassuring smile. "That's nothing to be upset about."

"You don't understand." Sareesa shook her head. "Ever since that first battle, I … I've seen you as a … as a monster."

Iyna stared at her. "What do you mean?"

"I've tried to hide it, but my hands have been shaking every day." Her eyes watered. "And each night I wake covered in tears and sweat, I … I can't stop thinking about that day."

Iyna remembered the Fyoreten rider she and Sareesa had killed on those blue lilies and lowered her head. "He would've killed us."

"I know that." Sareesa leaned against a wall, eyes looking down. "But seeing him lying there…" She turned to Iyna. "How did you manage to block the sight from your mind? How did you manage to keep moving forward?"

"I guess it was…" Realising the toughness of the question, Iyna perched on the ladder, staring distantly at nothing in particular. "I guess it was just my body moving by itself." A wave of guilt came over her. "I only really thought about what we'd done at Fiskior and Iorden." She shook her head. "Honestly, we should never've fought Fyoreten to begin with."

"That's why you let that group go." Sareesa's voice grew hopeful. "I had thought you did it so they could attack Erium."

Iyna sighed. "I simply couldn't bear seeing more of them pointlessly die, especially when *real* monsters are out there."

Sareesa stepped away from the wall. "I'm sorry I've been avoiding you."

"Don't fret about it." Iyna shrugged, letting herself lean back against the ladder rungs as she wondered what those Fyoreten soldiers must be doing now.

"Thanks for being honest." Sareesa went to the door and said, "Also someone called Niyaa came to see you."

"Niyaa?" Iyna shot up in surprise.

Sareesa nearly stumbled backwards. "Yeah, she's waiting outside."

Iyna's eyes widened. "Had no idea she came here." Remembering the times she'd tried to teach that girl how to fight, Iyna smiled with delight. "All right, send her in."

Sareesa opened the black door and Niyaa entered.

Iyna watched as her friend came bounding towards the lounge, nearly tripping on her long skirt. Niyaa embraced the commander in a sudden hug. "I'm so happy to see you again."

"I am too." Iyna placed her arms around her friend, hugging her back. "Can't believe how tall you've gotten. How've you been?"

"I'm good. Where I am now is an incredible place filled with friendly people."

"That's great," Iyna said as she thought about thanking Governor Seveck for taking care of the Edenor people. "Sorry I didn't greet you straightaway. Honestly, I didn't even spot you with the main group."

Niyaa giggled. "I … didn't travel with them."

"Then who?" Iyna released her grip, keeping her smile. "Are your parents here?"

Niyaa stepped back with an anxious look. "I'm here by myself."

Iyna stared at her. "You came without them?"

"Yes." Niyaa hesitated and took a long, deep breath. "Actually there's something I need to ask you."

"You can ask me anything." Iyna readied herself to disappoint her friend, knowing she'd be asked to restore Edenor.

Niyaa raised her voice. "I want you to stop this purge."

"Purge?"

"I meant expedition, I need you to stop this expedition," Niyaa pleaded.

Iyna stared at her for a long while before relaxing. "If you're worried about me, I'll be fine. There will be tens of thou—"

"That's not what I mean!" Niyaa shouted, grabbing Iyna's hand. "You shouldn't fight them. They're good people."

"What?" Iyna looked bewildered and slowly pulled her hand away. "You're not talking about the Beast Riders, are you?"

Niyaa nodded.

All excitement and joy vanished as Iyna stared wide eyed at Niyaa. "You're serious."

"They only look different to us, but believe me when I say they're good people."

"What is wrong with you?" Iyna demanded. "You know what they did when they came here!"

"Those ones acted out of anger." She grasped Iyna's hand. "But believe me when I say they mean no harm."

"No harm!" Iyna yanked her arm away. "They murdered the priest, the guards and Cairsie! They. Are. Monsters."

"We aren't!" Niyaa yelled.

Iyna stepped back unable to speak.

Niyaa gulped. "I'll prove it." She knelt down and untied her boots below her skirt.

Iyna unsettlingly asked, "What're you…" Her eyes widened in disbelief as unnatural streaks of deep blue and dark orange appeared where her friend's shins should be. Niyaa stepped out of the boots, and her feetless legs bent forward below the knees. Iyna staggered back.

Niyaa let her huge skirt fall to the ground, showing her curved lower legs bend and turn a yellow colour. "Having beast limbs doesn't change a person. They're just like anyone else."

Stunned, Iyna kept staring at those horrific legs as she stuttered, "What … what did they do to you?"

"They didn't do anything." Niyaa stepped closer with those abnormal limbs and reached to retake Iyna's hand. "*I* asked for this."

Iyna yanked her hand away and fearfully stepped away as the memories of the Beast Riders smiling at the fleeing villagers engulfed her thoughts. Without thinking, she had staggered towards the hallway, and her distraught body leaned itself against the wall with the lounge to her back.

Niyaa placed her hand on Iyna's shoulder. "I'm not your enemy."

Breathing heavily, Iyna was unsure of what to do and glanced to the black door. She focused on the repaired dent running through Felliet's emblem. She lingered on the sight of it for a long while as she thought about the calamity the Beast Riders had brought upon this village. Iyna straightened herself up and slowly turned to her mother's spear resting beside the door. "I don't know what they said or did to you, but I promise I will fix this."

As Iyna marched forward, Niyaa's grip on her shoulder slipped. "What are you going to do?"

Iyna tightly grasped her mother's spear and turned back to her old friend. "I will turn you back to normal."

"I don't want to be normal." Niyaa backed into the lounge. "This was my choice. I don't want it to be any other way."

Iyna tightened her grip around her mother's spear and marched into the lounge. Niyaa retreated backwards to the centre of the room, and Iyna pointed the spearpoint at her. "I don't want to make this hurt any more than it needs to."

Terror filled Niyaa's face and she desperately leapt to the side only for Iyna to swing the blunt spear handle, bringing her body to the ground. Iyna pounced, pinning Niyaa down. "I will not let them get their hands on you anymore."

"Iyna, please!" Niyaa struggled.

Holding her down, Iyna placed her legs atop her friend's young arms and turned toward the beastly yellow strands, raising her spear. Niyaa frantically kicked her lower legs against the ground, pushing them both back. Iyna was forced to lean in, bringing her face as close as possible to the nightmarish right lower leg.

She slid her right hand down the spear handle, aiming for the start of the strands and whispered, "I will fix you." Iyna brought her spear down, just as the leg bent, causing the spear tip to stab in the midst of the limb.

The severed strand snapped back, slicing across Iyna's face and forcing her to recoil off her body as Niyaa screamed in agony. She tearfully raised her head just as the unhandled spear leaned away, prising up another strand in the wound, painfully stretching it purple.

Niyaa reached her arm out and grabbed the spear, pulling it out of the seeping wound and hurling it to the far side of the room. She turned to Iyna, covering half her bleeding face as she rose to her feet. Seeing the rage in Iyna's eyes, Niyaa forced her body to stand, only for her cut leg to give way, causing her body to kneel.

As Iyna tried pouncing on her again, Niyaa's good leg sprang her away towards the ladder. Only thinking of escape, she grasped the rungs and climbed. Placing her wounded leg on a rung, Niyaa felt sharp pain coursing through the strands, and Iyna grabbed her other curvy leg. Without thinking, Niyaa kicked as hard as she could, striking Iyna in the head and forcing her onto the ground.

Not daring to look back, Niyaa pulled herself up each rung of the ladder till she finally made it to the glassless window at the top. She stared down at the grey wall below and glanced back at Iyna dazedly staring back from the floor. Niyaa seethed at her once friend, climbed onto the window's edge and stepped off.

Landing on the curves, she collapsed on the bleeding leg and cried out in pain. Glimpsing a soldier running along the wall towards her, she got up and limped her way to the wall's edge, falling into the shallow moat.

Hitting the mud and water, Niyaa collapsed under her bad leg, and the dirty water washed into her mouth. Gagging at the bitter taste, she clambered over the little mud bank and climbed up the rubble mound.

Reaching the top, she looked back and saw a bunch of soldiers gathering along the wall as their shouts and alarms blurred together. A hand grasped her arm, and she turned around in terror only to see Semy pulling her over the other side of the mound.

"Damn them!" he yelled as he noticed the blood staining the yellow strands. He knelt with his back to her, holding his arms to her. "Get on my back."

Niyaa put her arms around his neck and pulled her legs into his arms, and he ran away from the village, towards the hill. Hearing alarmed shouts grow distant, Niyaa felt tears trickling down her cheeks.

Semy jolted her upright. "Come on. We're nearly there."

She held on tighter and looked at the dark hill ahead.

Sitting up on the floor, Iyna put her hand to her forehead and felt the throbbing lump. Her cheeks were wet. She brushed her hand across her right cheek and found it covered in blood. She sighed at the thought of heated metal pressing against it and noticed her vision go blurry before she realised she was crying.

Grasping the ladder, she wearily pulled herself to her feet only to find the tears wouldn't stop. She rubbed her eyes and perched on the bottom rung as her blurred gaze drifted to the purplish boots. She wondered why Niyaa would side with those monsters.

Feeliath burst through the door, shouting down the hallway, "What's going on? Who was…" He stopped at the lounge entrance as he stared wide eyed at the gash across Iyna's face. "An assassin?"

She shook her head. "That was someone I knew," Iyna glanced up at the open window. "But now she's one of the enemy."

"Someone you know?"

"I guess not anymore." Iyna forced her body to stand. "Take a bunch of your men and chase after them." She marched to pick up her bloodied spear from the ground. "From now on, we will check everyone, no matter who or what group they travel in." She saw him still standing there and stomped her spear down. "Go after her, now!"

Watching him hurriedly leave, Iyna felt the crushing loneliness of the room and tightened her grip on her spear. She left the dreary building.

Chapter twenty-six – Comet Cycle

Eighth eclipse, thirty-second day

Trekking back through the desert, Niyaa kept her gaze low. While her leg wound had scabbed over, the pain of stretching it forced her into Semy's saddle the whole way, and worse yet, she had a constant reminder of that awful night.

As the gate of Lorish came into sight, she realised she would have to explain what had happened to her mom and the pioneers. Dreading such a talk, Niyaa sighed and leaned her body on Semy.

He patted her head. "You'll be resting in a nice soft bed really soon."

Not wanting to reply, Niyaa stared ahead and saw a bunch of beast people digging into the sand around the pink jagged wall. "What're they doing?"

Semy tightened his grip around the red scaly reins. "Looks like they're building extra defences."

Niyaa sat up straight and asked, "Did they know my plan wasn't going to work?"

Cabi answered, "It's just as a precaution. Besides, it gives everyone peace of mind."

Niyaa's body slumped against Semy once more as her failure weighed heavier. "There's no stopping the purge, is there?"

Cabi and Semy glanced at one another, unable to reply.

Nearly all the beast people were watching them from the new trench and atop the rough wall. Under the scaly curtain gate, a small crowd of curious and excited beast people had gathered.

Semy's and Cabi's snakeskin horses stopped before the gate, their dejected faces ending the curiosity and hopefulness of the crowd. Tovern came hobbling on his cane out of the disappointed crowd.

"Our mission has failed." Cabi raised her voice. "Upon seeing Niyaa's legs, the Felliet commander tried to kill her."

Niyaa looked around as everyone stared at the bloodied scab on her right curvy leg. The pioneer stiffly hobbled towards her horse.

Cabi continued, "However, I can at least say Felliet's army is small and ill equipped, so as long as we work together, they will easily fall before our walls."

The elderly pioneer seemed not to listen and stood beside Niyaa, glaring at the broken strand and placing his taloned palm lightly on the scab. Feeling his open palm on the scabby wound, Niyaa was overcome with failure and loss.

The pioneer turned to her face. "Why do you cry?"

"Because I"—she tried wiping the tears away—"because I failed."

"Look at me," he demanded.

Niyaa slowly looked into his bitter eyes.

He brought his taloned hands back to his cane. "Did you confront this Iyna person?"

Niyaa's voice croaked. "Yes."

"And did you tell her that we are monstrous creatures?"

She stared at him in disbelief. "No, of course not."

"Did you tell your friend to fight well in this next *expedition*?"

She felt her arms tense as her voice grew. "I told her to stop it from happening."

"Did you celebrate with your friend after—"

"I told her we are just like everyone else!" Niyaa shouted back before understanding the words that left her lips. She glanced at her yellow lower legs and realised she was truly a beast person, no longer part of Felliet or its people, and she stopped crying. "There is no difference between those with beast limbs and those without." She lowered her head. "I'm sorry I couldn't convince her of that."

"Hold your head high, Niyaa," Tovern said. "You should be proud to have taken such a risk to defend your kin."

Niyaa turned to him as the word kin swirled in her thoughts and noticed the beast crowd was looking at her with pride and gratitude. It became clear she and her mom were a part of this huge family, and all her unease faded.

The elderly man turned to Cabi. "Take fresh horses and go straight to Reeffewd. The other pioneers will be waiting." He hobbled back inside the walls, demanding, "And have someone properly tend to that leg of hers."

Niyaa kept staring at the looks of gratitude on the gathered faces. Semy moved his horse forward. "You see. No one here will judge you, for they know you did your utmost to help everyone."

A wide hopeful smile crossed her face.

The grey carriage seats felt too comfy and the weather too pleasant for such a dreaded, unavoidable journey to Sidium. Throughout the long ride on Erium's smooth road, Iyna kept her gaze lowered to the carriage floor, both avoiding the hilly landscape from the windows and the eyes of an elite couple sitting opposite. Occasionally, however, she thought about Barcial steering the carriage and tracked her fingertips across her long facial scar before shaking the traitorous memory from her thoughts. She needed to keep her thoughts only on the great chamber meeting.

The representative's wife got closer to her window, asking, "Are those Myklinn tents?"

Bartun leaned closer. "They are indeed."

Iyna raised her head and looked out the window. To her dismay, she saw vast fields of tents in enormous clusters of black, silver, blue, brown, iron grey and gold, behind which stood the grim black walls of Sidium towering far along the river.

Bartun glanced to her. "Seems our commander has finally awoken."

Iyna prised herself away from the fearful sight and asked, "Only the commanders need to go to the great chamber, so why have the expeditionary armies gathered here and not marched straight to Edenor?"

The representative leaned back in his seat. "Officially, Emperor Merchasious desired to have all the armies gather in one well-supplied location before marching as a single force." He narrowed his eyes. "Though he let our army remain in Felliet."

Vieceen turned to Iyna. "In this expedition we desperately need your army to distinguish itself."

Iyna sat up straight. "My soldiers are experienced and skilled. They will fight well."

Bartun shook his head. "We said your force needs to distinguish itself from all the other armies. That means you must truly leave an exceptional impression for every eyewitness out there and not just become another band of unruly fighters." He tensed his hands. "The future of Felliet will depend on it."

Iyna remembered the scornful faces of the Fiskior people and leaned back into the carriage seat. "Will Erium try to conquer us?"

He paused. "The real reason the emperor chose to gather the armies here was to display Erium's superior strength."

Vieceen pointed to the vast swathes of black tents lined before the approaching gate. "These men were given black iron chainmail, polished shields and good swords. They will be followed by numerous supply carts fully prepped with all the necessities they could ever need." She turned back to Iyna. "Essentially, this entire venture is a statement to demonstrate the Erium Empire is dominant over the rest of the federation."

Iyna grunted. "So he thinks Felliet's not even worth considering then."

Bartun gave a grim nod. "At a dinner invitation in his palace, he told me that directly."

She clenched her teeth, and the carriage crossed the river towards the black gatehouse.

He leaned forward, whispering, "We believe that if you distinguish Felliet as having a strong, albeit small fighting force, we can use that to form an alliance with Gildren, and possibly Myklinn Minor."

"An alliance?" Iyna felt a spur of hope. "Is it possible?"

Bartun grinned. "Thanks to a pair of elites working these past eclipses, it just might be."

Iyna relaxed. "How do you suppose I distinguish Felliet from the others?"

"Afraid that will be on your skills and cunning," Bartun answered.

Vieceen added, "Though it will be difficult with an oath."

"Oath?" Iyna asked.

"Officially, the reason the commanders are gathering here is to launch the expedition as one force. However, we believe it is more than likely Emperor Merchasious will have each of the commanders swear an oath that they only serve the interests of the federation."

Iyna crossed her arms. "You mean the interests of Erium."

Vieceen nodded.

Glancing to the passing layout of black homes and laden trading carts, Iyna smirked. "I think I have an idea."

Stepping inside the Gallery, Jornis found it abundant with stern guards, because for once, the granite stand seated all eleven members of the Elite Dictorate. As the overly extravagant doors shut behind him, Jornis exchanged mutually determined glances with Copias, and they marched forward, passing the opulent wall displays in their stride.

Nearing the stand with the midday day sun shining through the curved glass roof, Jornis observed the disgruntled expressions on all but one of the Dictorate. Only Pryias Lawver, sitting beneath her similarly lavish bronze crest, held an expression of neutrality towards the pair.

She spoke first. "Copias, if you would start by explaining your mission."

Before he could answer, Ovallian smirked at her. "Refer to him by his full name if you please."

Her lip curled. "Very well. Copias Lawver, if you would start by explaining your mission."

"I shall." Copias stepped forward, focusing only on Eythiam Zenth in the centre of the panel. "In the midst of the fourth eclipse of this cycle, the third expeditionary force comprising a thousand Erium spearmen returned from the desert. With only half of them returning and the subsequent raid on a border village, it became clear Felliet faces a strong, hostile threat from its eastern border." He took a deep breath. "Combining this with Erium's enormous militaristic and economic power, it was abundantly clear our nation is in a precarious situation. It was thus agreed Felliet would require allies."

Eythiam asked, "So why start with Gildren?"

Jornis stepped forward. "The initial reasoning was because we possess resources one of their siloins would be unable to obtain from their planned expansion. However, the further we investigated, the further it became obvious they too are in a perilous situation and would greatly benefit from a trustworthy ally."

Pryias narrowed her eyes. "You refer to the aggressive actions of Artor and Myklinn, correct?"

Jornis nodded. "With the additional threat of the Rauders along their coastline, it would be accurate to say Gildren is surrounded by enemies. The siloins of Gildren understand an alliance with Felliet is in their interest."

"That is good to hear," Eythiam replied. "Now, you two, as well as our newest representative, personally met with the emperor. Could you explain why?"

"It was intended to discuss Felliet's concerns with the tributary demand sent to Myklinn Minor, the decline of the priesthood in Rubium and the growing Rauder threat."

"But that was not what happened," Eythiam replied. "From what I heard from Bartun Coriate, the dinner took a very different course. Could either of you elaborate?"

Jornis hesitated, letting a brief tense silence fill the Gallery before Copias stepped forward. "It was orchestrated from the beginning as a way to demonstrate Erium's superiority over Felliet and the rest of the federation. They even had the audacity to serve fanbirds as the main dish." He lowered his gaze and tensed his arms. "Emperor Merchasious told us directly our country is a mockery on the world stage."

"It is deeply concerning to hear Bartun's explanation was correct." Eythiam crossed his arms and stared at Jornis. "However, you neglected to mention the person you focused your attention on, apparently even heatedly arguing with him."

Copias turned to Jornis who simply sighed. "That person, much like their other two guests, was brought in specifically to agitate us."

Ovallian leaned back. "Seems like it worked."

Pryias asked, "Do you know that young man personally?"

"I do not." Jornis answered the anticipated question and remembered the past lectures and arguments he'd had with his son. His mind conjured the joyous, playful laughter Vernon often shared with his mother, at which Jornis forced himself to hide his shame. "He is a stranger to me. I believe that young man was used by the emperor's sister solely to aggressively argue in favour of the emperor so if relations between our nations soured, he could be used as a scapegoat."

Copias said, "Looking at the past will not help matters. We need now to concentrate on what we can do in the present."

Eythiam turned to him. "So what do you propose?"

Copias raised his voice. "When Gildren's army passes through here, its commander will agree to an alliance with us. We will need to wait for the right date to announce it to the entire federation." He glanced to Pryias. "That should provide enough time for Jornis and I to travel to Myklinn Minor and work to establish a second alliance or at the very least, a mutual defence pact."

Jornis glanced at Copias, knowing they had never spoken of travelling together.

Eythiam stroked his chin. "It would appear we have very few options available to us. More disconcerting is the idea of the emperor's sister leading Erium's army through our lands." He darted his eyes to the other Dictorate members. "Does anyone have any other suggestions?"

Seeing their defeated faces give not a single response, Jornis felt vengefully delighted.

With each black step climbed, Iyna's bitterness grew as she neared the white walls of the great chamber, for she saw the towering black palace behind it. The sheer size of the emperor's house imposing over the entire city was disgusting, so she avoided looking at any of it. She noticed Bartun was strangely calm and composed as he walked beside her up the black steps. All the other commanders and representatives following them also were somehow relaxed.

Only when she reached the end of the black stairs with the huge open doors of the great chamber ahead of her, did Iyna realise she must appear calm and collected if she was going to speak for Felliet. She took a deep breath, easing much of her hatred and loathing before marching inside with determination.

Following a man in yellow silk alongside a commander in gilded chainmail beneath the observers stand, Iyna glanced at Bartun, but her eyes were drawn disturbingly ahead. At the far side of the pearl floor sat the emperor, arrogantly wearing a huge robe of black crystal and sitting on a throne of solid bronze. Perhaps the most arrogant thing were the words *where integrity prospers* engraved at the top of the bronze throne, for it clearly meant the betterment of the federation depended on the emperor himself. Looking away from the abhorrent sight, Iyna spotted a woman in full black chainmail standing next to a sheathed sword in the centre of the chamber and knew she would be Erium's commander. Dread came upon her as she pictured the emperor's sister trying to give her commands.

Bartun whispered to Iyna, "Do us proud."

He followed the man in yellow silk to their seats as she followed the gilded armoured commander to line up on either side of the woman in black.

With the last of the representatives taking their seats, Iyna heard the doors slam shut and noticed, behind the emperor's robe-covered legs, the four legs of the Federal Throne and the four threads tied around them. She seethed with rage at the disgusting simple design showcasing the emperor's superiority over the world's nations. She forced herself to take another deep breath while carefully hiding her fists behind her back.

Emperor Merchasious raised his voice. "For many long comet cycles since the first Beast Rider was made, we have sought to rid the world of this threat to our humanity. While my grandfather drove them from the federation, even giving his life during the first expedition, the Beast Riders stubbornly endured. Thus, in this final day of the cycle, I declare the beginning of a final expedition surpassing all that came before, to finally bring an end to the culling and rid the world of these creatures." His words echoed across the chamber, and his gaze settled on the woman in black armour. "Elleasious Imerial, step forward."

The emperor's sister stepped forward, head held high.

"Will you, Elleasious Imerial, guide this force across the vast desert and meet the Beast Riders in victorious battle?"

She raised her voice. "I will."

"Will you uphold your duty to the federation and finally rid this threat from the world?"

"I will."

"Then I declare you to be the head of the expedition. You shall have the decision to use your army to crush these monstrous animals as you see fit." Emperor Merchasious turned to the other commanders. "With the enormous scale of this venture, I must ask each commander here to make a pledge. They will heed the command of Elleasious Imerial, fully support the overall goal and seek no individual glory." He paused. "Now, who among you will be first to pledge themselves to this cause and to Elleasious Imerial's direction."

Iyna glanced down the line to see only the Therran at the far end unhesitatingly taking a step forward. The creature bent its naked, wheat-skinned legs and placed its palm on the pearl floor. "In vengeance for setting foot on the everlasting soil, the Therra swear to incinerate every Beast Rider, till they are naught but ash flowing with the wind. The Therra will follow the Imerial Elleasious."

The emperor gave a single nod. "Very good. Now who shall be the next—"

Iyna marched forward till she was in line with the woman in black. "I swear my army will fight for Felliet but will follow this woman's orders only if they don't endanger my soldiers."

The emperor scowled at her, and Iyna heard a familiar voice yell from the stand above, "How dare you try and divide this unifying cause!"

Iyna turned her head, only for all her anger to vanish as she saw Vernon standing up in the front row of the observers stand staring down at her.

Vernon's maddening eyes faded to utter shock as his dearest friend was revealed, and he watched the anger in her expression return. A mere moment later she turned her bitter gaze ahead, leaving Vernon slumping back onto his seat.

The man in gilded chainmail advanced, standing alongside Iyna. "The siloins of Gildren, in respect for our righteous soldiers and their families left behind, shall strive to see them safely return after this expedition. In light of this, I shall also object to any orders that will neglect the safety of my army."

The silver-armoured commander hastily stepped forward, announcing, "Erium holds no authority over us. My army will follow *her* command if I will it."

The atmosphere in the great chamber grew tense as the emperor turned his gaze to the last three commanders. "And what of you?"

The Riverveins commander in light blue, cloth padded armour walked forward, bowing his head. "Our soldiers are famed for their swift response both in supply and reinforcements. It would be a mistake to place us at the forefront of any battle, and as such we see no reason not to obey the command of your sister."

"Good." Emperor Merchasious turned to the commanders of Myklinn Greater and Artor, who glanced at one another before simultaneously taking a step forward.

The man with fur-covered chainmail spoke first. "Myklinn fights to win. We will follow your sister's orders."

The Artornese woman placed her hand on her chest. "The macemen of Artor will prove themselves fully committed to the safety of the federation. We also will follow Elleasious's orders."

Vernon breathed a small sigh of relief.

The emperor paused for a brief, reflective moment as he looked at the eight commanders. "To those who believe my sister is the type of leader to prioritise glory or grudges over duty, you are grievously mistaken." He glared at Iyna. "In this expedition you shall find no decision of hers to be foolhardy and will be wise to follow all commands given."

Vernon leaned forward as he stared at his friend and noticed her hands were tight fists behind her back.

The emperor relaxed his irritated expression and rose from the Federal Throne, announcing, "I shall thus bid you all a glorious hunt." The doors opened below. "Go now and ready your armies to depart at the first light of the new cycle."

Elleasious was the first to turn away and march for the doors, and the other commanders followed. Watching Iyna disappear below the stand, Vernon rose from his seat and hurriedly walked out of the observers stand as the emperor went onto the next agenda.

Passing the guards, Vernon stepped outside and saw the commanders already descending the black stairs, so he rushed down the white observatory steps.

At the top of the black staircase, he shouted down to her, "Iyna!"

She halted halfway down without looking back while the other commanders glanced disinterestedly at him and followed Elleasious away.

Vernon raced down the stairs and stopped a couple of steps above her. "Iyna?"

She stood motionless in her armour.

He stared at his friend and asked, "Why are you leading Felliet's army?"

She breathed deeply and turned to him. "Have you sided with Erium?"

Feeling attacked, Vernon became spiteful. "You *honestly* believe in Felliet?"

"Because we're weak and small?" Iyna asked.

"Because the elites are corrupt," he said. "You haven't experienced what they are like or what they have done."

"I've *experienced* plenty of people with names." She dismissively turned to the muster's square where a man in the same thin green chestplate over loose chainmail was waiting, "Some of them are in my army now and aren't corrupt at all."

Vernon stared at her in disbelief. "They are just the ones who are expendable. The higher elites care only for themselves."

"Says the one siding with the emperor."

"That's different." He took a step towards her. "He wants to bring the world together in an enduring age of peace and prosperity."

"Peace and prosperity?" Iyna asked. "Have you been to Fyoreten? Have you seen the people of Fiskior? They live in hatred and fear of Erium."

"You're wrong!" Vernon shouted. "I've been to Iorden *and* Fiskior. I have personally witnessed their homes rebuilt and livelihoods restored. Each of their families has already been given carts filled with clothing, food and furniture, far more than what they would have had before. Every Fyoreten citizen will soon see all the benefits the rest of the empire hold and without even facing taxes for many cycles to come. Their lives and the lives of their children will greatly improve now."

She shook her head. "They won't forgive Erium and its army for what they've done to them, nor will they give up on their fight to liberate their home." She turned away. "See ya, Vernon."

Watching his old friend march down the black steps, Vernon was left wondering how she could possibly think life under the Elite Dictorate would be better for the people of Felliet.

Bringing his ink feather to the parchment, Jornis suppressed his emotions as he guided his hand to write.

Dear friend,

I have returned safely from my journey, but at present I cannot meet with you for I am accompanied by someone uninvolved. Rest assured, however, all members of the Dictorate suspect nothing, and I can confirm the plan is proceeding smoothly.

I, however, need to reiterate that you must wait for my return before you act, for we will need the full support of our southern and western allies. Furthermore, the expeditionary force must be deep within the desert before we begin, as having nonaligned armies in Felliet territory will greatly complicate the situation. For now, focus on mustering support in all areas outside of Ellity.

S

Lining the edges of the page with egg whites, Jornis set a thick, irrelevant parchment atop the letter and smoothed them together, obscuring the vital words. After folding it, he used his precious stamper to seal it. Upon using his wife's seal, he stared longingly at the drying grey wax.

He took out a tiny iron pin from a concealed pocket and stared at its depiction of a bridge over a river of snakes. Jornis grinned and cheerfully imagined the Gallery's crests being torn down and burnt.

As Reeffewd's scaly gate rolled up, Niyaa saw her mom and Fewttyre waiting for them with a bunch of beast people, and the two of them ran to meet them. Niyaa climbed down from Semy's saddle and stumbled on her bandaged leg. Clinging to the saddle for support, she saw her mom's face fill with worry, so Niyaa tried to act calm.

Mysia wrapped her arms around her daughter. "What happened?"

Niyaa hugged her back and said, "Iyna's not my friend anymore."

"She did this to you?" Mysia broke from the hug and looked at the bandaged wound. "I'll make her pay dearly when I see her."

Niyaa turned away. "I don't know why she did it."

Semy climbed down from his saddle and spoke to Mysia. "Well if it helps, thanks to her, we now—"

"I don't want to hear it!" she shouted back. "What would've happened if she didn't return?"

"We would've never allowed that to happen," he argued.

Mysia furiously stepped towards him. "But you allowed this to happen."

"Mom, it's all right." Niyaa grabbed her hand. "I'm glad I did it."

"But your leg?" Mysia said in disbelief.

Niyaa smiled. "I don't mind if it meant I did my best."

"But"—Mysia stared wide eyed at her daughter—"you could've been killed."

Niyaa turned to the beast people gathered under the rolled-up gate and said, "I am really happy we came here; these people have done so much for us." She turned back to her mom. "I realised we both truly belong here now. So I promise I will do whatever it takes to make sure none of us get hurt again."

"But I don't want *you* getting hurt."

Niyaa darted her eyes away, unable to say anything that wouldn't disappoint her mom.

Mysia stared at her daughter and turned to Fewttyre as he muttered something to Cabi. "Can you see to her at least?"

He turned away from Cabi and walked to Niyaa and her mom. "From what Cabi's described, I believe one or more of the strands have snapped. It will take a while, but I assure you they will heal."

"Good." Mysia sighed.

Fewttyre bent his knees, presenting his back for Niyaa. "Let's get you to my lab."

As the sun lowered beneath the glistening black walls of Sidium, Vernon opened the tavern door and saw the long room filled with cheerful soldiers in all kinds of armour and colours. Pushing his way to the bar, he found Grayfern rushing to fill several tankards at once. When he laid eyes on Vernon, he pointed to the distant corner. "Your friends are over there."

"Thank you," Vernon replied over the unending commotion and laboriously navigated his way through the packed crowd of merry soldiers. He found Orfain and Lysia standing in the corner with full tankards in their hands.

She patted Vernon's back. "Isn't today a great day?"

He looked at her in confusion. "A great day?"

"Yeah," Lysia said. "The final expedition's starting, and soon we'll live in a world free of those monsters."

He stared at her without knowing what to say and noticed Orfain uncomfortably sipping his ale.

Lysia darted her gaze to the soldiers. "Since these men are committed to ridding us of those animals, I've said they earned a night of free drinks."

Vernon glanced towards Grayfern handling the swamped bar and leaned on the wall alongside his friends, unable to say a word.

Lysia took a hearty drink of her tankard, saying to Vernon, "I actually despised you after what you did to me in Ellity." She sighed. "It was the second time I've had to leave my home and change my name."

Orfain whispered, "So what's your real name?"

She stared into her ale. "It doesn't matter anymore."

The air between the three of them was engulfed in silence.

Thinking about how to improve the mood, an idea came to Vernon and he smiled. "You know, I know a perfect place where we can watch the comet."

Lying down in Fewttyre's lab, Niyaa stared up as the stars began their nightly twinkling. Completely relaxed, she turned to her mom standing beside the bed and was glad to see most of her worries had left.

Fewttyre nudged his chair closer to Niyaa's leg. "Now, I'm going to untie the bandage and take a closer look at it, so I need you to hold very still."

"All right." Niyaa returned her gaze to the glass ceiling just as a greenish, westerly glow arose in the night sky, and she said, "The comet's coming!"

Mysia looked up and smiled. "I think it's come to wish us fortune in this new cycle."

Niyaa's excitement faded as she asked, "Do you think Dad can see this from where he is?"

She stroked her daughter's hair. "I'm certain he has a great view."

Imagining him staring up at the same light, Niyaa relaxed and spotted faint ribbons of green fluttering across the starry sky.

Fewttyre asked, "Is he still in Felliet?"

"He was taken to the Atimah," Mysia frowned.

He stopped undoing the bandage and sharply turned to her. "Is that true?"

"The governor of Pelight had him taken away on the same night he took our belongings."

Fewttyre paused for a long moment. "What's his name?"

"Darryam," Mysia answered. "Why do you ask?"

"Just curious." He returned to his work, undoing the final layer of bandage. "It appears several strands were cut."

Niyaa raised her head. "Thought it was just the one."

"One on the surface, yes," Fewttyre said. "Underneath there are many more smaller strands, running throughout your leg."

Mysia glared at him. "Lucky it didn't strike the big vein."

"The main artery ends at the knee and splits into thousands of miniscule capillaries along the strands." He smiled. "You can imagine it like the veins of a leaf. Anyway, I will apply a special glue to the innermost strands which should help it heal over the next few days. After that, I will go layer by layer till every strand is back to normal."

"Thank you," Niyaa replied, lying back down. She watched in wonder as the twinkling sky above filled with incredible long ribbons of pale green as thousands of bright green dots shot across, leaving streaks of wavy blues in their wake.

She saw it, the huge comet of red, orange and yellow filling the sky overhead, leaving an enormous trail of green, blue and violet in its wake. Niyaa stared awestruck as the whole sky beautifully blended in a swirling, peaceful collage amid a canvas of twinkling stars.

Watching the common messenger gallop out of the inner, western gatehouse, Jornis heard Copias call to him and turned to see him rushing towards him.

Reaching the gatehouse, Copias asked, "I thought you were going to witness the comet from the plaza."

Jornis glanced westward, at the emerald glow emerging on the horizon. "The plaza is sure to already be filled with elites from every corner of the city." He glanced at the soldiers gathered along the ramparts and at the commoners gazing out of windows and atop their rooftops. "Here should be sufficient to watch the comet pass."

"But it's unheard of for an elite to view the comet from a mere gatehouse."

Jornis observed strands of green snaking from the horizon as the emerald glow radiated across half the night sky. "An ideal location is still ideal, even if others haven't heard of it before."

Copias didn't argue and instead stood beside Jornis, "Very well then."

A pleasant smile crossed Jornis's face. "Have you realised that you and I are unlike any other elites?"

Copias looked at him in confusion. "Unlike the other elites?"

He nodded. "It is rare of for an elite to travel outside Felliet, but to personally witness the main drivers of the world with his own eyes, now that is truly unheard of."

The young elite smiled. "With respect, it is the duty of the elites to dedicate their efforts solely to the roles they are assigned."

The two of them gazed up as thousands of shooting green stars flew overhead in streaks of arching blue.

"But I admit," Copias said. "After travelling in your company across the world, I have learned a great deal."

Jornis raised his head to the red light appearing on the horizon. "I truly believe you will grow to be a fine man in whatever path you decide."

The subsequent orange and yellow bands shone across the landscape as the bright comet filled the sky with its vast trail of blues and violets.

"I swear I will do Felliet proud," Copias stated as he gazed at the colourful sky.

The arduous question of how to convince Copias to his side engulfed Jornis's thoughts but he pushed it aside, for he could trust the young man would make the right choice when the plan unfolded. Jornis took a deep hopeful breath and watched the multicoloured comet pass overhead with Copias at his side.

Sitting next to Barcial at the front of the empty carriage with the bleak city long faded from view, Iyna glared at the surrounding green, yellow and blue hills. Barcial pulled the reins of the horse, bringing the carriage to a stop.

Iyna turned to him. "What're you doing?"

He pointed eastward. "The comet will be arriving soon."

She turned her head and saw a green glow filling the horizon. She leaned back without saying a word.

Barcial jumped down from the carriage seat, pointing to a nearby hill covered in untouched blue lilies. "We can get a better view from up there."

She shook her head. "I don't want to stay in these lands."

He marched around the carriage and held his thumbless right hand to her. "I don't either. But the comet will pass overhead regardless."

Iyna sighed and took his hand, reluctantly following him up the blue hill as the sky filled with green lines sailing across the night sky.

The two of them stood at the top of the hill as the sky above flooded with every possible shade of green.

"Tonight I want us to relax." Barcial sat down. "And enjoy every bit of this moment."

Iyna looked at him peacefully staring up at the colourful array, and a little smile crossed her face. She sat beside him and gazed up.

They watched as countless blue stars pierced the green sky above before all the blue flowers surrounding them opened their buds. The air was filled with a vast concoction of earthy scents and flowery smells all blooming together.

As she gazed at the reddened comet emerging from the east, Iyna turned to Barcial. "Thank you for being there for me."

He shook his head. "*You're* the one who's been there for me."

She leaned closer to him as they pleasantly watched the red, orange and yellow comet soar over them.

Racing up the unguarded steps of Elleasious's tower, Vernon guided his friends to its peak till they emerged standing on its empty black crystal circular roof. In the distance the horizon was already beset with a vast emerald glow as streaks of pale greens sailed across the sky.

Orfain patted Vernon's back. "I don't know why the guards out front let you through, but you've definitely chosen a perfect place."

"I agree," Lysia said as she leaned her hands on the glistening merlons and stared across the black city. Her eyes widened, and her voice became awestruck. "The city's glowing."

Vernon rushed to the nearest edge and saw every black crystal surface mirroring the colourful sky, transforming the entire city into a vast spectrum of glistening green.

Staring at each of the shimmering buildings, Vernon noticed a multitude of blue trails swiftly arching throughout the sky. He turned to his friends and watched Orfain gently place his hand atop Lysia's.

She glanced wide eyed at him before a pleasant smile crossed her face, letting her hand remain where it was. As the red, orange and yellow comet soared overhead, Vernon watched the two embrace and he politely turned away.

Both sky and city filled with beautiful concoctions of blues, purples and greens as Vernon optimistically watched the red comet leave for the next horizon.